SOUTHERN DISCOMFORT
Rita Mae Brown

"A woman of feist and, as the reader learns, fun. Spunk and humor and ability."

—*Los Angeles Times*

"Brown's characters...are full of wisdom and sass. Spirited, funny, and moving, this novel will appeal to Brown's many fans. It may also earn her some new followers."

—*Library Journal*

"A fast-paced novel... The portrayal of Blue Rhonda and her friends is tender, funny and even to its unexpected end, touching."

—*Chicago Tribune*

"This novel is spunky, hearty, moving... It is also raunchy, spirited and unrelentingly human."

—*Publishers Weekly*

Bantam Books by Rita Mae Brown
Ask your bookseller for the books you have missed

RUBYFRUIT JUNGLE

SIX OF ONE

SOUTHERN DISCOMFORT

SOUTHERN DISCOMFORT

Rita Mae Brown

BANTAM BOOKS
TORONTO · NEW YORK · LONDON · SYDNEY

Dedicated to Elaine Spaulding

This low-priced Bantam Book
has been completely reset in a type face
designed for easy reading, and was printed
from new plates. It contains the complete
text of the original hard-cover edition.
NOT ONE WORD HAS BEEN OMITTED.

SOUTHERN DISCOMFORT

A Bantam Book / published in association with
Harper & Row, Publishers, Inc.

PRINTING HISTORY

Harper & Row edition published March 1982
4 printings through May 1982
Bantam edition / May 1983

ISBN 0-553-23108-1

Published simultaneously in the United States and Canada

Bantam Books are published by Bantam Books, Inc. Its trademark, consisting of the words ''Bantam Books'' and the portrayal of a rooster, is Registered in U.S. Patent and Trademark
Office and in other countries. Marca Registrada. Bantam
Books, Inc., 666 Fifth Avenue, New York, New York 10103.

PRINTED IN THE UNITED STATES OF AMERICA

O   098765432

Acknowledgments

I write a book alone but I don't live alone in this world. Many people contribute in their various ways so that I can work. The following people have helped me and I remain grateful: Linda Damico, Colleen Moreland, Patricia Neal, her late parents, William and Marion Neal, Julie Florence, Betty Burns, Rebecca Brown, Catherine Ordway and my agent, Wendy Weil. I'd also like to thank the feline help: Baby Jesus, sixteen years old on July 14, 1981, Cazenovia Kitty and Louise. The dogs contributed very little to this book, but in case they ever get smart enough to read, I'll name them so their feelings won't be hurt: Tetsuo and Ruby. Thank you all.

A Note

If you don't like my book, write your own. If you don't think you can write a novel, that ought to tell you something. If you think you can, do. No excuses. If you still don't like my novels, find a book you do like. Life is too short to be miserable. If you like my novels, I commend your good taste.

Prologue

Blue Rhonda Latrec was eighteen years old and at the top of her profession. She was a first-class whore. On this hot day she plopped her butt on the front stoop of her small frame dwelling on Water Street. Blue Rhonda considered herself fortunate in her location, as the train station was just down the road. From the mouth of that beautiful structure poured a steady stream of new customers to supplement her regulars. Blue Rhonda was in business with a partner, Banana Mae Parker. Banana Mae couldn't have been much over twenty-five, but she refused to reveal her birthday. "A woman who'll tell her age will tell anything," Banana Mae frequently declared.

Blue Rhonda specialized in oral flourishes, while Banana Mae concentrated on other forms of carnal desire. This distribution of services caused no problems between them, or if it did, each partner kept it to herself.

Although they'd been working together for over two years, Banana Mae had yet to see Blue Rhonda naked. Whenever she'd tease her about her prissiness, Blue Rhonda's ready answer was, "Mother taught me to be modest." Mother taught her little else, for Blue Rhonda snorted cocaine every hour on the hour, swore with imagination, drank when she felt like it and was good enough at her trade to be in constant demand. Banana Mae was much more the lady.

Each resident views a city with a particular set of references. Blue Rhonda and Banana Mae looked at Montgomery, Alabama, in terms of sex. The town resembled a stud farm, although everybody lied through their teeth about fucking. Maybe the real difference between Blue Rhonda, Banana Mae and the rest of Montgomery's citizens was that they told the truth. In this world, lying, fornicating and thieving are prerogatives of the sane. Small wonder that the two women, or any prostitutes, for that matter, were regarded as nuts.

1918

"How about Bunny Turnbull chewing the rag?" Banana Mae started up.

"Rattling off her woes like mea culpas." Blue Rhonda sighed, relishing the sight of tiny Bunny wringing her bejeweled hands. Although Miss Turnbull ran Montgomery's best whorehouse, that never prevented her from behaving like a duchess. Or maybe she behaved that way because of it. "First, the house cost too much money. Her cook demanded Sunday morning off or a raise. The piano player costs, one of her girls snuck off and got married, and God knows, good help is hard to find."

"She's still got Lotowana. That's enough for any man." Banana Mae laughed.

"All three hundred pounds of her."

"Every now and then I think we ought to expand, open a house, but the worries—"

Blue Rhonda interrupted. "We're better off this way. Oh, Christ, here comes Linton Ray."

Reverend Linton Ray perceived his duty as saving these wretched women. The fact that they didn't feel wretched had no effect on his efforts. Deep down they had to be filled with loathing, they just had to be. In all his years of badgering he'd converted two prostitutes to his cause; nonetheless he did drive customers away. Fortunately he only made the rounds twice a week. The rest of the time he devoted his gargantuan energies to his Methodist flock of grocers, haberdashers and housepainters. Same difference. He minced over to the gray-painted steps.

"Good evening, Miss Latrec and Miss Parker."

"Good evening, Reverend Ray." Banana Mae minded her manners.

"Is this a lengthy visit?" Blue Rhonda forgot hers.

"Do not turn away the messenger of the Lord, for I bring tidings of great joy."

"I thought you used that line at Christmas." Blue Rhonda frowned.

"Miss Latrec, why do you resist our Lord and his only begotten son, Jesus Christ, who died that you might live?"

"I'm alive, ain't I?" Blue Rhonda stared at him.

"Yes," Reverend Linton Ray answered in his honey voice.

"O.K., so Jesus was a big success. He didn't say how I was to live. That's up to me."

"But you live a life of sin," he unctuously pointed out.

Banana Mae fanned herself and peered down the road. A customer was due in five minutes.

"Repent. Repent and God will forgive you all your sins." Linton loved to roll the word "repent" off his tongue.

"Good. May God forgive me for my sins, for I'm not about to dwell on them." Blue Rhonda spoke firmly.

"Someday you'll need the help of the Lord, Miss Latrec. You'll call on me then." Linton allowed himself the vision of a cowering Blue Rhonda, smiled, then headed toward Bunny Turnbull's house, where in the distance shutters could be heard slamming.

"If God were so almighty smart, you'd think he'd do a better job of hiring," Blue Rhonda declared.

"Amen," Banana Mae agreed.

A powerfully built man slid out from the narrow walkway to the backyard.

"Is he gone?" Karel Sokol asked in a thick Czech accent.

"To his reward, I wish." Blue Rhonda motioned for Karel to come on in.

"Nice to see you, Karel," Banana Mae welcomed him.

Karel nodded, pushed the screen door open and went inside. Blue Rhonda followed and quickly set about cannibalizing the next generation.

On the other side of the tracks, where the blood was bluer, Hortensia Banastre was enduring her own problems with the next generation. The pulsating red of the ace of hearts cheered her as she fingered the card. She liked to win, and she was about to win this poker game.

"What have you, Paris?" Hortensia demanded.

Paris expectantly put down a pair of kings and a pair of tens. Edward laid down three jacks. Triumphant, Hortensia smacked down four sparkling aces with one hand while gathering the red, white and blue chips with the other. Paris started to cry.

"Mother, you always win," Edward complained.

Paris, at age nine, did his best. Edward, two years older, shuffled the cards for yet another round of humiliation. Mother's little hour with the children descended each day like a sentence to the Bastille. If I ever have children, Edward thought, I'll ignore them. They'll grow up happy.

Her opponents and children stared at Hortensia with facsimiles of affection. If she noticed the distinct lack of warmth, Hortensia never mentioned it, but then warmth was not high on Hortensia's list of priorities.

Unfortunately for the children, it didn't seem to be too high on their father's list either. Carwyn Banastre managed the family's fortune, which was considerable. Marriage to Hortensia Reedmuller, a brilliant social match, afforded him no love, little sex and two strangers masquerading as sons. He concentrated on making even more money and on politics. Not that Carwyn was unkind; merely inattentive and distant. He became a useless appendage to his family, like a dewclaw.

Hortensia betrayed no signs of dissatisfaction with her marriage. She enjoyed her powerful social position, occasionally locking horns with her even more powerful mother, Lila Reedmuller, for control of Montgomery's upper classes. Hortensia, like a stiletto, was narrow, thin and sharp. Her pale-blond hair, ice-blue eyes and sensuous mouth caused a sensation among gentlemen. Like her mother, she would age well, but at age twenty-seven Hortensia gave no thought to aging. She shared with her husband an obsession for power. Hortensia wanted control over everybody and everything. If she couldn't win by charm she resorted to the club. When women around her fluttered over love, Hortensia thought them silly twits. She didn't believe in it and when she saw evidence of love in someone's behavior she considered it a suspension of logic, a temporary madness. If the fools married, time, which ground the days to fine powder, would wear down this passion. Love, never.

When love finally seeped into Hortensia's life, it was from a person so unexpected that the forbidden force of it damn near destroyed her.

The immaculate butler hurried into the paneled library. Before the words "Your mother is here" tumbled out of his mouth, Lila Reedmuller swept past him.

"Thank you." Lila spoke to him as though he were a water bug.

"Grandmama!" Paris charged over and kissed Lila's silken cheek. Edward kissed her also.

"Getting bigger every day." Lila patted them on the head. "Cards again, Hortensia? You know how I feel about women playing cards."

"Well, Mother, nobody's asked you." Hortensia's tone soothed while it stung. "Boys, run into the kitchen and ask Leone for cookies."

Paris put his head in Hortensia's lap. "Mother, can't I stay here with you?"

She pushed his head away. "No."

He touched her arm. "I'll be quiet."

"Go with your brother. Children are to be seen and not heard."

He withdrew and walked alongside Edward. As they opened the door they both turned and said, "Bye, Grandmama."

"Jigs for Coke!" Edward slapped Paris on the back as they left the room.

Outside the library, Paris turned to his older brother. "You always win when we say the same thing at the same time."

"You gotta be fast, Paris."

"But saying goodbye to Grandmama isn't really the same thing as saying the same thing at the same time."

Edward swung his arms like a soldier. "Why not?"

"Because you're expected to say goodbye to someone. That's being polite. 'Jigs for Coke' ought to go for something that's not expected."

"You're trying to skin out of owing me a Coke—that's what I figure."

Paris changed the subject. "In a deck of cards, what would Mother be and what would Grandmama be?"

"That's a good one." Edward skipped toward the kitchen, his favorite place in the house.

"Do you know what I think?" Paris burrowed into his subject. "I think Grandmama is the ace of diamonds and Mother is the king of diamonds."

"And Mother wants to be the ace." Edward mentioned this as an observation, not a criticism. "Can a lady be a king?"

"Mother says so." Paris slid ahead of his brother on the highly polished hallway and pushed open the kitchen door.

"Paris is so attached to you," Lila noted.

"He gets on my nerves."

"He's still young. He'll grow out of it and then you'll hardly ever see him."

"I always thought little boys were supposed to play outside and kill things."

Lila tilted her head. You never knew if Hortensia was serious or being smart. "Let's hope not. Are you giving a tea dance Saturday?" She paused, then sniffed. "What's that?"

"Narcisse Noir. I've worn it for the last five years, Mother."

"And I've detested it for the last five years. It smells like cat's pee."

Hortensia picked up the deep-green cards with the gold border.

Lila glared at the cards. "You give dances where ladies, and I use that term loosely, arrive in diaphanous clothing—which is to say they come half naked. You fling yourself at the head of every handsome man you see. You ride astride. You teach your sons cards. You—''

''I can do without the litany of my sins.''

''You're not in Paris, Hortensia. And given the war, it's a good thing, too. Montgomery shies from cheap fads, dear. This passion for what's modern makes you look superficial.''

''Montgomery sits between garbage and the Gulf, and I'd rather look superficial than stuffed.''

''Squandering a fortune to gain the good opinion of people who are not top quality strikes me as a foolish act.''

''I haven't noticed you restraining yourself when it comes to money.''

''I'm not here to discuss me; I'm here to discuss you. Are you giving that tea dance?''

''Of course I am. Would you like to come?'' Hortensia smiled.

''Is Jamison Chappell invited?''

''He said he'd jump the peony bushes on his big gray to start the party.''

''Give him up.'' Lila folded her hands together.

''There's nothing to give up. We're friends—friends.''

''Hortensia, I know perfectly well that your marriage to Carwyn lacks''—she paused, searching for the least offensive word possible—''excitement.''

''What do you know about excitement?'' Hortensia underscored the delicate word.

''I love your father very much, and strange though it may sound to you, we were young once.''

''Mother, I am not engaging in a physical relationship with Jamison Chappell or anyone else, except for my husband—on rare occasions. I'm tired of you accusing me of carrying on with every man I know!'' Hortensia's uncharacteristic bluntness had the ring of truth to it.

''I'm glad to hear it.'' Lila's reply was automatic. For all Lila's faults, she loved her daughter. She wished Hortensia could love a man even if it were not her husband, but how could a mother say such a thing to her daughter? Lila had watched Hortensia for twenty-seven years—a brilliant girl, a beautiful girl, untouched by emotion. Hortensia lived from the neck up. The rest of her was dead. Try as she might to reach her daughter, to sympathize, whatever Lila said sounded like criticism. And Lila warred with herself. Half of her longed to usher her daughter into the human race and the other half of her fought to preserve the stultifying social order over which she, Lila, presided.

The kitchen expanded with heat. Amelie, the cook, a slender black woman, cut up chicken while Leone Sokol filled the boys' glasses with lemonade.

"Don't you think Grandmama is the ace of diamonds?" Paris asked Leone.

"What?" She grabbed two peaches out of a wicker basket and put them before the brothers.

"Your grandmother doesn't approve of cards." Amelie split open a joint.

"No, I mean she *is* the ace of diamonds," Paris asserted.

Leone put her hand on her hip. "She's rich, if that's what you mean."

Edward rescued his brother. "Paris is talking about Mother's way to rank people. She taught it to us today. A deck of cards has four suits, right?"

"Hearts, diamonds, spades, clubs," Amelie sang out.

"I thought you didn't play cards, Amelie." Leone wiped her hands on her apron.

"How can I? My husband plays all day long. The cards never leave that man's hand." Amelie sank the knife into another chicken breast with new vigor.

"So people fall into suits," Edward continued. "Clubs are when you use force, so the lowest people are clubs."

"The worst person in the world is the two of clubs." Paris's eyes enlarged.

"Spades are when people work for a living. A man digs a ditch. That's next. Diamonds are smart and rich, but the best, the very best people in the world, are the hearts." Edward clapped his hands together, applauding the fact that he remembered everything.

"So an ace is high? What kind of person would be the ace of clubs?" Leone asked.

"A man who has courage," Paris said.

"Yes, but not much else. He rises because he's strong but not because he's good," Edward added.

"Are generals clubs?" Amelie was enjoying the conversation.

"I bet General Custer was the ace of clubs," Edward shouted.

"Well, what are you, Edward?" Leone laughed.

"I'm too young to know."

"I see." Leone walked over to the sink.

"But don't you think Mother and Grandmama are diamonds?"

Amelie, diplomatically, said, "Oh, I don't know."

This new world view puzzled Leone. "Don't you think your mother's a heart?"

Paris cut open his peach and began eating one half of it. Edward stared at the other half, then picked it up.

"Mother's the stone at the heart of the peach," he said, deliberately and quietly.

The two women ignored this statement. The sorrow of it was that it was true.

. . .

"Help! Help!" Lotowana, a triumph over gravity, ran down Water Street squealing at the top of her lungs, laughing at the same time.

Blue Rhonda called out from the upstairs bedroom: "Careful, Lotowana. The street's got enough potholes."

"Come on out here and gimme the chance to kick you one," Lotowana cheerfully called back, while eluding her ardent pursuer.

Blue Rhonda thumped down the stairs to join Banana Mae on the porch.

"Finished so soon?" Banana Mae watched Lotowana hit her stride.

"Press Tugwell was not blessed by nature," Blue Rhonda whispered. Her customer could be heard snapping suspenders.

"Save me! Save me, Banana Mae." Lotowana panted. She flung herself on the steps and the whole house shuddered. Dad-eye Steelman, all five feet of him, leapt on top of her and rolled off. Lotowana good-naturedly slapped him. "Stop it, you beast."

"Lottie, let's go back to your room," he pleaded.

"In a minute. I want to talk to my friends."

Dad-eye contented himself with fondling her breasts, those big sugared gumdrops, while she chatted.

"Nanner, gimme a whiskey so I can get a headache." Lotowana invited herself to a drink.

"Only if you tell me everything." Banana Mae hurried inside and reemerged with whiskey and glasses.

Blue Rhonda leaned forward. "Dad-eye, better grab all you can. If army recruiters get you drunk, off you go. Just stay drunk with your friends."

"Hush." Lotowana's voice hit the alto range. As she turned to Dad-eye it shot up to soprano. "Now stop it."

"I don't give a shit what the Kaiser does." Dad-eye leered.

"You'll get in it, just you wait," Blue Rhonda harped.

"Why? Let those crazy people on the other side of the ocean kill themselves. Got nothing to do with me." Dad-eye nibbled Lotowana's ear.

"Yeah, what's it got to do with us?" Lotowana echoed.

"Karel says it's a whirlpool and we'll all be sucked in." Blue Rhonda removed a beautiful tiny silver box from her meager cleavage.

"He's just a dumb immigrant." Dad-eye spat on the ground.

"Maybe so, but he came from those parts, he ought to know something." Banana Mae liked Karel.

"Ran, you mean." Dad-eye snickered.

Lotowana jabbed him in the ribs with her elbow. "Be nice or you won't get what you want most." He immediately sat up straight. Dad-eye lusted after Lotowana and he didn't want anything to get between him and that rotund castle of flesh, least of all World War I.

"America's all Europe's rejects." Blue Rhonda dipped her fingernail into the cocaine she kept in the silver box. "Some of us got here sooner than later, that's all." She took a sniff—"Wonderful for sinus"—and exhaled gratefully.

Dad-eye sipped his whiskey. "Wonderful for the digestion."

"Yoo hoo." A small voice caught their attention. Demure Bunny Turnbull motioned for Lotowana to get back at her station.

"In a minute," Lotowana yelled. "Slave driver," she muttered.

"That's what I want to know, Lottie." Blue Rhonda leaned over conspiratorially. "Does Bunny service any of her customers?"

"Bunny? Ha!" Lotowana roared.

"Everybody's got to have it sometime." Banana Mae couldn't imagine celibacy.

"Maybe she's gelded." Dad-eye giggled.

"I bet she's got a secret passion and you never noticed, Lottie. She's shrewd, that Bunny," purred Blue Rhonda.

Lotowana's eyebrows jerked upward as if by spasm. "She's smart, that's a fact. I'll see what I can see." For a fat woman, Lottie was quite graceful. She rose from the steps, thanked Blue Rhonda and Banana Mae for the refreshment and obediently headed toward her place of employment. Dad-eye trotted behind like a penny dog.

"He likes fat women the way a rat likes pumpkins." Banana Mae chuckled. "But that Lottie's a sweet soul."

"Uh-huh. Is Carwyn dropping by tonight?"

"I expect."

"You know, if he weren't married I bet he'd marry you."

"Hell, Blue Rhonda, nobody marries a whore." A trace of anger crept into her voice. Society people marry one another and that's that.

"Those Banastres are all magnolia upstairs, all skunk cabbage downstairs. You're too good for him." Blue Rhonda tapped her foot.

An elegant phaeton glided down the street, pulled by a pair of matched chestnut horses. The coach stopped in front of the little house on Water Street. Carwyn Banastre jumped out.

"I'm going on down to the station to see if I can find Placide Jinks. We need some more wood." Blue Rhonda touched Banana Mae's shoulder. "Hello, Mr. Banastre."

"Leaving us?" Carwyn's jet-black mustache curled upward. It gave him a permanent smile.

"For a spell."

"Good evening." He tapped his hat with his ebony cane.

As Blue Rhonda's erect figure receded, Banana Mae and Carwyn went inside. No sooner was the door closed than he grabbed her. With Carwyn Banana Mae never faked it. She loved him despite herself.

· · ·

Union Railroad Station commanded Water Street. Completed in 1898, it fell in architectural style somewhere between Victorian Gothic and Romanesque. Bartholomew Reedmuller, Hortensia's father, had helped conceive of the building, although he was only the number two architect at the time. Bartholomew, in the eighteen-year interval, advanced to become the darling of the Masons. Every time a new Masonic lodge was erected, the plans were usually those of Bartholomew Reedmuller. Each lodge progressed in homage to Egypt, the Sphinx and a variety of pharaohs' tombs. The sight of the station at 250 Water Street still stirred in Bartholomew a hot resentment. He dreamed of station doors as great Assyrian gates opening onto the desert of travel. Public buildings should be repositories of dreams, not just functions. Bartholomew thought buildings exerted a secret, powerful influence and their mystery should be heightened, not diminished. Apparently the only Americans sharing his philosophy were the Masons. Bartholomew half closed his eyes as he hurried from his train through the general waiting room out to the front of the station. The industrial majesty of Birmingham cried out for buildings, buildings and more buildings. Mr. Reedmuller spent half his time now in the upstart city and was just returning. Lila would have none of it and considered everybody and everything about Birmingham inexpressibly vulgar.

Just as Bartholomew passed through the doors, Blue Rhonda passed in. She adored the train station. Passengers spilled from cars like milkweeds. The ricochet of massed voices in the various waiting chambers made her feel a part of movement, of the future. She especially liked sailing through the general waiting room, where the gentlemen gathered. The sight of her generated comment. She then strolled into the ladies' waiting room, more for the irritation value than anything else. The town's proper matrons ruffled and clucked, then settled back on their behinds.

"Twitch, you damn broody hens," she said to herself. "The only difference between you and me is a piece of paper."

She walked out the door and a few paces past the ladies' waiting room to the colored waiting room. She stuck her head in the door. Placide Jinks wasn't there.

"Placide about?" she called to the assorted sitters, standers, waiters.

"Back by baggage, Miss Blue," a voice replied.

Around the train side of the building, Placide heaved huge steamer trunks off a wooden cart with large iron wheels.

"Placide." Blue Rhonda waved.

"Miss Latrec." Placide smiled. She was unlike any woman he'd ever known and he liked her.

"Can you or your boy drop some wood by?"

"Sure enough." He swung another trunk down. Thanks to heredity and his job, Placide looked like baby Atlas.

"Everyone's talking about the war today."

"Wilson didn't do such a good job of keeping us out," Placide replied.

"I never pay any attention to what politicians say. If I can't vote, why should I listen?"

Placide grinned at her. "You have a way of putting things, Miss Latrec."

"Why, thank you, Mr. Jinks."

"I'll be sending Hercules by. Working late tonight." He lowered another trunk. His oldest boy, Apollo, just the right age for a war, was threatening to enlist once out of school. Placide had endured the Spanish-American War. Black men weren't supposed to fight, so he languished in the stables with the rank of private. One filthy-hot day he'd been chewed out by a white buck lieutenant, boots gleaming. A terrifying explosion tossed Placide in the air like a rag doll. When he opened his eyes, blood covered him from head to foot, but he was uninjured. He looked over to where the lieutenant had been standing and what remained was his left leg from the kneecap down, standing as though planted in the ground, the boot still glistening.

Thoughts of war didn't upset Blue Rhonda. She was too young to know what it really meant. She did consider business. Troops moving through the rail station on their way down to Mobile meant a lot of business. She walked around the station one more time before heading home. The idea of boarding a lavishly appointed car thrilled her. Atlanta, New Orleans, Chicago, Richmond, Philadelphia, New York—the names written on the timetable provoked her imagination. If she made enough money she'd see those places. Being in Montgomery was itself a victory. She grew up in a tiny place, Hatchechubbee, in eastern Alabama, not far from Columbus, Georgia. She left home at age fourteen and spurned the textile mills of Columbus for the imagined glamour of Montgomery. The beautiful state capital, the White House of the Confederacy, Court Square fountain, haunted her with visions of a time just beyond reach. She knew even if she did visit those other cities she'd return to Montgomery, for she felt free here. She dawdled on the way home, hoping that by the time she arrived, Carwyn would be gone.

Hortensia rode her spirited bay, Bellerophon. Paris and Edward kept close to her on their ponies. Attired in a lavender riding coat, fawn breeches, black boots and a fawn derby with a veil, Hortensia evoked admiration or shock, depending on who was looking.

"Heels down, Paris. Yes, that's better."

"How am I doing, Mother?" Edward eagerly asked.

"Keep a light hand on the rein."

"Good evening, Mrs. Banastre." Richard Bosworth, a lawyer, greeted her as he left his office.

"Mr. Bosworth! Attending the Horatio Club tonight?"

"Yes, ma'am. I hope to see Mr. Banastre there."

"I'm sure you will." She granted him a smile, her white teeth shining.

Once out of earshot, Paris piped up, "Grandmama says you shouldn't be so friendly with people like that."

"Lawyers?" Hortensia knew what Grandmama was

about, but she might as well hear it from her own son's lips.

"The middle classes," he disdained.

"Who cares?" Edward was already egalitarian, a triumph, considering his family.

"They have silk hats but no families," Paris grumbled.

"They do so have families." Edward hadn't liked giving way to his younger brother when he was born and he didn't like it any more now, nine years later.

"Bloodlines," Paris pronounced. "And Grandmama also says they have comic tensions."

Hortensia sighed. "I believe my dear mother's line is: 'The middle classes will endure anything so long as they can make money and be allowed their comic social pretensions.' "

"Exactly," Paris bellowed, thinking he'd found an ally in his mother.

Hortensia bore no special affection for the middle classes. After all, they were in the middle and by social geography therefore boring, but they had their political uses. The Horatio Club was Carwyn's idea to knit a closer alliance between Montgomery's upper classes and the middle-class men. Carwyn was dedicated to the 1901 rollback of rights, which effectively cut off poor whites and all blacks from any kind of voice in politics. Better to have the lawyers, tailors, pharmacists wedded to those in power than to have them making matches with those without. He knew perfectly well a bond between the people with their noses in ledger books and the have-nots could end his reign and the reign of everyone like him. He also knew that an insurance salesman would much rather be seen with himself, Carwyn Banastre, than with the poor, regardless of color. Buying off the middlemen proved hilariously easy. It didn't cost a penny. Hortensia patronized the shops of those men in the Horatio Club and she invited their wives to a tea from time to time or to one of her balls, where they could mingle with the very rich. Lila Reedmuller hated such watering of good wine, as she put it, but then Lila put wreaths on the graves of the Confederate dead.

"Paris, in the future keep your opinions to yourself," Hortensia snapped.

Jubilant, Edward rose up in his stirrups. "It's Father!"

From the opposite end of Lee Street, Carwyn and Banana Mae rolled toward them in a gorgeous deep-burgundy open-air carriage. Carwyn was so sure of his position he dared to be seen with Banana Mae. Besides, he'd enjoyed two orgasms in the space of ninety minutes. For him that was a sexual miracle. He felt expansive, and a small gesture like a ride pleased Banana Mae more than the forty-thousand-dollar emerald necklaces he bestowed pleased his wife.

"It certainly is your father." Hortensia abhorred getting caught in this position. Better take the offensive. She touched the spur to her horse's flanks and cantered toward the as yet unaware twosome. Edward and Paris galloped after her.

Banana Mae observed a stunning woman approaching them. She'd never seen Carwyn's wife. Before he could say anything, Hortensia, shimmering in her anger and from the ride, was alongside.

"My husband, I presume?"

Banana Mae's mouth fell open.

"Hello, darling. You look marvelous." Carwyn never missed a beat. "Allow me to introduce you to an acquaintance of mine, Miss Parker."

Hortensia touched her derby with her crop. "Charmed, Miss Parker."

Banana Mae's mouth still hung open. The boy's finally caught up and immediately became silent.

"Are you dumb, Miss Parker?" Hortensia smiled that radiant smile.

Banana Mae turned red and stuttered, "Please to meet you, Mrs. Banastre."

"Have you a speech impediment, my dear?" Hortensia was redefining the word "sympathy." She shone her admiring gaze upon her husband's steely face. "Mr. Banastre, your concern for the welfare of those less fortunate than yourself is touching indeed." She returned her attention to Banana Mae. "I do so hope you recover quickly, Miss Parker." Hortensia wheeled her horse around and trotted off. Bewildered, the boys followed her.

"Mother, who was that nice-looking lady?" Edward innocently asked.

"One of your father's whores."

"She's the most beautiful woman I've ever seen," Banana Mae quietly commented.

"Good; you marry her." Carwyn sighed.

Rather than contain her fury, Hortensia decided to ride it out. She snapped her crop over Bellerophon's flanks, goading the boys. "Catch me if you can."

Hortensia had no business galloping down streets and alleyways, but once she felt the powerful muscles under her and the lick of wind on her face there was no stopping her. A low white fence tempted her. She soared over it, only to collide with Hercules Jinks, Placide's youngest son. The cart Hercules was pulling spilled its load of wood all over the dusty alleyways. Hercules, knocked flat, never saw what hit him.

Hortensia dismounted, rapidly tied Bellerophon to the fence and rushed to the stricken boy. "Are you all right?"

Hercules got up on elbows, gasping. She knelt down, but he waved her away and sat up.

"Wind," he whispered, taking deep breaths.

"I'm so sorry. Not only have I knocked you over; I upset your apple cart as well."

Paris, laughing, caught up with his mother. She snapped his knees with her crop. "That's enough, young man."

Edward stopped in a cloud of dust. "Is he in one piece?"

Paris opened his mouth and thought better of it. Hortensia replied, "I hope so."

Breathing regularly again, Hercules studied his assailant.

"You're one of the Jinks, aren't you?" she asked.

"Yes, ma'am."

"Let me make good my mistake. From now on you can deliver a cord of hardwood to our house every Friday."

"Yours is the house with the Corinthian columns?"

Hortensia was surprised that he knew his architectural orders. "It is. How do you know that?"

"Your father taught my father and my father taught me." Hercules stood up and towered over Hortensia, a tall woman herself.

"That must have been a long time ago." Hortensia petted Bellerophon.

"When they built Union Station. Daddy worked from the basement to the roof until he went off to the war. Ever since then he's studied architecture." Hercules brushed the dirt from his pants.

Hortensia stared at him. "Hercules, you are aptly named. How old are you?"

"Fifteen, Mrs. Banastre. I'll be sixteen come December."

"I see. Well, again, I'm sorry. Fridays." She seemed to float onto the saddle.

"Fridays." Hercules agreed, then went about picking up the mess.

At fifteen he was six feet tall, heavily muscled. He looked much older but he retained that peculiar sweetness boys on the verge of manhood often possess.

The screen door flapped behind her. Banana Mae found Blue Rhonda in the kitchen, drinking roped coffee.

"Want some?"

"No, thanks," Banana Mae replied. "Carwyn Banastre says the temperance people are getting stronger. Linton Ray's in on it, naturally."

"Fucktooth." This was Blue Rhonda's special noun for premier assholes. Linton Ray qualified.

"They say Camden County went dry."

Blue Rhonda took another fiery gulp. "If Camden County is dry, it's because they drank it all up."

Banana Mae drummed the tabletop.

"Well?" Blue Rhonda added more whiskey to her coffee.

"Well what?" Banana Mae avoided Blue Rhonda's eyes.

"What are you sitting on, missy?"

"My ass."

"You know what I mean."

"Nothing."

Blue Rhonda wrinkled her nose. "If that's the way you want to be about it."

"Oh, I saw Hortensia Banastre, that's all."

"That's enough."

"Have you ever seen her up close?"

"Only from a distance."

"Her eyes are ice blue. Really, Rhonda, ice blue. They're so clear you can almost see clean through them."

"What else?"

"She a bitch."

"Makes me wonder. What's she got to be so mean over? She has everything."

Banana Mae weakened and poured herself some coffee laced with whiskey. "People need more than money, looks and brains, I guess."

"What, for instance?"

"Love."

"Banana Mae, love! The last thing men and women do is get along. And if they did we'd be out of business."

Banana Mae stirred her potion. "You don't believe in love?"

"Not that kind."

"Surely it works sometimes. Some husbands must love some wives and vice versa."

"I figure his vice is her versa." Blue Rhonda thought herself clever.

"Haven't you ever been in love?" Banana Mae leaned toward her friend.

"I love you."

"Romance," Banana Mae prodded.

"No. Besides, what we have is better. You're in my corner and I'm in yours. What else is there? Sex? Sex doesn't hold people together. We're better off without that—between us, I mean."

"I should hope to holler." Banana Mae savored the whiskey.

"What about you?"

"That's how I got in this business, because of love."

"Some small-town fart in Hissop, Alabama, who screws you then dumps you isn't exactly my definition of love."

"Nor mine neither. Oh, why are we talking about this? It makes no difference. Let's go over to Bunny's. Lotowana is singing tonight. We'll close up shop. Mondays are slow anyway." Banana Mae brightened.

"Sounds good to me." Blue Rhonda stood up. "Banana, you know you can tell me anything."

"I know. You can tell me anything too."

Rhonda looked down at Banana's bright hair and wondered if she really could tell her anything.

• • •

The next Friday Hercules delivered hardwood to the Banastre mansion. Amelie met him at the back door and showed him where to stack it. When he finished his job she gave him a book about the work of Palladio.

"Missus says you're to have this."

Hercules held the book. "I'll read it and return it next Friday."

"She didn't say nothing about giving it back."

"I'll bring it back just in case."

Amelie nodded.

The Friday after that Amelie traded books with him. This architecture book contained engravings. From then on, every time Hercules delivered a load of wood or did an odd job at the request of Amelie, Leone or Hortensia herself, he was given another book. Unbeknownst to him, Hortensia often observed him as he received the next book. It took so little to make him happy. One book from the thousands in the Banastre library turned him giddy. She almost envied him. Hortensia knew education for his kind was not encouraged, but she couldn't see how learning about architecture would spawn another Nat Turner. Besides, no one knew he read her books but Amelie and Leone, and she did feel some responsibility for him after sending him flying across the alleyway.

Linton Ray strolled the cemetery behind the neat brick church with the cross of John Wesley on its steeple. He offered up small prayers for the dead, reserving his big guns for the living. The peacefulness of the graveyard invited him; no temptations here. Every Halloween the children of Montgomery divided up into two teams for the Great Witch Hunt. Screams, knocked-over tombstones, paint, desecrated his retreat, but he put up with it because the Great Witch Hunt was a town tradition. It was a glorified scavenger hunt, though more frightening, and whichever team collected the items on its list, followed the clues and found the Great Witch won prizes. Linton played it as a child, if he could remember back that far. Hard to imagine Reverend Ray playing at anything. The other day he caught his sexton, Cecil Romble, singing "Hello, My Baby." Linton pitched himself a fit and fell in it. Cecil Romble might never sing again after that display.

No drinking, no smoking, no dancing, no anything—this was Linton's creed. Unlike other good shepherds who fleeced their flocks, Linton believed every word of drivel he spouted. If he'd robbed his congregation, lived high on the hog, he would have been more comprehensible to Montgomery's citizens. Upright, self-righteous and joyless, Linton herded the one hundred or so souls under his protection. In his congregation the absence of feeling was declared a deliverance from temptation; emptiness was spiritual triumph. These poor souls were hollow as drums; it made them feel superior to everyone around them when they heard their own reverberations.

"Are you heading toward Water Street, Reverend?" Cecil asked, slyly jabbing Linton. "Those wicked women just don't seem to want no parts of the Lord."

"In time, Cecil, in time. We're on this earth to stamp out two great evils, the abuse of alcohol and the abuse of the body. Our bodies were made in God's own image; they must be kept pure!" Linton stoked his boiler.

"Indeed." Cecil returned to sweeping off the pathway to the cemetery.

"Progress is being made."

"Praise the Lord." Cecil swept harder.

"Some of our city's finer citizens frequent those dens of iniquity on Water Street."

"You don't mean it, Reverend." Cecil long ago learned to play dumb so Linton could feel smart.

"I think if I can present them with their sins"—he breathed forcefully—"they'll see fit to go along with our temperance program. Alcohol must be outlawed."

"A trade, sort of?"

Linton recoiled from business comparisons. "Certainly not. One thing at a time. First we stamp out this evil, then we're free to stamp out the other."

"Wise, Reverend Ray, very wise."

"Thank you, Cecil." Reinforced by bogus admiration, Linton finally headed toward Water Street, leaving Cecil in peace.

The sexton leaned on his broom, tapping his foot. He wasn't singing out loud but he was singing in his head. He also wondered if man was created in God's image, did that mean God had sex organs? For a moment the vision of a giant penis hovering over the moon startled him. He went back to sweeping.

Religion also guided the life of Ada Jinks, formerly Ada Goodwater. Holy rollers, Pentecostals and all other forms of spiritual exuberance infuriated Ada. She was an Episcopalian. The daughter of one of the black community's undertakers, Ada grew up with strong ideas about one's station in life. She deeply regretted that Palmer Institute was not opened when she was a schoolgirl. However, she propelled her children to Sedalia, North Carolina, where Charlotte Hawkins Brown pinched them like wet clay. Ada was rigid, relentless and regal. When Placide Jinks first met her years before, all he saw was the regal; the rest came later. Still, she was a warm woman if you went along with her, and she loved her husband and family ferociously.

She bore Placide five children—of whom three survived—while continuing her career as a schoolteacher in Montgomery. Ada's specialty was Latin, but she also taught English and gladly tutored any child who showed promise. Religion was Ada's inner concern; education was her outer concern. She believed it was the salvation of her race. Her children embraced her passion for learning, although Hercules as yet showed no signs of an intellectual career. Athena, her oldest, had graduated from Palmer Institute and now studied at Vassar. Apollo, eighteen, would graduate from Palmer this year and he had a good shot at Yale; failing that, he'd matriculate at Atlanta University and join Alpha Phi Alpha, if he didn't enlist first.

Ada had married beneath her, Placide being labeled a "striver"; he did well, though. He worked his ass off down at the train station and invested wisely, mostly in real estate. That plus the decent inheritance Ada's father left her when he died paid for these expensive educations. The Jinkses lived modestly, putting their money into their children rather than worldly things. And what children they had: beautiful, bright, well-mannered. No parents could be prouder of their offspring than Ada and Placide. Their only "failure" was Hercules. The boy dreamed of sports. He loved architecture but he didn't want to become an architect. Football, baseball, basketball, track and field— whatever the sport, Hercules beat everybody at it. He'd even taken up boxing, to the horror of Ada, who considered it truly low-rent. But there was money in pickup fights and Hercules, without a thought for himself, inevitably sent his earnings to Athena. Once a man twice his age split Hercules' lip in a fight. Ada swooned when her son snuck home that night. He bought her an outrageously expensive perfume and she half forgave him. Hercules' good nature and generosity won over everyone, even Ada. That, however, did not stop her from crabbing about sports, especially boxing. Such things were not done by "our kind of people." Ada repeated this so often that Hercules heard her voice in his sleep. Didn't stop him, though. Life bound him with restrictions not even becoming a doctor wouldn't remove. When he cracked a man firm on the jaw, blasted through a tackle or fielded a sizzling grounder, Hercules felt he owned the world. That's all he wanted from this life. Given the times and the temper, he was asking too much.

The sun, a golden monocle, glittered in a pale-blue sky. Lila Reedmuller trimmed her roses. Her blooms surpassed those growing on the capitol grounds. The kneeling and bending of gardening kept her fit, but mostly she loved to see things grow. Bartholomew had built a sumptuous greenhouse off the parlor of their Georgian home. One could sit amid eighteenth-century furniture and look into a jungle of seedlings, orchids, begonias. When the short winter passed, Lila flung herself into pruning, planting, planning. From the first crocus to the last hardy mum, she drew sustenance from the quiet life of flowers. Hortensia, her daughter, evidenced no interest in her mother's passion. Icellee Deltaven, a friend from childhood, joined Lila today, although her gossip skills exceeded her gardening skills.

"That youngest Bankhead girl is such a pistol, her father is sending her up to Washington, D.C., to school."

"A father with two daughters is not to be envied even if he is in Congress." Lila caressed a peach-colored rose.

"Tallulah could try the patience of all the giving saints, from what I hear." Icey adjusted her wide-brimmed straw hat.

"Where do you hear these things?"

"Grace is at Miss Martha's with Eugenia, the older Bankhead girl."

"And how is Grace?" Lila fairly skipped over to her trellis roses, Icellee's discontent with her only daughter being a worn topic.

"Takes Bunky to school and dreams of becoming an actress." Icey fanned herself with a handkerchief. "A Deltaven on the stage! I'll get apoplexy from that girl of mine, I swear I will. You know she sleeps with that vile little dog?"

"Bunky?" Lila laughed. "Be glad that's all she's sleeping with." Propriety never dimmed Lila's humor.

Icey flapped her with her perfumed hankie. "Wicked thing." She collapsed on a small wrought-iron bench and patted the seat next to her. "Sit a spell, Lila. The roses can wait."

Reluctantly Lila placed herself beside her. Icellee showed all the signs of gearing up for a bout of nostalgia.

"How I remember when we were in school! Where does the time go, Lila, where does it go?"

"Mmm." Lila keenly observed a shiny beetle attacking a prize white rose. She snapped it off.

"Bartholomew spends so much time in Birmingham. Don't you miss him?" On "him," Icey's voice rang out pure soprano.

"Always fishing. My God, I do admire your consistency. You were nosy in second grade and you're nosy now."

Icey pretended a huff. "No need to get contentious,

Lila. After all, what are friends for if we can't pry into one another's lives?"

"And announce it to the world."

Icey fluttered her hankie. "Lila! Lila Duplessis Reedmuller, how can you even think of such a thing? We've been bosom companions for thirty-nine years and I've never even intimated one syllable about you to anybody."

"Forty-three years, Icey."

"Speak for yourself."

Lila smiled. Icellee, finding her equilibrium, continued. "And I don't announce events to the world—just to Montgomery."

Lila laughed out loud and picked up Icey's hand. "That's our world, dear."

Icey wriggled around in her seat; the wrought iron lacked comfort. "Well, do you or do you not miss Bartholomew, and why don't you go with him to Birmingham?"

"Leave my garden? Anyway, twenty-five years with one man is a long enough time that I don't worry about him when he's away from home."

"He's still very good-looking."

"So am I." Lila saucily replied.

"I don't see how you do it. After Grace was born I blew up like a poisoned dog. You stay thin—and mean."

"You might try cutting down at the dinner table, Icey."

"I know, I know, but it's one of my few pleasures in this life—and I do have the best cook in Alabama, if I say so myself."

"That you do."

They sat quietly for a few moments, secure in the years of proximity. Lila, never one to sit still long, got up and returned to her roses.

"Stay put, Icey. I'll have Luzena bring you out a beverage." She walked over to a small fountain and rang a tiny bell near it. Luzena, a woman of Lila's years, peeped her head out the back door.

"Miss Lila?"

"Luzena, might you bring some lemonade for Miss Deltaven?"

Luzena's head disappeared behind the kitchen door.

"I still say Luzena's one quarter white." Icey considered herself an expert on bloodlines. The mixing of the races was her specialty, shared only among true friends. The philanderings of the white men in colored quarters was a source of hot pain for most of Montgomery's better ladies. Had they but known, it was a source of hot pain in colored quarters also.

"Shush, Icey. It's all water under the bridge, as they say."

"Ha!" Sexual dramas thrilled Icey no matter how old the news. Icey found Luzena's ancestry, with its whiff of wrongdoing, intoxicating.

"Are you going to be a Great Witch marshal this year?" Lila asked.

"Yes; you too?"

Lila tossed her head back. "I'm the Great Witch."

"You don't mean it!" Icey clapped her hands.

"Found out this morning."

"Oh, Lila, that's so exciting."

"I think so too. I can't wait until we sit down and make up clues."

Wistfully, Icey said, "I wonder if I'll ever get to be the Great Witch."

"You know how that works. There are so many groups to please, ruffled feathers to soothe. We've got to rotate the honor. Since it came to one of us, it will probably be five years before it returns."

"I suppose. Well, I'm delighted that you're the witchy-woo. Wait until your grandsons find out."

"They won't find out until the end of the hunt." Lila wiped her brow. Luzena brought out the lemonade in a silver pitcher on a little silver tray. "Thank you, Luzena. That looks so pretty."

"Yes, ma'am." Luzena headed back for the kitchen.

"Are those two still fighting like banty roosters?" Icey sipped her drink.

"Luzena and her husband?"

"Say, I didn't know anything about that." Icey's eyes enlarged.

"Oh, will you stop it?"

"I meant Edward and Paris."

"Brothers always fight. Sisters too."

"Of course." Icey took off her hat and fanned herself with it. "Amazing, though, how much Paris looks like his mother. Doubles." Her voice sank into its "secrets" key. "You know Carwyn was seen with that fancy woman. In public! In his fine, fine phaeton!"

Lila had hoped Icey wouldn't bring this up. "I know."

"Lila, isn't Bartholomew going to do anything about it? After all, you can't talk to your son-in-law about such behavior. It really is Bartholomew's place."

Lila kept sipping.

"Lila!"

"What, Icey?"

"What are you going to do?"

"I'm not going to do anything. The men of Montgomery have their cake and eat it too."

"How can you say such a thing?"

"It's true and you know it's true."

"Bartholomew must talk to Carwyn. It's bad enough he hangs over on Water Street like a blowfly over meat, but Jesus, Mary and Joseph, you don't bring it on the respectable side of town."

"Bartholomew will talk to him, but I don't want to know anything about it."

"Well, I do, so you can find out for me." Icey's burst of honesty struck her silent for a moment, then she had to laugh at herself. Lila laughed along with her.

"Oh, Icey, you are one of a kind—thank God; I couldn't bear another one."

Icey quieted herself. "How's Hortensia?"

"Herself."

Icey nodded. She had witnessed Hortensia from her first day of life on this earth.

Lila put down her shears and spoke as if to her roses.

"Whenever I go to dinner at Hortensia's I always feel that the table is set for someone else."

Icellee stopped fanning herself. She was having her troubles with Grace. She wondered if mothers and daughters ever understood one another, or did they come to terms when it was too late?

Karel Sokol visited Blue Rhonda once a week. His wife, Leone, abhorred sex. She was a good wife other than that. Karel would be halfway to Water Street and his underused rod stood at attention.

Banana Mae, Blue Rhonda and Lotowana languished on the porch.

"Here comes your six o'clock," Banana Mae reported.

"Hot as a forty-balled tomcat." Lotowana giggled.

Karel bounded up the stairs, greeted the ladies and vanished through the door. Blue Rhonda whispered, "Half an hour," to Banana Mae, who winked.

Once in her clean bedroom, Blue Rhonda sat on the edge of the bed. "Here, let me remove that nasty lump in your wallet." She slid her hand in his pocket, retrieved his wallet and brushed against his stiff prick. Karel grunted. Blue Rhonda tossed the wallet on her bed, then set about unbuttoning Karel's trousers. He usually stood up and today was no exception. Blue Rhonda stroked his penis and then began working in earnest. Karel was so ready it didn't take her five minutes. He slumped on the bed in gratitude.

"My legs feel like jelly."

"Lie down next time," Blue Rhonda advised.

"If I can wait that long." He pinched her cheek.

She fished her money out of his wallet and gave it back to him. She liked Karel. He was a decent man.

"There's no hurry, Karel. Relax. Maybe we can get you going again."

"Ah, I'm not so young anymore." He put his hand to his forehead.

She tactfully dropped the subject. Blue Rhonda figured her work was clean. Banana Mae twisted herself like a pretzel and the men sweated all over her. All Blue Rhonda had to worry about was whether to swallow it or spit it out. Karel recovered himself, buttoned back up and left early. Blue Rhonda rejoined her friends on the porch.

"You missed the best." Banana Mae knocked back a shot of whiskey.

"What?"

Lottie quivered in anticipation.

"Tell her." Banana Mae poked Lottie.

Words tumbled out. "Bunny was so het up she was ass over tit, I tell you, ass over tit!"

"Huh?" Blue Rhonda was intrigued.

"Linton Ray nearly drove her to cold-blooded murder. Uh-huh."

"What's that pissant up to now?" Blue Rhonda literally snorted.

"He told her if she'd join his temperance league he wouldn't trouble business."

"Fat chance." Banana Mae offered Lottie a slug of booze but Lottie leaned toward Blue Rhonda's coke, which she gladly shared.

"Maybe, but he said he's gonna start leaning on her clientele—if she don't go along with him, that is."

"I'll be damned." Banana Mae whistled.

"That's what Linton says," Lotowana innocently added.

"She's not gonna knuckle under?" Blue Rhonda tensed.

"No, but that old reverend is a slyboots. He'll muddy the waters, you wait and see." Lottie was right on that. She grabbed Blue Rhonda's knee. "Hey, Rhondee, where do you get such good stuff?"

"Press Tugwell, the pharmacist. A regular, you know."

"Get me some?"

"Sure." Her eyebrows knitted together, Blue Rhonda pondered Reverend Linton Ray. If he backed up his threat, something would have to be done about that man.

• • •

A clear night blessed the promoters. Most of Montgomery's male population, black and white, packed the makeshift wooden stands. Bare-knuckle fighting was brutal at best, murderous at worst. Cedrenus Shackleford, chief of police, conveniently turned a blind eye to the proceedings. Deprive the city of such bloodthirsty diversions and the city would surely deprive him of his job. Cedrenus quietly accepted payoffs, diligently applying himself to throwing drunks in jail on the night of a fight.

Placide Jinks accompanied his son to ringside. On the other side of the ring, Sneaky Pie took bets. Hercules was not favored to win, as his opposition was the best bare-knuckle fighter in Chicago. Sneaky Pie brought him down especially to wipe out this upstart, the boy wonder. Sneaky earned his name in the crime wars of the first decade of the century. Each immigrant group fiercely contested its own territory. Once a section of the city was under the domination of a warlord, he and his men moved into the next section, underground imperialism. The black section of Chicago, ripe with promise of profit, lured many a greedy man. Sneaky Pie heard the captains were planning a huge banquet to divide up territory and to try and settle differences in a less violent fashion. Posing as waiters, Sneaky and his men succeeded in serving poisoned pies to the guests, hence the name. After that the white boys left the black side of town alone, although they vowed to one day get Sneaky. He never expected to live long anyway. The danger heightened his appetite for all pleasures. Sneaky's face resembled an old wine cork, but those bright eyes never stopped scanning.

Hercules observed his opponent, a man in his late twenties, barrel-chested, with close-cropped curly hair. They called him Balthazar and he was ebony black, blue-black. The torch light seemed absorbed by his skin.

Placide arranged towels, buckets of water and smelling salts in Hercules' corner. "Your mother will kill us both for this. Balthazar is small potatoes compared to her."

Hercules smiled. He recognized Carwyn sitting in the front row, surrounded by his cronies. He wondered if he'd told Mrs. Banastre about the fight.

Bunny Turnbull, unable to control her girls over this one, brought them all to the fight, much to the delight of the men. Lotowana wore a dress of diaper-rash pink. Bunny, attired conservatively, poked a man in front of her. She handed him money and he placed a bet for her with Sneaky Pie.

Banana Mae was suffering from a cold, so Blue Rhonda stayed home to nurse her.

The two men met in the middle of the ring. The referee, Jake Rill from Birmingham, explained that hitting below the belt, kicking and butting were prohibited. If he tapped a man on the shoulder he must break. When the bell rings, return to your corner. Hercules and Balthazar nodded that they understood. The fight would last until a man was knocked out or threw in the towel.

When the bell sounded, Balthazar sprang across the ring. He peppered Hercules with punches, all easily blocked. Every now and then Hercules would slide a flicking left jab through Balthazar's defenses. It didn't look like much.

The first six rounds went the way of the first. Balthazar would try to intimidate Hercules, showering him with punches, and Hercules would parry and keep that light jab going. Both men were in splendid condition.

In the seventh round Hercules slipped and Balthazar, like a puma, pounced on him. He ripped open Hercules' cheek. The crowd roared. Hercules shakily pulled himself back together.

After that moment of suspense, the bout settled into a tremendous pounding match. That the two could exchange such blows and remain on their feet was remarkable. Sneaky Pie watched appreciatively. When he accepted the fight he didn't think this Montgomery kid had a snowball's chance in hell. A lot of money could be made off the Jinks boy, in the right hands. Sneaky just hoped he wouldn't lose money on this particular fight.

Lotowana shot up and down in her seat like a jumping jack. Bunny yanked her down. "Sit still, Lottie. No one can see from behind you." Even Bunny showed excitement. Her cheekbones glowed; she clasped and unclasped her hands.

Balthazar was a man in command of his art. If Hercules lost his temper the older man would move in for the kill.

By the twentieth round, blood matted the chest of each man. One eye of Hercules was swollen shut. Balthazar's ear kept filling up with blood from a wound in his scalp. He rhythmically shook his head to clear the ear. Their stamina was extraordinary. Balthazar reached deep within himself to find the energy to take the offensive. He slammed into the younger man like Thor's hammer. He beat Hercules back across the entire length of the ring. Hercules felt the ropes burn into his flesh. Balthazar pinned him with his left shoulder and tore into his body.

Hercules began to sag as the bell rang. He slowly dragged into the corner.

Placide popped smelling salts under his nose while a second threw a bucket of cold water on his face.

"Are you all right? Are you all right?" Placide knelt down to be at eye level.

Hercules opened his eye wide. "Yes."

"Do you want to stop?"

"I can take him."

"You know best," Placide counseled.

Hercules nodded.

The bell rang and he flew out of his corner. Balthazar blocked a straight right aimed at his jaw, but that left slipped by to irritate him and jar him. By now both men were crazed with fatigue and the desire to win. Hercules backpedaled and faked a slip. Balthazar, as he had in the seventh round, leapt onto his opponent, fully committing himself. As Balthazar dropped his guard to blast Hercules out of the ring, Hercules cracked him on the side of the head with a solid right. Balthazar hit the canvas. He swayed on all fours. Jake crouched over him and began the count. Balthazar staggered up just in time for Hercules to finish him off with a thundering uppercut. The crowd exploded. Hercules barely walked back to his corner.

Sneaky Pie pushed his way over to the young man. "Jinks, you need polish, but by damn you've got everything else!"

Hercules could only nod a thank you.

"You come see me in Chicago. I can make you rich, boy."

Hercules tried to shake Sneaky's white-gloved hand. "Mr. Pie—"

Sneaky hooted. "Sneaky, Sneaky. No one ever calls me Mr. Pie."

When Placide and his son came home that night Ada shrieked. However, as they counted the money, her shrieks subsided considerably.

"What are you going to do with all that money, son?" Placide asked.

Hercules spoke with difficulty, as his mouth puffed up.

"Athena wants to go to law school when she graduates from Vassar. This is for her."

Hercules didn't keep a penny for himself.

Carwyn and his friends enthusiastically discussed the fight as they rode back toward Water Street. It promised to be a night of ruinous pleasure. A few blocks from the train station, Carwyn saw his father-in-law approaching his coach. Bartholomew hailed him. Reluctantly, Carwyn sent his friends on their way while he joined Bartholomew.

"From the rumpus in the streets, I take it it was quite a contest."

"Hercules Jinks emerged the king of clubs." Carwyn swept his hat off his head.

"What?"

"You know, Hortensia's card system."

"That—I'd almost forgotten. She loves games. Lila too. I always think of the Jinks as hearts myself." Bartholomew sucked on his pipe, stalling.

"How is Lila?" Carwyn inquired.

"Fine, fine."

"I heard you had dinner with Smith again?"

"The Louisville and Nashville Railroad and I go back a long, long way." Bartholomew chuckled. He and Morton Smith, president of the railroad, stuck together when the governor of Alabama declared war on freight rates in 1903.

"He's a farsighted man," Carwyn mentioned.

"Yes, he is."

"Did he say anything about the war in Europe?"

"He thinks we'll finish it off for all of them." Bartholomew relit his pipe.

"We went in on the wrong side." Carwyn played with his mustache.

"Oh?"

"Let England and France exhaust themselves. Germany is the coming power. You, of all people, ought to appreciate that."

"How so?" Bartholomew actually hadn't paid much attention to the European conflict.

"You're the one who says the South can't look back.

'Relinquish the past to the dead.' '' Carwyn quoted Bartholomew's favorite line. ''The New South must be committed to industry. The way I see it, Germany is well on its way to being the real industrial key to Europe. France and England had their day. Like Birmingham, Germany is the future.''

''I'm not sure I follow that, Carwyn, but it's an interesting thought.'' Bartholomew blurted, ''See here, you can't be taking fancy women out in public.''

Carwyn figured this would come sooner or later. ''It was my mistake. It won't happen again, sir.''

Bartholomew sighed. ''I know how things are sometimes. I—Hortensia means a great deal to me. When I gave her to you in marriage I assumed you'd honor her. Don't disappoint me or humiliate her.'' He exhaled. ''Other than that, what you do on Water Street is your own business.''

''Yes, sir.'' Carwyn enjoyed social prominence, but he was still too young to challenge the strong hold Bartholomew's generation had over Montgomery society. He knew his time would come.

''Good.''

Curiosity got the better of Carwyn. ''Haven't you ever found that your wife was, uh . . . haven't you ever enjoyed other women?''

''Never.'' Bartholomew rapped out the word like a command.

• • •

Two cars, gleaming with brass, wasted space in the stables. Hortensia, spurred by her passion for everything new, bought them, toured around for a week, then got disgusted because the contraptions were forever breaking down. She regularly brought apples to Bellerophon. She poured affection into the animal that might well have gone to a human, but humans don't love one as devotedly as beasts. She'd discovered childbearing didn't supply what she longed for, either. All this business about children loving their mother—they didn't want to give, only to take. What they wanted was things or attention. If they didn't want toys, then she had to intervene in one more sibling squabble. Her restless energy fed her discontent. If she'd known what was wrong with her she might have tried to fix it, but Hortensia was not a woman to search inward. Instead, she rode faster, bought more jewels, traveled, threw sensational parties, and always wound up half bored and afraid that she was missing something.

Bellerophon, freshly groomed, shone more than the automobiles. A noise behind her startled Hortensia. It was Hercules Jinks. His face looked like a bruised plum.

"Good afternoon, Miss Banastre."

"Hercules, you look like hell."

"Yes, ma'am."

"Does it hurt?"

"Not much." He looked down the front of his shirt, which was covered with wood chips.

"My husband told me about the fight. He's a keen sportsman. It's about town that some Chicago people want you to make a career out of getting the stuff knocked out of you."

"Yes, ma'am."

"Well, will you do it?" she demanded.

"I'm thinking about it."

Hortensia fed Bellerophon another apple. "Faraway places and fame are seductive but not very satisfying, I think."

"I don't know."

"What on earth would possess you to tolerate such pain?"

"I like to win."

"Is that all?" Hortensia was incredulous.

"The money's good."

"That's a bit more convincing." She stroked the horse's neck. "Do you think it will make you happy?"

"Doesn't it make you happy?" Hercules simply wanted to know.

Hortensia wasn't prepared to be questioned. But Hercules caught her off guard. Besides, there was something about him. He was polite but not subservient. The Jinkses were that way; it could grate on your nerves.

"No."

Hercules was taught to emulate highborn people like

Hortensia. From a distance they looked like gods. Up close was a different story. Surprised and disquieted, Hercules wondered for the first time what makes anyone happy. If it wasn't being white and rich, then what was it?

"You have everything."

"You're very young, Hercules. I have nothing."

Part of him was angry at her. How easy for her to say money didn't make her happy. She could implicitly dismiss being white because she was white. Then, too, she should know her place, the top. She was supposed to uphold the system, give orders, provide an example. How could she question it? It was one thing for Hercules to wonder, but Hortensia should not. Having her above him, having anybody above him—a white person, a parent—relieved him of certain responsibilities. It unsettled him to consider assuming those responsibilities himself—even if society allowed it. But at this moment, the other part of him wanted to take some responsibility for Hortensia. Underneath the glamour she was raw. He wanted to protect her.

"Do you love your husband?" The words ran out of his mouth of their own accord.

Hortensia stiffened. How dare he? Then she stared at his injured face and thought him a combustible mixture of curiosity and innocence. After all, he was still a boy.

"No." She left the stable.

Blue Rhonda and Banana Mae met down at Bunny's to discuss Reverend Linton Ray. So far his campaign to blackmail clients into joining his anti-alcohol forces enjoyed limited success. Bunny, a natural planner, wanted to be certain they all stood together on this if it got worse. Her place of business reeked of Victoriana. As if that weren't bad enough, every room was named for a flower and decorated appropriately: rose, iris, pansy, tulip, petunia, orchid.

"Are we agreed, then, to keep this subject before our customers?" Bunny acted the chairman.

"Yes," all agreed.

"Good. I don't think anyone likes the way Linton is

going about this. He'll dig his grave with his teeth, that one.'' Bunny's light accent filled the room.

Bunny passed herself off as English but few people believed it. She came from one of the colonies: Australia, South Africa, Canada. However, her reserve and clipped speech set her apart from the other women, which was her design. Lotowana spied on her vigorously but couldn't find traces of affairs. Bunny managed her girls, counted her money and took great pleasure in its piling up. Still, Banana Mae and Blue Rhonda suspected a hidden lover somewhere.

The meeting concluded, Blue Rhonda and Banana Mae breathed in the crisp fall air as they walked home.

''Speak of the devil!'' Banana Mae griped.

''I think I'm gonna puke.'' Blue Rhonda squinted.

Linton oozed down the street. There was no escape.

''Miss Parker, Miss Latrec, it's God's will that I see you today.''

''God's fucked this one,'' Blue Rhonda whispered.

Upon them, Linton lost no time. ''You know of my great work here. Won't you join me in my crusade to end the evil use of alcohol?''

''No,'' came Blue Rhonda's swift reply. ''If people don't drink, they'll do something else. It's human nature.''

''We were expelled from the Garden of Eden for that very nature.'' Linton, ever the pedagogue, clasped his hands together.

''Who wants to live with a snake hanging from a tree?'' Blue Rhonda hated Linton.

''What's so bad about a nip of brandy, Reverend?'' Banana Mae baited.

''We must be clear of mind and clear of heart to perceive God and to perceive one another.''

''That's exactly why I drink, Reverend.'' Banana Mae's lips attempted a smile, but it was more a snarl.

''I don't quite follow, Miss Parker.''

''I see people quite clearly; I perceive them quite clearly; and I'd rather not know what I know.''

''Oh, surely you can't take such a dark view of human nature.''

"You do. Aren't you the one forever bleating about shitfire and abuse?"

"What?"

"For Chrissake, Linton, according to you the human race is a cesspool."

"You misunderstand me, Miss Parker, but I do believe alcohol leads us to the cesspool."

"Ha! You defraud the state by drinking water, because you cheat the vine grower, screw the tax collector and rob the merchant. I assist the nation by getting drunk." Banana Mae spun on her heel and walked off.

Blue Rhonda stood frozen in admiration. Before she could take off, Linton needled her.

"And you, Miss Latrec—do spirits pass your lips?"

"No, Reverend. I stick to cocaine." She ran after Banana Mae.

"That fartface gives me a spiritual ulcer. Petty, sanctimonious . . ." Anger stole her words.

"Banana, you laid him out to whaleshit. You were wonderful."

"Thanks." She paused. "He's not so easily put off. We're going to have trouble with him. He's like water. If he can't go through a problem, he'll find a way around it or simply wear it down like a stone."

"Then I say we give him a rat week." Blue Rhonda licked her lips.

Paris and Edward wriggled with excitement. Halloween night arrived at last. The two brothers would be divided, as the Great Witch Hunt specified that families be divided up between the two teams. The reasoning behind this was that it's a good thing for children to learn to cooperate with others, especially the little ones, who might have a tendency to lean on an older brother or sister.

Each team received ten clues. The first clue must be figured out by children in first and second grade. The second clue was for third and fourth graders, the third clue for fifth and sixth, and the fourth clue for seventh and eighth. The remaining clues were open to all. Older children couldn't help younger children with their clues, but younger children could help older. The range allowed in age was six to eighteen years old. All over town marshals were posted. These civic worthies, resplendent in black-and-orange sashes, monitored the proceedings. Marshals were carefully scattered about lest they lead the children to the clues.

Legend had it that the Halloween game was as old as Montgomery, which was incorporated in 1819. A father made it up to soothe his tiny daughter's fear of ghosts about on that night. Whenever it started, no resident could remember being without it. Odd how the little things stay with one. Citizens of sixty could recall vividly their participation on a winning team. Naturally, old-timers declared their clues were brainbusters. Kids have it easy nowadays. In fact, clues remained steadily difficult, graduated for age, of course.

On the other side of town, Blue Rhonda and Banana Mae readied themselves for Halloween. They donned sheets, made holes for eyes and squealed like the children down at the statehouse being divided into teams. Blue Rhonda and Banana Mae were not invited to the Great Witch Hunt, but they had concocted plans of their own.

"Got the corn liquor?"

"Yes," Banana Mae replied. She looked at herself in the mirror. The eye holes in the sheet were too small, so she took a scissors and enlarged them, nipping her eyebrows in the process.

Blue Rhonda also checked her image. "Hey, there's bloodstains on this sheet. Goddammit, wait until I get my hands on Euthabelle."

"She can't perform miracles. Bloodstains are hell to get out."

"She's a laundress; that's her job." Blue Rhonda pouted.

"You don't want to use a good sheet anyway. Now shut up and come on." Banana put her sheet back over her head.

Blue Rhonda followed, carrying a billy club. "We can take turns with that corn liquor if it gets heavy."

"There's another way to lighten that load," Banana suggested.

"Amen, sister."

Edward danced around in the crisp night air. He was on the Black team, Paris on the Orange. Before each team could be given their first clue they must vote on a captain. This honor always went to an eighteen-year-old, and most often a boy. People could tell you that an Orange captain of 1835 went on to become a Confederate colonel, or a Black captain of 1852 made a fortune in railroads. As it turned out, most captains did well in this world; a few dengenerated into drunks or scoundrels, but not many. Lila Reedmuller was Orange captain of 1891. She was one of the four girls ever chosen for that honor, and Lila went on to reign over Montgomery society and to play politics, so it was gossiped. Tonight she swooped about her cherrywood library in her black witch's cape, to the merriment of dear friends and Bartholomew. Within the half hour she'd have to creep along Montgomery's streets to her hiding place. From Orange captain to Great Witch—her two childhood ambitions were realized. From the vantage point of being forty-three they appeared unheroic, but it was fun to be the Great Witch, even if one knew better.

Orange team elected Charles Scott Venable captain. A handsome boy with a scientific mind, he would provide steady leadership. The Blacks picked Alexander Fleet; imaginative, high-spirited, he was temperamentally opposite Charles. The rotund Chief Marshal handed out Clue One.

Charles read it to his Orange team. "Here's the church, there's the steeple. Open the doors, there are no people."

Alexander did the same for his baby Blacks, as he called them. "Hey diddle diddle, the cat and the fiddle. Find the little puss and you've solved the riddle."

The Great Witch Hunt covered a two-square-mile territory. The game rarely ventured into the further reaches of its boundaries because it was important for the children to know the limits. It made the riddles easier for the small ones and kept them from getting too tired. As the clues became harder, the geographic limits became more frustrating. More than one team was tempted to wander off, but they lost so much time in doing so, they usually lost the game.

"We have to go to a church, but which one?" Paris offered his teammates.

Another small child figured, "One that keeps its doors open."

Mary Bland Love, the darling of the seven-year-old set, screeched, "Saint Matthew's. The Catholic church always keeps the doors open."

As some of the little ones started in the direction of the church, Charles called them back. "Now are all you first-clue people agreed on this? Let's not run off if anyone thinks it's wrong."

No hands shot up.

"O.K., then, to Saint Matthew's." Charles headed up his small army.

Downtown Montgomery shuddered under the tramp of tiny feet. The Black team tore off at about the same time as the Orange. The game usually started this way. The teams remained even until they got into the more difficult clues. After that is was anybody's guess. The Blacks turned a corner and found their clue pinned to the door of Mother Goose Café. A cat-and-fiddle sign squeaked in the light evening air.

Alexander read Clue Two. "There was an old woman who lived in a shoe. Find her, you'll know what to do."

As his third and fourth graders argued over this one, all the Blacks heard a roar.

"They figured out Clue Two." A bigger girl leaned over a third grader. "Hurry up."

Orange's second clue read, "Yo ho ho and a keg of rum. If you don't find this one you're very dumb." A bright kid who was also chubby yelled, "Mason's Candy Store." He remembered the huge Rumtopf keg sitting in the front window.

In a state of tension, the Blacks, already worried about time, thundered over to the Regenbogen Shoe Salon. A small advertisement in the corner of the window showed the old woman in her shoe, surrounded by children, all wearing the latest styles. Clue Three hung on the door.

"Mighty Samson avoided this place. You come and we'll improve your face," read Alexander.

At about the same time the Oranges grabbed their Clue Three, which was right where the fat kid said it would be.

"Jesus slept in one, so they say. But mostly this one's filled with hay," Charles's deep voice rang out.

Blue Rhonda and Banana Mae clambered across town in their high-button shoes. The jug passed between them whenever it proved too heavy. Banana Mae went beyond the call of duty to lighten their burden.

"Slow down, Nanner. You'll never make it to Marshal Post Thirty."

"I can drink anyone under the table."

"That's not under dispute. Tonight you need to be sharp."

"All right, then, gimme some toots."

Blue Rhonda fished out her small silver box filled with coke. "Hold up a minute. Here." Banana leaned over and sniffed some of the powder from Blue Rhonda's long fingernail.

"Are you satisfied? I'll be alert and I promise not to take another swig"—Banana raised her right arm and the sheet pulled up, revealing her dress—"for at least five more blocks."

Oranges and Blacks mastered their third clues without too much trouble. The Blacks stood in front of Philpotts' Barbershop and the Oranges massed inside Bazemore's Livery. The next set of clues took one group to a pawn-shop and the other to the hospital. The fifth clues proved a bit more difficult, but Orange's "From where I sit I see you talk, but I can't move my feet to walk" took them to the statue of Jefferson Davis. Blacks decided, as quickly, that "People come and people go, I remain through all the flow" could only be the train station. Even the sixth and seventh sets of clues didn't slow them. However, the eighth set tested everybody.

"Read it again, Alex," a Black cohort called.

Alexander studied the clue and read it for the third time. "Relatives come, quite devout. You can dress him up but you can't take him out."

The team investigated clothing stores, but that didn't make much sense. If you bought clothes, why couldn't you or whoever you bought them for wear them? Someone suggested dressing up animals. Other members of the team sat on the ground.

Oranges fussed over their clue: "I tell the truth and make it pay. Find me and you're on your way."

A little boy screamed, "What's that?"

The group had a vision of two white ghosts flitting down an alleyway.

"I want my mother," piped a tiny voice.

"Don't worry, honey. Ghosts are supposed to be out on Halloween night," an older child reassured.

"Let's scare those little chips off the old block!" Banana giggled.

"We haven't got time. If we don't get to Marshal Post Thirty before the game's up, we lose our chance."

"You'd have made a great overseer, Rhonda," Banana clipped. "Too bad you were born before the War."

They clambered along. Quickly Blue Rhonda stopped and Banana Mae, who wasn't watching, smacked into her.

"Hey," Banana bitched.

"Shut your trap," Blue Rhonda hissed. "There he is."

A block away, Reverend Linton Ray paced his beat like a soldier on guard. Both teams passed him in their searching. Like the other marshals, he didn't know the clues, so he would only know the game was won when the Chief Marshal rode to each post announcing a good time was had by all. He absentmindedly clutched and unclutched the Bible in his hands.

"Stick to the plan," Blue Rhonda whispered.

Banana Mae nodded and sprinted out in front of the reverend. She danced around, making scary noises. Meanwhile, Blue Rhonda snuck up behind him.

"Why aren't you with the other children?" Linton asked.

"Woo, woo," Banana kept on in a tiny voice.

"Go on, now, you can't scare—"

He slumped to the ground. Blue Rhonda crowned him with her billy club.

"Jeez, you hit him hard," Banana worried.

"Whenever you hit anyone on the head it makes a crack. Come on, do your stuff, girlie."

Banana took out her corn liquor and poured it all over Linton.

"Pour some on the Bible, New Testament," Blue Rhonda advised.

"O.K."

"The disciples only got wine. This ought to wake them up."

"Rhonda." Banana Mae shook her head.

When the jug was empty, she carefully placed it in Linton's hand.

"Let's get out of here." Blue Rhonda grabbed her partner. They burned the wind racing home.

The Orange team pieced together their next-to-last clue and were at the newspaper office. The final clue, which was identical for both teams, was handed to Charles Venable by the city editor. It read: "There once was laughter, there once was light. Now I'm alone in the blackest night."

Traditionally, the tenth clue, which led to the Witch, was the hardest. This one proved no exception. From a few blocks away the Oranges heard a shout. The Black team finally mastered their eighth clue, which took them to Sonneborn Funeral Parlor. They were frenzied to get through their ninth clue. They knew the Oranges were ahead of them; each team sent out a scout to report the progress of their opponents.

The ninth clue for the Black team maintained the Halloween spirit: "I say nothing but I tell all. You'll find the next clue pinned on the wall." Alexander proved his worth as a captain. In an inspired moment, he shouted, "The Ritz Theater!" The team feverishly charged over to the movie house, to find the last clue. It was now a dead-even race. Whoever got to the Witch first had the game.

"Anyone got any ideas?" Alex asked.

"It can't be a store, because they're always dark at night," an older boy volunteered.

"Laughter—an old theater," a girl called out.

"The Capitol Theater was torn down last year." Edward spoke up. "What's around that's empty?"

"The Bainbridge estate!" Alex leapt into the air.

Three beautiful daughters lived in the Bainbridge estate, a handsome Greek Revival mansion, before the War. Each daughter came to a bad end. One died of typhoid. The second killed herself when her husband died at Gettysburg, and the third lived on into the 1880s, only to be murdered in her bed by her lawyer. Not one daughter produced an heir, although the rumor was that Vicky, pregnant, refused to marry her lawyer lover and he smothered her. She'd always said to her closest friends he was good enough to bed but not to wed. She suspected he wanted her for her money, and getting her with child seemed a sure route to the altar. No one really knew what happened, but the decaying house remained as a question mark, a symbol of two lives: one for the street; one behind closed doors.

Blacks flew to the huge house. Lila, broom in hand, met them under the pillars. Appropriately enough, bats darted in and out of the eaves. About ten minutes later the Oranges arrived on the lawn. Winners received a little silver witch's hat at the end of the black-and-orange ribbon. Engraved in the other side was the year. Everyone got candy. Children compared clues, and the losers, typically, declared their clues were much harder. The competition faded amid the candied apples and floss candy.

"Just wait, Edward, I'll win." Paris eyed his brother's shiny medal, tears in his eyes.

The real shock of the night came when the Chief Marshal rode upon Linton's prostrate body. He nearly fell off his horse from the reek of alcohol. Before the rooster woke up on the first of November, the whole town buzzed with the news of the preacher's downfall.

"How was I to know it would backfire?"

"Rhonda's right, Bunny; it seemed a good idea at the time." Banana Mae stoutly defended her friend.

Lotowana wiggled. "Wish I'd been there. The dried raisin. Wish you'd split his head clean open."

"I thought he'd learned his lesson," Blue Rhonda said. And so he had. From now on Linton Ray would concentrate on the wives of men who frequented Water Street or local drinking establishments. The painter, at last, found his palette. Trying to convert individual prostitutes and drunks had proved less than perfect. Now he'd weld together a mass of malcontents and bring pressure to bear on his enemies, the sinners.

"Who could stop drinking?" Banana asked. "Even if someone could stop drinking, isn't it my inalienable right as an American citizen to get snookered?"

"There's plenty of Americans that would be glad to take that right away from you," Bunny mentioned.

Lotowana's caterpillar eyebrows fuzzed together. "I can't say as Reverend Ray's got any men with him. It's all their women."

"He's got some men," Bunny informed her.

"Those aren't men; those are males who call their wives 'Mother.' " Banana smirked.

"What's wrong with people? I mean, what's a little drinking and fucking got to do with anybody else?" Blue Rhonda spoke whimsically.

"Yeah, what's it to anybody but the person doing it?" Lotowana picked up the banner.

"Obviously, it means something to Linton," Bunny said, sighing.

"Maybe he's not getting any." Blue Rhonda laughed.

"That's unnatural, you know, really unnatural," Banana said. "God made animals to fuck; us too. If we weren't supposed to fuck, then God wouldn't have made us with conjoining parts."

"Conjoining?" Lottie leaned forward.

Banana Mae made a circle with one hand and pierced it with the index finger of her other hand.

"Oh, that." Lottie nodded in agreement.

"It's not just Linton's clean-up campaign. It's morality for some of them, but it's power for others. They want to see if they can force you to bend their way instead of going your own way." Blue Rhonda's lips compressed.

"So greedy they'd steal our share of sunlight," Bunny agreed.

"Well, he's not going to go away." Lotowana folded her hands.

"These damn temperance leagues spring up all over like fleas. What's happening that so many people are willing to worry about something so . . . so superficial?" It took Blue Rhonda a while to find "superficial."

"I think it has something to do with the war," Bunny put forward.

"That's over in Europe, and who cares if a bunch of Limeys, Krauts and Frogs kill each other off?" Lotowana had no time for war talk.

"I don't much care what those people do, myself. If they can't learn to get along, let them kill each other. Good riddance, I say." Banana Mae seemed sure of that.

"Except, we're in it too. Makes no sense to me." Blue Rhonda's voice lowered.

Bunny picked up her line of thought. "That's what I mean. Don't you see? When something big like a wolf lurks at your door and you can't kill him or get rid of him, you pick on someone smaller than yourself. If you beat up your child or your wife, then you can feel victorious."

"Until the wolf comes through the door." Lotowana rooted around in her bag for tobacco.

"Exactly," Bunny trumpeted.

The little group quieted for a while, as the thought was upsetting. Finally, Blue Rhonda broke the silence. "You know, when they found Linton he rattled on about a choir of angels. Not only did they think he was drunk; they thought he was nuts."

"Everything would have been all right if that big lump hadn't raised up aside his head." Banana frowned.

"There are those who think he fell down, plastered, and those who think he was hit over the head." Blue Rhonda took a toot.

"For Christ's sake, next time don't act alone. Let's talk this out between us." Bunny sounded imperial.

"Who died and made you God?" Blue Rhonda, ever hostile to authority, got her back up.

"Hey." Banana Mae punched Rhonda in the arm. That settled her for a minute.

"I didn't say I'd give orders. I just said we should discuss these things together. After all, we are in the same trade." Bunny really was the natural leader of the Water Street women. For one thing, she had the most at stake, having the largest establishment.

"That's a good idea, Bunny." Banana smoothed things over.

Rhonda quickly came out of her sulk. "I was sitting here thinking."

A catcall from Lotowana stopped her. Lottie peered down at her huge bosom and brushed off an imaginary flake of tobacco to avoid the glare.

Rhonda continued. "We don't care what everybody says about us or we wouldn't do what we do. Other people seem to care. I can't imagine that anyone would give a shit what anyone else thinks about them."

"People are weak," Banana said. "They go along with the crowd."

"Look at the French Revolution." Bunny displayed her learning.

"I don't give Jack Shit about the French Revolution." Blue Rhonda considered history what happened two hours before. Anything beyond that was not worth attention.

"Nonetheless, the policies swung one way, then the other, thousands of people were murdered, all in the name of public safety, and in the end they wound up with another dictator. They were as well off with the king. And the great mass of people, the ones whose safety was in jeopardy, sat through it all like a slug."

"Where'd you learn all this, Bunny?" Lotowana was impressed.

"I finished high school, you know. History was my favorite subject." She smiled.

"Where?" Blue Rhonda crept up on her.

"Bri— Why, in Sussex, of course."

Rhonda slumped back in her seat. "As I said, anyone who cares what anyone else thinks is stupid."

"Right." Lotowana loved such talk.

"I mean, have you ever seen engraved on a tombstone: 'She Was Well Liked By All'?" Rhonda roared on.

"No." Banana Mae tapped Blue Rhonda's hand. "Time to go."

Once Blue Rhonda warmed to a subject she'd beat it into the ground. Banana Mae employed all her persuasive powers to pry Rhonda out of Bunny's living room. Blue Rhonda was now holding forth on why fishing was cruel. In her mind, this was connected to worrying about people's opinion of you. Finally, Banana Mae resorted to bribery. She got her home on the promise of cooking spoon bread.

Carwyn watched his sons bicker over a baseball. He blamed their failings on Hortensia. Edward he liked because he could talk to him, carry on a reasonable conversation. Paris, absorbed in his desire for Hortensia's affection, barely noticed his father. Carwyn didn't like his own son. He kept it to himself but it came out in other ways.

He and Hortensia lived as signatories of an armed truce. It never occurred to him to wonder if she had a life separate from her social and familial obligations, an inner life. It never occurred to him that he as well might have an inner life. Carwyn viewed the world directly; he simply wanted his own way. He gave little thought to anything or anybody. His political ties were to preserve his power, and by extension, the power of his class, race and sex. He assumed everyone like him thought like him. In the main he was right, but there were a few rebels out there, and more, he was creating the conditions for rebellion in his sons. Each son would choose a different path, but the die was cast: they'd turn away from their father's world.

Hortensia glided into the library to find a book.

"Hello, dear," Carwyn said.

"I didn't know you were in here."

"I've been watching the boys fight. Can't you do anything with them?"

"No."

"I don't see why not. My mother kept me in line."

"I'm not your mother."

"Well I know it."

She slammed the book on the table. She'd had a day of it anyway. The boys were cranky; one of the maids was out sick; she felt as if she was coming down with something herself. Father Time honed his scythe on her spirit.

"You're their father. You do something about them."

This argument rolled off Carwyn. He ignored it. Hortensia became angrier. "You had these children as an act of inattention."

"On the contrary, I remember it quite well."

Though he bore no affection for his wife, he liked to go to bed with her. Carwyn remained vulnerable to that beauty.

"You look for the belt and hit below it." She picked up her book.

"We understand a great deal about one another, my dear, and we don't like what we know." He stroked his mustache. He hated her but he wanted her. His father was right when he said, "Women—you can't live with them and you can't live without them."

"Yes." She stared at him. He was a good-looking man, yet she felt nothing but disgust. As she wheeled to leave the room, he grabbed her around the waist and kissed her. He liked the struggle. If he could get her in bed after a fight it sharpened his appetite, although she seemed to have no feeling for it at all. He didn't much care, as it was for his pleasure.

"Keep your eunuch's kisses to yourself," she spat.

Furious, Carwyn struck back. "You should have been born a man, my dear."

She met him with, "Apparently that's a misfortune we both share."

She'd rarely examined herself or her marriage. She lived with it. However, she now understood that her marriage was a nerve ending in a dead hand.

Ada Jinks scraped at the corner of the floor with a paring knife. Her bum rose like the full moon. Hercules scrubbed down the floor that morning as he was told to do, but that wasn't enough for Ada. On Saturdays, off work, she propelled her titanic energies into keeping everything and everybody clean. When her children were small she bathed their little hands so often it was a wonder they weren't raw. Age increased her mania for cleanliness. She knew errant fuzzballs lurked in the corners, and by God, she would get them out. Placide attended to the outside chores all that day. The grunting and groaning of his spouse prevented his enjoying the rest to which he felt he was entitled.

"Ada, calm yourself."

"I can't rely on Hercules to do the corners. If you want something done right around this house you have to do it yourself." She picked up two strands of fuzz and put them in the trash bucket.

"The floor shines like glass. Come on, honey."

"Placide, I can't stand a dirty house."

There was no getting around her. Athena, home from school for the week, clambered down the stairs.

"Where are you off to?" Ada sternly asked.

"India Overton's."

"Why don't you leave that poor old woman alone?" her mother quizzed.

"I like her. She knows things."

"Horseradish, that's what she knows." Ada jabbed in the corner.

"She knows the healing arts."

Ada glared at her eldest. "A handful of herbs and dandelions do not add up to the healing arts."

"Mother, not everything comes out of a book."

"Telling your mother about the world, are you?"

"You don't know everything."

"I do not suffer fools gladly, miss," Ada boomed.

"I don't know why I bothered to come home," Athena moaned.

"Don't you talk to your mother that way even if she is wrong." Placide rustled his evening newspaper for effect, and that fast, Athena bolted out the front door.

"Wrong!" Ada complained.

"Let her be. India Overton spins a good tale. If Athena wants to eat dandelions, she deserves them." Placide folded his paper.

"Too clever by half."

"I guess we spoiled her." Placide smiled. "But, honey, what's the use of having children if you can't spoil them rotten?"

"We never agreed on that, my dear husband."

"I know. I married a Prussian general in disguise."

Ada put her hands on her hips. "Just keep talking, Mr. Jinks."

Hercules dashed in from the back door. "Hi, Mom. Hi, Dad."

"Slow down!" Ada commanded as he skidded across the floor.

"Sorry. It's so beautiful out today that I ran all the way home. Guess I forgot to stop."

"Another architecture book?" Placide eagerly spied a book in his son's hand.

Hercules showed it to his father. "Isn't it something?"

"You read it first, then I'll read it," the father advised his giant offspring.

"How about this for a system: you use a red bookmark and I'll use a blue. So we can read it together. Whoever is finished for the day can put it on the dinner table."

"Hercules, you might amount to something in spite of yourself." Ada attacked a new corner.

He said nothing, but shrugged his shoulders.

"Do you know what Athena's doing over there at India Overton's?" Ada demanded.

"She teaches her country medicines and tells her about slave days. Athena likes all that history stuff." Hercules didn't think a thing of it.

"Why is she so interested in all this?"

"Wants to be a lawyer."

Ada's expression changed to one of beatific delight. "She never told me."

"She's afraid you'll make fun of her and tell her to get married," Hercules said.

"What?"

"You're always at her because she doesn't have a proper beau."

"Placide, do I do that? The way I feel about education! Why, there's all the time in the world to get married. Do I do that?"

Placide stuck his nose deep in the paper. "Yes, you do."

She applied herself to her corner, embarrassed.

Placide laughed behind his paper. Hercules laughed too.

"Did you see Mrs. Banastre today?" Placide inquired.

"No," Hercules replied.

"Do you usually see her when you get these books?"

"She leaves them with Amelie. I've only spoken with her once. I told you before, Dad."

"Good," Placide exhaled. "You must be careful with those people."

"The Banastres?"

"Along with the others. You have to be careful."

• • •

Grace Deltaven dug her heels into the sidewalk, compelling her mother, Icellee, to grab her with both hands and yank with all her might.

"Grace, you will accompany me."

"No."

Bunky, Grace's dog, with poached-egg eyes, yelped as he was squeezed under his mistress's left arm.

"I will not change my mind. I will not change my mind. I will not change my mind!" Grace screamed.

"Shut up, bitch!" Icellee lost control.

For revenge, Grace let loose Bunky. The beast nipped Icellee's high-button shoes. She tried kicking his guts out but he darted away.

"Call him off."

"Let go of me, then I'll call him off."

"No."

"Sic her, Bunky. Bite her good."

Bunky ducked between Icellee's slow-moving legs and sank his sharp little fangs above her ankle. Icellee released her daughter and hopped around on one foot.

"Rabies, I'll get from the vile creature. How could you? Your own mother."

"I told you to let me go."

At that smug retort Icellee swung her whole weight around like a discus thrower and whacked Grace with her packed purse. She caught her offspring square on the jaw. Grace tumbled over backward. Bunky sped to his mistress, licking her face between ferocious growls at Icellee.

"Now we're even, miss."

Crying, Grace pleaded, "It doesn't matter what you do. I won't change my mind."

"We'll just see about that." Icellee swayed like a cobra over her fallen daughter.

Grace scooped up Bunky and reluctantly followed Icellee, who seemed to have grown larger, more powerful, after the encounter.

Lila Reedmuller witnessed the contest from the vantage point of her front porch. She considered walking out to greet them, but decided to give both women a chance to calm down.

Icellee, gaining speed, marched up the steps of the graceful mansion. "Lila, do something."

"Haven't you done enough?"

Grace, ten feet behind, rubbed her cheek with her free hand. Bunky continued growling. Her eyes lowered, Grace mumbled her hellos to Lila and took a seat on the porch chair. "I'm not changing my mind even if you gang up with Mother."

"Do you see what I put up with?" Icellee pitied herself. "She's been like this since September, and she's getting worse."

"Come on, ladies, let's go inside. It's a bit chilly out here."

As the combatants flung themselves into the parlor, Bunky wriggled free of Grace and curled up in front of the fireplace. He watched Icellee with suspicion.

"It's my life," Grace argued.

"I'm your mother. I'm responsible for that life and I won't have you throw it away."

"Same problem?" Lila offered Icellee sherry, which she readily took.

"I'll say. She's never been the same since she met that Bankhead girl."

"Tallulah has nothing to do with it." Grace defended her friend.

"Ha. That fat hellion is so wild she's only allowed

home for the holidays. I knew once you got thick with her sister trouble would follow."

"I wanted to be an actress long before I met anyone from Jasper, Alabama." Grace drew out "Jasper" until it hissed. Bunky flattened his ears against his head.

Lila positioned herself between the two women. "Grace, it's a very difficult life."

"I don't care. I want to do something. Be somebody."

Icellee leaned around Lila in order to give Grace her famous freeze stare. "Marrying well and living in Montgomery isn't good enough, eh?"

"No."

"It's proved quite acceptable to Lila and myself."

"I'm not Lila, or"—she paused—"yourself."

"Is it so important that a carpenter in Chicago know your name, or a bootblack in New Orleans?" Lila gently chided her.

"Yes—no. That's not why I want to act." Grace wanted Lila to understand. She'd always liked her. "I want to do something that comes from inside me, that doesn't bore me. Aren't you ever bored, Miz Reedmuller?"

Icellee raised up on her haunches to smack Grace. Lila intervened and Bunky bared his fangs. "Don't ask a personal question of your betters, young lady."

"That's all right, Icey." Lila patted her friend's shoulder. "Grace, there have been moments in my life when I thought I'd die of boredom."

Icellee's eyes popped open. "Lila."

"You've never been bored?" Lila asked her.

"I'm not answering that in front of a recalcitrant, ungrateful child."

Lila continued. "There were mornings, more so when I was younger, when I'd wake up and look out the window and wonder: Is this it? Is this life?"

"And that's why I want to act."

"What makes you think you can't get bored or hurt on the stage?" Lila smiled.

This idea never occurred to the rebellious girl. "Well, I just wouldn't, that's all. I couldn't possibly. Anyway, I'd get to be different characters, and I'd be so busy learning my lines, I just wouldn't."

"Perhaps." Lila folded her hands.

Icellee gazed into the fire. She'd been bored plenty in her life, and although Grace did not add to the boredom, she added to the aggravation.

"Even if I get bored, it's still my life." Grace clamped her jaw.

Lila took Icellee's hand. "It is her life."

Icellee wriggled in her seat.

"Icey."

"I know. I don't want her to throw it away. You know the kind of people who inhabit the theater."

"You know the kind of people who inhabit Montgomery." Lila smiled again.

"Things sure are different than when I was a girl. My father would have locked me up. There's no discipline anymore, Lila. Her classmates are just as bad. They all have ideas of their own."

"Be that as it may. I don't see how you can stop her."

The three sat like stones. Icellee knew she had to give in. Grace silently glowed. Lila wondered why you make all your mistakes on your own children when you can so clearly see how to help other people's children.

• • •

"The Halloween witch drinks human blood and crunches up bones." Edward's voice cackled.

"I'm too old for that." Paris feigned indifference.

Edward kept cackling. Paris continued to assemble a little locomotive engine.

"Heh, heh, heh, heh." Edward swooped down on his brother, knocking him backward.

Paris socked him. "Stop it."

Edward cackled louder. What he was really mad about was the fact that Paris had discovered his hiding place for money. Piggy banks no longer thwarted his little brother. Edward hid change in a shoe box in the back of his toy chest and put the few dollar bills he had between the pages of a dictionary, figuring his brother, averse to books, would never find them. Paris found them and when Edward went to check on his cache, like Scrooge, he found nothing. An accusation met with the usual denial. Maybe the witch trick would scare Paris into confession.

"Whooooo, blood and bones. Yum."

"I hate you." Paris's lower lip trembled. He'd heard from older friends about Dr. Jekyll and Mr. Hyde. Maybe Edward was undergoing a transformation.

The subsequent screams and rumble of furniture brought Hortensia up to their room. Paris flew to her side and Edward, still furious, kept after him.

"He stole my money, Mother."

Paris ran around his mother's skirt and Edward chased him. She grabbed Edward's shoulders as he seized a hunk of his brother's hair. He let go and Paris disappeared under Hortensia's long skirt.

"Mama's boy, mama's boy," Edward chanted.

"Enough!"

Edward shut up.

From underneath the skirt Paris called back, "I am not a mama's boy."

"Paris, get out from under there."

"No, he'll kill me. He said he would." Paris, crouching down, now looked upward to behold the formidable underpinnings of femininity. He couldn't see anything except what looked like ruffled bloomers, but the odor was sweet and warm.

"He took all the money I hid in the dictionary." Edward sounded like a prosecutor.

She released her elder son and spoke to the younger. "Out!"

"No." Paris clutched a leg hardened by years of riding.

Losing her own temper, she swatted him through her skirt. "When I say 'get out,' I mean get out."

His head popped out and a half kick from his mother greatly speeded his departure. In full view of a glowering brother and an irritated mother, he sprang to Hortensia and wrapped his arms around her waist. She pried him loose.

"I didn't steal his money. I did not. I did not."

Edward, writhing, but determined not to appear hot-headed again in front of his mother, reached down and picked up the battered train engine. "Then where did you get the money to buy this model?"

Paris gulped, then smoothly replied, "Grandmama lent it to me."

"At an interest rate?" Hortensia's lip twitched upward.

"Why, yes, that's exactly what she did." Paris beamed.

"Darling, you know Grandmother attends church regularly?"

Paris answered, "Sure, I know that."

"There's a law in the Bible against usury. Your grandmother wouldn't lend you money at an interest rate." Hortensia fought back the laughter. He was so easy to catch in a lie.

"I didn't use anything!" Paris screeched.

"My money." Edward veered within striking range and Paris clung to Hortensia again. This time she smacked his hands.

"Let go of me, Paris. I've had enough of this behavior. You will repay your brother every penny."

"I didn't steal it."

"Then you'll repay him anyway and become your brother's keeper."

"Ugh." His beautifully formed lip curled over his teeth.

"It's good discipline. You can start by cleaning out the attic. I'll check on you later."

Shrewdly, Paris said, "Can I go through all the old uniforms and stuff?"

"After you get the junk out first."

Edward considered this. "When you're finished with the junk I'll help you with the uniforms."

"No you won't." Paris smiled maliciously. "It's my punishment."

Sparks flew again. Hortensia, bored and impatient, stated, "One more argument, one more, and no riding lessons this week, nor fencing. If you can't get along, then dislike one another quietly for today." Edward bowed his head. "Edward, while Paris works upstairs, why don't you go down to Granddad's office. He said he has some old things there you might look at before he throws them out."

"Really, Mother?"

"Really. Now go on."

Edward shot out of the room. Paris returned to his mother for one more hug. "You're so mean."

"Next time, don't take your brother's money. And don't ever lie to me."

"What's so bad about my train engine? He could play with it too."

"That's not the point. It was his money. If you'd learn how to save, you could buy lots of things."

A lesson on economics was worse than cleaning the attic. He made a great show of leaving the room and trudged up to the next floor, complete with sniffles.

Hortensia returned to the small reading room off her bedroom to try one more time for a few minutes' peace.

Paris resembled his mother except that his pale-blond hair was curly. He looked like a little angel. Even in the cradle, ladies had oohed and aahed over him.

Edward, the salt to Paris's pepper, was dark like his father. He usually covered up for Paris. It wasn't so much that he loved him, but with distant parents, his brother supplied an emotional center.

Hortensia observed this and assumed the two had little need of adult interference, except on those occasions, like today, when they got into a fight. She congratulated herself on the fact that they took care of one another and let it go at that. For Edward she felt some warmth, but toward Paris she was curiously empty. She felt estranged from him even when he was in the womb. If she'd wanted to discuss this with anyone, she never did; there was no one she could or would talk to anyway.

She sat in her big wing chair before the fireplace and covered her legs with a plaid blanket from Scotland. She was recovering from last night's social triumph. She threw a party with the theme "The Future." Betty Stove, her closest rival for leadership of the younger set, arrived as Electricity. The light bulbs sprinkled in her hair caused a sensation, particularly when they shorted out. Hortensia concluded that electricity was yet to be perfected as well as Betty Stove.

That party over, she fidgeted in her chair, searching for a new toy, a new anything. One day without a goal, no matter how superficial, upset her. A light knock on her door startled her.

"Miss Hortensia?"

"Yes, Leone."

"Hercules Jinks read up all the architecture books. Do you want to start him on something else?"

Hortensia opened the door. "Why? Did he ask for something?"

"Oh, no, ma'am. He's returning the book and it's the last on the shelf."

"Give him what he wants." Hortensia closed her door, then opened it again. "Never mind, Leone. I'll speak to him."

The stairs barely rattled as she slipped over them.

Hercules stood stiffly in the middle of the library. He'd never been in the big house except to drop off wood by the side of the kitchen. Leone dragged him into the library and he wanted out of there. At the sight of Hortensia he became motionless.

"Hercules, you've read all the architecture books?"

"It seems so, Miss Hortensia."

"What next?"

"I— You were kind to allow me to use your library."

"You haven't read everything in here yet. Come on, what next?"

"Thank you, but—" He looked beyond her left shoulder. Those ice-blue eyes were hard to look into.

"If you're going to be indecisive, I'll make up your mind." She walked over to one side of the room. "Your mother teaches Latin, does she not?"

"Yes."

"Then best start on the classics, to please her."

"Thank you." He grinned. Ada would gobble up the books like candy.

Hortensia handed him Terence. She didn't let go of the book. The two stood there holding opposite ends of the volume.

"Do you read Latin?" she asked.

"Barely. I'm the dumb one in our family."

"Modest might be a better word." Unconsciously she pulled the book toward her. Hercules kept his feet firm, but she threw him off balance. Embarrassed, he finally let go of the book and Hortensia reeled backward. Hercules quickly caught her. Falling, she grabbed him around the neck. As if by instinct, Hercules kissed her. Realizing what he'd done, he started to pull away, except that Hortensia kissed him back. The two profoundly shocked one another and themselves.

"Forgive me, please forgive me." He was shaking.

"You didn't sin alone, Hercules." She gave him the book. He took it and vanished. She stood in the middle of the library for a very long time after that.

Providing for the needs of their clients filled Blue Rhonda and Banana Mae's hours. Most of the men who visited them sought simple relief from a confusing sexual code. Their imaginations ranged no further than a blow job, the missionary position, or on a few rare occasions, rear entry. Even Carwyn rested content within this limited framework. Naturally, more pursuits were available at Bunny Turnbull's house, but the gatherings were less sexual than convivial. The men dutifully followed the women of their choice upstairs, got laid and trotted back down to join in the singing, drinking and merriment. Anything out of the ordinary would have been gleefully reported by Lotowana. By now Dad-eye Steelman shadowed her like a penny dog. The attention flattered her, but sometimes he got in the way.

A mild sensation rippled through the small community when Minnie Rue and Leafy Strayhorne opened a house to rival Bunny's. They decorated it as a restaurant and even served good food, but the delight of Montgomery's men was that on the menu, *le plat du jour* was a new sexual position. The men learned various tricks at Maxim's, as it was called, and then demanded similar contortions from Bunny's girls, or even Blue Rhonda and Banana Mae. Bunny, faced with a competitive crisis, decided to fight fire with fire. She initiated threesomes, different prices for new and different positions, and for major holidays, roaring orgies. The contest with Maxim's sharpened her wits. She relished the fight. Whenever she passed Minnie or Leafy on the street, she oozed propriety. In private, she excoriated them as degenerates. However, business boomed.

Blue Rhonda and Banana Mae maintained their cottage industry. The wildest they got was with Cedrenus Shackleford, chief of police. His new twist was getting sucked off by

Blue Rhonda while burying his head in Banana Mae's bush, licking away. The two had never worked in tandem before. After Cedrenus unloaded, all three of them sprawled on the bed for a breather.

"We ought to work on our timing." Blue Rhonda looked at Banana Mae.

"What?" Cedrenus asked, barely audible.

"Oh, nothing," Blue Rhonda replied.

"Say, if I get a second wind, how about I fuck you in the asshole, Blue Rhonda? You can sit on me while I lie on my back and Banana Mae can squat over my face for another go-round."

"My mouth is my fortune, Cedrenus. I leave all the other joys to Banana."

"Come on, Rhonda. It'll do you good," he cooed.

"Nope."

"No one can get Rhonda on her back." Banana sat up.

"Hell, Rhonda, that makes no sense." Cedrenus raised himself on his elbows.

"I'm too young to get pregnant."

"There's ways to fix that," he advised.

"Yeah, and none of them work." She dangled her legs over the edge of the bed. Christmas preyed on her mind. She hadn't bought one present and the holiday lurked around the corner.

"How did Linton Ray's temperance rally go last night?" Banana changed the subject.

"The usual collection of battle-axes and half-wits. Fair number of them, too." Cedrenus attempted to remain neutral on all subjects. He wasn't above thumping the Bible when it was useful to his advancement, but Linton disgusted him. Cedrenus's world view coincided with most people's: You say one thing in public and do another in private.

A loud knock on the front door jolted all three of them from the bed. Before Banana Mae could dress and answer it, the door opened, then slammed, and one of Cedrenus's men shouted upstairs.

"Chief, trouble at Maxim's."

Cedrenus buttoned his pants crookedly, tossed on his shirt and put on his boots, forgetting his socks. Halfway

down the stairs, he struggled with his uniform jacket. Blue
Rhonda and Banana Mae fell in behind him, raging with
curiosity.

"How many men do we need?" Cedrenus assumed a
fight had broken out, or worse, that Linton had organized
a much unwanted demonstration.

"Just you and me." The young man's mustache quivered.

As if to answer his question, Lotowana and Bunny hit
the front door at the same time and nearly became wedged
in the opening as they tried to burst through simultaneously.

"Step back, Lottie," Bunny commanded.

The voice of her employer had the ring of God to it;
Lottie made way for the diminutive Bunny. As she bounded through the door she saw Cedrenus and Dick Carver.

"Oh, so you know." Bunny slowed her pace.

"We don't know nothing. Tell or I'll die!" Blue Rhonda
demanded.

Dick opened his mouth, but nothing came out.

Lotowana, finally through the door, blurted, "Judge
O'Brian's deader than a doornail."

"Who killed him?" Cedrenus wanted all the facts before he ventured over to Maxim's.

"Nobody, exactly," Dick stammered. This story was
going to be hard to tell.

"He died in the saddle." By now Lotowana was laughing.
Bunny jabbed her with her elbow. Everyone acted like a
total twit. Bunny decided to take over.

"This is due to Minnie Rue's latest craze," Bunny
began. "Tonight was history night."

"What?" Blue Rhonda couldn't believe this.

"You haven't heard nothing," Lotowana spiced the tale.

Bunny went on quietly. "Yes, you were to come as a
famous figure from history, and for a high price, mind
you, you could do whatever you pleased—if you get my
meaning—as long as no real damage was done to life and
limb."

"Obviously, damage was done." Cedrenus figured two
men must have fought over a girl.

"Well." Bunny paused. "You see, the Judge always
admired Napoleon, so he came dressed for battle. Each of

the girls represented a battle. By the time he got to Austerlitz he suffered a heart attack.''

"As blue in the face as a crab," Lotowana volunteered.

"Chief, we've got to get his body out of there and back to his chambers." Dick sounded worried.

"If we bring up a wagon, that'll attract attention." Cedrenus was trying to digest the information.

"You'd better get him out of there before he gets stiff." Lotowana was only too helpful with her vivid details.

"We've got some time before that happens, Lottie," Cedrenus assured her.

"Why not roll him in a rug like Cleopatra?" Bunny suggested.

Blue Rhonda applauded. "Yes."

Cedrenus looked at Dick and Dick looked back.

"You got a rug, Bunny?" the chief inquired.

"I sure do. We'll meet you over at Maxim's. Come on, Lottie, help me carry it."

Cedrenus took off his jacket. "I'll come back for this later."

"Can't we help?" Blue Rhonda hated to miss anything.

"Keep watch on the streets," Cedrenus said.

Banana Mae and Blue Rhonda crammed into their coats and raced over to Maxim's. Minnie Rue hovered, close to cardiac arrest herself. Leafy, skinny and mean, kept her head. When Bunny strolled in the door giving orders, it went down the wrong way with Leafy.

"Just who the hell do you think you are, Turnbull?"

"I'm here under the aegis of Chief Shackleford." Bunny brushed past Leafy, who didn't know what aegis meant.

"Huh?"

"Do what she says." Lotowana swelled at the idea of her boss being party to such an event.

The two women put the rug down and unrolled it. As they unrolled it, the rug was all mice turds and no wool.

"Damn those buggers," Lotowana cursed.

"Can't be helped." Bunny concentrated on the task. "Where's the body?"

Minnie tearfully pointed to a crumpled mass in the next room. His beautiful uniform stank of piss and shit and his face really was blue. Neither Minnie nor Leafy bothered to button his trousers, so his member flapped lifelessly as the women picked him up and deposited him in the rug.

"I hope it was worth it, Judge," Bunny grumbled.

Lottie could barely bend down, but the four of them managed to roll him up in the rug. Minnie recovered herself somewhat.

Three knocks on the back door meant the chief and Dick were ready. The two had waylaid Hercules Jinks. No way would Hercules argue with the chief of police. He had recently acquired a sturdy gray horse to help him haul more wood. The men stashed wood under the back stoop, then placed the body in the cart and delicately arranged a few logs over it. Blue Rhonda and Banana Mae vigilantly patrolled the alley and front street.

"Hercules, we'll meet you back at the courthouse, side door." Cedrenus patted the horse.

"Haven't you ever seen a dead man before?" Banana Mae asked, walking by the cart.

"Yes," Hercules answered.

"You're long in the face." Banana liked the young man.

"Don't like to see anyone die." That was a lie, as Hercules had been moping around for days.

"Get on," Cedrenus commanded.

As the clip-clop of horse's hooves faded away, Blue Rhonda and Banana Mae walked back with Bunny and Lotowana.

"Doesn't that Leafy have the whitest complexion?" Lotowana marveled.

"No doubt from all those rocks she's been living under," Bunny snapped.

It was rare, but men did die down in the whorehouses. Bunny prayed that this wouldn't leak out. She feared Linton could use it, slyly, in his campaign.

Hercules, Cedrenus and Dick placed the body in the Judge's chambers. Getting off his uniform turned their stomachs a little, but they managed. As they left the courthouse, Cedrenus thanked Hercules and said, "I owe you one." Hercules nodded and drove off. The Jinkses were well respected by all people for their tact and discretion. Cedrenus knew Hercules wouldn't even tell his parents, so if the story leaked, it would have to come from Maxim's.

The next morning, Judge O'Brian was discovered at his desk by his secretary. She advanced the explanation that he'd worked late that night and died of a heart attack. However, no one could explain the mouse turds in his hair.

. . .

Muscular sphinxes smiled in repose at Bartholomew; yet another Masonic temple was pinned to his drawing board. If Stanford White struck out in one direction, Bartholomew stumbled in another. Intellectually, he believed in industrial progress, yet his work gleamed with a repressed mysticism, a secret pull away from the machine. He had celebrated his fiftieth birthday on the twenty-ninth of July, but now, the week before Christmas, his half century crowded in upon him. He felt the past riding on his shoulders like a parrot on a pirate's back. He felt old, although physically he was sturdy and energetic. He avoided the four great Western narcotics: alcohol, religion, drugs and sex. O'Brian's sudden death disturbed Bartholomew. Oh, he knew about the Judge's Achilles' heel, but what man doesn't have a vice somewhere? The Judge was a man like any other. Bartholomew knew he'd miss him. The last ten years he'd bidden goodbye to too many friends. Montgomery was beginning to resemble a cemetery with lights. He looked at a commission he'd completed—a huge Birmingham house in Stockbroker Tudor. Suddenly he thought he would burst with contempt for all he'd done and all he believed. His work was bought and sold piecemeal. He never really got the chance to let his imagination soar, for his generation didn't want imagination, it wanted conformist comfort. He no longer felt like an architect; he felt like a lackey. The New South seemed anything but new—old wine in new bottles was more like it. All the blather about honor, ideals and sentiment. Sentiment was the soft outside of cruelty. However, he'd seen the giant cities of the North: Chicago, New York, Philadelphia. They seemed no better. If anything, their citizens were more hypocritical. In the South, if someone hated your guts he usually told you so.

He swept his arm across the table, sending his T-square and utensils flying. The pathetic clatter only made him feel weaker, smaller.

The one triumph of his life was his marriage to Lila. They'd grown together over the years instead of apart. The passion of their younger years had turned into passionate companionship. They still enjoyed the congress of the flesh; not as often, but Lila moved him always in a deep physical way. Observing the marriages of his associates, he knew his was priceless, his wife a marvel. He could talk to Lila about anything, but tonight he was shamefully embarrassed at what he took to be self-pity. There was little room in Bartholomew's makeup for honest self-doubt, so when it came he confused it with self-pity. Besides, would he not belittle her life by telling her he felt he was becoming worthless?

He'd failed as a father, although he secretly wondered if anyone could have been successful with Hortensia. She was strong-willed and aloof in the cradle. He regretted not siring a son, but then who knows how the boy would have turned out? Maybe it was all for the best.

He walked over to his workroom window and stared at the street below. Garlands decorated street lamps and doors were festooned with colors. A fat woman with a shawl hurried by carrying a package. Christmas 1918 would precede New Year's 1919. Bartholomew shivered. He had always been able to project himself into the future, but tonight 1919 was blank. He saw nothing.

He laughed to himself, and thought, Human beings don't understand themselves until it's too late to do anything about it.

Beckoning on the wall was a small, exquisitely wrought dagger given him years ago by Hortensia. Like a jack-in-the-box, the idea popped into his head that he would plunge that dagger through his heart. Suicide had never remotely occurred to him before. The mere thought of it unnerved him. As though put in a trance by this terrible thought, he glided over to the dagger and touched its merciless point. Why not just end it all? He wasn't in distress, yet he couldn't find anything to live for, and worse, he felt like a charlatan. He stood there eyeing the dagger. He had the power to end his life. It was almost intoxicating.

Tears exploded down his cheeks. He hadn't cried since his mother died, twenty years before. The sobs shook him so much that he leaned against the wall, and finally slid down it to sit and cry as though he were four years old again and found his adored puppy crushed by a wagon. He cried to escape the self that does not lead to darkness. He cried because he was lost, because he understood his life was finite and his body limited. He cried because he'd lived a life of reason and reason had failed.

He didn't know how long he'd cried. His head ached and he slowed down a little. He thought of his wife. How could he leave her alone? He thought of his daughter. Someday she might need him. He thought of his friends. How could he repudiate all their days by ending his? He thought of the poor sons of bitches who stood at Thermopylae and died because they believed in their Athens. Could he die just because he was afraid? He thought of the wretches who'd perished from Europe's vicious plagues throughout the Middle Ages. He thought of people living on through those horrors and the pains of their bodies for which there was no relief. If they persevered, uneducated, terrified, oppressed, who was he to turn his back on life?

He stood up, pulled a handkerchief from his breast pocket and blew his nose. He picked up his T-square and other tools, carefully putting them in their proper places, then he tossed on his overcoat to start home.

As he walked through the city in which he'd spent his entire fifty years, he suddenly realized that it isn't your freedoms that keep you alive; it's your obligations.

• • •

Betty Stove presided over the annual Christmas Eve Ball, which had been the responsibility of her family on her mother's side since they first came to Montgomery, shortly before 1819, when the city was incorporated. A small band of Dutch, attracted by the possibility of wealth, land and adventure, migrated from New York, where many of their families had resided since Peter Stuyvesant. Betty's mother, Beukema Toe Water-Van Aken, an energetic sixty, planned the ball along with her daughter. All of Montgomery's gentry came: top hat, tails for the men, costly gowns and stunning jewels for the women. Here and there a military uniform shone.

Betty wore a pale-blue gown designed by Poiret, referred to by her husband as Porous. She looked radiant, and for once Hortensia forgot to be competitive. Other things preyed on her mind. She'd sent over to Hercules Jinks a Christmas present through Amelie. She still couldn't decide if she'd done the right thing, but she wanted to give him something to show she wasn't angry. Then, too, he might have forgotten, being so young. She found a book of engravings of famous boxing matches. She wondered if he liked it, or if he'd unwrapped the present yet.

Carwyn danced with all the ladies, including his mother-in-law, who was easily the most beautiful woman of her age, eclipsing many a younger lady. Bartholomew, too, never left the dance floor unless it was to fetch a glass of champagne for a partner.

The ballroom in the Stove mansion was smothered in white, with red ribbons on the columns and door mantels adding a touch of brilliant color. Mistletoe hung from the tip of the central gigantic crystal chandelier. A small orchestra played on the balcony built expressly for that purpose. Beukema and Betty provided smart favors for their guests: a silver pipe cleaner for the gentlemen, and a lovely silver bookmark for each of the ladies. The favors were engraved with the date.

Grace Deltaven impressed everyone by her short solo with a group of women carolers. As if to mollify Icellee's nagging concern, quite a few people told her that her daughter was so beautiful and accomplished the whole world should see her. Naturally, no one said directly that Grace should go on the stage, but their comments helped Icellee a little bit.

Everyone conceded that Betty was undoubtedly one of Montgomery's most splendid hostesses, and if Beukema ever retired from rigorous social duties Betty would assume them smoothly. Such undercurrents of competition between hostesses ensured Montgomery a lively social season. Mr. Peter Stove, a genial, towering blond, renowned for prowess on the polo field, gloried in his wife's success.

The dancing, feasting and laughter went on until sunrise. Those that didn't attend midnight services hopped into their carriages and caught the early morning service.

Riding home in the soft glow of sunrise, Lila and Bartholomew exchanged stories. Peregrine Cranmer passed out before three o'clock; Grace broke the heel of her pump thanks to exuberant dancing; Vera Fetterolf and her husband still weren't talking to the Alton Riddlebergers over last summer's horse race. Their horse lost and they swore Riddlebergers' Currier got a false start. The usual stuff.

Lila kissed her husband on the cheek. "Bart, I haven't seen you this happy in a long time."

" 'Tis the season to be merry—and I have you, don't I?" He kissed her on the lips.

"God bless the day I met you, Bartholomew Reedmuller." Lila's eyes glistened.

He put his arm around her and whispered, "I loved you then. I love you now. I'll love you until the day I die. And if there's a way to love after death, I'll figure it out."

She hugged him and kissed his neck, his hands, his face.

"Lila, it's taken me fifty years, but I finally figured out the only reason to be alive is to enjoy it."

She laughed, and kissed him again. "Merry Christmas."

Hortensia and Carwyn rode home in anything but conjugal bliss. He'd bought her a choker and a bracelet of rectangular sapphires, bordered on each side with diamonds, also rectangular and of the same size. The stones were so carefully set that you could not see a space between them. He presented these to her before the ball so she could wear them. Carwyn felt a vague sense of guilt toward Hortensia and the gifts helped him overcome it; also, he certainly didn't want his wife overshadowed by someone else. Her jewels provoked admiring comment. She gave him a rifle with an inlaid stock and a sensational chestnut thoroughbred. Hortensia had changed somehow, and Carwyn couldn't figure it out. Before, she was cold to him; now she seemed thoughtful but almost indifferent. He couldn't put his finger on it. They chatted about Bartholomew dancing all night. They agreed that Grace Deltaven possessed a marvelous voice, but this actress idea was disquieting. Betty Stove thought of everything; yes, that gown must have cost the equivalent of a battleship. It was all very polite; each was trying to be decent.

When they arrived home, the boys were wide awake under the Christmas tree. Edward loved his set of lead soldiers and Paris had received a toy fire engine with pumps and hoses that worked. He lost no time in turning it on Edward's soldiers. Typically, they gave perfunctory thanks for the clothing and other less spectacular presents.

Later that day, a fight broke out between them. Paris threw half of Edward's soldiers in the fire. Livid, Edward struck his brother, a soldier in his hand. A deep four-inch gash sent Paris reeling, but it didn't prevent him from opening up his pocket knife and stabbing Edward's hand. The point of the blade ran clean through the fleshy part by the thumb.

After the boys' wounds were stitched, their horrified parents packed them off to their rooms in disgrace. Carwyn sat in the library, Hortensia in her reading room. It became another silent day.

Cookie stars, red beads and popcorn decorated the Jinkses' tree. Everybody came home for Christmas. Athena played big sister and drove her brothers to rebellion. Once she calmed herself, good spirits were restored. A fat Christmas ham baked in the kitchen, and the smells of oranges and rum filled every room of the house. Athena lined her specimen jars along the ledge of the window in her room, and Ada shrieked when she saw them. Little frogs floating in alcohol were not her idea of proper decor for a young lady. Athena's insistence on the cultivation of a scientific mind, her claim that criminal lawyers had to know about anatomy for murder trials—nothing could budge Ada, who demanded she carry those pickled creatures into the shed at the back of the property.

Shouts, giggles, squeals reverberated everywhere. Ada could restrain her family, but not over Christmas. The natural high spirits of the children and Placide himself eventually rubbed off on "Madam Cato," as the family called her. Her *"Delenda est Carthago"* was "Education is the hope of the Negro race." Placide put it better when he said, "Put your money in your head, then no one can take it from you."

Each person received a practical gift and an imaginative gift. Ada's practical gift from the whole family was a typewriter. The contraption weighed a ton. Her impractical gift from her husband was an illuminated manuscript. Placide had spent most of 1918 tracking down what he wanted and then paying for it. Surprised into silence, she finally burst into tears. Placide and the children fussed over her and loved on her until she recovered herself. She swore it was the very best Christmas of her life.

"There's one more present left under the tree," Placide noticed. He picked it up. "For you, Hercules."

"It must have been buried amid all the wrappings." Ada took it from Placide and handed it to Hercules.

He opened what was obviously a book, and smiled when he discovered it was about boxing.

"Nifty beans," Athena said.

"No slang in this house, miss." Ada frowned.

"Who's it from?" Athena peered over her brother's massive shoulder to read the inscription.

"It says, 'Would that life were as simple as sport,' signed, 'Hortensia Banastre,'" Hercules read.

"Odd inscription," Athena noted.

"Well, it was thoughtful of her to remember you, Hercules. You will write her a thank you." Ada rose to set the table.

"Yes, ma'am," Hercules replied.

"You're doing a fair amount of work over there." Placide pinched popcorn off the tree. He munched on the corn. "Mrs. Banastre never struck me as a particularly philosophical woman."

"I think she is, quietly so," Hercules said.

"What makes you say that?" Ada carefully arranged her table settings.

"She's unhappy and so she reflects on things."

"It's not a happy marriage, all of Montgomery knows that," Athena called out from the kitchen.

"She throws parties and is beautiful. I can't see her thinking much about anything. Those people don't think." Apollo, previously silent, put in two sarcastic cents.

Hercules warmed up. "How can you say that about someone you don't know? People are one way on the outside and sometimes another on the inside."

"I thought you hardly ever saw her." Athena folded napkins.

"I don't, but you can feel things from people, can't you? It's like fog; you can't see exactly, but you can make out shapes." Hercules' almond eyes opened wide.

"That's true, son, that's very true." Placide headed for the kitchen to help his wife.

Later Christmas evening, Athena dissected a snake for Hercules' benefit. She and Hercules bore a strong resemblance to one another although she was slender where he was broad. Athena fascinated her brother with her knowledge. Apollo passed on the tiny autopsy, especially after a huge meal, although he was usually curious about such matters.

"It's amazing how creatures are put together." Hercules' eyes watered from the formaldehyde fumes.

"Like a puzzle." Athena showed him where the stomach was located. "I'd really like to cut a human someday. I think you should pay doctors when you're well and have them pay you when you're sick," she said, carefully pulling out the brain with tweezers. "I wouldn't mind being a doctor, but I think Apollo will become one. Anyway, I like to argue, take things apart and put them together."

"Have you ever been in love?" Hercules peered at the elongated victim instead of looking at his sister.

"There was a fellow back at Palmer I liked, but I don't think it was love. Fat chance of meeting anyone at Vassar. And I can't go on weekend parties, now, can I?"

"How can people tell?"

"Beats me, but they sure act a fool. Why?"

"Just wondering."

"Are you fancying someone?"

"I guess I am. I feel so strange when I see her. My heart pounds and I can't think of anything to say. I want to run away but I—"

"Maybe you've got a heart murmur or a speech impediment."

"Smartface, just wait until it happens to you."

"Not me. I'm not falling in love."

"I'm engraving every word on my pea brain." Hercules groaned in concentration.

Athena poked around inside the snake. "I'm sorry, Hercules. No one ever made my heart pound."

"She's so intelligent, and she's so . . . so fine. And she's married."

Athena looked up from her task. "Hercules!"

"Don't worry. I don't stand a snowball's chance in hell, but I love her all the same. I've spent the last four months hiding it from myself. I might as well own up to it and get over it somehow."

"You stay away from married women."

"Her husband ignores her. How anyone could ignore a woman that beautiful is beyond me. She doesn't love him. I know for a fact she doesn't love him."

"O.K., but that doesn't mean she loves you."

"I know that. I don't think she could ever love me. I'm too young, besides."

"Stay clear. Did you tell her how you feel?"

"Of course not." He paused. "I kissed her once by mistake, though."

"By mistake?"

"It's too long a story to tell, but she kissed me back. A real, true kiss."

"You're crazy, Hercules."

"You haven't heard the worst part." He took a long breath. "She's white."

"Oh, God!" Athena dropped her scalpel.

• • •

The women down at Water Street went all out for Christmas. Lotowana received a green velvet dress from Bunny. Behind her hand, Bunny let it be known that it cost her a pretty penny, as there were yards and yards and yards to it.

Linton Ray appeared, lecturing these sordid souls on the true meaning of Christmas. The season being what it was, everyone took it with good grace, except for Blue Rhonda, who said Linton Ray was such a bunghole he could screw up a wet dream.

Banana Mae gave Blue Rhonda an art nouveau silver mirror with a lady swirling around the edges. Rhonda presented Banana Mae with a handsome fur wrap made from red fox to match her hair. No one could tear that fur off Banana Mae for the remainder of the day.

Minnie Rue and Leafy Strayhorne gave Bunny Turnbull a new Persian carpet as a mute thank you for the great service rendered. Bunny softened her line toward Minnie and Leafy after that.

Lotowana sang carols at Bunny's Christmas open house, joined in by whoever was in the mood. Lottie's voice sounded silver. It never ceased to amaze people that such purity of tone could emerge from that bulk.

The star of Christmas was Blue Rhonda, who found the perfect present for everyone as well as the perfect comment on the season. To all assembled at Bunny's during one more bubbly toast, Rhonda trilled, "Here's to my birthday. Christmas you have to share with Jesus."

Banana Mae reapplied her makeup after a session with Carwyn. He had asked that she sit on him, facing him, while he sat up also. Banana figured he'd put in time over at Maxim's. Blue Rhonda, fresh from providing Karel Sokol with joy, trotted in.

"How do you like my new perfume?"

Banana Mae wrinkled her nose. "Not so hot. Is it a late Christmas present? Two weeks late."

"Oh." Blue Rhonda betrayed her disappointment.

"See that new girl down at Maxim's?"

"Charlene?"

"Isn't she pretty as a butterfly?"

"And as smart, too," Rhonda remarked in her charity. "Let's go to the movies."

"I'm still recovering from *The Kiss of a Vampire*."

"Nanner, one scary movie. You liked *The Perils of Our Girl Reporters*."

"That's true, but I hate sitting there in silence. It'll never take the place of theater, you know."

"Aren't we high and mighty?"

"Besides, I thought you were broke."

Rhonda twirled a black curl. "Just got paid."

"You belong to the consider-the-lilies school of finance. You've got to start putting money away."

"Now you sound like Bunny Turnbull."

"I'm not that bad." Banana Mae checked a stocking. "But you could invest, or buy land, or—"

"I don't give a bug's ear. I could be dead tomorrow, then what good would all that planning do me?"

"Just trying to be a friend."

"Yes, Mother."

"It's too cold to go out to the movies."

"What about the train station?" Rhonda felt stir-crazy.

"Have you got a wild hair up your ass, or what, girl?"

"I feel like seeing people."

"They don't feel like seeing you."

"I hope Lotowana trips and falls on you, Snotnose."

Banana tugged at the offending stocking. "It's me; I'm in one of my moods."

"On the rag?"

"No; which reminds me, you are so scrupulously clean I never see you wash out anything, throw out bloody petticoats—you amaze me."

"Cleanliness is next to godliness."

"Cleanliness is next to impossible. I don't see how you do it."

"Yeah, well, I'm descended from Merlin."

"I've never seen you read a book, even a newspaper, Blue Rhonda. How do you know about Merlin?"

"My mom used to read to me about Camelot," Rhonda informed her without a whiff of nostalgia. "So come on, why are you singing the blues?"

"More like the mean reds, really." Banana Mae leaned her elbows on her vanity. "I realized today after Carwyn left that he never asks me one thing about myself."

"What do you talk about?"

"Him or sex."

"You could shit in your shoe. That'd be good for ten minutes of conversation."

"Thanks, Rhonda."

"Well, what do you expect? If you go to a stable you talk to the groom about horses. Go to a whore and you talk about sex. Their wives don't listen to them, so we do. Sometimes I think people need to be listened to more than they need to fuck."

"I wonder." Banana slapped some more powder on her face. "You're right, I know you're right, but I feel like a function, not a person."

"I guess." Rhonda thought little about her profession. It brought in money. If she formulated a philosophy about it she was keeping it to herself, and Rhonda rarely kept anything to herself.

"Do you ever feel sorry for some of the men we see? I do sometimes. I mean, do you ever feel a kind of sympathy for them?"

"Sympathy lies between shit and syphilis in the dictionary."

"Rhonda, melt those splinters of ice in your heart."

Blue Rhonda smiled. She relished playing the tough girl.

Gazing at herself in the mirror, Banana Mae said wistfully, "Someday my prince will come."

"Yeah, in your mouth."

Banana shook her head. "I give up. Let's go to the movies."

Hercules stamped his feet, then opened the back door. He had one foot inside when his mother and father pounced on him.

"Where have you been?" Ada demanded.

"Working."

Placide handed him a telegram, unopened. "For you."

Hercules gingerly took the yellow envelope.

"Open it." Ada was impatient.

"Let me get my coat and boots off, will you?" He hung his coat on the peg by the door and carefully took off his boots. Then he opened his telegram.

"FIGHT IN CHICAGO STOP FAT PURSE STOP WIRE ANSWER STOP IF YES WILL SEND EXPENSES BY RETURN WIRE STOP BE

HERE MARCH 1ST STOP FIGHT MARCH 15TH STOP SNEAKY PIE.'' Hercules reread the telegram to himself.

"I smell a rat.'' Ada crossed her arms over her chest.

"He has to make up his own mind,'' Placide said.

"I can certainly tell my son how I feel about boxing.'' Ada paused dramatically. "And what's more, on the Ides of March. It's the unluckiest day of the year!''

"Mother, you're the only person in the world still mourning Julius Caesar.'' Hercules kissed her cheek and firmly said, "I'd like to go.''

Ada let out a howl.

"Ada, that's enough. He's his own man.''

"He just turned sixteen in December.''

"Are you sure about this, son?'' Placide affectionately asked.

"Yes.''

Hercules needed to get away. He couldn't put Hortensia out of his mind, and each day hung around his neck like a stone. The chance to make money was a good excuse.

Amelie wished Hercules good luck. He'd explained to her that he wouldn't be delivering wood for the next two weeks but his father would fill in for him. He left the kitchen and hurried through the backyard. A whinny from the stable and Hortensia's voice tempted him. He didn't want to talk to her; he wanted to see her without her seeing him. She was so beautiful. He stood by the door but he couldn't see anything; he could only hear Hortensia fussing over Bellerophon. He leaned forward to get a better look and she caught a glimpse of him.

"Hercules!''

"Good afternoon, Mrs. Banastre. I dropped by to tell Amelie that I'll be gone for a few weeks.''

"Where?''

"Chicago. I'm going to fight there.''

"Oh.''

He couldn't tell if her face registered concern, worry, or if her expression had anything to do with him.

"It was nice to see you again.'' He backed out of the door.

"Hercules.''

"Yes, ma'am.''

"I appreciated your thank you letter.''

A note of hope and enthusiasm crept into his voice. "It's a wonderful book. I've studied every engraving."

"Here, let me wish you luck."

She motioned for him to come over to her. Reaching in her jacket pocket, she pulled out a silver whistle. "It's all I have here, unless you'd like a bridle"—she laughed—"or one of the horses."

She did care for him. He knew it. "Thank you, ma'am." Hercules held the whistle in his open palm.

Then Hortensia, as if outside herself, did what she couldn't think of. She could act but not think. She knew she was wrong to do it but she couldn't stop herself. She also knew she wanted Hercules and she'd never wanted a man before in her life. The fact that it came so late to her made him all the more irresistible. She placed her gloved hands on his face and kissed him. He drew away but she kissed him anyway.

Hercules had never slept with a woman. He thought his head would burst and he kept his body away from her because he had the biggest hard-on and he certainly didn't want her to know that. It was a very long kiss. Finally, he kissed her back and pressed his body against hers. She kissed him harder.

A second of lucidity shot across her brain. "This could ruin both of us."

"I don't care," he said, and by that time he didn't.

They climbed up in the hayloft and Hortensia tossed a blanket over the hay. It was cold but she removed her clothes. Hercules covered her with another blanket. He ripped off his clothes and got under the covers.

Hortensia was every description of Aphrodite his mother had ever read to him. Her breasts were full and firm. He could span her waist with his hands. Riding made her strong, but even so he was afraid to embrace her. He felt she'd snap like a matchstick. But she hugged him with all her strength and bit his neck, bit his enormous chest, and drove him crazy. He had heard enough about making love, but hearing it and doing it are two different things. All the blood in his body must have rushed to his cock. He fumbled around.

"Slow down," she whispered. "There's no rush."

She kissed him some more, then gently guided his cock into her. He couldn't believe how hot and soft she was. He feared he'd come right then, but he managed to hold off for a few minutes. Hortensia moved underneath him, placed her cheek next to his, and pushed him rhythmically. He lost control and exploded.

Afterward he didn't know whether to run like hell out of that stable or caress her. Hortensia held him like a baby.

"Was that your first time?"

"Yes," he whispered.

She didn't say anything but she rubbed his back and head.

"Mrs. Banastre."

At that she roared, "For God's sake, Hercules, call me Hortensia."

He touched her cheek. "Hortensia, I love you."

She kissed him again, as though he were an angel, and try as he might, Hercules couldn't help himself; he cried.

• • •

Wood-burning, tobacco and cooking odors hung inside Lila's house. Spring took its time arriving, and she missed the fragrance of flowers. Her greenhouse produced orchids, so some natural color greeted her.

Lila had noticed Hortensia's recent high spirits. Her daughter behaved like a different person, affectionate and easy to please.

Icellee buzzed with her own observations concerning Hortensia. She ran through every available and unavailable man in town, but not one of them seemed right. Icellee knew Hortensia had to be having an affair, but with whom? Lila agreed silently; she wouldn't give Icellee the satisfaction. She, too, wondered, Who could he be?

Each day before he left for Chicago, Hortensia met Hercules in the stables. The day he left, every train whistle she heard pierced her heart. The first week of his absence was tolerable; the second week was pure hell. Her stomach reacted as though she'd eaten sulfuric pancakes. She had to see him. She couldn't live without seeing him. She concocted a plan to go to Chicago. No one wants to visit

Chicago in March, but she had family there on her mother's side, who'd made a fortune in the stockyards. The families saw one another at large gatherings. She told her mother she wanted to see Reuben and Martha Duplessis. When Lila's eyebrow shot into her hairline, she further explained that she needed time away from the squabbling boys, and most of all, from Carwyn.

"Hortensia, I am not deaf, dumb and blind," came Lila's swift reply.

Hortensia blanched. She was so on edge she thought maybe her mother by some miracle had found out. "Whatever do you mean?"

"I mean you're transformed. You're acting like you've got spring fever before spring. In fact, I've never seen you so happy or so . . . jumpy."

Hortensia swallowed.

Lila sipped a bit of sherry. "I'm not criticizing."

"I know, Mother."

"But it is odd, wanting to visit Chicago now."

"Would you feel better if I sailed for Saint Petersburg?"

"Given the war, no."

"I'd love to see the palace."

"Hortensia, I know we've never been close, but don't shut me out." Lila blurted, "I know perfectly well you're in love. I'm a woman too, remember."

Hortensia blinked, astonished. Part of her wanted to tell her mother, tell somebody, but this news would affect Montgomery the way World War I was affecting Russia. She quietly said to an anxious Lila, "Mother, I wonder if there aren't too many years of silence between us."

"I haven't been a perfect mother. I don't know anyone who has."

Seeing the hurt on her mother's face surprised Hortensia. It was not until she had accepted and given love that she could see who else loved her. She was shocked to see how much her mother cared.

"You've been a good mother. I think I was born cut off from other people. It had nothing to do with you. I'm finding my way back." Her voice rang quiet and pure.

Lila reached over and smothered her hand in both of hers. "We're all such mysteries. I used to worry that your aloofness was my fault. I can stand on ceremony. Then I wondered was it the people around you or was it something you were born with—a kind of strong natural reserve." She paused. "It doesn't matter. I'm glad to see you blossoming. He must be an extraordinary man."

"He is," Hortensia confessed.

"Does Carwyn suspect?"

"No."

"For the love of God, honey, keep it that way. He can run all over town, but if he ever suspects you are—"

"Rotten unfair."

"I'm not saying I approve of extramarital—well, you know. But you married young and there was little love in it."

"Actually, I felt rather like I was a corporation merging." Hortensia laughed.

Lila frowned at herself, not at Hortensia. "I'm partly to blame for that. I was so dazzled by the match; it was a very good match on our terms, you know. I forgot to see if you loved him. And then again, I married your father at seventeen. How handsome that man was! Perhaps I put myself in your shoes and assumed you felt the way I'd felt those years ago."

"No one forced me to marry Carwyn. I did it of my own free will."

"Thank you, dear, but I wish I'd been more perceptive."

"I'd always envied you, your marriage with Daddy."

Lila was surprised.

"Sometimes I thought you two were playacting, but the older I got the more I realized it's a true marriage. I couldn't fathom what that meant until now. Oh, Mother, there's no hope for me. I love him so much I could die for him. There's nowhere to go."

Lila moved from the chair to put her arm around her child's shoulder. "Keep your head; no matter what happens, keep your head."

"Yes, Mother."

"Is he married?"

"No."

"Does he want to marry you?"

"That's impossible."

Lila, assuming that divorce was unthinkable, missed the implication. "But if it were possible, would this man marry you?"

"I think he would."

"He's in Chicago, of course."

"Yes."

"You can't trust Reuben and Martha; they've always been vicious social climbers." She thought for a moment. "But you can trust your Great-Aunt Narcissa. She's been through this herself."

"Aunt Narcissa?" The idea that the eighty-year-old woman had once nourished a secret lover floored Hortensia.

"During the War, when the family was still here. Her husband was in the army and she met a naval officer down at Mobile."

"What happened?" Because of her own status, Hortensia devoured information about other illicit lovers.

"Killed in sixty-three. Narcissa recovered her poise but never her spirit. That's what Grandmother used to say about it, but I think Narcissa reeks of spirit!"

"Did her husband ever find out?"

"Peregrine? If he had misgivings, he kept it to himself. Men have a funny way of ignoring what they don't want to know. Actually"—Lila's eyes twinkled—"I think women are equally bad. I'll send Narcissa a wire today. When are you leaving?"

"Tomorrow."

"Poor thing; if she doesn't want you, you aren't giving her much choice."

"I could stay at a hotel."

"Hotels are for people without relatives."

"Mother, you aren't going to tell her?"

"Certainly not. I'll just tell her not to mind your comings and goings."

"Speaking of which, I'd better go. I promised Edward I'd watch his fencing lesson." Hortensia started for the door, then wheeled around and ran over to kiss Lila. "Mother, thank you."

Lila kissed her back. "Remember, Hortensia, no matter what: keep a cool head."

• • •

Sneaky Pie didn't walk into a room so much as he insinuated himself into the future. Somehow you knew this man would always be around. His cuff links lay on his sleeve as fat as hen's eggs. He wore a soft yellow jacket over a teal-blue vest, which he wore over a pale-pink shirt. His pants were dove gray and he wore spotless spats. How he kept them clean in the slush was simple: he never walked anywhere. Sneaky Pie rode in state. He had so many retainers that a simple two-block journey looked like the progress of Henry VIII. He loved jewels as much as Henry did, but he drew the line at three wives. Six was too much for any man to handle. Sneaky thoughtfully installed Hercules in a nice apartment not far from the gym. Sneaky was not a trainer. He was a gambler, a bon vivant and an efficient killer of his enemies. He put Hercules in the hands of one Roxy. Roxy had no last name. He and Sneaky formed a friendship before the gang wars. Roxy was loyal and, better, he knew more about boxing than anyone else in the Midwest.

Hercules thrilled Roxy. He'd never been given the gift of such superb raw material. The boy lacked polish and he needed ring smarts, but what power and endurance! Roxy threw every gut-busting exercise he could at the kid and Hercules breezed through it. Harder was the ring work, where Hercules' inexperience showed up again and again. Roxy would stand at a corner, towel around his sweaty neck, hurling instructions to Hercules. Like a burr, Sneaky stuck around to observe the lessons, and his machine gun laugh surmounted even the groans of the boxers.

Each night Hercules folded into bed and dreamed of Hortensia. Sometimes he couldn't believe it had all happened. Why would she love him? Sometimes he strained so hard to remember her face he couldn't remember her at all. Other times she was so vivid in his mind he smelled her perfume and felt her smooth skin. Those times were the hardest. He couldn't write letters. The chance that a letter might fall into the wrong hands was too great. They'd agreed on that before his departure. Sometimes he thought he'd take all the money from this fight, if he won it, and the two of them could run away somewhere. He'd heard that France was a good place for people like them, but with the war, how could they possibly get in? Then he thought he could double as her driver or some kind of servant and they could move up North and masquerade until the war ended in Europe. Other times he thought he'd enlist to solve the dilemma. He loved her desperately, as only a sixteen-year-old can love.

• • •

Torches flashed in the twilight like large fireflies. Linton, as many had feared, was on the rampage, with his band of revengeful wives, peppered with men wearing steel-rimmed glasses and hats to hide balding pates.

At first they contented themselves with smashing a few liquor shop windows. Given that the owners were at home, they met no resistance. Pumped up with this seeming proof of their invincibility under the banner of Our Lord, they headed for their secondary target, Water Street.

Placide was on the night shift down at the train station. The faraway rumbling and specks of light pulled passengers out of the waiting rooms to watch. Linton's fulminations were old news to town folks, but tonight he meant to get the prostitutes.

Blue Rhonda and Banana Mae were steady customers of Placide's. They paid promptly for their wood and for whatever repairs they needed. Bunny paid, but she was as tight as the bark on a tree. Still, the women treated him and his sons with decency. If he ran fast, he could warn Blue Rhonda and get back to work before he was missed.

Press Tugwell, the druggist, was bumping up and down on top of Banana Mae. He divided his time equally between the two women.

Rhonda was joyfully sampling the latest gift of cocaine he brought her. A pounding at the back door scared her.

"Goddammit!" She spilled some coke on the floor. "Who in fucking red hell is it?"

"Placide, Blue Rhonda."

She hastily opened the door at the sound of that familiar, troubled voice.

"What's the matter?"

Puffing, he put his hand on the doorjamb. "Looks like Linton's coming this way with an army of Bible-thumpers."

"Jesus H. Christ on a raft."

"You tell the others. I must get back to work."

"Thanks, Placide. I'll make it up to you."

"No bother, Blue Rhonda." He left as quickly as he'd come.

She shut the door and flew up the stairs, racing into Banana's room without knocking. Press writhed in ecstasy.

Banana lifted her head. "This better be good."

"What?" Press was not yet aware of Rhonda's presence. He froze in mid-hump when he finally sensed another person in the room.

"Reverend Ray's on his way with a mob. Sorry, Press."

"Oh, no!" Bewildered, Press tried to pull up his trousers while lying atop Banana Mae.

"We've got to warn Bunny." Banana slid out from under her burden and he rolled off the bed like a rolling pin off a kitchen table.

Press kicked around on the floor. "I've got to get out of here. If my wife finds out, she'll kill me."

"Hell, Press, she's probably in the mob." Rhonda snickered.

"Look at a woman's mother before you marry her. That's what she'll turn into." He sputtered, snapping his suspenders, struggling to his feet. "My father warned me, but oh, no, I knew better. Holy stinking shit."

"You'd best go out the back door and tear up the alley." Banana handed him his coat.

"What if someone sees me?"

"Hide in the cellar," Banana suggested.

"No, don't do that. They could put a torch to the house."

Press's eyes were so big when he heard Rhonda, they looked all white. "Oh, God!"

"Get packing." Blue Rhonda practically carried him to the door.

"Get the guns," Banana yelled, as she rummaged through her bureau drawers to find her old .38.

Rhonda yanked a shotgun out of the hall closet. She

stuffed shells in her purse, her pockets, the hat she slapped on her head.

The glow of torches about four blocks off spurred both women. They flung themselves through Bunny's front door. The piano player didn't miss a beat. Bunny put her hand on his shoulder. He stopped.

"Linton's got himself a gang," panted Banana Mae.

"Heading straight for us!" Blue Rhonda popped two shells in the shotgun for punctuation.

The men jumped out of that house like fleas off a dead dog. One fool dove headfirst through a window.

Lotowana lifted the top of the piano bench, with the player still on it, and withdrew a six-shooter. "I'll kill that bastard."

Before Banana blinked, every woman in the house was armed.

Bunny took over. "Mabel, tell Minnie Rue and Leafy. Then get back here."

"I'll kill him." Lotowana quivered.

"Let's flip for it." Blue Rhonda hated him just as much.

"Don't you want to protect your house?" Lottie figured this would occupy Rhonda.

"They'll come for the big ones. We're small fry."

This disgruntled Lottie, as she wanted Linton all to herself even if she got sent up the river.

"How about we each take a window?" Banana Mae flattened herself by the window next to the door.

"There may be another way out of this." Bunny ran her fingers through her hair. "Quick, Blanche, go over to Minnie's and get them all to come here—and tell them to bring the choir robes."

Blanche hit the door before Bunny took the next breath.

"I wanna kill him," Lottie wailed.

"Shut up, Lardass," Bunny sharply reprimanded her.

Lotowana towered over Bunny. "I wanna kill him."

"And ruin all of us? That's what he wants."

The noise of the mob could now be clearly heard. They weren't ten minutes away.

"Nobody but a damn fool wants to die." Rhonda sided with Lottie. "Kill him."

"If there's violence, the police have no choice but to shut us down." Bunny's lips compressed.

"Oh." Banana Mae understood.

The click-click of high-button shoes on cobblestones alerted Rhonda. She checked her window. "The competition."

Minnie and her girls filed through the door. Each girl carried a robe.

"Good evening, Miss Turnbull." Minnie never forgot her manners in this sugared rivalry.

"Likewise, Miss Rue."

"Trouble?" Minnie put on a brave show to keep her troops in line. Leafy stood behind her.

"We'll see." Bunny smiled, for the same reason.

The women, half terrified, took heart, but they mumbled to one another, confused.

"Each girl put on a choir robe. Give the extras to my girls. Make sure Lottie gets one. On the double."

They followed orders.

"Where'd you get all these?" Blue Rhonda buttoned her purple robe with the pale-blue trim.

One of Minnie's employees whispered, "History night."

"Huh?" Rhonda fluffed up her sleeves.

"Peter Stove dressed up as a bishop. We had to sing while he desecrated the altar—if you catch my drift." She giggled.

"Peter Stove?" Blue Rhonda exclaimed.

"Ecclesiastical desires are a patent item," Leafy sniffed.

"All right. Everyone around the piano. Those of you not in a robe bring up a chair like a meeting." Bunny was everywhere at once. "Lottie, you sing every other stanza as a solo."

"I wanna kill him."

"The shortest distance between two points is not always a straight line." Bunny propelled her to the piano.

The crowd oozed down the street.

"Does everyone know 'Beautiful Savior'?" Bunny called out.

Most heads nodded.

"Sing like angels." She clapped her tiny hands together.

The piano player cracked his knuckles, then began.

Heedless of Linton haranguing his flock, the women sang on.

From outside the catcalls eventually died down. His followers stared at Linton as the words "Sodom and Gomorrah" tumbled from his lips. Sensing he was losing his audience, he closed his mouth for a moment. He, too, heard the beautiful solo from inside, followed by a fairly well-tuned choir. A faint clatter barely threw him off. Blue Rhonda had forgotten to remove her hat and when Banana Mae jerked it off, the shotgun shells bounced on the floor.

Her timing perfect, Bunny opened the door. "Fellow believers in the forgiveness of our Lord and Savior, Jesus, who died for our sins and rose again from the dead, please come in and join us for our weekly devotional."

Listening to this, Banana Mae leaned over and whispered in Blue Rhonda's ear, "Do you think Jesus rose from the dead?"

"Maybe he was full of yeast." Rhonda returned to her singing.

The crowd strained to catch sight of the fully equipped choir. When Lottie sang another stanza, her voice was so haunting a few women got misty.

Again Bunny beckoned. The singers appeared not to notice the unusual gathering at their door.

Fuming, Linton yelped, "A trick of the devil!"

"Where there is no faith, devils are a necessity." Bunny struck the right tone.

One by one, the women at the edges of the mob stole away. Within minutes the crowd evaporated, leaving Linton and two diehards. Frustrated beyond endurance, he ripped off his coat and stomped on it.

Bunny closed the door and the women sang until certain they were safe.

"Party!" Rhonda threw her arms around Lotowana's neck. Rapturous, she even kissed Bunny. The women went wild and stayed up until dawn, singing songs of quite another sort.

Admiringly, Banana Mae shook Bunny's hand. "You're a genius."

"I just threw a little Christian stardust in their eyes." Bunny raised her champagne glass to heaven.

• • •

Great-Aunt Narcissa darted about like a hummingbird. Her hands revealed great age, but nothing else about her did. Narcissa believed the blow that does not break one's back strengthens one. She retained a love for life despite its injustices, and she retained a healthy disregard for conformity. She considered Chicago a city of private wealth and public squalor, but enjoyed its undeniable energy. Her greatest contempt was reserved for the so-called pillars of society; herdsmen of the sacred cows, she called them. It was Narcissa who invented the card-ranking system with Hortensia one summer when everyone luxuriated on Mount Desert Island off the coast of Maine. Her greatest regard was for the people they both dubbed hearts.

"You're so kind to receive me on such short notice." Hortensia sat in the cherrywood library. Narcissa poked the fire although her servants would gladly have done that for her.

"I was going to entertain the Caliph of Baghdad, but I told him to come another day."

"Where would you put his harem?" Hortensia joined in.

"Why, down at City Hall, where they belong." Narcissa whacked another log. "Hungry?"

"No. I thought I'd take a little ride and then come back for dinner, if that suits you."

"Suit yourself. I eat when I'm hungry. I'm usually hungry at six. I'll sit at the table with you, though, if you're late, and regale you with my wit."

The black cab stopped outside Roxy's gym. Hercules had mentioned the gym before he left, and he also mentioned Sneaky Pie. Hortensia hired a hack since she decided against trusting Narcissa's servants. The driver took the note inside.

A sweaty Hercules emerged, closely tailed by a cursing Roxy, who tried to throw a coat over the young giant's shoulders. Hercules moved to the cab with the speed of light. When Roxy caught up with him and wrapped the coat around him, he glimpsed the most beautiful woman he'd ever seen and his smile was like a crack in old plaster. White women with black men was nothing new to Roxy. He'd seen everything and regretted most of it. But this white woman was high tone and utterly gorgeous. Hercules glared at him and Roxy faded away. Hortensia opened the door to the cab and he got in.

"I can't believe you're here! I can't believe it!" He exuberantly kissed her.

"I couldn't stay away." She kissed him back while pulling the curtains with one hand.

"Come to the fight." He kissed her some more.

She drew back for a little air. "Darling, I don't think I could watch you get hurt."

"If you're there I'll fight like a Titan, I swear. Oh, please come, Hortensia. All kinds of people will be there and you won't be conspicuous." He kissed her ardently, then sat back in the cab, his hand on his forehead. "No."

"What's the matter?"

"I can't make love to you until after the fight."

"I don't care. I just want to see you, to hear your voice, to watch your face. I don't care."

He wrapped his arms around her. "But think of the celebration we can have after the fight."

"Hercules, you probably won't be able to walk." She laughed at him. He was the sun, this young man.

"Just you wait."

Roxy returned to harass him. More training. Hortensia told him where she was staying, but if possible she'd visit him in his quarters. It would be hell to wait three more days, but somehow they'd manage. She promised to come every day to watch him practice.

Over supper, Narcissa noticed Hortensia's fevered glow. She said nothing as she devoured yet another piece of beef Wellington.

"When's the last time you played cards, Hortensia?"

"I usually play each day with the boys."

"Remember our game?"

"I taught them."

"Hmm." Narcissa changed the subject by a quarter turn. "I'd say you found your king of hearts."

Undaunted, Hortensia teased her. "Trusting your woman's intuition, Auntie?"

"Intuition is a suspension of logic due to impatience. I practice it all the time." Narcissa laughed.

Hortensia admitted she'd found her heart at last, as well as her ace. The rest she kept to herself.

Humanity in all its diversity crammed into the arena. Hercules placed Hortensia under the care of Sneaky Pie. She sat at ringside, splendidly dressed, wearing a veil.

When the two men met in the middle of the ring and touched gloves before the start of the battle, Hortensia forgot her worry and became caught up in the incredible excitement surrounding the event.

Roger Boatwright, the opponent, danced in his corner. He was the best fighter in the Midwest. After this victory he intended to go after the heavyweight title. The name Roger Boatwright didn't electrify the imagination, so his promoter called him "The Butcher," due to his reputation for mauling, pulverizing, disfiguring his opponents. No one but Sneaky, Roxy and Hercules' sparring partners thought Hercules had a chance.

When the bell rang the two blasted one another. Disdaining his opponent, Roger figured he didn't need to feel out this kid; he'd blow him off the canvas. Hortensia shivered as the men pounded hot flesh. She half expected sparks to fly. Fearful as she was for her lover, she was enthralled by his beauty in the ring. She knew how perfect his body was but she'd never seen him like this. Hercules was so awe-inspiring, athletically, that he seemed an instrument of God. Roger came at him like a bull. Hercules unleashed a right at his temple that was so mighty one expected to hear thunder. Roger bent over like a jackknife. He folded face down on the canvas and took the count of ten. Ice water finally revived him.

The crowd, stunned and disappointed because they'd expected a long match, remained quiet for a few moments, then erupted in cheers. Clearly this young fighter was a phenomenon. Sneaky knew he had a great one. This fellow could take them all, and he'd trot him around

America, around the world, to prove it and to make a fortune.

That night Hercules proved he could stand up. They made love all night. They did things they didn't know existed. They floated on a current of high energy and Olympian love.

When Hortensia snuck into her room at 7 A.M., Narcissa, up for an hour and sipping coffee in the library, heard her tiptoe upstairs. She smiled and then took a shot of straight gin to remember the occasion.

• • •

A bitter-cold wind whipped off the lake and howled through Chicago. Temperatures dropped way below zero and snow fell heavily, only to be blown into huge drifts. Hortensia and Hercules huddled under four blankets and a heavy bedspread.

"Good God, how do people live in this?" Hortensia rubbed her feet against Hercules' feet.

"Now you know why Yankees are so mean."

"No wonder. And there's nothing to do when it gets like this. People ice skate or sleigh ride and that's supposed to be fun. Frostbitten noses and wet feet—fun!"

"I'd like to try skiing once." He put his arm under the pillow under her head.

"Fine. You can try it by yourself. I'm not going down a hill on two sticks."

Hercules laughed.

Hortensia had to leave for Montgomery the next day. Hercules and Sneaky Pie were still debating over his next fight. Staying in Chicago didn't appeal to Hercules. He liked the city fine, although not the weather, but he loved Montgomery for all its faults. He was willing to travel to wherever there was a fight—but he was living in Montgomery and that was final. The lure of furs, women, high living, seduced most everyone. Sneaky was amazed that it had no effect on Hercules. Roxy fussed, but Hercules said he could train at home and he'd arrive two weeks early for any fight so Roxy could work with him. There was no

question of Roxy's moving to Montgomery. His view of
Southerners was "They're so dumb they ain't even ignorant."

"Did I ever tell you about the time I got into a fight in
fourth grade?" Hortensia asked.

"No."

"I conduct imaginary conversations with you all the
time. When I finally see you, I can't remember what I've
said and what I've imagined. I hate being repetitious, so if
I tell you the same story twice cut me short."

"You've never told me the same story twice."

"Good," she breathed into his neck. "Do you ever
think about whole conversations with me when we're
apart?"

"Sure."

"Really?"

He smiled. "I think everyone does that when they're in
love."

"Oh. I've never been in love before." She bit his ear.
"How do you know about these things, buster?"

"Ouch!"

"Have you ever been in love before?"

"No, but my mother is the love expert in the family."

"You're lucky to have them."

"I know. You've got to meet my sister sometime. She's
going to be a lawyer. Actually, I wish you could meet all
of them. They're so smart."

"So are you."

"Not like the others."

"Honey, you're very smart." She rubbed his curly head.

"I don't feel very smart," he sighed. "I know you've
got to plan ahead, learn a profession, but there isn't
anything I want to do. I like physical things and there's not
much I can do with it. I'll keep at boxing for a while."

"There's nothing wrong with that."

"I know, but I look around at those old punch-drunks
down at Roxy's. Who wants to end up like that?"

"You'll know when to quit."

"I don't worry about that. I just wish I knew what I
wanted to do or—"

"You will."

He looked at her. "Do you feel you have a purpose in life?"

Hortensia absolutely never carried on conversations like this, but with Hercules she talked about everything and anything. She asked questions of herself she'd never asked, and together the two of them laughed over the silliest things.

"No. I got married, produced sons and threw marvelous parties. I was bored, but—oh, I don't know. I can't see that I do one useful thing in this world, but then again, I can't see why I should."

"What do you mean?"

"I mean there is no meaning."

"Life has meaning."

"For whom?"

Hercules earnestly replied, "For us, for God, for everyone."

"I envy you your belief. I figure we're all here like the animals, only we're a little more clever. If we have a purpose we make it up, but it doesn't really mean anything."

"I don't know. I'd hate to think I was here for nothing."

"Exactly. Where did this nagging need to have a purpose begin?"

"In the nighttime," Hercules said.

"What?"

"Don't you get scared at night?"

"Sometimes, but what's that got to do with it?"

"When you're scared you make up things to give you the courage to go on. I bet the whole human race was terrified until we discovered fire. We must have had thousands of years to invent stories to get us through the night. Maybe we invented a purpose out of that fear too."

"Well, Hercules Jinks, you've solved an eternal dilemma." She pulled a hair on his arm, and teased him.

"Thank you," he said.

"It's as good an explanation as any. I never think of those things."

"Do you have to go back tomorrow?"

"Yes." She put her head on his chest.

"What will we do when I get back home?"

"Sneak around and hope we don't get caught."

"Why don't we run away? We could live here."

"Carwyn I could leave in a minute, but I can't leave the children. I'm not even sure I love them, but I do feel I belong with them."

"Take them along."

"Oh, Hercules, think about it. Carwyn would let me go before he'd relinquish his sons. The future lies through a womb. His sons are his high cards; he'll not part with that future."

"We can't keep meeting in the stable. Sooner or later someone will catch us." He sat up, then quickly sank back into the covers, as it was wicked cold even with the fire blazing. "Dad and I deliver wood to some people down on Water Street. Maybe they'd rent us a room or we could rent a house. You could get out in the afternoons."

"Down by the red-light section?"

"I can't think of anywhere else."

"How could I get in and out without being recognized?"

"It'd be strange, but what could anyone say?"

"A hell of a lot, I should think." She chuckled.

"Huh?"

"They could say I was down there buying one of those whores for myself."

This took a moment to sink in. "Oh." Then he brightened. "But who would even think of that?"

"Hercules, everything goes on in Montgomery. Ladies sleeping with ladies is the least of sins."

"Wouldn't you rather have people think that than know about us?"

"The truth is I don't care what anybody thinks, but I know if my husband finds out he'll kill you for sure, and probably kill us both for good measure."

Hercules knew the penalty as well as Hortensia, but it was disquieting to hear it spoken aloud. They lay in silence.

At last Hercules spoke. "I'll ask Blue Rhonda. She'll think of something and she'll know if there's any place to let."

"Blue Rhonda?"

"Blue Rhonda Latrec. She's something."

"Where do they get these names?"

"She probably made it up. Her real name's probably Tillie Crouse or Mary Lou Bumps." Hercules was playful.

"How about Euthabelle Pitts?" Hortensia loved their spontaneous games.

"Beulah Sweitgart."

"Vergie Armpreister."

"Vida Scudder." Hercules grinned.

"Sophonsiba Rill."

"This is it, Hortensia, the ultimate name. You can't top this one: Wilhelmina Charity Goodykoontz."

"Yolanda Yucatan?" she shouted, high on the fun of it all.

Hercules lowered his voice and said in triumph, "Now you know how Blue Rhonda got her name."

Stunned, Hortensia looked at him. "You devil—and you know, you're probably right."

They screamed and rolled around in the bed like two puppies fighting over a bone. They finally settled down, with Hortensia under the covers biting Hercules' big toe. When she came up for air, they couldn't stop giggling.

"I haven't laughed this much since I was ten years old and I was in church with Mother." Hortensia gulped to catch her breath. "I opened a hymnal and out fell this awful dirty handkerchief, or snot rag, if you care to be so crude. I couldn't stop laughing. The harder my mother poked me, the more I laughed. Everyone in the pews turned around; the preacher raised his voice to go over my howls; and finally Mother got so mad she hauled me out of church and whaled the daylights out of me. That did it, too. I thought, All this bullroar about love and Christian tolerance, and here is my mother giving me a whipping because I was laughing in church. I decided right then and there that Zeus and the gang made a lot more sense."

"That's it!" Hercules grabbed her.

"Now we're running away to Greece."

"No. You can join Linton Ray's crusade against alcohol and prostitution. You could come and go on Water Street as you please."

"Hercules, that's crazy."

"That's why it'll work."

"Hercules, I loathe those people."

"His women followers all have husbands who frequent the ladies of the night.

"God knows I've got that. But, darling, I mean those people are, well, of a different class. No one who knows me would believe it."

"I'm not so sure, and not all the women are—what would you call them?"

"Middle class." The words shivered with understated venom.

"Hortensia, it's either that or disguises." He was firm, then he melted. "You do want to keep seeing me, don't you?"

She kissed him. "I'd die if I couldn't see you. For the first time in my life I feel alive. Maybe I don't have a purpose, maybe I don't know anything, but I feel alive!"

"O.K. I'm talking to Blue Rhonda Latrec."

"Blue Rhonda Latrec." Hortensia repeated the name and they each suffered another attack of giggles.

No one imagines growing old. Every time Narcissa passed a mirror and saw that old face staring back at her, it came as a rude surprise. She remained young in her mind. How could her exterior be so out of whack with her interior? If she never accepted the limitations of age, she at least grew accustomed to it.

Sitting at her Louis XV desk, she wrote into the one hundred twentieth volume of her journal. She'd begun keeping one at age fourteen and found it gave her life some structure. Narcissa had never thought anyone would read it. She kept it to put events in perspective. Humans think whatever happens to them is unique. It's all happened before.

Aside from writing, reading history was her greatest satisfaction. The relentless stupidity of humankind through the ages gave one the comfort of consistency.

She'd finished writing the sentence: "As you understand yourself more, others understand you less," when Hortensia, puffy-eyed, appeared at the doorway.

"Come in."

Hortensia sat across from her great-aunt. "I finished packing. The train leaves in two hours."

"Would you like some tea or coffee or gin?"

"Nothing, thank you."

Narcissa didn't waste time. "When will you see him again?"

"In about a week, I suppose."

"He lives near Montgomery?"

"Right in town."

"How convenient and dangerous."

"Aunt Cissy, one minute I feel like dying, and the next minute I'm so happy I feel like I could fly. I don't understand myself at all."

"Do you have to?"

"What?"

"Understand yourself."

Hortensia blinked and Narcissa just smiled.

Finally, the younger woman asked, "Wouldn't it make it all easier?"

"Probably not."

"But you don't know the whole story."

"What's there to know, my dear? You're in love with one man and married to another. The particulars are merely"—and she waved her hand—"fripperies."

Unconvinced, Hortensia mentioned, "He and I come from vastly different social backgrounds."

"Good. Maybe you'll learn something."

Hortensia leaned forward to say more, but then stopped herself.

Narcissa closed her journal. "Great love always works at cross-purposes with society."

"I never thought about love."

"Being an old lady, I have all the time in the world to think about everything. It's one of the great advantages of age. The disadvantage is that no one listens to you." She laughed.

"I'm listening."

"I know, dear."

"So you don't think I'm a fool?" Hortensia earnestly inquired.

"The fools are the ones who never love. It's love that

makes us human. Otherwise we might as well be mosquitoes.''

"You make it seem so simple.''

"It is. Either you live your life, or you let other people live it for you.''

"What do you think he's up to?'' Lotowana scratched her nose.

"An affair of the heart, I suppose.'' Blue Rhonda put on her best woman-of-the-world face.

"But why wouldn't he get a place over in colored quarters?'' Lottie asked.

"And have his mother sniffing around? Everyone knows Ada Goodwater Jinks is fierce about moral issues.''

"Ummm,'' Lottie replied.

"No one notices much over here.''

"Wrong, Rhonda. Everyone notices everything. We keep it to ourselves, that's the difference.''

"Maybe. Banana was glad to get the rent, I can tell you that. All her harping about property, investing—you heard it all. So she buys this tiny house and then it sits for a few months. I thought she'd fuck twenty-four hours a day, she was so worried about keeping up her investment.''

The two laughed over their coke and whiskey.

"Banana's got her ways.'' Lotowana dipped her tongue in the amber liquid, then licked her lips.

"Don't we all?''

"So you know nothing about who Hercules's got back there?'' Lotowana returned, ever the homing pigeon of gossip.

"No, I haven't had time to snoop around. Now, Lottie, is this curiosity all your own, or is Bunny up to something?''

"Bunny?''

"Don't play coy with me, Lots; your boss is the nosiest woman ever lived.''

Lotowana giggled. "She is, isn't she?''

"See, I knew she put you up to it.''

"Well, if the truth be told, I'm as nosy as she is.''

"Go on, Lottie; confession is good for the soul.''

"I hate to miss anything.''

"Ha. Working over there at Bunny's, how could you miss anything?''

"Come on, Rhonda, do you know what's going on?"

"No, I don't. Honest injun. But figure it out. It can't be some regular old love story, or Hercules would marry her, right?"

Lotowana digested this. "Right."

"So he's doing something out of the way."

"A man?" Lottie couldn't picture Hercules hard at it with another man.

"Maybe, or maybe he's got someone back there who's married."

"That makes more sense."

Rhonda continued, "It's gotta be serious."

"Couldn't you snoop around a little?"

"Sure, I could do a lot of things, but you still haven't told me what Bunny's up to. You don't expect me or Banana Mae to believe she's simon-pure."

Lottie's face reddened. "I swear, I swear—I spy on that woman day and night and I don't see anyone, I don't hear anyone. She lacks the urge."

Blue Rhonda folded her arms across her meager chest. "I don't believe it."

Palms upward, Lottie exclaimed. "You watch her, then."

"When I get the time."

"Where's Banana?" Lottie asked.

"Buying fabric for new curtains. Very nesty."

"Tell that to Bunny. Those flower rooms like to tear my ass with boredom." Lotowana sniffed a little powder and glanced at the Ansonia clock on the mantel. "Dad-eye Steelman's coming by. I gotta get back to work. He's so damn little he always falls out."

"Lie on your side. He won't know the difference."

Lotowana hit the door as Banana Mae was coming in. They exchanged pleasantries before Lottie skipped down the road.

Banana looked at Blue Rhonda and smiled. "When Lotowana leaves the room it's like the tide going out."

• • •

Blossoms covered trees like colored powder puffs. Azaleas took over when tulips left off. Montgomery glowed in soft April light, resplendent in her best season. Spring infected everyone. Hortensia felt like Persephone rescued from Hades by Demeter. Her radiance dazzled everyone around her. She felt so glorious that she was extra-attentive to Carwyn. Hortensia was so in love with Hercules that her abundance of goodwill spilled over. She thought she'd find Carwyn more offensive than usual once she had become lovers with Hercules, but the opposite happened and it confused her. She began to look at Carwyn as a man, instead of as her husband. If anything, she understood him better and she tried to make his daily life happier. Entangled in meetings, political smokers and his small but persistent vice of gambling, he wasn't home more than before, but when he was there he found life pleasant. The few times he made love to Hortensia she was compliant. That surprised her enormously. She thought she'd hate Carwyn's touch but she barely noticed and she didn't feel unfaithful to Hercules. Carwyn was her husband; she owed him something. The passionate lovemaking with Hercules enabled her to experience every moment as special. She counted those moments, too, until she could see him again. Tuesday and Thursday afternoons were their times. To Leone's delight, Hortensia swapped coats with her. Looking only slightly like her own cook, she'd hurry down to Water Street. If anyone noticed her, she was too caught up in the affair to care.

The small white frame house sat behind Blue Rhonda and Banana Mae's house. It was at the end of a long lot and she could slip in on the alley side. The rooms were neatly wallpapered and quite clean. Hercules moved a good bed in and that was their only furniture except for a sofa in the parlor and a small wooden table and chairs in the kitchen. The cupboards were painted white with red stencils and the table was also white with red stenciling. The decor couldn't have been simpler, unless they'd lived in a monastery. Hortensia loved that little house more than she'd loved any place in her life. She'd always been triumphantly materialistic, reveling in her jewels, Bechstein piano, sables, and European furniture looted from the palaces of crumbling empires. Now she realized that beautiful though those things were, she'd used them to fill her emptiness. With Hercules she didn't need anything but him. He superseded jewels, paintings, antiques. When he was in a room he was all she saw and all she wanted to see. The clean simplicity of their surroundings accented their love. She felt that if she could live in this little house forever with Hercules, that's all one could ask from life and it would be a very full life.

Banana Mae figured out that Hercules spent Tuesdays and Thursdays with someone. He'd be in there at times alone, unloading groceries or sweeping out the rooms. She figured he was working up to make the break at home; soon he'd live there full time. It's only natural that a child leave home right about his age. If they stay on longer they never quite grow up. Banana had shot out of her house like a cannon. She was sixteen and she'd never returned. She saw little purpose in remembering her family, a collection of half-wits if ever there was one. At least Hercules came from better people.

Banana Mae was curious, but not like Blue Rhonda. Rhonda was curious about everything. Once she had caught a cockroach with a glass jar. Rather than kill it, she punched holes in the lid, fed it moldy lettuce and watched it intently. Disgusting was the only word Banana Mae could apply to the brown bug with its tiny wings and spiky legs. Rhonda was fascinated. Nor could she bring herself to kill it. With great ceremony, a cockroach Declaration of Independence, she released it in the backyard despite Banana's protests that it's a filthy bug.

To alleviate the tedium, one day Blue Rhonda poured cinnamon honey over Karel's cock. The thick, sticky substance roused him to great pleasure and Rhonda liked the taste. Afterward she poured him a tall glass of rum while she made do with a small gin.

"Do you ever get homesick, Karel?"

"No; do you?"

"For that jerkwater town in eastern Alabama? I'd have to be nuts to go back there."

"That's how I feel about Prague, and now there's really nothing to go back to. Just wait; Eastern Europe will fold up like a busted hand in poker."

"Who knows? They may come out ahead."

"Rhonda, with Germany on one side and Russia on the other, how long could they last even if they did come out on the side of the winners? You don't know Europe. It's a collection of hatreds and conceits going back to the Roman Empire. We were tribes then and we're tribes now. That's why I came here—to get away from all that crap."

Blue Rhonda listened. She couldn't imagine what life was like over there. "You sure know a lot."

He put his arm around her shoulder. "You're nice to say that. I do miss some things, I guess. There's a café in Prague with a frog sign hanging over the door. I miss the beer at that place and I miss duck the way my mother cooks it. And the uniforms! Ah, Rhonda, the uniforms of the Austro-Hungarian Empire are something to see—gold braid, furs, bright reds and deep blues, every color of the rainbow, and shakos with giant plumes."

"I don't miss anything so grand, but you know what I do miss, sometimes in the fall?"

"What?"

"Getting a new book bag, ruler and pencils for school." She half laughed at herself.

"We remember the damndest things, don't we?" He stretched himself.

"Hey, I'll go out with you if you go the back way. I want to peek in Banana's rented house to see what I can see."

Karel wagged his finger at her. "Is that nice?"

"No, but I'm doing it anyway."

Tiptoeing out the back door, Rhonda explained that Hercules rented the place. Karel feigned interest in her surmises. Rhonda's liveliness and lack of concern for what others thought about her is what held his attention. He didn't give a damn what Hercules or any other man was up to.

When you're supposed to be quiet is exactly when you want to fall on the ground shrieking with laughter. Her hand over her mouth, Rhonda snuck around to the back door of the little house. Two light coats hung on pegs. As he waved goodbye to Rhonda, Karel noticed that one of the coats looked familiar. He crept up to the back door.

"That's Leone's coat," he whispered.

"Couldn't be. She's at work." Rhonda felt as if she'd stepped into quicksand.

"Goddammit, I ought to know my own wife's coat."

"There's more than one coat looks like that. Don't get all het up over nothing."

"We'll soon see." He opened the door and walked in. Leone had embroidered her initials on the back inside collar, and there they were, "L. S."

Rhonda watched in horror. Without hesitation, Karel started up the stairs to the second floor.

Whispering vainly, "Don't; Banana Mae will kill us," she pulled on his suspenders, but he dragged her along.

Feet could be heard smacking against the floor, and as Karel reached the top of the stairs Hercules was there to greet him.

"What are you doing with my wife?" Karel bellowed.

"Nothing," Hercules truthfully replied.

"See, I told you, Karel. Now come on and leave him alone. I'm real sorry about this, Hercules."

"He's lying. You don't expect him to be fucking my wife and tell me, do you?"

There wasn't much Rhonda could say to that one, except that she couldn't imagine Hercules wanting Leone in the first place, and she sure as hell wasn't going to say that.

"I'm not seeing your wife, Mr. Sokol," Hercules calmly said.

Karel attempted to push past Hercules, but the younger man held him in place with one arm. Rhonda was on the other arm, edging him down the steps. Karel's face shone red as a cock's comb; his voice rattled the windows.

"Leone, get out here. If you don't show yourself, I'll kill you when you get home."

The bedroom door opened. Hercules flew to it and tried to block her emergence. Karel was right behind him, dragging Blue Rhonda with him.

"Don't!" Hercules begged.

Hortensia pushed the door open anyway. She was wrapped in a soft, dusty-rose robe bordered in pink. Karel and Blue Rhonda gasped as much from the knowledge of who it was as from how lovely she looked.

"Don't punish your wife for my deeds, Karel." Hortensia's voice cut.

Embarrassed, Karel babbled. Rhonda tugged him away

from the door. He finally found his voice. "What's Leone's coat doing hanging by the back door?"

"I gave her a new coat weeks ago in exchange for this one. You ought to pay more attention to your wife."

"Come on, Karel. Hercules, I'm as sorry as I can be."

"Who are you?" Hortensia stared at her.

Hercules answered, "This is Blue Rhonda Latrec, Banana Mae's partner. Blue Rhonda, this is—"

"I know who she is," Blue Rhonda answered.

"You two are heading for a pack of hell," Karel said.

"We'll be there a lot faster if you don't keep quiet." Hortensia was cool.

Karel saw the look in Hercules' eyes and felt sorry for the fellow. "I'm not saying anything."

All three turned to Blue Rhonda. She burst out, "How can I not tell Banana Mae? I tell Banana everything."

"Try," Hercules quietly said.

"I believe your partner knows my husband."

Blue Rhonda moaned.

Hortensia went on, "She might be tempted to tell him what she knows, so it's better she doesn't know anything."

Rhonda puffed out her little chest. "Banana's not like that. She's the Rock of Gibraltar."

"I'm sure," Hortensia agreed. "But try, Miss Latrec, please try to keep this secret."

"All right."

As she walked back to her house, Blue Rhonda's stomach gurgled; her head ached. She wished she didn't know anything. I don't know if curiosity killed the cat, she thought to herself, but it could make cat or human miserable. Aside from feeling sorry for Hercules, she was wretched that she couldn't blab all.

Hercules sat on the edge of the bed, with a vacant look that belied his worry. Hortensia rubbed his neck as she sat behind him.

"Honey, we've got to get out of here. Please let's go. We can do all right in Chicago."

"Hercules, all my money is in my husband's name. How far do you think we'll get?"

He turned around. "I'm making good money off these fights. We'll be all right."

"How long will that last? Even if you could keep it up for years, I wouldn't let you. Little by little that kind of punishment creeps up on you." She ran her finger around his ear.

"Then I'll find another job after that. I'm strong and I work hard."

"Darling, you'll be a black man saddled with a white woman. How many friends do you think you'll have?"

"I don't care about anyone but you."

"What I meant was you might not find it so easy to get work."

"Roxy saw that you were white. I can work. I can always work. We may not have a social life, but we'll have one another."

"What about your family? This will kill your mother."

Hercules breathed deeply. "She'll learn to live with it. It's my life, not hers."

She knew he was right and he was willing to risk everything, to move, to start life in a strange city. She wanted to go desperately, but invisible bonds held her to Montgomery. Strongest was her responsibility to her sons; her lack of tenderness for them did not weaken her sense of duty. The less apparent, but telling, bond was her position in the town. She liked being top dog and she wasn't eager to part with that. On the other hand, she couldn't live without this man. Night after night she'd lie alone in her bed and wonder why God had blessed her and cursed her with this love. Why blacks and whites lived on opposite sides of the Grand Canyon didn't puzzle her. She accepted as natural the division of the races. She knew it was grotesquely unfair, but she had no plan to correct it, and she couldn't imagine how two strands so long separated could be woven back together. Yet she and Hercules had managed to do just that. Slowly she realized not only that was this a love affair, but that her view of the world she lived in was being altered. But she was not yet prepared to run away.

She kissed his cheek. "Darling, I do want to go with you, but I need time to think."

"Maybe you don't love me enough."

"No, oh, please don't say that, don't think it. I—I need to put my house in order, so to speak." She kissed him, drawing him down on the bed. He kissed her back and started to sit up, but she pushed him down again and slid her hand under his pants until she found his cock. It never took him long to get rock hard. She unbuttoned his pants and slid them off. She kissed him and played with him and sat on top of him, rubbing his head, massaging his temples. When he begged to go inside, she teased him some more, finally sliding on him and slowly moving. For a good twenty minutes she tormented him, now slow and now fast, until neither of them could take it any longer.

Afterward she kissed him and told him she loved him. It would take her time, but she was trying.

"Are you afraid?" he asked. "I'll protect you."

"I know you will. I wonder if I can protect you. I feel as though I'm dancing on a volcano."

Hercules' eyes shone so light and clear. "Maybe everyone is; they don't know it and we do."

The war provided Grace Deltaven with a golden opportunity to hone her acting skills. She practiced relentlessly on the boys graduating from high school. At the mention of enlistment, her large violet eyes filled with tears; she'd brush her hand across the young man's hand and then gaze downward. This produced an electric effect and Icellee beat off the boys with a stick. Her front porch would be lined six deep. Montgomery noted both Grace's beauty and her ability to wrap men around her little finger. As to her acting ability, time would tell. With or without talent, Grace was bound to conquer. Lila and Icellee prevailed upon an old mutual friend, Illona Pagent Reynolds, to house Grace in New York while she studied at the acting academy. Illona's daughter, Peppermint Reynolds, suffered from the identical malady, so the girls could emote together. Peppermint, so named because her father had amassed a fortune in the candy business, owned a perfect profile. She was one of those girsl who would have to grow into her face. A flurry of letters from Montgomery to New York and New York to Montgomery contented Grace while she counted the days until she could burst forth like a comet.

• • •

Tending her orchids, Lila Reedmuller was also obsessed with the future. She felt impending disaster, but from what direction? Was it the war, or was it closer to home? She mentioned her premonition to Bartholomew. He didn't make fun of her, said perhaps she had second sight. Lila had never had a premonition in her life. Bartholomew said that didn't matter; it came to you when you needed it.

Ada Jinks felt more than premonition. She knew Hercules was up to no good. This was compounded by the fact that Apollo announced he would enlist as soon as he graduated from the Palmer Institute in June. Ranting and raving rolled off Hercules' back. Apollo was too far away to yell, so she wrote letter after letter. Placide felt pride mixed with fear that his oldest son would choose such a path. He knew Apollo had no idea about what he was getting himself into. Armies are dependent on youthful male ignorance. Like Hercules, Apollo had made a decision that would forever close the door on boyhood. His father had to admire him for that.

Crystal balls, tarot cards, the future itself, bored Blue Rhonda Latrec. The future was a drug people fed themselves so they could get through today. She desired nothing but the present—and to forget her past. She suffered a small scare when Minnie Rue cornered her at a party over in her establishment. Minnie traveled to Columbus, Georgia, on business and briefly stopped at Hatchechubbee, Alabama.

"I had myself a Coca-Cola at the soda fountain." Minnie grinned, looking like a shark. "And I asked the fellow behind the counter if he'd ever heard of you. Said he didn't."

Rhonda held her head up. "Minnie, I hope you don't think I called myself Blue Rhonda Latrec back in Hatchechubbee."

"What is your given name, then?"

"I'll never tell."

"Well, how old were you when you left home?"

"Fourteen, but I was big for my age." Rhonda glared.

Minnie checked her out from head to toe. "I don't know, Rhonda—there's something mysterious about you."

"Bullshit. You tell me one woman here that uses her right name, yourself included."

"Lotowana."

Rhonda grimaced.

A flicker of victory shining in her eyes, Minnie went on, "No one could imagine a name like Lotowana, so you know that's real. And I think Bunny's last name is her real name."

"That doesn't count. Bunny's far from home, so what's it matter to her? As for Lottie, well, she's Lottie. What else can I say?"

"So come on, what's your real name?"

"Bag it, Minnie. What's yours?"

"Minerva Raines Desfors." She laughed.

Blue Rhonda joined her. "That's ripe."

"So what's yours?"

"I'll tell you this, Minnie. If you outlive me, you'll know it, and my name's even funnier than yours."

"What are you hiding?"

"Same thing we're all hiding: a past that doesn't match our present."

Rhonda mentioned this conversation to Banana Mae.

"Minnie's got the searching eye," was Banana's reply.

"Well, I don't like it."

"Come on, Rhonda, the worst thing in the world is not to be talked about. You love it."

Prudently, Blue Rhonda decided to let that fly by. As for Banana Mae's given name, Banana told her once and she'd forgotten it. All she did remember was that it was Irish. With Banana's red hair, one would figure that out sooner or later.

Rhonda burned to tell Banana what she'd seen in the little house, but she restrained herself. For one thing, Banana Mae still cared for Carwyn, although his fascination for her had faded somewhat. He spent more time over at Minnie's, sampling the position of the day.

Instead, Blue Rhonda turned the conversation to Reverend Linton Ray, and they both agreed he'd stick to fighting the demon alcohol for a long time. Then they got into a fight because Blue Rhonda wanted to wear navy blue. Banana screamed that no woman ever wore navy blue before Easter. Blue Rhonda retorted that Easter was just around the corner. No matter. Some rules could not be broken. As Rhonda sulked, Banana Mae marveled that Blue Rhonda's mother could have been so stupid as to ignore the basics.

• • •

Senator Bankhead wired Carwyn to come to Washington for two weeks. Hortensia smothered her excitement as best she could. She rode with him to the train station to make sure he was really going. When the giant locomotive pulled in, steam hissing, she viewed the machine as her deliverer. Mechanical devices fascinated her. Trains meant progress, speed, an end to provincialism. Few people questioned the fact that it forever altered humans' conception of time as well as distance. The sun gave way to the clock. Between timetables and the industrial whistle, humankind would never again feel time as did their ancestors or the beasts in the field. A grid dropped over the human race; the hours bound one as securely as a cell.

The first week of Carwyn's absence, Hortensia and Hercules luxuriated in being able to spend the nights together. Once he even came over to her house. Hortensia had never been happier. The only sting of reality came when Paris asked her why she kissed that black man he saw. She remembered she did kiss him goodbye by the back door. The child must have been lurking about. Rather than lie to him, or let him sense that he had the upper hand, Hortensia very calmly explained that the man in question had done many things for her. She kissed him same as the rest of her friends. This satisfied Paris somewhat and he dropped it.

Toward the end of the second week she cherished each minute with Hercules and dreaded Carwyn's return. It wasn't so much her husband as it was the sneaking about. That Friday she arrived at the little house early. Hercules thought he could finish his rounds and be there in the late afternoon.

On the way to the house he stopped by the station to see his father. Hercules wore a plaid jacket Hortensia had given him, as she said his old jacket was thin as a bee's wing. Even in springtime the dampness from the Alabama River would creep up on you.

The two men walked down the tracks. Placide wanted to check a boxcar on a siding; he thought it might be on the wrong track. Placide pushed the heavy door open.

"This thing's full of pianos. I swear this is the wrong load."

Hercules stuck his head in. "Do they always crate them like that?"

"Yes." Placide hopped down. "I'd better go back and check the freight sheets one more time."

Father and son walked back between the ties, as it was easier than walking on the myriad of curved rails leading into the station and the sidings. An engineer backing up his locomotive bumped the boxcar, but he was not aware of it. It started rolling toward the two men. Hercules turned his head and saw the yellow car hurtling toward them.

He leapt off the track.

Placide stared at the car, frozen. Hercules jumped back on the track and literally picked his father up and threw him to the side. He couldn't fully get out of the way in time. When the car roared by, Placide picked himself up and beheld Hercules, lying on his back, his left leg cleanly amputated above the knee.

"Hercules!" he screamed.

"It's all right. I'm alive," Hercules panted.

Blue Rhonda, on her daily stroll to the station, observed the accident. Cursing her prissy pumps, she ran close enough to see the fountain of blood gushing from Hercules' thigh. She yanked off her shoes, and running, yelled over her shoulder. "I'll call an ambulance or get the stationmaster to call."

Placide tore off his shirt and ripped it into strips. He applied a tourniquet, loosening and then tightening it. He knew if his son didn't get help soon he'd bleed to death and if the tourniquet stayed on too long it would kill what was left of the leg. Blue Rhonda was now by his side.

The ambulance arrived, pulled by two sweating horses. The stationmaster, in his haste, automatically called the ambulance number he knew. It was the white amublance. The three attendants ran over to Hercules.

"We don't take coloreds," the tall, skinny one said.

"You've got to take him, you've got to!" Blue Rhonda's veins stood out on her throat, her voice unusually deep.

"For the love of God, man, make an exception," Placide cried.

"Sorry." They got back into their ambulance and drove off.

Blue Rhonda raced back into the stationmaster's office, sobbing. Appalled at the mistake he'd made as well as at the refusal of the three white men, the stationmaster shrieked into the phone. As he hung up, he reassured her, "They'll be right here."

Blue Rhonda hurried back to see if she could help in any other way. Hercules began to get woozy. He knew he wasn't going to make it. He held his father's hand. Placide knelt down, his son's head in his lap. Rhonda got down on her knees as well.

"Hercules! It's Blue Rhonda." She didn't know if he was cognizant or not.

He opened his eyes and smiled at her. She could hear the ambulance in the distance.

"Can I do anything for you?"

"Yes," he whispered. "Tell her I love her. Ask her to live for me."

Placide caressed Hercules' cheek. "Don't talk like that. You'll be fine; just hang on."

The black attendants came up the track with a stretcher.

"I'm dying. I can feel it." He reached up to touch his father's face.

Tears wrecking her makeup, Blue Rhonda vowed, "I'll tell her."

The attendants lifted him onto the stretcher. One bent over the track and picked up the leg, and tossed it in the back of the wagon. Placide climbed in back. Rhonda waved goodbye.

• • •

Banana Mae was slicing bread when Blue Rhonda came into the kitchen.

"What's wrong?"

"A boxcar ran over Hercules Jinks and cut off his leg. He's bleeding to death. He's probably already dead."

Banana sat down hard. "Oh, no, not that sweet boy."

Blue Rhonda cried, "There's more. We've got to go back there to the little house and tell his lover."

Banana put her hand on her heart, already sympathizing with the nameless woman's plight.

"Banana, his lover is Hortensia Banastre."

She stopped breathing; her eyes almost bugged out of her head. "What?"

"You heard me. Now we've got to go back there and tell her before she goes looking for him and finds out the wrong way. She could show her hand and ruin herself."

"Why should I care what happens to her after the way she treated me?"

"This is no time to be petty. How would you feel if you saw your husband riding around with a fancy woman?"

That had some effect on Banana.

Blue Rhonda traced the tablecloth pattern with her index finger. "It's the least we can do for Hercules. She couldn't help falling in love with him, I guess." Rhonda looked Banana Mae in the eye. "Come on; she's no one to help her now but a whore."

Banana Mae stood up and squared her shoulders. "Let's go," she said quietly.

When they told Hortensia, she was in the kitchen baking up corn bread as a surprise for Hercules. She never cooked or baked, so she thought he'd enjoy it all the more. She looked at the two women like a deer who's been shot, runs a few paces, and then falls dead. She repeated the same question: "Where did you say he is?" When the full import of Blue Rhonda's message hit her, she made for the door. Both of them restrained her. She fought them, screaming and wailing.

As a concession, Blue Rhonda agreed to take her to the funeral home. She figured that by this time the body would be there. Only if she saw him dead would Hortensia believe them.

Rhonda realized a scene over in colored quarters would do no one any good. There seemed no other way to settle down Hortensia, who in her grief was almost as strong as Hercules.

Between the two of them, Blue Rhonda said she herself would take Hortensia to the funeral parlor. Banana Mae faced the equally unwelcome task of calling on Lila Reedmuller to warn her of what had transpired, and to see if she would accept her daughter into her home after all this. For certain, Hortensia could not be left alone.

Blue Rhonda managed to get Hortensia in through the back door of Jefferson's Funeral Parlor. Placide sat in the front room. Exhausted, he needed to pull himself together before going home and telling Ada.

When Hortensia saw Hercules' body laid out on the slab, she didn't scream or make any sound. She flung herself on him, kissing him, trying to revive him. Blue Rhonda thought her heart would break. She pulled Hortensia off.

"No, no." Hortensia battled her.

"Time to go home," Rhonda softly said.

"He is my home," Hortensia sobbed. She made an animal sound that sent chills down Blue Rhonda's backbone. Placide heard it too. He pushed open the door and saw Hortensia. He was beyond shock at who she was. All he thought was: Poor woman.

Lila, a pale fury, met Banana Mae at the back door. It took some fast explaining on Banana Mae's part or she would have been tossed out on her ear. Lila couldn't believe what Banana Mae was telling her. On the other hand, it was so preposterous she couldn't be making it up. When Blue Rhonda finally delivered Hortensia, Lila perceived that the two women had performed a great service to her family. There was no time to properly thank Banana Mae and Blue Rhonda, though she did the best she could under the circumstances. Hortensia wept and begged her mother to kill her, to put her out of her misery. Distressed at the sight of their daughter's suffering, neither Lila nor Bartholomew could condemn her. Lila wisely packed a bag and unobtrusively got on the night train up to Chicago with her daughter. Her only hope was to get Hortensia to Narcissa's and to stay with her until she returned to the land of the living. She left Bartholomew to lie to Carwyn when he returned.

As though struck by lightning, the rooms of the Jinks house vibrated with terror and sadness. Placide sent telegrams to Athena and Apollo. When he told Ada the news, she took it like a Roman matron of the Augustan age: no tears, hysteria or complaints. She knew her husband endured a worse ordeal than hers, since he had witnessed Hercules' death.

They sat in the parlor. Neither could eat and there wasn't much to say.

Placide didn't tell his wife about Hortensia at the funeral parlor. There was no reason for her to know that.

If Placide accepted the injustices of this world, Ada did not. She asked him once more about the white ambulance turning away. As night wore on and Hercules' death became more final, Ada became more distraught, yet still very much in control, showing no overt grief.

"They treated him like a dog."

Placide's eyes, bloodshot, and suddenly old, gazed at his wife. "What could I do?"

Ada spoke firmly. "What are we to do? I tell my children to get an education, work hard, be respectful. Do you think it makes any difference?"

"This isn't the time to speak of such things," Placide answered.

"When is the time to speak of such things?" Ada whispered. "It doesn't matter what we do; we're still niggers."

What Blue Rhonda and Banana Mae saw was explainable but not justifiable. Both women, born and raised in Alabama, appreciated the racial caste system, but like most caring people they somehow assumed that it wasn't all that bad. After all, had they ever heard a black person complain? It was especially hard on Rhonda, for she would forever see the white ambulance pull away.

After informing Bunny and Lotowana of events minus the information about Hortensia, the two friends trudged back home. The night shone with silver-gray low-hanging clouds. They could smell the river. The beauty of the evening underscored their sadness.

The felt a rancid mist fall over them. Banana Mae knocked back the booze to dull the pain. Blue Rhonda snorted cocaine, hoping it would help, but all that did was make her senses sharper.

"The home was beautiful." Banana Mae crossed her legs under her on the couch.

"What home?"

"Reedmullers'."

"Oh." Rhonda faced her on the opposite end of the davenport.

"I guess most of the money is hers. He can't make all that much."

"Men don't mind taking a woman's money. They mind taking orders." Rhonda spoke this without malice. "I don't know about Mr. Reedmuller, though. I think those society architects get big fees."

"Maybe." Banana Mae poured another glass. "How is it that some women get on one side of the tracks like Lila and Hortensia and some of us get . . . here?"

"How the hell should I know?" Rhonda didn't think her side of the tracks was all that bad. What's more, she was certain it was more fun.

"It's not fair."

"Banana, who cares? Life is what you make it. You can be anybody, anywhere, and you'll decide more than someone will decide for you."

"I wish I could believe that."

"You think fate or God put you here on Water Street?"

"Well, it wasn't all my doing!" Banana heated up.

"So being born like Hortensia wasn't all her doing— and look at her now. I wouldn't trade places."

"I agree with you there." Banana eased away from a full-scale attack of self-pity. "But heartbreak is one thing, being shoved aside or plain pushed around is another. And that's what I mean. It just isn't fair. If you're born on one side of town, the right color, the right sex, life is a lot different than for someone like you and I."

"I don't give a shit. I'm as good as all those swells."

"They don't think so."

"So what?" Now Rhonda got mad.

"That's what I mean."

"For Chrissake, Banana, it doesn't matter who you are or what you are—there's always someone to look down their nose at you."

"I'd be a helluva lot readier to suffer in Lila Reedmuller's mansion than here," Banana replied.

Rhonda's voice was sharp. "Do you think for one minute that the pain is any different?"

"No," Banana wearily agreed, "but one's place on the social ladder is a benefit at any time other than something like what we just went through."

"But I don't care." Banana's hungering after social respect mystified Rhonda. All she wanted to do was live and let live.

Banana changed the subject and said, with a glint of the devil in her eyes, "Is there any man I can look up to without lying on my back?"

"Ha."

"And another thing. You never lose your heart to any man. I'm so dumb I still care about Carwyn Banastre."

"I told you long ago you've got my heart. Men are business."

Banana tossed a needlepoint pillow at Rhonda's curly black hair. She caught it and tossed it right back at Banana Mae. In seconds the two were rolling and fighting on the floor. Rhonda, slightly stronger, finally pinned Banana Mae to the floor.

"Uncle, uncle." Banana gave up.

"I'm not your uncle."

"Rhonda, you let me up."

"No. I'm gonna sit here on top of you and read *War and Peace*."

This reply sent a half-looped Banana into giggles. Rhonda held her shoulders down. Then, quite unexpectedly, she kissed her. Banana laughed through it. Rhonda persisted. Finally, Banana Mae kissed her back.

"You don't kiss so bad for a girl."

Rhonda kissed her again.

"O.K., that's enough."

"You didn't mind it so much." Rhonda's face was red.

"No."

"Let me make love to you."

"Rhonda, I may be a whore, but I'm not a queer."

"Hell, you do everything else. Just once, for...curiosity's sake." Rhonda kissed her again.

"If we're going to do this, we might as well be comfortable." Banana smiled.

Once in Banana's bedroom, Rhonda stripped to her slip. She never wore a corset, so she had time to help Banana out of hers. Why anybody desired an hourglass figure was beyond Rhonda. It was too much trouble. Rhonda pushed Banana Mae on the bed and kissed her, kissed her breasts and eventually worked her way down to Banana's crotch. Since the men who came to Banana generally had little desire to perform acts of oral sex on her, this came as a delight.

Afterward Banana snuggled next to Rhonda. "Are you O.K.?"

"Oh, sure. I came when you did."

"With your slip still on?"

"Never underestimate the power of a woman."

"Rhonda, I swear to God, you're nuts."

Blue Rhonda laughed. "I never said I was sane."

Banana Mae was in no danger of becoming a lesbian. Still, she appreciated Rhonda's gentleness and concern for her sexual pleasure. "I never thought I'd like anything like that."

"Mmm."

"Women really are mysterious." Banana's eyes opened wide. "Why, I mystify myself."

"And you're calling me nuts?"

They fell asleep, little realizing that often after a death the need for sex was ravenous, overpowering—as though Nature were trying to replace one of her own.

• • •

Lila and Narcissa watched over Hortensia day and night until they determined she was stable enough not to kill herself. Her return from the brink of self-destruction was aided by the discovery that she was pregnant. After weeks of discussion they agreed the child would live with Hortensia, but as Amelie's child. Since Amelie's husband had run off for the seventh or eighth time, she would probably be glad to live up on the third floor of the house. Covering pregnancy and birth isn't easy, but women have been doing it for centuries. Hortensia stayed in Chicago until the baby was born. She named her Catherine.

1928

Prohibition slowed down not one soul in Montgomery. Reverend Ray gloried in his great victory, but it was as hollow as a bootlegger's shinbone. Minnie Rue served fruit juices with her *plat du jour* that would knock you flat on your ass. Bunny Turnbull discreetly inquired as to her customers' medicinal needs and readily supplied them. Banana Mae, weaned on whiskey, continued to suckle the bottle. Delivery of contraband required imagination and cash. Other than that, business continued as usual. Perhaps better. The generation who fought World War I reveled with an abandon not seen since the restoration of Charles II.

If ever a person was in tune with her time it was Blue Rhonda Latrec. Born in 1900, she hit the twenties as she hit her own twenties. Angular, built exactly right for the clothes of the day, she mixed peacock blues with purples, and even wore white before the official beginning of summer. Blue Rhonda never did fill out, whereas Banana Mae ripened a bit as she coasted into her early thirties. Not that she discussed her age. Lotowana may have gained a pound or two over the years, but at her size it barely mattered. She flashed her snaggletoothed smile, won during a wicked fistfight a few years back, and still sang like an angel. Bunny Turnbull took to wearing rimless glasses when she went over the books, which was often. Gray laced her hair, but her figure remained trim.

"Do you think we ought to advertise in the paper?" Banana Mae asked Blue Rhonda, who was reading the evening news. Banana Mae needed attention every second and Blue Rhonda had been quietly reading for over ten minutes. Drove Banana crazy.

"Huh?"

"Advertise in the paper."

Blue Rhonda dropped the paper on her chest. "Sure. I can see it now: 'Cocksucking. Special Discount on Sundays.' "

"That's your ad, not mine. I mean something to bring in new business or passing travelers. You know, something about rooms to let or . . . I can't think of the right words."

"We could rename this place Pussy Hall, hang out a shingle, put a half-page ad in the paper. Keep cooking, Banana."

"Smartass. I was only trying to improve our financial station."

Blue Rhonda gave up on reading the paper. "We do fine. We've got our regulars and new business drops in. Which reminds me, isn't tonight Cedrenus Shackleford's night?"

"Yeah; he phoned and said he'd be late." Banana's cheeks were permanently rosy from the booze.

"One of Minnie's girls gave birth this morning." Blue Rhonda ran errands all day and didn't know if Banana had heard.

"Lottie told me. Minnie's got a passel of bastards over there. Her girls ought to be more careful."

"At least you heard it from Lottie. I had the misfortune to run into Minnie herself. She can talk."

"Amen."

Blue Rhonda continued, "You know Minnie. She relates every event to herself. So once she'd informed me of the miracle of new life, she then goes on to tell me she weighed seven pounds at birth. I said, 'Yes, and your tongue weighed nine.' Well, you should have seen her face!"

"That'll dampen her for all of two days. What do you bet she'll be over here Thursday, running at the mouth again?" Banana hooted.

"Two days—is that your bet?"

"I'll bet you that hat down at Fuller's Millinery."

"You're on!" Blue Rhonda loved a bet. Her penchant for gambling got so bad right after the war that Banana took seventy-five percent of her earnings from her and invested it in real estate. Blue Rhonda let her do it; even she knew money burned a hole in her pocket.

The two women lived together for over a decade. They were like a happily married couple in all respects but one: they didn't sleep together, except for that one fling after Hercules died. Rhonda took up gardening—she said for her nerves. Her azaleas, dogwoods, magnolias, plus all the annuals she planted every spring and fall, lent cheerfulness to the property. She landscaped the grounds to the little rental cottage in the back, and in good weather croquet and lawn parties filled her time. She painted both houses sky blue with sparkling white shutters. Bunny and Minnie ran houses, but Blue Rhonda and Banana Mae provided a home, and a good home at that. No wonder their customers stayed with them over the years to become members of the family. Their regulars were men trapped in marriages of convention or marriages that long ago lost their fizz. The fact that they enjoyed themselves with the two women proved to be as seductive as sex itself.

"Aren't those peepers driving you wild?" Banana interrupted Rhonda's reading one more time.

"The tree frogs?"

"Hell, yes. What in God's name do they say to one another?"

Blue Rhonda patted the head of Attila the Hun, a ferocious cat who'd adopted them about a year ago. "They're all out there telling one another they're princes."

Banana paused, then her eyes narrowed. "It's the end of the day. You're slipping, girl."

"It could have been worse. I could have told you the only way you'll find your prince is to kiss a lot of toads."

That shut up Banana Mae long enough for Blue Rhonda to finish reading her paper.

Catherine at age ten never walked when she could run. Her father's energy and athleticism raced through her body. Her skin was the color of coffee with cream and her eyes were a light hazel. Loose reddish curls bounced on her hair like a jolly cap. She was curious, outgoing and friendly. Except for Carwyn's study, Catherine could go anywhere in the house. She could often be found at Hortensia's vanity, dipping her fingers in pots of rouge. If she wondered about her parentage, she didn't betray it. Amelie made a convincing mother. Hortensia masqueraded as Aunt Tense. Catherine was in awe of her real mother, who moved through the rooms like a dancer and could command an entire gathering with a turn of her head.

Hortensia loved the child as she had never loved anything in her life save for Catherine's father. Once when talking to Lila about Hercules, she said, "I have been in sorrow's kitchen and licked clean all the pots." Since those terrible early weeks ten years before at Great-Aunt Narcissa's, that was the only occasion on which she spoke of Hercules. Hercules' brief life didn't alter the fact that he was here; Catherine was her proof of that.

Carwyn immersed himself in politics. He got the thrill out of it he used to get from racing. Like many people in similar situations, he chose to ignore what was under his nose. As far as he was concerned, Catherine was Amelie's child. He justified Hortensia's extraordinary interest in the girl by telling himself her sons were grown and a woman needs children. Catherine worked her charms on him too. He found the smiling, exuberant child irresistible. He'd never relaxed around his sons and possibly never would. It could be that he was that much older, in his early forties, or it could be that little girls elicit a response sons do not. On his way home, Carwyn would often stop and buy her some book or toy. The two would then engage in conversations which he would recall months and years later for his own amusement.

"What did you learn today?" Carwyn asked this of Catherine each evening when he came home.

Her eyes brightened. "Today we learned about the English winning the French and Indian War on the Plains of Abraham. That's why we speak English instead of French, but isn't it sad that the general died?"

"Most generals die fat in their beds—or somebody else's." Carwyn's mustache curved upward.

"They don't die in wars?"

"No."

Catherine pondered this. "That's not fair. Generals are supposed to die in wars."

"Did you learn anything else?"

She tossed her Raggedy Andy doll in the air. "Oh, in Bible class we learned about Jesus 'scending to heaven after forty days—but I already knew that."

"You're long on Jesus."

"Sure. I know everything. I know all about Virgin Mary, Joseph, Peter and all those guys."

"Very impressive. Here, I brought you something to keep you out of mischief." He handed her a brightly colored rubber ball.

She grabbed it with excitement. "Thank you, sir." She threw it in the air and Carwyn caught it, holding it before he'd give it back.

"Tell me one more thing, Miss Fireball. Do you believe everything you learn?"

Undaunted, Catherine replied, "No. I believe most of it, I guess, but some things make me wonder."

"Like what?" He pitched the ball at her. She caught it with her left hand.

"If I tell you, will you promise not to tell?"

"Word of honor."

"Well"—her little voice dropped in seriousness—"what I don't understand is Jesus going back up to heaven. If he loved us so much that he came down and made himself a person and suffered, then don't you think he should stay here so we could all see him?"

Carwyn wrinkled his brow and she went on: "He lives forever and ever, so why can't he live here on earth? If I could see him I could believe so much easier—couldn't you?"

"Yes, I believe I could."

A whistle from outside caught her attention. She was halfway through the door before she remembered to stop and thank Carwyn again for the rubber ball. Carwyn laughed, watching her skip out. For him she existed as a free spirit. For the rest of Montgomery, Catherine existed as a moral question mark.

The University of Virginia endured the sons of the South. Mr. Jefferson had founded it as an institute of higher learning. What Paris Stuart Banastre learned there had little to do with T.J.'s high hopes for young men. Paris at twenty haunted the local whorehouse on Fifth Street. He gambled compulsively. If he cracked a book it never showed, but he maintained his good manners and earned a gentleman's C. He considered anyone who studied a grind. Gentlemen didn't study; they enjoyed life. His philosophy was simple: Let other people work. As long as the Banastre fortune lasted, Paris need not concern himself with such desultory topics as paying the bills and being responsible. He glittered, beautiful as his mother but in a thoroughly masculine manner. His curly blond hair and ice-blue eyes unnerved women, as well as a few male professors. Welcomed at the great estates which encompass Albemarle County, Paris was known as a perfect dinner guest. A few shrewd heads glimpsed the hollow, even cruel, person underneath, but Paris's chatter kept most from looking too deeply. Besides, in Charlottesville everybody was far more interested in drinking than in really knowing anybody.

His most outrageous exploit as an undergraduate, one that nearly got him thrown out of Beta Theta Pi, a fraternity accustomed to exploits, involved the death of a much beloved English professor. The professor was not particularly beloved by Paris, who stole his body out of the mortuary and placed it, correctly attired, in the classroom in time for Milton's *Paradise Lost*. The young men blanched at the sight of their glass-eyed literary lion. When the corpse passed gas, one undone lad screamed, "If it can fart, it can walk," and tore out of the classroom. Hours later they found the fellow near to death himself from alcohol poisoning.

Paris faced a phalanx of angry deans; pissing pederasts, he called them. Then he had to apologize to the bereaved family and finally had to make good whatever damages were done to the body. With the exception of a few overzealous blowflies laying eggs in the old man's orifices, the body was as good as new. After all, what were funeral directors for but to clean up the effluvia of death and make a bag of bones look good for its final social extravaganza? Paris performed all these ministrations, calmed down for two weeks and then promptly set about raising holy hell one more time. He was becoming legendary even in a school habituated to high spirits.

When home he maintained his customary distance from his mother and father. "The sperm donor" and "the sperm receptacle" were how he described them. He quickly figured out that his mother's love for Catherine was not untainted by blood, but he had not figured out who the father was and he was certain his own father ignored the whole thing. Like everyone, he found Catherine disarming. He gave her a Raggedy Andy doll, and when he bothered to pay attention to her he found her curiously beautiful.

Edward also had attended the University of Virginia, where he'd studied history and politics. He was now in his first year of law at Yale. The day he announced his intention to go to New Haven was the only time he could remember his father getting upset. Southern men don't venture farther than Princeton, was all Carwyn could sputter. Edward moved on to Yale and buried himself in books for his first year of law school. The campus couldn't hold a candle to the grounds of the University of Virginia, but Edward liked the people and appreciated the intellectual quality of those around him.

Paris's misdeeds filtered up to him even in Connecticut. Perhaps if Paris had not been his brother, Edward could have secretly relished the outrageous behavior of the young man. However, everything his brother did seemed a blot on the family, its reputation, and Edward's own future. It was bad enough that people whispered behind their hands about Catherine; with Paris it was open humiliation.

What time he had to himself he filled by seeing all of Grace Deltaven's films. She'd become a great star. Though she was six years his elder, the two had been on many a Halloween Witch Hunt team together, and Grace always answered his letters. Despite her exalted status, or perhaps because of it, she was touched by these letters from a hometown boy now studying at Yale. Edward seemed so normal, and in fact he was.

Grace's life was anything but normal. Those early years studying in New York had frustrated her, but she stuck to it. Grace was never meant for the stage; her beauty and remoteness waited for the camera. It was her good fortune to grow along with the film industry. Once lured to California, she spent three long years in films that were cranked out in five days. The pace nearly killed her: up at dawn, always on call, and sometimes working as long as people could keep their eyes open. But she persevered. What she lacked in talent, she made up in bullheadedness. Once the reign of the vamp weakened, the cool beauties moved in. Grace was aided by the strange fact that her eyes, very pale, seemed to generate light. On film this gave her an almost mystical quality. She became an enormous star, finally. No longer did she have to make a film a week or stand on her feet from sunup until sundown. She picked her scripts. When she played a difficult scene, violins sobbed off camera. She strode through the studios with her two white borzois. Other film stars flung themselves at her feet, as well as Europe's vagabond nobility. She was rumored to have beautiful lovers, male and female. She was rotten with money and she was achingly dissatisfied.

First of all, artistic triumphs were not hers. She was a commercial queen but no critics sang paeans to her ability. Her petulance on this count was justified. She really was good, but critics didn't understand film; they still rated people on theatrical terms. New York cultural snobs wouldn't set foot in Hollywood unless they were dead on a train. The money couldn't possibly compensate for the loss in prestige or the vulgarity of mixing with "those people." Grace, like the rest of her cinematic peers, engaged in constant bickering with the Knickerbocker Crew, as they dubbed them.

What's more, Grace had affairs but no real, deep love. She found something wrong with every man and woman she met. She began to wonder if her mother, Icellee, and Lila knew about this termite in her soul. Was that why they'd warned her off such pursuits when she was full of dreams? Or were they just two dear Southern matrons who couldn't imagine life outside Montgomery? Well, she'd see them all over the summer, as she'd told everyone in town she was taking a month off in June, come hell or high water. She said she wanted to visit her family. True enough, but even more, she wanted to get out of California.

The public was beginning to get wind of the bizarre behavior of its silver-screen darlings. A few scandals had erupted over the last few years to reveal a corruption unimagined. Of course, if the local worthies of Pocatello, Idaho, had bothered to look in their own backyards, they would have found proportionately as much whoring, drinking, doping and other thrills to keep them busy. However, why spoil the fun?

Grace understood the need of her co-workers to do some of the things they did. Everyone knew Mabel Normand didn't get on dope of her own free will. Nobody could blame her. As for the rest of the dirt, Grace didn't blame anybody. She looked at other actors in the film business with a kind of pity. At the mercy of producers, these people, often from modest or poor beginnings, teetered on the edge of fear. They'd come so far so fast, and they all knew the rug could be pulled out from under their feet in a minute. Some of the devils actually cared about the quality of their work, of the film as a whole. Those were the ones who really went crazy. Grace told herself she was in it for the fame, fortune and fun. However, she wasn't having any fun.

• • •

Lotowana sat on the front porch at one, perhaps two, with nature. A hot hopscotch game frayed the temper of Blue Rhonda.

"Banana Mae, you stepped on the line."

"I did not." Banana looked to Lottie for confirmation.

"How can you see when you're hopping?" Rhonda persisted.

"We need an umpire." Bunny fingered her tossing stone. Rhonda and Banana Mae had conned her into the

game by promising to register to vote if she played.
"Come on, Lottie, either ump or play."

"I'm too old." Lottie was all of thirty-four.

"Bullshit! You're too fat." Blue Rhonda was still angry
at Banana Mae.

"Let's not forget our manners." Bunny tossed her stone
and it landed on square eight with a satisfying smack.

"It hurts my feet to jump." Lotowana stayed glued to
the porch.

"Yeah; well, it hurts to live." Rhonda took off her
shoes. She was getting serious about the game.

"It must be that time of month, Blue Rhonda, because
you're a pure-D bitch." Lotowana sniffed.

Banana Mae opened her mouth. "I've known Rhonda
for over twelve years and I have yet to see her get her
period."

"You all make such a to-do about it. I simply go
about my business and you never know the difference.
Cramps are all in the mind." Rhonda threw her shoulders back.

"In that case, would you mind speaking to my ovaries?
They haven't heard the message." Bunny sailed through
eight and was on number nine.

"Maybe Rhonda don't have ovaries." Lotowana smiled
and looked amazingly like Buddha with hair.

Hearing this, Blue Rhonda fired back, "Don't forget to
pluck the hairs on your chin, Lottie. Even though it's a
double, a few sprout out."

"Press Tugwell told me that after thirty your hormones
change and that's why you get hair on your chin." Lottie
indignantly stood up.

"Press Tugwell doesn't have both oars in the water,"
Banana Mae said.

Bunny picked up the conversation. "I've heard that
too—about hormones changing. I know I need eight hours
of sleep, and even five years ago I could get by on six.
Things change with age."

"Yes; it's harder to get drunk." Banana laughed.

"You drank enough last night to knock the rear wheel
off a Cadillac." Blue Rhonda folded her arms across her
chest.

Banana Mae ignored that. "Rhonda, we owe Minnie Rue a dinner."

"Wrap it up and send it to her."

Lotowana giggled at Rhonda's reply.

"Speaking of dinners, I sat between Minnie Rue and Leafy the other evening. You remember, when I was over there getting all the girls to register?" Bunny's tiny eyebrows slanted upward. "What a mistake. I could barely walk the next day; my ankles were black and blue."

"That's like sitting at the table when you're a little girl and giving your brother the elbow every time Dad would make an ass out of himself." Lottie joined the game. She was light on her feet despite her bulk.

"In Baltimore?" Bunny asked.

"Ballimore." Lottie made it to three, pronouncing her city's name as only a native can do it.

"Did you ever think it was fate that brought us all here?" Banana gazed off. A train whistle shrieked.

Blue Rhonda rubbed her tossing stone in her palm.

"We're here now, so it doesn't matter how we got here." Lottie was not one for philosophical discussions.

"I won," Bunny gleefully reported.

"That was upsies. Now you've got to do downsies." Banana Mae thought she'd win this game.

"Enough is enough. I kept my end of the bargain; now you all register."

"There's no one to vote for." Lotowana pouted.

"Pressing the flesh and passing the buck, that's politicians."

"That may be true, Rhonda, but a vote is a vote and you don't want to see Linton Ray get in the statehouse, do you?"

"No," came the swift reply.

"As for President, who cares. I wish Douglas Fairbanks would run." Lottie sighed.

Banana Mae jiggled her hat into place.

"Where'd you get that hat?" Bunny stared approvingly.

"Won it from Blue Rhonda in a bet."

Some of Rhonda's good humor returned. "I'll bet you

that same hat I can beat you in hopscotch upsies and downsies.''

Lottie held the hat while the two went at it. Rhonda became her old self again. She'd been to the doctor that day. He took a battery of tests. She had mostly good days, but every now and then she'd sink, so she snuck off to the doc's. Rhonda had a feeling she had something and when she worried she got snappy. But the game and her old friends took her mind off it, plus she really did feel better.

Placide Jinks rolled a little cart down the road. Seeing him, Blue Rhonda halted the game a moment.

''My cuttings.''

Row after row of little sprouts lined the cart. Each was carefully marked with the common name and the Latin name, as well as with instructions.

Blue Rhonda beamed. ''That's beautiful. I never saw anything like that.''

Placide smiled. ''You know Ada. She never does anything halfway.''

Bunny and Lotowana inspected the source of Rhonda's rapture. The organization was impressive, but Lottie couldn't get excited over minuscule green shoots. Bunny, still posing as English, felt it her national duty to appreciate gardening, although you'd never catch Miss Turnbull with her hands in the dirt.

''Prince of Wales clematis.'' Bunny hummed authoritatively.

''Bunny, get your long nose out of my plants.''

Blue Rhonda unobtrusively paid Placide and arranged to get the cart back to him next day. The hopscotch game needed finishing. She wanted that hat.

Once Placide was out of earshot, Lottie garbled, ''Poor man.''

Bunny nodded. Hercules' death had soon been followed by Apollo's getting killed in the war. Athena finished her education and married into a fine Atlanta family, and now practiced law in that city.

''The last thing life is is fair.'' Rhonda was on sevens on the way down. Banana was two numbers behind.

"That goes for you too." Banana pointed at Rhonda's foot. "You're over the line for your throw."

"What!"

She'd finished her sevens and was tossing for sixes, and her right foot just edged the toss line.

"Gunboats." Banana issued judgment on Blue Rhonda's not very delicate feet.

• • •

"Mom, are Paris and Edward ever coming home?" Catherine ran her finger around the icing bowl Amelie was using. A slap on the hand stopped that.

"They get a spring break. They'll be here in a few weeks."

"May I lick the bowl when you're finished?"

"If you grease the pans." Amelie motioned to the cake tins stacked next to her.

Catherine rubbed lard along the sides and bottoms of the tins.

Hortensia came into the kitchen. "Sweetheart." She kissed the child. "Marble cake, Amelie?"

"Yes, ma'am." Amelie was a fine baker.

"How was school?" Hortensia asked.

"We have to learn all the capitals of all the states by Friday." Catherine moaned.

"Slaughterhouses of the imagination." Hortensia frowned.

Catherine stopped greasing the pan to stare in admiration at Hortensia. Her vocabulary, her clothing, her beauty—everything about Hortensia fascinated the child. A little tap from Amelie awakened her to her task.

"When you've finished your chores and licking the bowl you can come riding with me." Hortensia kissed Catherine again.

"Thank you, Aunt Tense."

After Hortensia left, Catherine matter-of-factly said to Amelie, "Willy Patterson called me a zebra today."

"A zebra?" Amelie poured the batter into the overgreased tins.

"Yeah; he said I was half white and half black. I pasted him one right on the nose."

Amelie smoothed the batter in the pan. No reason to react and give Catherine more to think about. "Willy Patterson got what he deserved."

"Right." Catherine put her hands on her hips. "But, Momma, I don't look so much like the other kids. Did I have a white daddy? You can tell me. I won't think less of you."

Typical of Catherine was her straightforward manner and her openness. Amelie was touched by the child's attempt to consider her feelings. By now Catherine was old enough to know the races don't mix, or if they do, they sure do it in secret.

"Honey, your father was not white; I can promise you that." Amelie placed the tins in the oven.

"Haven't you got a picture of him? I'd feel so much better if I could see him." Catherine dutifully held the oven door open.

The request was more than justified. Amelie had no idea if a photo of Hercules could be found. "Honey, I don't know. Let me root around in my things when I get a minute."

Later that day Amelie told Hortensia all that transpired.

People gossiped. As long as humans have tongues they'll wag them. Someday perhaps Catherine would be told of her true beginnings, but certainly not now. Hortensia knew she could send Amelie on any errand with confidence, but somehow she felt she should run this errand herself. She knew Placide Jinks knew the truth. Blue Rhonda, who had stayed a loyal friend despite the social Grand Canyon, whispered to her about Placide in the funeral home. But even without that information Hortensia could tell that Placide knew by the way he greeted the child whenever he saw her. Hortensia decided to seek out Placide and ask him for a photo of his son.

Gleaming like polished mica, the engine regally pulled out of the station. The railroad men called her the Bolshevik, for the huge locomotives were built for the Russians near the end of World War I. When the revolution ripped apart the nation, prior contracts were voided. American lines bought the engines. Distinctive by its size and proportion, the Bolshevik was one more technological glory in the service of railroads. Service steadily improved, comfort kept apace. The extraordinarily wealthy owned private cars, lavishly appointed. Silver toilet fixtures, silk-covered ottomans, down-filled beds infested these rolling palaces. Many brought their own cooks, staffing a kitchen. Others, wealthy or regular folk, descended upon the dining car, where a great cook was considered as essential as the engine itself. Every presidential candidate, theatrical star or common thief entered Montgomery through its station unless he traveled on foot. As the riverboat waned the railroad waxed. The high rollers formerly found in the velvet casinos of paddle wheelers now rocked rhythmically on the rails, but the same excitement pervaded their comings and goings that once enlivened the docks. Placide helped build the station, and except for the interruption of the Spanish-American War he worked there for over thirty years. Montgomerians considered him a fixture as much as the state capitol.

Infrequently clabberfaces would disembark and harangue the man. They were usually brought up short by a resident, who would explain that there were good blacks and bad blacks, and Placide was a good black. If he ever hungered for social respectability, that hunger died long ago with Hercules. He didn't give a damn whether he was "good" or "bad." Placide did his job, was considerate, and lived in his own world, far away from the world around him. He retreated behind all the external deference, thinking his own thoughts and expecting little from the world. Folly, it was all folly. He worked hard, made a decent amount of money, educated his children, lost his two sons to death. His daughter flourished. That was something. But all that struggle seemed meaningless now. Ada believed. How she still believed. The cruelties of this world lashed her like a whip. She ran that much faster, worked that much harder. Ada was a great power in her community. The more chaotic life became, the more Ada insisted on order, routine, logic. Placide didn't cross her. He was wise enough to figure out this was her way of surviving, just as his drifting into an attitude very close to Buddhism was his way of surviving. Not that he was religious in any respect. He simply fed off his own resources and those of nature. He no longer cared for the world of men. A sunny day pleased him and the bite of damp winter pleased him. Whether death would please him he'd find out in due time. If death didn't please him, his only concern was meeting it with grace. Every day was a gift. Life was to be endured, sometimes enjoyed, and if possible, transcended.

A brief lull in traffic allowed him to watch the sun's glint on the tracks while he smoked his pipe. A foggy, throaty voice pulled him around. Hortensia Banastre stood before him.

"If smoking a pipe could make me feel as peaceful as you look, I'm tempted to try it."

Placide smiled and they exchanged pleasantries. Hortensia wanted to place Placide at ease as well as herself. In many ways, she thought, Placide was much like a woman: what was unsaid was as powerful as what was said. Well, she hadn't come down to the station to bumble about.

"I hope this isn't an impossible request, but might you have a photograph of Hercules?"

A look passed over his face. Sorrow or surprise, Hortensia couldn't tell. He answered evenly, "I'll bring one by tomorrow."

"Thank you, Placide. Thank you very much."

He'd heard about Willy Patterson's crack. He didn't know if the request had anything to do with that, but more than likely it did. He also knew Catherine socked hell out of that big-mouthed brat. Like Hercules, so like Hercules. A conspiracy of silence surrounded Catherine. Amelie, by way of Hortensia's approval, allowed the child contact with the Jinkses, although Catherine did not yet know her relationship to them. Placide hadn't told Athena, but she'd figured it out thanks to that one long-ago talk with her brother. As to Ada, he never told her. Placide knew Ada's will and ferocious sense of family. A struggle between Ada and Hortensia would do no one any good; least of all, Catherine. Ada knew her place, but if she had any idea who Catherine was, she'd try to wrench the child out of the Banastre home. Underneath it all, Placide also knew that Hortensia needed Catherine far more than Ada did. He couldn't understand how she'd got tangled up with his son . . . poor damn fools in a tragedy. Out of respect for Hercules he kept an eye on Hortensia, and also out of affection for the woman herself. You could never trust whites, but he hoped Hortensia was the one exception which proves the rule—for Catherine's sake and possibly for his own. He'd like to believe that one of them didn't have two faces and half a heart.

The next evening, when Hortensia came back home she found a small framed photograph of Hercules which Placide had delivered. Sitting in her small dressing room, she put the photo to her heart, then took it away to look at again. She'd almost forgotten how he really looked. The picture brought back the force of him, the smell of him, the heat, the passion, the love of him. Oh, God, he was so beautiful. He was so young and so was I. She cried and the cries turned to sobs. A little rap at the door startled her.

"Aunt Tensie, are you all right?" Catherine heard her on the way up to her room on the third floor.

"Yes, dear, I'm fine. Go upstairs with Mother. I'll be out in a bit."

There was a slight, indecisive pause, then Catherine said, "O.K.," and her footsteps receded.

Hortensia walked over to the window, holding the photo. She didn't know if there was a God, but in case there was, she prayed, "Please don't let that child suffer for my past. Whatever sufferings are to come to her, put them on me. Spare this child."

She looked at the photograph again, Hercules' full, firm lips so serious. What liars pictures are. If only she could see him throw his head back and laugh, his teeth sparkling, his skin shining. He was the king of hearts. If only they could have one more day. Facing empty days which stretched into months and years, she learned she'd never go insane nor would she kill herself. Surviving his death taught her she would live. She would have gladly swapped her life for his. Hercules had more to offer the world than she did.

The stars glittered overhead. Venus was a large pinhole

in the sky. She thought, At this hour the Big Dipper pours light over his tombstone. Hercules' grave was a fixed point in her emotional life. The other coordinate, the point moving into the future, was Catherine.

• • •

Blue Rhonda dumped half her closet on her bed. Rummaging through blouses, skirts and a mountain of petticoats, she cursed cruel fate.

Banana Mae leaned against the doorway to better observe the multicolored slag heap. "Are you about ready?"

"I haven't got a thing to wear."

"Stay in bed then." Banana never could fathom Blue Rhonda's ritualistic dispersal of a perfectly good wardrobe.

"That's what I like about you, your compassion." Rhonda selected a fire-engine-red blouse and held it under her chin.

"I always think of that as your flaming asshole blouse." Banana ducked as the blouse was immediately aimed toward her head.

"I need something bright to bring out my complexion."

"Complexion, hell; what you need are tits."

Sadly, Rhonda gazed downward at her two nubs. Then she picked an emerald-green blouse from the pile, slipped it on and discreetly stuffed a few silk hankies in her top.

"Why bother?"

"Why not?"

"Everybody in Montgomery knows you've got the world's smallest bosoms." Banana pronounced "bosoms" so it sounded like "bosooms."

"All I want is a little curve. There's no need to be nasty."

Sighing, her partner checked her lipstick. "Are you about ready?"

"No, I am not about ready, and quit rushing me. Rome wasn't built in a day." Banana tapped her foot, which further burned Rhonda. "Look, why don't you just go on ahead of me? You're disturbing my creative powers. I need to think about this."

Eager to get to the party, Banana was relieved to take off. "O.K. See you there—and don't wear that new skirt of mine. I'm saving it for this Saturday night."

"I promise." Blue Rhonda buttoned her blouse, and as soon as she heard the front door slam she raced into Banana's closet and took out a lovely silk skirt, almost as thin as her blouse. Too bad, Nanner, she thought; you shouldn't have given me the idea. However, Banana's waist was smaller than Rhonda's. She bitched, moaned and sucked in her breath three times before she finally got the thing buttoned. She was skinny as a wire but devoid of all curves. Banana, much fuller, still had the smaller waist. Rhonda skipped down the stairs, as eager to get to the party as to see the shock on Banana's face. She couldn't resist tormenting Banana, and as it was mutual, the two were rarely bored. She opened the back door to call the cat before she left. A figure stood outlined in the moonlight by the little house. She squinted. Yes, there really was someone out there. Closing the back door behind her, Rhonda walked toward the little house.

"Who's there?"

The figure, a woman, moved and then, for whatever reason, stopped.

"It's Hortensia Banastre."

Blue Rhonda was stunned; her voice cracked. "Are you all right?"

"Yes, I'm fine."

As she drew near her, Hortensia seemed made of pale beaten gold. Maybe she was a night angel or a sister of Venus. Whatever she was, she stopped Rhonda cold. Remembering herself, Rhonda asked, "Would you like something to drink?"

"No, don't trouble yourself."

"It's no trouble if you'd like to come inside."

Hortensia said, "You're very thoughtful. I came back to see this house once more, just once more. I'm sure you're wondering why I'm here."

"I'm wondering why it took you ten years to come back."

Hortensia looked at Rhonda's strong, angular face. Nothing beautiful about Rhonda, but there was honesty in those eyes and a rare kindness which never pushes itself on anybody. She felt that she could talk to this woman, not because Rhonda saved her honor but because there was a curious quality of pain, of understanding, of being outside.

"I owe you a great deal, Miss Latrec."

"Call me Blue Rhonda, and you don't owe me anything."

"Thank you all the same."

"It hasn't changed much, has it?" Rhonda motioned to the house.

"No, but I have."

"Ten years is a long time. We all change. Why did you come back?"

Hortensia noticed the lovely flower beds. "You've got a green thumb."

Rhonda felt like saying, "And a golden mouth," but didn't.

"I came back because I needed to, because I looked at a photograph of Hercules tonight and I haven't seen him or anything of him since he died."

"Oh."

Hortensia turned to fully face Blue Rhonda. "I wish I had your courage."

"What courage?" Rhonda was confused.

"You do as you please and the hell with rules and regulations made by somebody else. Before he died Hercules asked me to run away with him. I said I'd have to think about it. I know now I never would have done it. I lacked the courage and I probably still lack it. I couldn't break the rules openly." She laughed at herself. "But I could break them in secret." Drew in a breath. "But then who doesn't?"

"Don't be hard on yourself, Miz Banastre. I'm not so brave. I couldn't get any lower, if you consider where I came from. You had a lot to lose."

"Yes—and a lot to gain."

Hortensia's horse whinnied behind the house and Attila the Hun scooted around the corner, dashed under the boxwoods, reappeared and proceeded to rub himself vigorously against Rhonda's legs. She bent down and hugged him to her stuffed chest. "He loves to scare animals, especially horses. I always wished we'd kept horses.''

"It's all cars now anyway." The tall woman put her hand on her hip. "How can you cooperate with an automobile? Riding is teamwork. Did you ever ride?"

"A couple of times. I mostly fell off." Blue Rhonda shivered. "Won't you please come in?"

Hortensia blinked and then graciously accepted. "I'd very much enjoy a cup of tea."

Hortensia sat at the sparkling clean kitchen table although Rhonda asked her into the parlor. She liked the kitchen better, probably because it reminded her somewhat of the kitchen in the little house. Rhonda was thrilled with Hortensia's presence. She knew it would never happen again, but she also knew that she was probably the only person aside from Hercules to ever see Hortensia minus the encumbrances of her position, minus the protective wall between herself and the world.

"Try some honey," Rhonda suggested.

The two drank their tea. Hortensia leaned forward to better look at Rhonda's blouse. "That's very handsome."

"Thank you."

"And the skirt is really smashing."

Rhonda giggled. "It belongs to Banana Mae. She bought it for a party Saturday night, but I swiped it. Is she going to bust a gut when she sees me in it!"

"I always wanted a sister so I could swap clothes."

"Well, with Banana you don't exactly swap. Every time I borrow anything she inspects it to see if I've loosened a button. A real fuss—but she's O.K."

Blue Rhonda felt expansive. "Do you ever feel like your body is a blouse?" Hortensia was puzzled. "I mean, that you put on flesh like a blouse, like you're a stranger in your own body? Your spirit is different? I—well, sometimes I look at everyone and I don't feel like I have a body, exactly."

"I don't think I've ever felt quite that way, but sometimes I feel like a pair of giant eyes, watching. Is that what you mean?"

"Sort of." Rhonda swallowed some more hot tea while

Attila purred over a gnawed fishbone. "I guess what I was thinking of is sometimes I don't feel like my body. I know what I mean." She clapped her hands together. "You and Hercules were in different bodies and different colors. That's supposed to be wrong—uh, am I being rude?"

"No. I'm really interested."

"But the colors didn't matter, did they? You loved him. His spirit."

"Yes, I did."

"Well, don't you see, Miz Banastre? I've thought about this before, too. It's God's joke."

"Color?"

"Yes, color and everything. God put beautiful spirits into these bodies, all kinds of bodies. There's men and women and white and black and beautiful and ugly and old and young and oh, just everything. And we dumb humans are confused by the outside. We keep looking at the outside instead of the inside, so we say, 'I don't like that man, he's a nigger—or he's a Catholic.' Pretty soon we start killing each other because of these bodies. And God laughs because we're so stupid. We can't see anything. He put spirits in every one of us and trees"—Rhonda looked at a happy Attila—"and cats and everything. So maybe we aren't the same outside, maybe we are unequal, but inside, the soul is pure. All souls are equal. If only we could see the soul. Some people do and they understand the joke and maybe they find happiness. I—" She fumbled for her thoughts, a connection, and then said with finality, "We are one."

Hortensia absorbed this outburst. Rhonda's face was cherry red. Hortensia touched her hand. "I don't know if that's true or not, but I hope you are right—I very much hope you are."

They finished their tea in silence. Hortensia rose to leave. Rhonda walked outside with her, back into that brilliant moonlight. She held her hands so Hortensia could step in there and mount up without difficulty.

"Blue Rhonda, I enjoyed tonight. Thank you." She gazed down at her funny face and thought for that moment Rhonda's soul did shine through. "How odd that we live so close to one another..."

Rhonda finished her thought for her. "Same town, different worlds."

Hortensia's smile caught the moonlight. "Ah, but we are one."

. . .

Payson Thorpe blew another line. Grace backed off from the embrace. Payson smelled ninety proof. The director, Brad West, lean as a hound, yelled, "Cut." Usually tolerant, Brad was nervous because he was already over budget on this goddamned costume drama. If Payson wanted to drink up his own career, fine. When he started drinking up Brad's, that was another matter. As if things weren't bad enough, Aaron Stone had just walked onto the set. Aaron Stone had changed his name from Steinhauser, played polo each weekend and aped a Wasp establishment he both worshiped and despised. Like most people without a place, he propped himself up by humiliating those underneath him. Brad West summed up Aaron one day when he said, "Stone's either at your throat or at your feet." Today Stone was at everyone's throat.

"Can't you sober up that faggot?" Aaron shouted.

The crew, accustomed to his insults, appeared not to notice.

Grace noticed. "He's sick."

"I'd be sick, too, if I drank the swill he does." Aaron puffed on a Havana. "Kick him in the ass, Brad. He'll love it. Better yet, jam an umbrella up there and open it."

Payson was drunk but not deaf. "I'd rather be a drunken sodomite than a fat Jew."

The entire cast and crew held their breath. Aaron wanted to repudiate his Jewishness but have Gentiles respect it at the same time. You can't have it both ways.

Reeling with fury, Aaron could barely speak. Hauling his considerable gut over to the now smiling Payson, Aaron backhanded him. Payson's head snapped back. The epaulets of his uniform shuddered. He quickly recovered and calmly kicked Aaron Stone in the crotch. Roaring like a bull, Aaron doubled over.

"I knew kikes didn't have any balls." Payson laughed,

dusted off his hands and walked off the lot. The picture was eighty percent completed. Unless Stone was a total fool, he couldn't fire Payson. It would be too expensive to reshoot all his scenes. If it was a question of pride or money, Payson knew perfectly well Aaron would go for the buck every time; who wouldn't? If Aaron blackballed him with his cronies, so what? There were other producers in Hollywood and Payson Thorpe was a very big star.

Grace loved Payson. He was a dear friend. Why he steered straight for the rocks she didn't know. She quietly left the set, perched in her creamy white convertible and drove after Payson. There'd be no more work that day.

Clear, sparkling sunshine bounced off the stucco buildings. She could almost smell the orchards surrounding the small city. When she pulled into the driveway of Payson's enormous mansion up off Sunset Boulevard, she sat still for a moment and relished the view. What a magic place! Payson greeted her, drink in hand. They sat by his endless pool, served by a variety of stunning servants.

"Payson, you've got to stop drinking."

"Work is the curse of the drinking class, darling." He toasted her. Payson was nearly forty, athletically built and terribly attractive. His pencil-thin mustache accented straight teeth and sensuous lips. His hair was almost black and slicked back. Undoubtedly he was one of the most fabulous-looking men to ever walk the earth.

"I'm serious. You can't keep it up. If you don't ruin your health you'll ruin your career."

"Nothing lasts forever." He swallowed the contents of his glass and it was replaced immediately. "Forgive my bad manners. Would you rather have some cocaine?"

"Not today."

"Oh, Gracie, ever the Southern beauty. You hardly drink, never sniff. Do you fuck, darling?"

"Every chance I get."

They both howled over that. They had arrived in California within a year of one another: two kids full of ambition and without malice. The ambition was fulfilled; the malice came later. He knew of her secret longing to become a true actress, and he also knew that underneath that splendid castle of flesh lived a lonely woman who wanted love but didn't know how to give it. He was exactly the same. He was a solid friend but a rotten lover. Payson never really believed anyone loved him. Before any of his lovers could get close enough to wound him he managed to find something wrong with them and dismiss them.

Grace touched his hand. "You've got to apologize to Aaron Stone."

"That filthy kike. He started it."

"Aaron's not known for his charm, but he's got a knack for selecting good material, and more, Payson, much, much more—he's going to take over that studio."

"Levy will never bow out."

"Of course not . . . but Stone will take over that studio."

"Christ almighty, I hate that scum." Payson knocked back another drink. "I hate 'em all. All the goddamned Jews, immigrants and flotsam that's washed up on our shores. They care about nothing, these people."

"Our people were immigrants once."

"In sixteen sixty." Payson's family was as old and distinguished as Grace's. Like her, he'd had to fight like hell to be an actor. It just wasn't done among the Thorpes. Acting was for the lower classes.

"Be that as it may, you've got to smooth things over."

"He struck me. He insulted me. He's lucky I didn't kill him. They're not like us, Gracie. Their ways and beliefs are one hundred eighty degrees away from us. You know what a Jew prays each night before he goes to bed?"

Grace shook her head.

Payson growled, " 'O dear Lord, on the day I succeed may my best friend fail.' No honor, I tell you. No honor."

"Look, I detest Aaron Stone as much as you do, but there's good and bad in every bunch. Anti-Semitism is beneath you. Forget it."

Grace's prejudices were reserved for the insensitive and the vulgar. She cared little about anyone's lineage. Whatever gnawed at Payson Thorpe, Jews in general had become a handy target.

"Seen Naja lately?" Payson abruptly switched the subject.

"Every now and then. She's going to have a great hit with *Red Sun,* you know."

"Yes, I hear it's a marvel. Be out in a month?"

"Looks like it."

"Want to go to a premiere with me?"

The only time Payson looked better than when he was naked was in tails. He was the perfect escort. Grace readily accepted.

"We've known each other a long time, haven't we?" The glass touched his lips and then he put it back down without taking a drink. "You've seen me through so much, Gracie, so much, and I guess I've seen you through a lot too. I suppose George was your worst."

"And then he became your worst." She laughed. George had played them both for suckers. But he was endowed with a large phallus, a quick wit and refined manners.

"And Naja." Payson looked at Grace with sympathy.

"She's . . . I don't love her. I don't think I loved George either. I did love my dog Bunky, though." She smiled. "And I love you."

"Comparing me with a dog? Should I hump your leg?"

"What's to become of us?"

"Damned if I know, and I don't think I much care anymore." In a gust of honesty Payson continued, his deep voice reverberating like that of a Russian singer. "Grace, I've done everything and everyone. I've seen everything and it doesn't mean much. I'm going to be forty next week and I can't think of one useful thing I've done."

"Is this an attack of Protestantism?" Grace tried to cheer him.

"No, or if it is, I don't know it. I feel suddenly old."

"You look anything but."

"You're such a darling. I also suddenly wish I had children."

"You?"

"Me." His voice softened. "It's quite cruel that two men can't have a baby."

"Perhaps not." Grace finally took a sip. "The ancient Greeks believed women were for children and men were for pleasure."

"Have you ever heard the Arabic expression: 'A woman for duty, a boy for pleasure, a melon for ecstasy'?" He smiled. "I'll switch to melons. They don't demand expensive wristwatches."

"I don't want to frighten you, Payson, but Aaron could nail you to the cross over homosexuality."

"Darling, if you nailed every homosexual in Hollywood to the cross, the town would be deserted. Wasn't that the Roman form of punishment? To crucify criminals and plant them along the Appian Way—like marigolds. Imagine, the road to San Francisco would be thick with corpses."

"And if they added all the bisexuals and the heterosexual philanderers, the line would stretch to the Atlantic." Grace laughed. Sexual restraint melted under the California sun. Thank God, she thought.

"Cheers." He toasted her.

"Still, I tell you Aaron can get you. Look what they did to Roscoe." She referred to Fatty Arbuckle, whose career had been destroyed over false charges of rape and murder. By the time he was acquitted the damage was done. One of the biggest stars in the business now directed films under pseudonyms, when he could get the work. As far as ever getting in front of the camera again, forget it.

Recalling that scandal, Payson lost sparkle. "But why would Aaron kill the goose that laid the golden egg?"

"To get even, and more importantly, to put fear in the heart of every actor and actress in this burg. The message is: We can make you and we can break you."

"The public does that."

"To an extent, but you've got to get in front of the camera for them to see you."

"I'm a star, remember. I've established myself."

"And we're all asking for higher salaries. If Aaron can wipe you out, a lot of people will think twice before ruffling producers' feathers. And as for the public making a star, yes, you're a great one. But the studio publicity department helps. If the dung is thick enough it can cover you, and Aaron would do it."

Payson leaned against the back of his chair. He knew Grace was right. He was more vulnerable than he thought. He may have seen everything and done everything, but though he was slightly bored he wasn't bored enough to give up his position.

"Apologize."

Payson's eyes narrowed. "Darling, Aaron would love that. He could see me grovel and then destroy me anyway once the profits for the film were safely in the till—say about a year from now?"

Grace knew that was true. Thousands of people would love to be in Payson's place. If Stone did smear him, few would stick up for Thorpe. That also was true. Hypocrites and cowards, she thought with contempt; this business has made us hypocrites and cowards. I hope to God I've the strength not to desert a friend in trouble.

He stood up and took off his maroon silk robe. Every muscle in his body was defined. "Care for a swim, darling?"

"Go ahead."

"There are suits in the pool house." He rolled on his side and swam to the other end of the pool and back. As he touched the edge of the pool by Grace's foot he shot out of the water. "Grace, I've got it."

"Clap again?"

He quivered, cheeks rosy. "Marry me!"

"You're driving without your headlights."

"No, it's the answer. Stone can't take two of us down at once, and if you marry me, well, I'm safe—and we could have children."

She stared at him.

He got down on his knees. "Darling, you can fuck whomever you please. You can bring him or her home. We can fuck them together. You can keep an apartment for trysts. You can do anything you want. Anything. I'm serious. I love you. You're the best friend I've got. Whatever my faults, I'd be a good husband. You know I would."

She gently put her hand on his cheek. "I believe you would, Payson."

He wrapped his arms around her knees. "Please, Grace, please. I swear I'll do anything you want. I'll give you anything you want. I'll give up booze."

"Will you?"

"I swear it. I'll give up men too, if you want." That one was harder, but Payson was willing to try.

"No. Shedding one vice is enough for me." Grace smiled.

"Does that mean you'll marry me?" He was so incredibly naked, body and soul.

"Yes." She kissed him on the lips.

Payson kissed her lips, he kissed her knees, he kissed her hands. He wept. "Oh, God—oh, dear God. Thank you, Grace, thank you." He jumped up and yelled for his butler. "Jericho, Jericho, bring me every bottle of booze in the house, in the guesthouse, from all the cars."

Perplexed, Jericho did as he was bidden. Payson took each bottle and emptied it into the pool. His staff came out on the lawn to watch.

Grace roared. Payson was in a transport.

"Everybody, everybody who works for me—everybody in the world—I want you to know that Miss Deltaven has just consented to marry me."

The entire staff burst into applause. Then Payson said under his breath to Grace, "I suppose you'll want to wear the gown, darling."

* * *

Icellee Deltaven fought against the big head, but even a matron of distinction could succumb to the clarion call of publicity. Lila Reedmuller and Hortensia firmly held that publicity was for the rabble. Getting one's pictures in the papers was for people who needed to be known by the unknown. Everyone who mattered knew one another anyway. Certainly Icellee believed that, but each time she thought of the wedding her skin crawled with anticipation—it was either that or fleas.

Grace, shrewdly, decided to be married in Montgomery. Aside from shrewdness, marriage was an activity to take place before one's family, and Grace had no intention of tying the knot in California, where no one was connected to anyone. Then, too, *Sword of Vengeance* would be released across the nation during the week of her marriage. The opening would be held in Montgomery. A nice touch.

Aaron Stone, much as he would have liked to crush Payson, was being given another card to play—the wedding. Preparations for the wedding so involved Icellee that she was losing weight. The Episcopal church, whose interior was cream and forest green, would film nicely—all that light against the dark. Grace chose Peppermint Reynolds, her old chum from New York theater days, as her matron of honor. Tallulah, a star herself now, was one of the bridesmaids. The other bridesmaids were old schoolmates, most of whom still lived in Montgomery. Payson's best man was John Gilbert. The women of the city frothed at their collective mouths—not one but two of the biggest male stars in filmdom.

The wedding, set for June 11, aroused more comment than the opening volley on Fort Sumter. Cedrenus Shackleford drew up a plan for mob control which ensured that he would be on the church steps in full uniform. Grace and Payson carefully trimmed their guest lists, but the number still came to six hundred no matter what they did. Payson's father was long dead, but his mother, a formidable Savannah dowager, presented difficulties. Mother would march into Montgomery with every cousin, shirttail cousin and retainer she'd known for all of her sixty-three years. Housing all this watered-down blood required a logistics general. Icellee prevailed upon Lila, who accepted the burden.

The party would be held at the Deltaven mansion. Naturally, the whole goddamned house and all its twenty-seven rooms had to be refurbished; every piece of silver, brass and pewter polished; every window cleaned until it squeaked; flowers carted in from every greenhouse and farmer in the city. The preparations for the house alone consumed three months' time and a hefty sum of money.

"Oh, God," Icellee screamed. "All the servants will need new uniforms."

The long dining room with its Sheraton table, chairs and sideboard echoed with Icellee's gripes. The walls had just been recovered in a shimmering peach moiré. The wainscoting was an ivory white and the floor, a deep walnut herringbone pattern, was waxed to perfection. Three women servants polished Icellee's silver plus the wedding presents that were arriving every day.

"You've got two weeks left, Icey. The uniforms will be ready."

"Put Leone on it too."

"If need be," Lila agreed.

Icey disdainfully observed one maid. "We need another color."

"Icellee."

Realizing her potential gaffe, Icey added, "Uniform. That's just too dingy. Oh, why did it take me this long to notice? The women will wear a pale blue, I think, with starched collars, of course. The butler really must be in eighteenth-century attire for this. After all, it's a grand wedding and it won't do to have the butler in tails—he'll look like one of the guests."

"Yes, dear." Lila knew Icey relished all the bother.

"Dark red for his coat and a gold brocade for the waistcoat, fawn breeches, white leggings, black shoes." She tapped her wrist. "The rest of the men can be attired as footmen. Same color scheme but simpler."

"The color scheme is beautiful but the fabrics are quite expensive. No one would notice if you used something less elegant."

"Of course they would. I can't let Montgomery down. This is the most important thing since General Lafayette visited here in eighteen twenty-five!"

"Our people might notice, but no one else would. Honey, the California contingent wouldn't know the difference between a footman and a coachman."

Shocked, Icellee sucked in her breath. "Lila, you can't mean it. One learns these things by the time one is ten years old."

"If one is Southern."

"But even"—Icellee stopped and pointed in front of her body so the maids couldn't see—"know."

"Southern is Southern."

That sunk in. "Perhaps you're right. But when you see them on a screen they certainly act proper."

"Yes, well, I was only suggesting you might economize."

Grandly, wishing she had a large audience, but knowing the maids would spread the story all over their side of town and it would then immediately reach all the white homes through the kitchen door, Icellee emoted. "Thank you, Lila. You're such a sweetheart to think of me, but I can't economize when the honor of Montgomery is at stake. If I bankrupt myself it will be worth it, if for nothing else, to show the world there are people of quality in America." A dramatic pause. "What's a hundred thousand dollars compared to that?"

Lila smiled. Icellee would spend about fifty thousand dollars. A vast sum, but dear Icey could not resist gilding the lily.

The wedding permeated Water Street. Blue Rhonda, Banana Mae and Lotowana read every magazine and newspaper they could get their hands on. Bunny Turnbull, consumed with curiosity, felt it too obvious to read papers. Instead, she slyly pumped those people she knew to be in Icellee's employ. Some of the men frequented her establishment.

"Two hundred thousand dollars!" Bunny proclaimed.

"No!" Lotowana was blinded by the sum.

"Orinzabe Jones told me, and he is in a position to know."

Orinzabe was chief gardener at the Deltaven estate.

"If I ever even saw two hundred thousand dollars I'd think I'd died and gone to heaven." Blue Rhonda wistfully imagined all that money neatly stacked in her bedroom.

"I'd give anything, anything, to be inside that church." Lottie, for the only time that anyone could remember, lamented her station in life.

"Wouldn't you like to go, Bunny?" Blue Rhonda showed all signs of a brainwave.

"Of course I'd like to attend Miss Deltaven's wedding." Bunny sniffed. "I'd also like to live forever."

"Would you give anything to go?" Blue Rhonda pitched her voice lower for effect.

"Rhonda, what are you up to?" Banana, the reluctant partner in many a Rhonda scheme, blanched.

"Answer my question." Rhonda addressed Bunny.

"How much?" Since Bunny worshiped Mammon, she related everything to dollars and cents.

"Not one penny." Rhonda grinned like beans.

Lotowana looked at her boss and then at Blue Rhonda.

Lottie wasn't slow but she lacked imagination. She never had one clue as to what Rhonda would pull.

"All right, Rhonda, what's the bet?" Bunny never dreamed Rhonda could get her in that church.

"If I can get you in the church as a guest, a true guest, will you, Bunny Turnbull, agree to tell the three of us here the story of your life, including details of an intimate nature?"

Incredulous, Bunny stammered, "But why would you want to know?"

"I'm curious." This was the God's honest truth. The more mysterious someone was, the more Blue Rhonda had to know everything.

Thinking herself safe, Bunny said, "All right." They shook on it.

Rhonda beamed.

"The only way we'll get in that church is to build a Trojan horse." Banana Mae knew that story.

"Well, what do I have to give?" Lotowana wailed, fearing she'd been left out.

"Oh, Lottie, you don't have to give anything." Rhonda dug in her purse for her silver coke box.

"Why not?" Lottie was perplexed.

"Because I like you very much." Blue Rhonda spoke with sincerity.

Bunny wiggled in her seat. What did that mean—that she was a shit?

Deftly, Banana Mae said, "She likes you too, Bunny, but you're distant." Bunny listened, somewhat embarrassed that her feelings had showed. "That's why Blue Rhonda made the bet. She likes you, so she wants to know more. I do too."

"English reserve." Bunny accepted the explanation. She *was* distant. She didn't mean to be, but by both upbringing and experience she'd learned to reveal little, to live on the surface and to keep her emotions to herself. And she was in a business where one could get hurt fast.

"Rhonda, I don't put anything past you, but this time I think you bit off more than you can chew," Banana said.

"We'll see," came the singsong reply.

"Now, about Linton Ray's campaign," Bunny began.

"I don't think he'll ever risk bringing a crowd down here again, so we're spared on that count. Since mobs don't work, he's switched to plain old politics. And this prohibition victory puffs him up, the tick. If he gets in that statehouse, we're in for a lot more trouble than if he unleashed a tidal wave of Bible-thumpers on us."

"It might keep him so busy he'll forget about us." Banana was naive when it came to politics.

"He's a fanatic. He'll use the statehouse as both a pulpit and a whip," Bunny said.

"We should kill him." Blue Rhonda's reactions were pure, immediate and emotional. Bunny, had she been born a man, would have made a good politician. She concerned herself with the practical. Ideology attracted her about as much as religion. She thought systems were for the weak, people who needed rules, regulations and answers. She had standards, but in order to get anything done you had to make compromises. The trick was in striking the right bargain. Her mind was clear, dispassionate and sharp. Bunny knew the forest from the trees.

"Kill him now and the whole hive will attack. He's like a queen bee," Bunny replied.

"What if he died months after the election?" Lotowana was like Rhonda in respect to Linton. Get him.

"That would depend on whether he was in office or not. Murder seems like a solution, but if we discredit him or block him, that's better than making a martyr out of him."

"Like the time Rhonda clunked him on the head and doused him with rotgut." Banana enjoyed the recollection.

"We'll have to be more subtle this time, and we haven't got that much time, either." Bunny brooded.

"Got any ideas?" Lotowana asked.

"No, and that worries me." Bunny's lips compressed.

"I'll ask Cedrenus if there's dirt on Linton," Banana volunteered. Weasling information out of Cedrenus was so easy it almost shamed her.

"He's without vice. He's so inhuman." Bunny's voice rose. Linton did nothing except preach, pray and proselytize.

"Why don't we all think about it and meet again next week? Between the four of us we've got to come up with something." Banana Mae wanted to go shopping.

"That's debatable. We're at a dead end, I'm afraid."
Despondency crept into Bunny's high voice.

Rhonda blinked. "Debatable . . . Let's debate him."

"Rhonda, you're crazy," Banana said.

"Who wants to be sane?" Rhonda fired back. "I think
we should debate him. If he's a candidate, then he can't
back down."

"Sure he can," Bunny said. "We're not candidates."

"He does have a vice and that's pride. You strike him
there and he'll have to strike back. He's proud as a
peacock." Blue Rhonda was on target.

"Yes, but we can't debate him." Banana was growing
impatient.

Lotowana, steadily soaking up the argument, spoke the
obvious: "Why can't the other candidate debate him?"

"He could," Bunny said.

"What's he care about us?" Banana was right.

"He could be made to care. We've got a bloc vote here
and we could round up others if we're careful. We see a
lot of people."

"Why not just buy him outright? That's what other
people do."

"Magnus Stove drips money," Banana said.

"You'd think everybody would vote for him." Lotowana
assumed money and breeding solved all problems.

"Not with Linton posing as a man of the people.
Keeping men like Magnus out of office is the only revenge
insurance salesmen, auto mechanics and farmers have."
Bunny grunted.

"I thought his father hankered for high office." Blue
Rhonda remembered Peter Stove's attempts to run years
back.

"The son has a much better chance. Peter's over the
hill." Banana knew that much. "Say, why couldn't we get
to Magnus through his father? He's the one with the
bishop fixation over at Minnie's."

"Too heavy-handed," Bunny warned. "Look, what we
need to do is find a man to talk to Magnus. Magnus
doesn't have to defend whores and booze; all he has to do
is reveal Linton's single-mindedness. People worry about
crops, wages, prices more than they worry about liquor, if

the truth be known. You can't legislate morality. It never has worked and it never will. All that does is make people more dishonest, more cynical. Magnus needs to skirt the whole prohibition business and stick to bread and butter.''

"Let's sleep on it. We'll think of the right man to approach him and Magnus need never know we were behind it." Banana checked her watch.

As they collected their hats and purses, Blue Rhonda asked Bunny, "What's really so dangerous about Linton in the legislature?"

"He'll make sinners into criminals," she answered.

• • •

Blue Rhonda had never asked a favor from Hortensia. Lila, shortly after her return from Chicago when Hortensia had the baby, sent over a sum of money to pay off the mortgage on the small rental cottage behind the main house. The money was returned. Lila and Hortensia should have known that while the two women were ladies of the night, they acted with honor. But then women from different social positions had no opportunity to really know one another, and few well-bred ladies would ever be in the company of a common whore. Blue Rhonda and Banana Mae had earned their gratitude, but after returning the money they earned their respect.

When Blue Rhonda requested invitations to the wedding, Hortensia had no choice but to get them somehow. Because of her moonlight meeting with Rhonda she was eager to get the tickets. All of Alabama wanted to attend that wedding; why shouldn't Blue Rhonda? She's better than half the people who will be there, Hortensia thought.

With Rhonda's information, Hortensia knew Lotowana would present the least difficulty. Put her in the choir. What if a few people recognize her or her voice? The recognition will be a testimony in itself. As for the other three, that was not so easy. She decided to beseech Icellee for invitations for three distant relations. Of course, Icey would rant and rave and then give in. After all that Lila was doing for Icey, she couldn't very well refuse.

When Hortensia told Lila, she thought her mother would

pass out. Once she recovered herself she perceived the
humor in the situation. Mother and daughter conspired like
two naughty girls filching nickels out of the offering plate.
Blue Rhonda, Banana Mae and Bunny would have to sit in
the back pews. Some of the men would recognize them,
no doubt about that. The two of them prayed they'd be
able to detect who and when. It was too juicy to miss. As
for Blue Rhonda's saying whom she was connected to—
that was sticky, but really all they needed was the printed
invitation. After that they could get lost amongst the six
hundred people. They didn't need to claim relationship to
Hortensia, and better, there would be so many outsiders at
the church and the reception the three women could talk
with them. None of the other women present would know
a thing. The egg would all be on the faces of some of
Montgomery's finest men.

Actually, Hortensia was far more concerned with Paris's
behavior than with the Water Street women. Ever since he
and his brother had come home for summer vacation
they'd been like two banty roosters. Both she and Carwyn
were tired of picking up emotional tail feathers. The latest
source of concern was Paris's dallying with the daughter of
one of their friends. One doesn't take girls of good family
to bed without marrying them. Paris couldn't give two shits.

When Bunny found a wedding invitation on the silver
tray by her front door, she sat down out of shock. Later
that day the three squealed with excitement. A bet was a
bet and Bunny would pay up after the wedding. O Lord,
she thought, in the future remind me never, never to
underestimate Blue Rhonda Latrec.

"Avoid maturity at all costs." Whether Payson Thorpe
knew it or not, that was his motto. Notoriously unreliable,
he was so charming one couldn't stay angry at him.
Absolutely no one believed he'd keep his promise about
booze, not even Grace. He fooled them. Not one drop of
alcohol passed his lips. Nor did he take it intravenously.
He consoled himself by cavorting with a very famous,
ruggedly masculine baseball player. Once dry, he discovered
sex was better than he'd ever remembered.

He wanted to make a good husband for Grace. Having

witnessed the heterosexual couplings and uncouplings around him, plus the loveless but correct marriage of his parents, he was glad the union with Grace would be based on temperament, companionship and background rather than romance. He wondered if he should sleep with her on their wedding night. Sex probably wouldn't be a big part of their marriage, but he was capable of it and a wedding night is once in a lifetime, or should be. Since Grace understood him and he felt he understood her, the pressure was off. He was under no obligation to get the erection of the century. Proving yourself to a woman or to anybody exhausted men. Payson rejoiced that he was free on that count.

They chose to be wed at noon, so he would wear a morning suit. He loved the soft pearl-gray hat and the striped trousers. He looked smashing in those clothes. Clothes excited him as much as they excited Grace. His suits were made in London and the buttons on the ends of the sleeves actually worked so he could roll up his coat sleeves. He would wear a creamy brown tweed, roll up the sleeves and have a fire-engine-red handkerchief in the pocket.

Men who cared little for their appearance repulsed him. Payson fervently believed that you are your own work of art. In his case, he rivaled Michelangelo's *David*. If beauty is a curse and a blessing to a woman, it may be wholly a curse to a man. Even if she's beautiful, the woman still waits for the man to approach her. More than one modern Aphrodite sat alone on the weekend. Not Payson. He could approach anyone, male or female, and that person was his. He coasted on that all his life. To his credit he was bright, and this gave him wit, but he ignored his intellect and the dry rot began to tell. Secretly he hated himself for not having gone to college. Acting is no profession for a man. He loved the money, the adulation and the ability to submerge himself in characters, but he hated taking orders from a director and he knew himself well enough to know he wasn't director material. He was stuck in what he considered a feminine position; he didn't realize that he was an artist. He took his talent so lightly that he thought since it was easy for him it was easy for others. Payson's instincts were inspired. Like Grace he was made for the screen, but unlike Grace he illuminated his characters. Whenever Payson acted, the viewer believed he was that character. You never knew he was acting. On those few occasions when he could sit still long enough, he'd read the Greek plays of Aeschylus, Sophocles, Euripides and Aristophanes. In those days only men could act because the theater was a temple. The writing of plays and the acting of them was an offering to the gods. That perspective softened the humiliation of being treated like a dog by short men who wore riding boots, carried crops and shouted through megaphones. He had always wanted to work with D. W. Griffith, but Griffith was on the way out. At least *he* was a director who treated actors with respect.

Payson feared his days as a leading man were numbered just as Griffith's days were numbered or perhaps anybody's. The thought of playing avuncular roles or middle-aged kings didn't appeal to him. Why couldn't one stay young forever?

He had no interest in politics, considering it an occupation for the vicious and the mediocre. Revolution or reaction, it was all the same to him. His loyalties were reserved for people, not ideas. While he was irresponsible in many things, he was not irresponsible when a friend's back was to the wall. Whether his friends were Fascists, Communists or plain old Republicans mattered little to him. What was important was were they good company? If a friend had said to him, "Let's go to Russia and ride with the Reds," or "Let's go to Germany and march with the Brownshirts," he would have done either, because a friend asked and for the hell of it. Payson couldn't resist adventure. It was precisely that physicality, that excess of energy, that electrified his film performances. And it was precisely that disinterest in political sympathies that could land him in a peck of trouble. But then Payson waltzed on a tightrope; it was part of his charm.

"Christ, there's Our Lady of the Vestibule."

He and Grace, hoping to enjoy a private dinner, had walked into a Hollywood restaurant, only to find Sally Maddox, the gossip columnist, waiting like a spider in the middle of an expensive web.

"You mean Sally Nine Hairs," Grace whispered. Sally wore a wig to cover her sparse hair.

"The lovebirds." Sally swooped upon them.

"Miss Maddox, what a surprise." He flashed his famous grin.

"So many rumors fly around. Now, before I print one word I want the truth." She turned to Grace. "Is it true your wedding is costing half a million?"

Grace loathed Sally but spiting her served no useful purpose. Leave her to the mercy of time, she thought. "Mother doesn't discuss money with me, but half a million?" Then she looked at Payson and cooed, "But I'd gladly spend a million to marry Payson."

"Darling." He kissed her.

Sally's face froze at the midpoint between a social smile and the desire to say, "What a bag of shit."

Payson continued, "I'm the luckiest man in the world."

With an icy smile Sally agreed. "Yes." She babbled a few more niceties and then evacuated the premises.

Once at their table, Payson rumbled, "Even Orestes got rid of the Harpies. We'll never get rid of her."

"Sally likes to suck the marrow out of broken bones." Grace checked herself in the stunning gold compact Payson had given her. "How's slugger John?"

"Standing at home plate." He pulled out a cigarette. "I won't bring men into the house if you don't want me to."

"Payson, I know we're getting married, but I'll be the same Grace after as before."

He eyed her. "Will you?"

She laughed. "You're getting potty about all this."

"I don't know if I'll be the same. For the first time in my life I feel as though I'll have a home, some stability. I'll have you."

"That you will, and I warn you: I give as good as I get."

"Don't I know it." He looked at the menu. "Shall we start with oysters on the half shell?"

"Anything; I'm starved. Had fittings today. I feel like a pincushion."

"Did you read my latest script yet?" Payson tried not to appear too anxious.

"I did. Finally you can shed your sabers."

"You liked it?"

"Payson, the part is wonderful. I love the idea of you in a murder mystery, and the dialogue is very good."

"I'm not getting any younger, you know."

"What's that got to do with *Murder at Sunset*?"

"One of these days I just might quit acting and work for a living."

"Not one of your tirades against acting." She winked. "There's plenty of misery in this life, so you might as well be miserable on the top as on the bottom."

"I've got a present for you." Banana Mae tempted Blue Rhonda.

"Will it make me scream and foam at the mouth?"

"Yes." Banana hid her hands behind her back.

"It's rabies."

"Here, silly."

Blue Rhonda unwrapped the small package. "Banana, how beautiful. Thank you." A small pair of diamond earrings glowed in her hand.

"If we're going to the wedding we can't look like poor relations."

Blue Rhonda put on the earrings and then admired herself. "Speaking of rabies, another girl over at Minnie's came down with you know what."

Banana's face wrinkled. "The curse of our profession."

"That and pregnancy."

"So far we've been lucky."

Blue Rhonda strutted in her new jewelry. "What's that old expression: 'I'd rather be lucky than good'?"

"That's it. Come on, we'll be late."

A few hundred people packed the old hall. Its once deep-sapphire curtains hung limply by the long windows. The troops were out. Linton's followers, conspicuous by their dress—modest and out of date—sat on the right of the center aisle. The other people, far more heterogeneous, sat on the left. Bunny, Lotowana and quite a few of the girls scattered themselves throughout for effect—and spite. Blue Rhonda cherished dumping her behind on the long pew so hard that one of Linton's ladies bounced upward as though on a seesaw. The first hour of the debate hovered between tedium and tedium. Once they reached the issue of taxation, property owners and businessmen perked up. For a fledgling, Magnus Stone showed promise. His replies, questions and statements were concise, well thought out and spoken in clear English. Linton, as was his wont, scattered about polysyllabic adjectives like cannonballs at Gettysburg. His standard jeremiad against the evils of alcohol wasted time because half the audience was the converted and the other half did as they damned well pleased. Everything would have ended in a draw if the question of state control of railroad freight rates had not come up. Magnus pushed for no interference, while Linton, without any clue as to what he was talking about, took the opposing view. Foolishly, Reverend Ray figured he should set himself against anything and everything Magnus was for. Sensing he was slipping, he started on prostitution. The connection joined in his brain because he associated the railroads with the station at 250 Water Street, and the reminder of Water Street he associated with the "soiled doves," as he called them.

"... and so I say to you, good citizens of Montgomery, can we afford a cancer like this to grow on our fair city? Can we afford our young men to be enticed by these sirens of wicked pleasure? Remember the words of Saint Paul . . ." Here for a moment he forgot the exact words of the old misogynist, so he improvised: "Let a man live without congress with a woman. If he cannot restrain himself, then let him take a wife and cleave to her ever after." A few fans fluttered; it was warm. "If I am elected, I promise I will labor to stamp out this vice as I labored to stamp out liquor. God's work must be done in all places and at all times, whether in your home or in the legislature. Onward, Christian soldiers."

His side applauded.

Magnus's reply tore like a barb. "This nation was founded on the separation of church and state."

Bloated on his own oratory, Linton railed, "For a true believer there can be no separation of church and state."

"You are a Methodist, are you not, Reverend Ray?" Magnus's tone stayed level.

"Yes." This was uttered with a heavy dose of superiority.

"Then you are a true believer?"

"Of course." A flicker of disdain crossed Linton's features.

"I take comfort in your certainty, Reverend Ray, but the legislature contains Lutherans, Episcopalians, Presbyterians, even a Catholic, I'm told. Theology is not their concern, sir, but rather the governance of this state."

Had he been a politician, Linton would have realized he had skipped into a trap, but he was so consumed by his own beliefs, so absolute in their correctness, that he couldn't understand why other people did not agree with him. "God is everyone's concern."

"One hopes so," Magnus said, "but he is especially your concern because you have been trained as a minister. Wouldn't it be a better service to your God to utilize the skills you have developed rather than switch horses in midstream, as it were?"

A murmur rippled throughout the right side of the hall. The left side basked in the surgery.

"God's work is everywhere, young man. If it is his will that I serve him in the legislature, then I will do so."

"I beg to differ with you, Reverend," came the silky reply. "It is the will of the people that will decide whether you sit in the legislature. This is a democracy. For that privilege we fought a war against the British."

The murmur expanded into outright jabber. Blue Rhonda squirmed with excitement. She raised her hand but a stern stare from Bunny canceled that. The meeting broke up after that exchange. Magnus shook hands with well-wishers. Linton moved down a side aisle to leave, but Blue Rhonda stepped in his way.

"Let me ask you a question, Reverend." She would have given anything to draw a razor across his huge Adam's apple.

"What?" He was irritated. He couldn't understand how he had lost his hold on the audience.

"If a person is really Christian they shouldn't fear death, right?"

Wearily, as if explaining something to a dull child, he said, "Christ died for our sins. Through him there is life everlasting. Embrace Jesus and you have nothing to fear."

"I'm so happy to hear that. You could do us all a big favor, and yourself too, if you'd do yourself in."

"Huh?"

"We humans are such a rotten lot. Why don't you join Jesus and enjoy eternal bliss? After all, you're too good for this earth."

Banana yanked Rhonda away and Linton walked off.

"Rhonda, you can be so mean sometimes."

Rhonda buttoned her lip. Her vengeful streak could get the better of her. Plus she felt off, and that brought it out.

She jollied up as they all took the trolley home.

Stepping inside the door to their house, Banana lit a lamp and then shrieked, "Rhonda!"

Attila the Hun had killed a rabbit and sat hunched over it in the parlor. Attilla hadn't taken one bite out of the creature—it was his love offering. Rhonda understood cats, so she petted him, fussed over him and then gave him some milk. While the wiry tabby lapped his treat, Rhonda disposed of the dead animal. Banana slowly came off her hissy fit.

"How could he!"

Blue Rhonda washed her hands. "That's the nature of the beast. You can't hate a cat for killing any more than you can hate a man for fucking—or a woman either, if she'd be honest."

"Mmm." Banana was squeamish. "What in the hell was a rabbit doing in downtown Montgomery?"

"Buying a pair of shoes, I guess," Rhonda deadpanned.

* * *

Concealing Lotowana's dimensions would have challenged Merlin. In her choir robe she resembled an Arab encampment minus the camels. Tactfully positioned in the back of the host of voices, she still attracted some notice.

Blue Rhonda, Banana Mae and Bunny, all shielded by large hats, sat in the rear of the splendid Georgian church.

Icellee Deltaven, formerly called "Monster Mama," as she rivaled Lottie's bulk in her later years, had dropped a ton from all the work and emotional excitement. She looked younger than anyone could remember. Near the front sat Lila Reedmuller and the Banastres. The church seethed with anticipation.

Outside, Cedrenus Shackleford perused the thousands of people who jammed the steps of the church, spilling into the church grounds and down into the street. People were dressed to the nines just to stand outside.

Grace's wedding was the biggest news since the resurrection—and fortunately more people could observe it.

Payson was so nervous that John forgot his friend's pledge and offered him a drink. Mr. Gilbert usually had a supply within easy reach, his hip pocket. Payson refused. He was amazed to discover the conventional thoughts which scurried through his mind, but was too nervous even to be embarrassed at this tie to the rest of the human race.

Grace, on the other hand, appeared totally composed and ungodly beautiful. The dress alone would have endowed a small college. Since her father had died years ago, Bartholomew Reedmuller would give her hand in marriage. Hair brilliantly silver, he would have been hired for the part by Central Casting. As his own marriage was successful, he viewed his task with reverence and joy. If Bartholomew, the original straight shooter, had been told of the more private arrangements of the bride and groom, he would have dismissed it. Since he couldn't conceive of such things, they didn't exist. Fond of Grace, he prayed for her happiness. When your family is your fortress you can withstand all hardship. He pitied those who never find a true mate. Hortensia crept into his thoughts.

"Daddy Reedmuller, are you ready?" Grace snapped him into the present.

"Yes." He suddenly wanted to cry.

Their music cue sonorously bathed the room.

Payson and John caused a sensation, waiting at the altar. Banana swooned. Blue Rhonda had no intention of appearing so captivated. However, she couldn't take her eyes off either of them. Neither could Paris, who, standing next to his mother, looked like her twin. Edward's heart knocked at his rib cage. If only he were ten years older. Grace glided down the aisle majestically. Edward suffered a wild moment when he thought he'd leap out of the pew and abduct her. The silliness of it only underscored his schoolboy infatuation, and he knew it. Hortensia watched impressed, more by the spectacle than by the principals. Lila watched Icellee as much as the bride and groom.

Icey's ponderous bosom heaved. Head erect, she was every inch the grand matron bestowing her daughter on a handsome prince. Marriages are as much for the parents as for the betrothed. Payson's mother, shepherding her terribly correct Savannah regiment, sat in the pew opposite Icey's. It was a toss-up as to who would upstage the other. Mrs. Thorpe still considered Montgomery, Alabama, an upstart town. Her coastal snobbishness could be equaled only by a Charleston or a Richmond lady. Southerners are acutely aware of degree. Mrs. Thorpe comforted herself with the balm that Grace wasn't from Birmingham. If she'd had any idea that three whores sat in the back row, the old biddy would have shit a brick.

As if all that theatricality weren't enough, there was the pastor. His voice boomed out the holy sacrament of marriage, his expressive eyes rolled heavenward at exactly the right moments, he laid it on with a trowel. Grace almost started to giggle until she observed Payson; his eyes were glassy. My God, she thought, what am I getting myself into?

Peppermint Reynolds was thinking the same thing about her old friend. She'd been around long enough to know sex and love were rarely connected, despite all the propaganda to the contrary. Payson loved Grace. She wasn't sure that Grace understood the distinction between sex and love. Most women didn't. She was afraid that Grace regarded Payson as a glorified roommate whereas Payson regarded Grace as a soulmate. "Who knows how it will turn out? I've given up trying to figure people." Pepper noticed a very fat woman in the choir, winking. "Not at me, I hope.'' She cast a sidelong glance down the altar and saw John Gilbert wink back.

Betty Stove whispered to her mother, Beukema, ''It's a marriage made in heaven.''

Dryly Beukema rejoined, ''In time, one of them may feverently wish the other one were up there.''

The emerald lawn withstood the combined weight of six hundred guests and countless servants. The Savannah caucus quartered themselves near the rose garden. The California group wisely posted themselves by the buffet tables, which must have run the length of second base to home plate. The Montgomery guests, reticent at first, finally broke the ice with the Californians. The laughter proved too much for the Georgians and eventually everyone blended together. It was Icelee's greatest triumph. Photographers ferreted around the party. Icellee notified the head coachman to beat them off, but as her order was half-hearted he only went through the motions.

Hortensia and Lila, emboldened by the gaiety, even nodded and chatted for a moment with their ''distant relations.'' Banana Mae desperately wanted to close the distance between herself and John Gilbert, with the express purpose of relations. However, she couldn't jeopardize Hortensia and her mother. Lila, bubbling with good humor, pinched Hortensia every time a Montgomery gentleman spied the three women and gulped. Bold as brass, always, Carwyn took them in tow and introduced them to the California people. Hortensia noticed this and bore no grudge. That had all been very long ago.

Payson kissed their hands, as did John Gilbert. Banana stumbled nearly in a faint. Rhonda hissed for her not to make an ass of herself, but Mr. Gilbert was really divine. Tallulah held court under an immense magnolia.

Amazement rippled through the crowd when the wedding cake—it had to be one story in height—was wheeled onto the center of the lawn. As they cut the cake they did look beautiful: Payson, older, handsome in a cosmopolitan way few men ever achieve, and Grace, who at that very moment would have put Helen of Troy in the doghouse. Sally Nine Hairs, forgetting for a moment her vendetta on all talent, wished them well.

Payson was so enraptured with the moment and with Grace that he hardly noticed Paris Banastre. That was a first. Paris maneuvered around Mr. Gilbert, decided he was resolutely heterosexual, and flushed out other game. Of all people, he visited his golden presence upon Betty Stove, old enough to be his mother. That was the attraction. Paris hungered after the new. He'd never seduced an older woman, so why not Betty? She was tall, accomplished and attractive. Her husband depended on her, encouraged her social activities and physically bored her. A sitting duck. Edward recognized all the signs of what was to come. This was one day he wasn't going to be his brother's keeper. He kissed the bride. Grace thanked him for his letters.

"Remember the time you insisted Clue Three meant Kleiser's Butcher Shop with all those bones?" She smiled.

"Darling, whatever are you talking about?" Payson queried.

"The Great Witch Hunt. I'll explain it to you on our honeymoon."

Edward envied Payson more than any man at the reception, but since Grace had picked him he was determined to like him. "It's an old Montgomery custom. Your wife and I were always on the Black team."

"My wife." Payson opened like a flower. "You're the first person to call her my wife."

So many people demanded their time that the conversation shortly terminated. Edward moved on to other guests, delighted to have been so close to those lavender eyes.

Aaron Stone—he had had to be invited—picked a moment to quiet the crowd and then ostentatiously presented the couple with his wedding present. They would star in the biggest-budget film yet produced by the studio, a tale of a nurse during the war and her fallen aviator lover. This would be filmed as soon as each party was finished with prior commitments. The assemblage applauded, but the Montgomery and Savannah contingents considered the episode in poor taste. One doesn't call attention to oneself at another person's wedding. Gifts are displayed at the gift table. If Mr. Stone had any breeding, he would have had his intention printed on a cream-white card. This would have been propped up on a silver tray. Naturally, the guests would have read it and much favorable comment would have been generated. This way he removed the pleasure of one person's going to another with the news. Shortchanging the bearing of good tidings was as bad as making yourself the star.

At last the couple managed to get away, driven by a coach-and-four to the train station, where an entire private car had been placed at their disposal by the president of the Louisville and Nashville Railroad, as a wedding present. From Montgomery they would ride to New York, where they would board a ship and head for Europe. Their honeymoon was to be a month in Vienna, a city loved by both. After that, they'd return to Hollywood and work.

Placide placed their baggage in the car. Grace, who knew him from childhood, introduced him to Payson. Later, when she finally got around to inspecting her trunk, she found that Placide had left two exquisitely bound books as a wedding present from himself and Ada. One was *The Three Musketeers*. Grace had loved Alexandre Dumas as a little girl. Payson received *The Man in the Iron Mask*.

"What a gentlemanly thing to do." Payson fondled the deep-red book.

"Placide is a heart."

"A what, darling?"

Grace told him about the card ranking system Hortensia had taught her. "It's become a kind of inside scorecard among certain of us from Montgomery."

"What am I?" Payson was so eager.

"I always thought of you as the king of diamonds, but I may have to revise my opinion."

"I'd like very much to be a heart." The train lurched and he bumped into a sumptuous couch. "May I kiss the bride?"

Grace, amused, said, "Of course."

He kissed her with an energy that surprised them both. One thing led to another and they celebrated the fusion of soul and bodies so popularized by novelists of the day. Grace loved it. She had no illusions that Payson would strike his colors, nor did she want him to. But she was very happy he could perform his duty with such lurid vitality. Besides, he had a fat cock.

On the ship Payson read *The Man in the Iron Mask* and raved over it. After the mystery film and then their war film, he must make this picture if he had to finance it himself.

As it turned out, *The Man in the Iron Mask* would be his greatest role. People would return to that performance as the high-water mark of silent films. Unbeknownst to Payson or Grace, he would join the cinematic immortals and inspire an entire generation of male actors, like a touchstone. It would be his last role. Mercifully, neither one could pierce the future.

• • •

"I think it's wonderful that Walter Reed conquered the dreaded mosquito, but I rather wish he had focused his attentions on the flea." Bunny unceremoniously pinched one off her dress.

"Bugs gotta eat too." Blue Rhonda fixed them all drinks. Banana Mae, Lotowana and even Bunny were porous with drink. But thanks to the heady mixture of movie stars, social snobs and those few good people who just happened to be rich, they burned it off fast.

The afterglow of the wedding and the party hung about them like halos over the Last Supper. Each woman ruminated on the day. For Banana Mae it was both the thrill and the disappointment of seeing how the other half lives. The other half winds up acting depressingly like everybody else, only their manners are more highly polished. Blue Rhonda reveled in a good time. No more or less. She didn't much care if she was on the bottom or the top of the social order, as long as she was alive. Lotowana felt like a child in a fairy tale. The Deltaven home seemed wrapped in a mist of cotton candy—it was all so beautiful and sweet. Lottie, like Blue Rhonda, was glad to see it all. She didn't really care about belonging to that world. Lottie cared for her singing and a hot toot or cold drink. Bunny watched with an eye toward business—after all, half of her customers attended the wedding. She noticed their wives.

Seeing a man's wife made providing for his sexual need much easier. And then too, she enjoyed picking up pointers on the refinements of serving, table settings, etc. Of course, meeting John Gilbert and Payson Thorpe wasn't so bad.

Blue Rhonda pulled out an exquisite cigarette case of gold with a stripe of rubies diagonally pulsating across the top.

An appreciative murmur escaped Bunny's lips. "Still a member of the consider-the-lilies school of finance?"

"A client," Blue Rhonda airily replied.

"Honey, you'd have to work on that fella until your teeth fell out to afford this." Lotowana took the desired object out of Rhonda's hands.

"I got a discount."

"She did," Banana chimed in, "but still."

"O.K., O.K. So I disrupted my financial plans, carefully laid by Banana Mae. I had to have it. Anyway, I only sold off one little building."

"What in hell were you sniffing about in church?" Lottie couldn't take her eyes off the cigarette case. "You, Rhonda, of all people, getting sentimental over a wedding."

"I wasn't crying." Blue Rhonda grabbed back the case. "Taking a sniff. I felt a little weary."

"Old Hardhearted Hannah shed a tear? Mercy." Banana set out some fruits and small cakes. Lottie consumed a cake before Banana put the tray on the table.

Bunny peered at the obese woman. "Haven't you eaten enough today?"

"Just because you peck like a bird at food doesn't mean I have to." Lottie defiantly ate another cake.

A lull followed. Blue Rhonda quietly played with her magnificent cigarette case, then dropped it in her dainty string bag. She withdrew a tiny square gold box, also with a diagonal stripe of rubies across it. Dipping in with her very long pinkie fingernail, she filled her nail, placed it in her nose and sniffed.

"Our ancestors knew what they were doing when they took snuff," Rhonda sighed.

"Snuff is tobacco," Bunny informed her.

"I know that. Think of this as bleached tobacco."

Rhonda packed up her other nostril. "And now, Bunny dear, out with it."

Bunny arranged her skirt, gulped a drink and removed one shoe. "Blisters."

Banana Mae and Lottie stared at her. Blue Rhonda's eyebrows shot upward and met in her forehead like an inverted V. Bunny avoided looking at Blue Rhonda. After a dramatic pause, Bunny began.

"I was born in Brisbane, Australia, through no fault of my own. My father made barrels. Aside from selling barrels, he also filled some full of brine and pickled things. He was a Scot and a Presbyterian. Mother, for a reason known only to her, was a Catholic and she determined I would have a Catholic upbringing. I have not a clue as to whether their marriage was happy or not, because my sister and I were trotted off to boarding school at age seven." Bunny swallowed a bit of her gin. "I was wretched the first few years, then I grew accustomed to it. Children do, I guess. I wore my knees out genuflecting."

"Religious?" Blue Rhonda tried to imagine Bunny in a natty uniform complete with heavy brown shoes.

"Theater." Bunny smiled. "What I really felt was the sense of theater. It took me a while to figure out that I didn't give a fig for the church. That momentous occasion occurred when my favorite nun, Sister Mary Joseph, died suddenly. Of all the nuns, those harbingers of iron discipline, she was the only person who displayed any kindness towards us. Well, I prayed and I prayed for God to restore Sister Mary Joseph. He saw fit to leave me with the resident sadists and took the good sister to himself. That's when I decided it was all a gilded crock of shit." Her eyes narrowed, then widened again. "My first act of revenge was cutting out huge footsteps from red heavy paper and pasting them down from the cross, along the center chapel aisle and into the ladies' loo."

Lotowana emitted a shriek of appreciative laughter.

"Then I tied up all the kneeling benches. I also wrote 'between the sheets' on the Mother Superior's hymnal."

"Huh?" Blue Rhonda questioned.

"So when she'd open her hymnal to sing, oh, let's say 'Ave Maria,' she'd see 'Ave Maria between the sheets.' I ruined every damn hymn in the book. Lightning did not fry me on the spot, so I continued in my blasphemies surreptitiously for the remainder of my school days—which didn't last long. Around age fourteen, I discovered a sin more engaging than worshiping the fatted calf—sex.''

Lotowana clapped her hands together. Now Bunny was on ground she understood.

''The blacksmith's assistant, Rudolph Distol, helped me discover it. I'll never forget his name.'' Bunny dumped her other shoe and crossed her legs beneath her. ''Mother Superior got wind of it and I was tossed out with appropriate disgrace. My own sister, the silly ass, decided to become a nun—to atone for my sins, I suppose, and to save herself from any and all temptation. May she wilt in her wimple.''

''Wimple?'' Lottie blinked.

''You know, the white band over their foreheads. Oh, does it get hot in Brisbane! I bet she's down there sweating hogsheads. To make a long story short, I fled my native land. A female Aeneas, I thought. Sailing across the seas—the world is so big. Got to England first. Tried to earn a respectable living, but aside from being a maid or a governess, what can one do? And the wages! I quickly perceived the wages of sin were more equitable. So I studied at a high-class whorehouse. No, I didn't participate in the activities. I served as a maid. That kept me free of the madam's influence, mostly. It never hit her that I was soaking up the business, and since she didn't consider me one of her girls she didn't interfere in my comings and goings. Saved up enough for passage to America and by age eighteen here I was.''

''Why America?'' Banana wondered.

''Because you people are more dishonest about sex than even the English or the Australians. There's a fortune to be made here, and I've done just that.'' Her pleasure was enormous.

''In Montgomery?'' Rhonda gobbled a cake.

''My dears, the South appreciates a well-run house. Half of the men are riddled with guilt over sex. They pay for the relief and for you to shut up. The other half doesn't know the meaning of the word guilt or conscience and they pay you because they want a crackling good time. I love it here.''

"I still can't figure you in a Catholic girls' school." Banana giggled.

"I obeyed Christ's teaching. I became a fisher of men."

"Tell us when you're going to walk on water, Turnbull." Blue Rhonda held up her glass in a toast.

"What about love?" Banana asked.

Bunny played with her shoe by picking it up on her big toe and dropping it again.

Lotowana quivered in curiosity.

"Lottie, you've got lips like Pandora's box." Bunny aimed her shoe in Lotowana's direction.

"I don't know any Pandora, but I ain't telling, if that's what you're fussing about."

Satisfied with the small ripple of caution in Lottie's eyes, Bunny continued. "I loved Rudolph, but what did I know? There was a nice man in Manchester once, but I failed to fully return his affections. I think I took more men to my bed out of pity than out of love." She sighed. "I got bored with it."

"You don't go to bed with anyone?" Rhonda was incredulous.

"No."

"How about once in a blue moon?" Banana Mae enjoyed sex, or perhaps she enjoyed the power it gave her over men.

"No." Bunny laughed at them. "Honestly, no. Once the novelty wore off I moved on to other things."

"What else is there?" Lotowana prodded.

"I don't expect you to appreciate this, but I'm interested in the forest, not individual trees."

"Bunny, we're not lumberjacks," Blue Rhonda pointed out.

"All this carrying on about men and women, women and men, feuds, broken hearts, young love. There are other things in the world aside from mating. Like politics, for instance."

"Oh, that." Lottie seized another cake. If Bunny shied off at sex, she might as well get pleasure from eating.

"People get so wrapped up in their little lives they miss what's around them and what's being done to them."

Banana stared at Bunny. A failed romantic, she needed to understand this very opposite frame of mind. "You mean like Linton Ray? If we hadn't gotten ourselves together, he could have reached into our individual lives."

"Yes, that's what I mean. And not just here in Montgomery." Bunny, animated by finally being able to talk about what interested her, even allowed herself a few hand gestures. "Wall Street—why, it's the biggest crap game in the world. I like to read the papers and follow the stocks. We're manipulated, you know, manipulated by those few on top. Watch them and you can get ahead yourself, and you'll also know when to store nuts for the winter."

Business represented a lower form of life as far as Blue Rhonda was concerned. Fashion, films and sports occupied her—those and a ripping good time. She thought of Bunny as a rubber band that had been left out in the sun. She'd lost her snap.

"If you read history books, that helps," Bunny rambled on. "Not that history repeats itself. I don't believe that for a minute, but you can pluck a thread here and there that also runs through our time."

"Even if you figure everything out and stay on top" —Blue Rhonda became unusually serious—"what difference does it make? We'll all be dead. Let tomorrow take care of itself, I say."

"You were the one who wanted to know about all this," Bunny reminded her.

"Isn't there any more juicy stuff?"

"That's juicy to me. You know everything that goes on inside my establishment." Bunny glanced at Lotowana, whose face turned instantly impassive, thereby revealing her guilt. "That's juicy. I'm not, or at least I'm not by your standards."

"Don't you ever get lonely?" Banana downed the contents of another glass.

"Not much. I have the girls to talk to and Lottie's been with me so many years she's more like my sister than my sister. I have you, too."

"Yes, but still, don't you sometimes wish there were a person out there who really understood you, loved you and protected you?" Banana, after the wedding, softened.

Bunny paused. "Sometimes." She picked up steam. "It's too much to ask, Banana. If you get a high card dealt you in this life, you're ahead of the game. Very few of us ever get more than that. I'm content."

Blue Rhonda glowered at Banana. "Don't get moony. *I* love you."

"You're a woman." Banana stated the obvious.

"Cuts no ice." Rhonda leered toward belligerence, then withdrew.

"It is true that I'd rather us be together like two neutered cats than ride the roller coaster with a man." Banana frowned. "You can't live with them and you can't live without them."

"Right." Lottie slammed her drink on the table in agreement and broke the glass. "Damn, I'm sorry."

"Don't worry about it." Blue Rhonda left the room and came back to clean off the table. She brought another bottle.

Surprisingly Bunny said, "I don't think two women living together is like spayed cats. Love and sex are no respecters of society's rules."

Blue Rhonda wondered if Bunny knew about Hortensia. She'd never let that cat out of the bag. "See," Blue Rhonda chided Banana Mae.

"I was thinking." Lotowana's clear voice cut off Banana's reply. "You and your sister are two halves of the same coin."

The other women all turned to look at her.

Lotowana said, "She's a nun and has nothing to do with sex, right?"

"Right," Bunny answered.

"And you run a house and get rich from it." Lottie waited for Bunny to nod in assent. "Sex is in the middle of everything for her and for you too."

Perplexed looks greeted this idea. Lottie sputtered, "I can't say what I want to say, but I know it's true."

"I think I know what you mean," Bunny soothed her,

"but my sister and I are still on opposite ends of everything. She's a Christian and I am not."

Banana pooh-poohed this. "We're all Christians. If you're baptized, that's it."

"That can't be enough." Rhonda found a drop or two of water unconvincing stuff. "You've got to do good deeds."

"That's not what my daddy used to say," Lotowana chimed in. "He said all you got to do is accept Jesus as your savior and you sail through those pearly gates. Uh-huh."

"So you can murder one hundred people, believe in Christ and play a harp when you're dead?" Rhonda was scandalized.

"That's right. The God's honest truth." Lottie evidently chose to embrace Jesus secure in the knowledge that this did not interfere with daily life.

Bunny matter-of-factly explained her position. "I believe in Christianity but I'm incapable of practicing it. You can't make money and believe in Christ. It's one or the other. Either you live like Jesus and renounce worldly goods or you go out and make a buck."

"I'll have to think about that." Blue Rhonda scratched Attila's head. Attila appeared interested in theological matters.

Inspired, Lotowana proclaimed, "Render unto Caesar that which is Caesar's."

"That means don't meddle in politics." Banana dimly remembered Sunday school.

"It means pay taxes." Rhonda clarified the quote.

"Taxes are political," Bunny coolly noted.

"Amen!" Banana laughed.

After Bunny and Lotowana left, Rhonda turned to Banana Mae. "Australian, and her sister's a bleeding Catholic!"

"Beats all."

"Do you believe you can get into heaven even if you're rummy?" Blue Rhonda blurted. "All you have to do is believe in Jesus?"

"No. An honest person in China doesn't go to heaven because he doesn't accept Christ but a murdering American gets in—of course I don't believe that."

Blue Rhonda's mouth turned up at the corner. "Maybe

so, but I tell you that's powerful stuff if you're flopped on your deathbed. No wonder people want to believe."

"We're all a long way from that." Banana knocked back one more drink and called it a day.

Monday morning the newspapers choked with pictures of Grace and Payson, the reception—in fact, anything and everything to do with the wedding. Some sharp fellow down at the paper put Blue Rhonda's picture in the paper. She looked quite smart in her diamond earrings, a glass of champagne in her left hand while her right hand was extended to greet Aaron Stone. Icellee sat at the breakfast table, exhausted from her labors. She had nothing whatsoever to do with Water Street or its inhabitants, so she didn't recognize Blue Rhonda. Betty Stove and her mother did, and when they called to offer condolences spiced with outrage, Icellee pitched a fit, then passed out, her face crumpling into her perfect George III tea set. Two weeks elapsed before she would show her face in public, due to the burns, she said.

The seventeen-year locusts hatched in 1928. As they emerged from larval slumber, their celebration of release from such a confining dormancy rattled windows. Light-brown casings littered the tree trunks; even the sides of houses were dotted with outgrown skins. Their eyes popping out of their heads, the insects looked like tiny bulldogs. Shiny green-black, they had waited a very long time to work their will on the world. All this intense activity rubbed off on the human population. Such a commotion would not be heard again until 1945.

From the far recesses of Bangs, Wright and Brittingham, Edward appreciated their thunder. The high ceiling fans plowed through hot molasses air. He was glad of this summer job at such a reputable law office, but he looked forward to returning to Yale. He assumed he would come home to Montgomery to practice, once graduated.

As Edward diligently applied himself to the confusions of the law, Paris squandered his energies in bed with Betty. He thought she'd fall like a ripe apple, but it took him almost a month of constant attentions, flatteries and flat-out lies before he achieved his objective. The dust had yet to settle from his dishonoring of a young lady his age before he literally plunged into a lady twice his age. This generational rapture abruptly turned sour when Peter Stove arrived home early one afternoon to find his wife in the arms of Montgomery's Adonis. Paris dove out the window, leaving Betty to her fate.

At first Peter carried on as though he had uremic poisoning. His rage subsided when Betty tearfully apologized and just as tearfully told him she knew he was hardly free from sin. Peter blanched. After delicate questionings, he decided Betty knew nothing about his own ecumenical council. He magnanimously forgave her and she generously forgave him. Theirs wasn't a bad marriage but rather a stale one. They put a good face on it. Chances were that Betty would never again stray, but whether Peter could actually give up parading around Minnie Rue's in bishopric splendor was debatable.

"I know we said the subject was closed"—Peter picked up his sterling silver hairbrush—"but whatever did you see in that pup?"

Eyes still red, Betty replied, "He paid attention to me. He said I was lovely." A wave of grief engulfed her and she stopped.

With a sliver of insight, Peter sat beside her on the bed. "You *are* lovely."

"Really?"

"Yes." He ran his fingers through his graying hair. "I thought you knew."

"Once you thought I was pretty, and—"

"I think so now, today." Women need constant attention, Peter reminded himself. Why his wife didn't know he liked her looks, her, after all these years was beyond him. He really did like her. But why does she need to hear it? Why can't she go about her business? It occurred to him that he was her business.

Betty rested her head on his shoulder. "Do you think anyone lives happily ever after?"

Such a question had never once entered his mind. Without conviction Peter said, "Of course they do. But you have to take the rough with the smooth." He stood up.

"Where are you going?"

"To break that chicken's neck."

Betty bounced to her feet. "No!"

Angry all over again, Peter growled, "You love him."

Sensible, finally, she said, "I don't love him and I never would love him."

"And I'm going to kick his ass into next week." It was bad enough that his wife slept with Paris in the first place, but that he then flew out the window made Peter even angrier. It seemed to him that if you dallied with a woman of your own class, you ought to stand by her if caught. "He's young enough to be your son."

"If you can have young women, I can't see why I have to go to the grave without pleasure."

"That's diff—" Peter caught himself: "Unfortunate. It's not right for either party to break the bond of trust between them." He sighed. "These things happen, but Paris Banastre! He is young enough to be your son."

"You're repeating yourself, dear. And it's because of our son that I don't want you to make a scene. Magnus will win this election barring mishap. Let's not have the sins of the mother visited upon her son."

She was right but that was cold comfort.

"The least I can do is talk to Carwyn. He's got to do something with that boy," Peter vowed.

Hortensia picked up a calling card from the silver tray by the front door. Ladies let it be known what day and what hours they would receive visitors. Thursday afternoon was her day for such pleasantries, but she'd run into town unexpectedly. The white card with simple Roman lettering had the right-hand corner turned up. That meant it was a social call. If the corner was unbent, then the call was of a more structured nature: business or politics.

Carwyn spun through the door, nearly knocking over his wife. "Did I hurt you?"

"No. What's the matter?"

"I just had the most extraordinary conversation with Peter Stove. He accuses Paris of spoiling Betty. Betty!"

Nothing Paris pulled seemed farfetched to Hortensia.

"His face was empurpled with rage. I thought he'd hit me."

"Empurpled?" Hortensia enjoyed Carwyn's brief flurry of description.

"Mottled." Carwyn, settled a bit, asked, "Do you believe it?"

She led the way into the sumptuous drawing room. "I don't know if I believe it, but it is well within his range of reckless abuse of personal relations."

Carwyn knew this to be sadly true. "Do you know what else he said? He said that Betty told him Paris's smile was bruising. What's that supposed to mean?"

"I think you'd have to be a woman to understand that."

Assigning that which he couldn't bother to sift through to the feminine came easily to Carwyn. He preferred life in compartments, emotions being the compartment farthest from reach. "I curse the day I begat that brat on you."

With a flash of humor, Hortensia told him, "You said we needed the future heir and a spare."

"So I did. We succeeded with the heir and the spare spares us no amount of humiliation."

"Whatever he does, I suppose we're partly to blame."

Startled, Carwyn stopped lighting his cigar in midair. "To blame? For what? We put a roof over his head, food in his belly, and provided him with the best education money can buy. He has no excuse. None." He lit his cigar with finality.

"He is of an age where he's responsible for himself, but I sometimes wonder."

"There's nothing to wonder about. We did our duty. Look at Edward. He's turned out admirably."

"That he has. But our sons aren't a pair of shoes. They were different from the day they were born. It's almost as if they arrived ready-made."

"I don't know anything about that, but I do know Paris will come to a bad end. I pray he doesn't take this family's name with him."

Hortensia stared at her husband of twenty-two years. "I never felt close to Paris. Do you?"

Taken aback by such honesty, especially from Hortensia, he said whatever came into his head. "No. No, I never felt close to either of them. I never even felt close to you."

"Likewise."

Carwyn hadn't expected to reveal that, but the lid was off. "You know, I thought of you as an emerald. Deep inside burns a cold flame. I always wanted to heat you up. I never could."

"That wasn't entirely your fault." Hortensia felt a sympathy for him, previously unknown. She regarded him as an alien under the same roof.

"If I hadn't wanted you so bad I wouldn't have hated you so much. Every time I saw you I was reminded of my own failure."

"Wanting someone is a failure?"

"No, not being able to touch you. We were unsuited for one another." He unbuttoned his vest. "Strange, though. I thought you hated me too. Then years ago that changed into a resigned tolerance. I liked it better when you hated me." Carwyn smiled oddly. "At least when you hated me I was important to you."

Her back straightened. "Carwyn, I regret our marriage. I regret my own foolishness. We hurt one another by ignorance and later by intent. I suppose I was—or am—an emerald."

"Queen of diamonds, maybe?" Carwyn ranked people too. It was a seductive system.

"If I was remote, you might consider that I was also far away from myself."

"What's that proverb? 'We get too soon old and too late smart.' I wish I could start all over again. Don't you?"

"I don't know." A picture of Banana Mae Parker flashed before her. Sitting next to Carwyn in that splendid phaeton. She could see that moment as clearly as if it were right before her. She was livid with Carwyn not because she loved him but because he had compromised her in public. Banana Mae radiated love or perhaps merely excitement. She wondered if Banana Mae did love him. She wondered what happens to women like that—especially Banana Mae and Blue Rhonda, who were good at heart. They grow old too. A chill iced her fingers. God, life could be cruel and absurd. She looked at her partner and for the first time she wanted to know about him. "Have you ever loved anybody?"

"I love you. I never felt close to you, but I loved you."

"Carwyn, you indulged yourself on Water Street relentlessly." A flicker of indignation crackled.

"A man has needs. That's got little to do with love. I don't go much anymore."

"A convenient explanation. How do you know I didn't have needs too?"

"You sure as hell never displayed them around me."

"Approaching forty gives one such clarity of vision." She mocked them both kindly. "I think women come to realize what you call needs later in life than men do."

His cigar fizzled. Knitting his brows as though concentrating solely on the act of relighting, he asked her between puffs, "Have you ever loved anybody?"

"Mother, Father; as Edward grew up I loved him."

"No, no—love. Romantic bombast."

"Yes."

Carwyn had half expected that reply. "Did I know him?"

"Not well." She hastened to say, "Some things are better left alone. What matters is that he taught me to look outside myself. My mirrors became windows."

With an astonishing gentleness he said, "I'm glad."

The two of them sat in a peaceful accord until Paris slammed the door, whistling all the while. Carwyn motioned to Hortensia. "Let me handle this. It might get rank." She left by the door into the drawing room.

He swept in, golden. "Father, the only living Ostrogoth."

On his feet, Carwyn growled, "Sit down. I want to talk to you."

Going through the motions, Paris alighted on the brocade davenport.

"Paris, Peter Stove informs me you have been sleeping with his wife."

"If he'd sleep with her, then I wouldn't have to."

"Damn you!" Carwyn towered over his seated son. "Have you no respect whatsoever?"

Paris ignored that remark. After all, what was there to say?

"You can't go about sleeping with other men's wives. For the love of God, Paris, the woman is the same age as your own mother."

A wicked flicker crossed that perfect face. Paris was attracted to his mother. Whether he'd ever work up to trying to sleep with her was hidden in the back of his brain, but if he couldn't have her, then he didn't mind hurting her. She pulled him as the moon pulls tides, far away yet profoundly powerful.

"Matters with the Loves are not yet sufficiently settled. That poor child refuses to go out in public for fear she may see you and break down."

"Send her to Tunis, then."

"Paris"—Carwyn maintained an even tone—"if you don't straighten up you're the one going to Africa. You have no other purpose in life than to ruin your name."

"Get off your high horse. You rolled over on Water Street many a night. I'm not stupid."

"Don't you talk to me like that," Carwyn spat. "I'm a man. I've got faults. But visiting a whore is not nearly the same as messing around with respectable women."

"If they mess around, as you put it, then how can they be respectable?"

"You know what I'm talking about. This is not an exercise in semantics."

"Whores bore me."

"What do you mean?"

"I mean I'm not paying some floozy to pull my pecker. What's the fun of it if they have to do it? I might as well stay with my best friend." He made jerking-off motions with his right hand.

This inflamed Carwyn. "You're not natural."

"And sinking your fork into a painted hole is natural?"

Revulsion seized Carwyn. "The issue is not debatable. You are forbidden to ever do this kind of thing again. If you do, I'll throw you out of this house forever."

Paris's life with Carwyn was an accumulation of threats. Some his father enacted, others he did not. Although he'd never before said he'd put him out, Paris was not overly worried.

"Am I understood?"

"Yes," came the lackluster response. Paris rose to go upstairs and bathe.

"Paris."

"Yes." He didn't bother to turn around.

"If you don't care about your mother and myself—and we've made our mistakes—you could at least show some concern for your brother."

As he walked away, Paris intoned, "Old, dutiful Edward." Then under his breath he muttered, "Probably never been laid."

The stairs resounded with Paris's ascending footsteps. Carwyn thought to himself that his son was a catastrophe with legs.

• • •

Sweltering heat sidelined many an individual imbued with the Protestant work ethic. Not Ada Jinks. Not a hair out of place, not a smidgen of dirt or sweat on her dress, she drilled the subjunctive into Harriet Wilson, a student on her way to college. Harriet may have entertained no plans to attend college, but Ada would get her there anyway. Besides, Harriet was a fine student, motivated enough to study all through the summer. The Wilsons couldn't pay, but Vida Wilson, Harriet's mother, took in the Jinkses' ironing. Placide's shirts sparkled. Ada was loath to admit any woman could be as clean as herself, but she had hot competition in Vida.

Harriet finished her lesson with but one mistake. Proudly, Ada dismissed her with the next day's assignment. Ada nursed a high opinion of herself, but she never credited herself on another's ability to learn. Her focus rested entirely on the student and the subject matter. Teaching came naturally to Ada. Placide said that was because she liked to give orders. Perhaps, but she did love seeing someone grow and she liked making that possible.

After Harriet left, Ada cleaned house. Lately she'd taken to wearing a surgical mask for this activity.

"Anybody home?" Placide called from the kitchen.

"In the front room."

Placide walked over to kiss her. "Will you take that thing off your face?"

"It keeps the dust out of my respiratory tract. How many times do I have to tell you?"

He unhooked the mask. "Kisses are kisses and dust is dust."

She enjoyed her buss on the cheek and then started to pull the mask up again.

"How can I see your sweet lips? Besides, this is my home, not a hospital."

Cajoled, Ada removed her mask.

"Ran into Amelie today," Placide casually mentioned.

"What's Two Ton Tessie up to?"

"When that man of hers ran off she did eat, didn't she? You ought to get one of your university friends to do a study on that, honey. The relationship of fat women to broken hearts."

"You're in a good mood."

"Hotter than the hinges of hell, but for some reason that makes me feel good."

"Bakes out the arthritis, that's why. Now tell me, what'd Amelie say?"

"Not much. She wondered if you'd like to tutor her little girl, Catherine. The child's bright and I also think it would be a relief to Amelie and the entire Banastre household if some of her boundless energy were channeled toward lessons."

"She's a bright child. Martha Seddon had her in class last year." Ada smoothed over her skirt. "I suppose I could see how we work out."

"The Banastres would pay handsomely." He'd meant to say Amelie.

"It's wonderful the way they've taken to the child. I think Carwyn is the father. It just strikes me as odd they'd go out of their way . . ." She trailed off, as she didn't need to say it.

"Maybe. I rather doubt it."

"Something doesn't add up over there."

"Well, sweetheart, it's none of our business, is it?"

She agreed. He continued, "On the subject of the Banastres, I was waylaid by Gabriel today." Gabriel's true name, Xavier McLanahan, had dried up over the many years she lived in Montgomery for the simple reason that the woman could not keep her mouth shut. Hence Gabriel. A good fifty years ago, when they were both girls, she'd once heard Icellee Deltaven utter, "Encourage gossip. It oils the social machine." Being small, Icellee had no doubt picked it up from her mother. It made a great impression on Gabriel. As is the custom, the little girls had stopped playing with one another after a certain age, but Gabriel maintained the connection in her mind.

"Did the trumpet of our times blow?"

"Seems Paris enjoyed intimate relations with Betty Stove." Placide tried not to laugh.

"You don't mean it!" Ada pretended to dislike gossip, but underneath it all she was eager for scandal too good to be true. It confirmed her view of human nature. Then again, you don't feel so bad about your own life when you see other people botch theirs even worse. Gossip exercised a restorative power.

"Amelie didn't say anything?"

"No. You know she's one-hundred-percent true blue."

"Where in God's green earth did Gabriel come up with that one? It's so fantastic it must be true." Ada caught herself on the brink of enthusiasm.

"I can't imagine that Betty or Peter would let slip. Surely the Banastres wouldn't say a word."

"Those two must be in a state of advanced mortification," Ada commiserated.

"Actually, I think it's harder on the older boy."

"I wouldn't put it past Paris to rat just to see the havoc."

"Bet it was Marilee Brook. She's still furious over the way he dumped her last year."

"Babbling Brook." Placide smiled.

"Or Mary Bland Love, his latest victim." Ada displayed a wealth of knowledge about Paris, betraying her avid interest in who did what to whom.

Placide enjoyed her charade of being above it all. The little chinks in the armor only made him love her more. One could forget sometimes that Ada was human.

"Not Miss Love; she's not vicious and I hear she remains distraught."

"That'll teach her men are nice to look at but you don't want one in the house."

"Ada."

"You're the exception that proves the rule."

"Brother!" He shook his head. "You know what I think? It's a long shot, but I think Reverend Ray got wind of it and is making sure the story gets all over town. He thinks immorality in the family will hurt Magnus Stove at the polls."

Placide could see behind the scenes. Ada admired that ability. Her knowledge came more from books; his knowledge came from people.

"As far as we're concerned, it doesn't matter who gets that seat. Even so"—she attacked a fly, which audaciously invaded her house—"that's Byzantine."

"I'd call it dirty pool. Paris will cause a great deal of grief before he sees the far side of tomorrow. I worry about that."

"He stays out of our side of town."

"Isn't it you who says we are all responsible for one another?"

"Placide, don't quote me to myself. I'm talking about our people, not their people. There's nothing we can do about him even if we wanted to."

"I wanted to work in the garden today, but I think I'll wait until it cools off."

"You won't get out there until November, then."

Appreciating her comment, he unbuttoned his shirt and headed for the back door.

"How old is Catherine?"

"About ten," he replied.

"Might be fun."

Later, as he worked in the garden, chest exposed, she stuck her head out the back door. "You're still the best-looking man I ever saw."

"Don't you forget it, girl."

A loud crack reverberated over the field. Hortensia righted herself in the saddle. Polo was not for ladies, but she'd heard a group of women fielded a team down in Dallas, Texas. If Texans could do it so could Alabamans.

It took some convincing on her part, but many of the town's equestriennes came round. They were getting the feel of it. Initially the little group caused a sensation, but Montgomery soon returned to normal. Women flew airplanes, so what's a little polo? As long as the ladies hosted winning parties and bore the requisite amount of sons, much could be forgiven. A few old roosters crowed disapproval, but the twenties loosened many a restraint. The Great War, a decade behind them, haunted those people who fought in it and affected everyone who lived through it. Carwyn from time to time would still toss down his newspaper and curse England and France, who sucked up the peace table. "Our boys died for what? What in hell did we get out of it? Europe is a goddamned cesspool." Germany struggled with impossible reparations. Their fragile democracy tottered. Carwyn read German and subscribed to a number of publications from that nation. Their news upset him the most. Down at his club, most of the men felt as he did: The Allies were fought to a standstill. We came in and finished the job for them and came home with filled coffins instead of coffers. He could understand fighting a war for national defense or even for territory, but he could see neither in that conflict. The shattered Austro-Hungarian Empire lay about like so many bits of glass, waiting for some giant to glue it back together, cockeyed. Above all he detested the Soviet Union. Profit sang a siren's song. For the life of him, he could not grasp communism in any way, shape or form.

Hortensia occupied herself with Catherine, with her new passion, polo, and with a certain as yet unclarified hatred of dead convention. Europe seemed very far away. Her only international concern was that America would steer clear of any uproar in Europe, Asia or the Arctic. After the last chukker the women often stayed together for a drink. Hortensia was appalled at how little they knew of the world outside the boundaries of Montgomery's upper classes. Politics barely existed for them. She knew she was woefully uninformed, but they were flatly stupid. Lila, an eager political analyst, paused to tell her that people are only interested in politics if they have a shot at power. Hortensia began to believe her mother.

She'd brought Catherine and Amelie with her this afternoon. The practice was cut short because the ponies lathered up, and if they wouldn't suffer heat prostration the riders soon would. Catherine clapped her hands as Hortensia trotted off the field.

"I want to do it!"

"Keep riding and grow up," Hortensia called out to her.

Catherine eagerly took the bridle of the pony although she had to stand on her tiptoes to reach it. Hortensia dismounted.

"Banny, mother's milk." Sugar Guerrant held up an inviting martini.

"In a minute." Hortensia handed the pony over to her groom.

"You were born on a horse, Miss Hortensia," Amelie said.

"Almost."

"I want to ride as good as you." Catherine glowed.

"Practice, my sweet. Are you walking up the stairs backwards for your legs?"

"Except when I'm in a hurry."

"Good."

Catherine pulled off Hortensia's riding gloves. "When I grow up I want to be just like you."

"I'm not worth imitating, honey. Be yourself."

"No, Aunt Tense. I want to be like you. I wished I looked like you. You're so beautiful."

She dropped her arm around Catherine's shoulders. "Beauty keeps people from you. Never wish for that." Catherine blinked and Hortensia pulled her closer. "If a woman is considered beautiful, very few people ever get further than that. Men—well, you'll learn about men later. Let's say that men pay attention to you for all the wrong reasons and an awful lot of women hate you."

"Hate you? How could anyone hate you?"

"That's easy. Women compare themselves to you and feel inferior. They also live in the silly fear that you'll steal their man."

"How can you steal a man?"

"I don't know, darling, I never stole one. It makes them

sound like a loaf of bread." Her full lips opened, her teeth sparkled. "If you are beautiful, very few people ever really see you. *You*. It's a terrible thing to go through this life without anyone knowing who you are."

"I want to know who you are." Catherine's innocence shone like an icon.

"I believe you do. I hope when you are my age you won't find your Aunt Tense a disappointment."

"I'll love you more. I promise I will." Catherine stopped. "How old are you?"

Amelie clucked disapproval. Catherine looked at her, then at Hortensia. She wasn't sure what she'd done wrong.

"I'll tell you, but in the future it's preferable not to ask women their ages. I really don't give a fig, Miss Curiosity, but plenty of my sisters do." She put her hands on her hips. "I'm thirty-seven."

Catherine stared at her. Thirty-seven was an eternity. "Oh."

Sugar walked over and handed Hortensia a delicate glass. An appreciative sip followed.

"Sugar, you remember Miss Catherine Etheridge."

"Why, you're so big, Catherine. I barely recognized you." Sugar nodded to Amelie.

"Let's repair to the tent, madam." Sugar placed her hand at Hortensia's elbow. The rest of the gang engaged in lively talk, their laughter tinkling over the chewed-up grass.

"Can I come?" Catherine asked.

"No, dear, this is for grownups."

"But Miz Guerrant said not one second ago that I'm big."

"Bigger, yes; grown up, no." Hortensia patted her head.

"It's because I'm piebald, isn't it?" Catherine flatly stated. Amelie's eyes registered horror.

"What?" Hortensia inquired.

"Piebald, pinto—half black and half white. I don't fit anywhere, do I?"

Sugar Guerrant felt her heart sink. For one flutter of an eyelash she had a sense of the child's displacement, and worse, an insight into what Southerners used to call "our special problem." Our special problem emigrated to the huge, impersonal Northern cities, where relief was not forthcoming. The black diaspora achieved no promised land.

Shaken but in control, ever in control, Hortensia quietly said, "I can't lie to you, Catherine. You're going to find many a door slammed in your face because of your color. However, joining adult women for illegal spirits is not one of those doors. You're too young."

Catherine considered this. Amelie took the child's hand. "Now why'd you go and say a thing like that?"

"It's true. It's true I don't belong." The voice wobbled a little.

Sugar gently took the girl's other hand. "Darlin', it really is because you're still a little girl."

"But what happens when I'm a big girl? I still won't be able to play polo with you all." Tears welled up.

Hortensia said, with a sadness Sugar never glimpsed, "Catherine, even those of us who are supposed to belong often feel outside. I don't know if anybody belongs to anything. But you belong to me and to your mother. If all else fails, you have us. Isn't that better than overriding the ball with a bunch of white women?" She smiled unexpectedly.

Catherine remained silent, then with deliberation replied, "I'd rather have you and Mother than anything—but I still want to play polo."

"We'll address that question when you are ready to play polo. If there's a way around it, over, under or through it, I expect we'll find it. Now why don't you help Joe rub down Augustus?"

The two women slowly moved toward the tent. Sugar's eyes were moist. "God, don't it tear your heart?"

"Yes."

"I don't think much about race. People get so crazy over it. I never heard anything like it. That sweet child."

"You never hear anything like that because Negroes learn to lie to us from birth. It's lie or die."

"Do you really think so, Hortensia? I'd hate to think my

Sandra lies to me. She's been with me since I was tiny. I don't know what I'd do without her.''

"You might need her but you're not going to sit down at the dinner table with her.'' Hortensia cut to the bone not to hurt Sugar but because she saw things for what they were.

"How could I? We'd both be so uncomfortable.'' Sugar, upset, bounced from one emotion to the next: pain, pity, anger, defense, resignation. "I didn't start all this. I didn't ship those poor souls over here. What can I do about it? You can't treat people like equals if they're not. I'm not saying we're better; I'm speaking strictly socially.''

"I know. What makes you think I've got an answer? I don't eat with my servants either. Maybe sitting at the table isn't the place to start.''

"There's nothing we can do. Even if we tried, our husbands would kill us.''

"Sugar Guerrant, since when has your husband stopped you from doing what you want?''

Sugar's ability to control her husband was a subject of discussion. Everyone wanted to know how she did it. Men sure couldn't get an edge on Tom Guerrant.

"Going out and changing the world is beyond even my legendary powers.'' Sugar's usual personality returned to her.

Hortensia twirled her glass. "Still, if we wanted to, if we truly, truly wanted to, I think we could change the world.''

This was too much for Sugar to consider. Not that she wouldn't get back to it, maybe, but she needed something refreshing from the tent. Absentmindedly she spilled the beans. "There are moments when that child looks so much like you.'' Horrified at what she'd said, she scrambled. "But when people live under the same roof they do come to resemble one another in gesture and tone. Have you ever studied Icellee and Grace? It's like looking at the same person at different times in their life. Of course, now that Icellee's picked up pounds, the resemblance is not so pronounced.''

"Yes.'' Hortensia's lips compressed. She knew people wondered, but wondering and knowing were two different things. As Catherine attended the black school and basically associated with her school chums, lightning had not struck yet.

"Have you heard from Grace?" Sugar liked Hortensia. Not that she knew her, although she'd grown up with her. Hortensia was cool. She'd changed a bit over the years, grown more relaxed, even a little warmer, but you never really did know what she was feeling. She'd tell you what she was thinking if you asked, but she'd rarely tell you what she was feeling. Sugar sincerely hoped she hadn't offended or hurt Hortensia.

"Yes. The honeymoon was a huge success. They crawled over every cobblestone in Vienna, danced every night, and the last week—about now, I should say— they're going to Paris. They are smashing together, don't you think?"

"God, yes. I like my old Tom, but Payson Thorpe he ain't." She sighed a suffering sigh.

"That's a blessing, I think."

Alerted, Sugar perked up. "What do you mean?"

"Hen party." Dottie Damico joined them. She still wore the helmet.

"Hey, are you two swapping secrets?" Devadetta Corinth sidled over. Devadetta acquired her name at birth, like most of us. They said her mother had imagination.

"Girl talk." Sugar saucily waved her crop.

"You mean there's another language?" Devadetta reached over the sloppily concealed bar for another drink. Short and slender, she was a courageous player and would go for it every time.

"We were discussing Grace and Payson, vultures." Sugar laughed.

"Hens. Don't be testy, Sugar. We can't rely on the women's pages in that miserable rag of a newspaper. We've got to rely on one another. Now what about Payson and Grace?"

"Well, I said that my old Tom was a love but he was no Payson Thorpe, and Hortensia uttered, as the Delphic Oracle, mind you, 'That's a blessing.' What do you mean?" All eyes now turned on Hortensia.

"Good Lord, are you all that starved for news? I don't

know what I mean. I just have a feeling something will hurt them."

"Second sight. Marge Palmer has it," Dottie hummed.

"I don't think I'm sporting secret powers." Hortensia really didn't know why she'd had that sudden rush of feeling about Payson and Grace.

"Oh, it comes and goes, like a bird flying in and out of the window. That's what Marge says." Dottie spoke like an expert.

"A bird flying in the house means death." Devadetta shuddered.

"Balderdash and bilgewater!" Sugar boomed. "Spare me old wives' tales."

"Perhaps you'd like old husbands' tales," Dottie jabbed. Tom Guerrant was a notorious philanderer. Sugar could get anything out of him. He adored Sugar, but wandered, he thought, in secret. Wives are the last to know, but after all this time Sugar would have to be comatose to miss it.

"Who cares if hubby strays from the reservation, as long as he comes home and as long as you work for the same goal?" Sugar lashed back. Catherine's remarks weakened her usual control.

Devadetta saved the day by dumping on her own superstition. "Maybe Grace and Payson are too beautiful, too rich, too talented. Hortensia may be onto something. There are people who have nothing in their lives, so they latch onto someone else's; they become either disciples or assassins."

Dottie frowned. Devadetta rolled on. "When someone is high on the mountain, there are people who, out of envy, jealousy or plain evil, have to dethrone them. Grace and Payson are like a king and queen, sort of."

Sugar found her balance and spoke to everyone's relief. "I bet you're right."

Hortensia chatted with her team for another half hour or so, but she felt quite far away from them all, as though she were standing on another planet observing them through a telescope. Everybody's got problems, she thought. It was a very unoriginal idea, but true.

• • •

The open stalls of the market burst with summer corn, carrots, enormous turnips, pattypan squash and many other vegetables. Lottie, an iron filing to the magnet of food, lovingly cradled a titanic tomato. Blue Rhonda, immune to culinary creativity, inspected the buyers and sellers.

"This tomato's as big as I am."

"Yes, I'd classify that as a major tomato." Rhonda took it from Lotowana's hand and pretended to fall to the ground with it. Out of sheer devilishness she tossed it up in the air. Pure-D panic broke out on the face of the wiry little man behind the stall. Lottie caught it with ease.

"Rhonda, you can't behave for one minute."

"You wouldn't like me if I did."

"That's probably true." Lottie paid the man. "I want some sweet corn."

"Mac's got the best."

Bunny's cook bought all produce and meat for the house. Keeping a good table insured business. Bunny swore sex and food were related. Lottie disagreed from one end and Blue Rhonda disagreed from the other. Lottie nourished no quarrel with the cook, but occasionally she liked to pick up a few things for herself or the whole house. The colors of the foods neatly arranged and sprinkled in their little stalls attracted her as much as the prospect of eating it all up. Some proprietors put tomatoes in one bin, edged with parsley, corn next to that, throbbing purple eggplant beside the corn, and so forth. Lottie felt it was better than a painting because of the end result.

The flower stalls engaged Blue Rhonda. She'd fallen for a batch of insouciant sweet williams. If Rhonda had a green thumb, Lottie's was poison. She couldn't grow a weed. She considered Rhonda a magician.

"Bunny recovered from her confession?"

"My, yes. Rhonda, you're buying up a mess of those dainties. How are you going to get them home?"

The seller offered to drop them by after market closed.

"The horse knows the way." Rhonda winked at him. He was a customer who blasted through the door once every four months, when he could no longer hold it.

"He's got a truck, Rhonda."

"Lottie, sometimes I think you don't have the sense God gave a goose."

"Huh?"

Rhonda kicked her shins and motioned her to shut up at the same time. This was no easy task for Lottie. As they walked away she winced. "Why'd you go kicking me? You're the meanest thing ever lived."

"He's one of my clients. The shy kind."

"Oh-oh." Filled with understanding and secrecy, Lottie forgave Rhonda the kick. "You never mentioned him."

"Now you see him, now you don't."

"I've got a couple of those myself. You know who I miss sometimes?"

"Who?"

"Dad-eye Steelman. That man was crazy about me, a crazy fool."

Rhonda thought he was like the mouse in love with the elephant. "Poor bastard."

"They found him in a ditch clutching one of those spiky German helmets. I hate to think of him lying over there. He should be home, even if he's dead. He never wanted to go in the first place. Got drunk with the boys and enlisted, so they say."

"I sure as hell don't want to go home when I'm dead. Anyway, this is home."

"I don't like to think about it. Dying." Lottie inspected some chickens hanging by one foot. "But I think of him at the strangest times. It's like he pops into my head as though he were trying to tell me something."

"He's whispering from the grave, 'Roll over, Lottie, you're crushing my foot.'"

The comment struck Lottie as so absurd that she laughed. A feather floated off one of the chickens. "People reach from the other side."

"Yeah, and a bear don't shit in the woods." Discussions of what couldn't be proved either irritated or bored Rhonda. "You like Jimmy Hale?"

"Jimmy?" She squinted her eyes. "He's tolerable. Got bad breath, though. I don't expect I'll ever find anyone to fuss over me the way Dad-eye did. I didn't know how good I had it."

"Everybody says that as they get older. Better watch out, Lottie; next thing you'll go completely gray on me."

"Wasn't that sad, Banana Mae asking about being lonely?"

Rhonda snorted. "Sad, a boil on her behind. She's got more friends and excitement than anyone could want. She gets soft as a grape when she's in her cups."

Lottie saw a squashed grape in a teacup. "I don't know."

"Banana half wants to get married. That's not going to happen. Why she can't be content with me is a huge failure on her part."

Lottie fingered a pure white pattypan squash. "Friendship really is more important than love. All this caterwauling about love, love, love. It grates on my nerves." She placed the squash on the hanging scale with a little black rim. "Wait until these babies go up a nickel a pound. Every time I turn around, something is more money. Placide raised the price on a cord of wood seven dollars."

"Be fair, Lottie, that's for cherrywood and birch. You can't hardly find that. Pine's cheap as ticks."

"O.K., I'll go along with you there, but Rhonda, this charging more for less has got to stop. Bunny moans about it every day, but she's right. She says, too, that everybody's living on the margin."

"Margin—outside the lines in a notebook. That's us."

"No, it has something to do with stocks. I don't understand it, but Bunny says people are getting something for nothing and there will be hell to pay. She studies and studies those figures. I don't see why she bothers. She's put everything in real estate and gold."

"It's all pie in the sky to me. If I can't hold it in my hand I don't believe it."

"Me too." In her hand Lottie cradled the squash. She'd purchased it, but she wanted to admire it before she put it in her carry bag.

"You hear about Paris and Betty?"

"Who hasn't? He's wild as a rat. I also hear Beukema pitched a running fit."

"Not a fit and fall in it, but a running fit, a true running fit?" Rhonda's gait quickened.

"I mean to tell you, honey, up one side of the house and down the other, squealing about her daughter. Foaming at the mouth too. Gabriel told me everything."

"Take it with a grain of salt. Gabriel embellishes. She calls a spade a delving instrument."

Lottie giggled. "Talk a tin ear on you, but that colored woman knows everything. She even keeps books on the children. Said Catherine, Amelie's little girl, is taking up summer studies with Ada Jinks."

Rhonda waited a second, then put out a feeler. "Did she say anything else about Catherine?"

"No."

"About her father, I mean?"

"Some people think it's Carwyn, but she doesn't look at all like him, so that theory's shriveled. Amelie never had a reputation for mixing, but then a woman can lapse." Lottie drew in her breath on the "lapse." Her life was one long lapse. "Don't I know it. But we may have the story backwards."

"What do you mean?" Rhonda said much too loud.

"I don't rightly know. One hears rumbling, but it's too farfetched."

"Like what?"

"Like that Hortensia is the real mother."

A hollow laugh exploded on Rhonda's face. She prayed she didn't look as transparent as she felt. "Ridiculous. She couldn't show her face in this town and you well know it."

Half convinced, Lottie said anyway, "Well, Rhonda, the rich get away with a hell of a lot in this world. She was away a peculiarly long time some ten years ago."

"Ten years ago Carwyn acted like a damn fool in our house, yours and Minnie Rue's. I bet she left him flat to teach him a good lesson. He calmed down."

"I never thought of that. But the world's full of open secrets. You know about that lady in Mobile, Royal Pumpelly, she has herself a black-boy lover. Everyone in the town knows about it. He sneaks out the back door at dawn, but who's he fooling? And she goes about big as you please and no one dares say a word. Her family owns the goddamned town.''

"And her husband's been dead for years and she's always been high-strung." Rhonda discovered logic in the nick of time. "Hortensia Banastre has her husband, whatever his prior faults. It makes no sense at all that she would take such a chance, and even more, he'd find out.''

That struck Lottie as more than likely. But she persevered. "I thought she hated him, myself. And men don't see what they don't want to see.''

"Lottie, it makes for a good story but it's like talking about the man in the moon. Everybody says they see his face up on the moon, but when you look through a telescope and get close, there's nothing there.''

Piling up the crisp greens on the scale, Lottie admitted Rhonda was right. Rhonda knew Lottie, reveling in the logic of it all, would tell what she'd heard as though she invented it herself. Rhonda felt a strong bond with Hortensia. She found the woman's beauty intoxicating and maybe that made her secret all the more tragic. At any rate, Rhonda cherished a secret of her own, so her protectiveness toward Hortensia and Catherine was wily and fierce. She regretted she'd probably never be able to have another good talk with Hortensia, but they lived at opposite ends of the ruler: Rhonda sat on one and Hortensia on twelve. Given Catherine's status, she might be able to know her a bit. She'd seen the girl around and about. Placide once introduced them and Rhonda made Catherine laugh.

"You're looking peaked, Rhonda.''

"It's only temporary. Death will cure it.''

Lottie hit her. "You're awful. I know you've been to the doctor. You got the clap?''

"No. You sure know a lot.''

"I worry about you.''

"There's more little white cells in me than red, or they're heading that way. That's all. I need lots of iron.''

Lottie's eyebrows, thin as daddy longlegs, shot up over her nose. "Iron?''

"Brings back the red ones.''

"Oh. Collards will do it for you. Eat lots of collards.''

"They coat my teeth.''

"Rhonda, you can't have everything.''

As Lottie selected onions, Rhonda absentmindedly peeled off some of the paper skin. "Hey, I heard a good one today. What do you get when you cross an onion with a donkey?"

"What?" Lottie fell for it.

"Most times you get an onion with big ears, but once in a great while you'll get a piece of ass that'll bring tears to your eyes."

• • •

Racing up the stairs, Paris tripped on Catherine's Raggedy Andy doll. She'd carelessly dropped it. He cursed, picked it up and dusted it off. His room was at the end of the long hall on the second floor. Catherine and Amelie lived in servants' quarters on the third floor of the other end of the house; a third-floor hall led to their rooms. He sat the doll in front of his door, went in and opened his closet. A fraternity brother was giving a large party, an end-of-summer affair. A pair of white trousers should do it. He rummaged through his shirts. A little knock on the door didn't slow down his inventory of clothing.

"Come in."

Catherine entered, doll in hand. "I lost Andy. Thanks for finding him."

"You abandoned him on the stairs."

"Oh. I was late for my lesson."

"Latin today or history?"

"Latin. You know what?"

"What?" He settled on a pale-blue thin cotton shirt with hairline stripes of mint green.

"Mrs. Jinks and I speak Latin to one another."

"*Amo amas amat?*"

Catherine swung her doll. "We started out memorizing all that junk but then Mrs. Jinks decided we'd talk. I could memorize and read later. This way it's like a code language."

"I had no choice but drill, drill, drill. I think it's all a bloody bore."

"Do you? I like it. I especially like it when Mrs. Jinks tells me about Pericles and Augustus and those guys."

Catherine liked Paris because he was fun. Her contact

with him was sporadic, but his lack of concern for adult preoccupations put him on her level in some ways. Edward was sweeter but he didn't get out of line. One time before he went off to school last summer, Paris showed her how to stand on a horse bareback. Like his mother, he was a fine rider. Catherine also inherited that ability. They said it came down from the Duplessis family, Lila's line; Bartholomew and all the Reedmullers had to be strapped onto a horse. She had learned not to rely on him, but if you caught Paris in the right mood he outshone all others. Small as she was, she sensed his halo of violence. As this quality didn't bear down on her, she wasn't afraid of him, but she could almost smell it when he was in the same room with his brother or mother.

"Where are you going tonight?"

"To a party."

"I went to a party last week, kid stuff."

Paris laughed. "Getting big for our britches."

Catherine stood on one leg to see how long she'd last. "Piggy Latham cried when he couldn't blow out all the candles on his birthday cake. Weenie butt."

Paris collapsed in a dark-green wing chair by his fireplace. "Ah. Push me the hassock."

She placed it under his feet.

"Thanks. I need a breather before facing the rigors of high society."

"What'd you do this afternoon?"

"Played nine innings of red-hot baseball, Beta Theta Phi against Phi Delta Theta."

"Who won?"

"They did, thanks to piss-poor pitching on our part. What can you expect when everyone's from different schools? We should have practiced."

"Who was the pitcher?"

"Me." Paris pointed accusingly to his breast.

Catherine put her hand over her mouth and giggled.

"I'm better at first base but—"

"Tell me a story. About baseball."

"A short one. I haven't got a lot of time." He motioned for her to sit on his lap. She jumped on the edge of the armchair and dumped her doll in his lap. "Ever hear about Mighty Casey at the bat?"

"No."

"Me neither. Let's try another one."

He launched into a tale about the World Series of 1919. She leaned over, raptly attentive, and tumbled into his lap.

"Catherine, you're heavy. Now sit still."

She settled into his lap.

"The shortstop knew nothing of the plan, but . . ."

Her body heat gave him half an erection. Titillated, Paris maneuvered her with his left arm and placed the Raggedy Andy doll over his crotch. As the story rambled on he suggested she play with her doll. She wasn't much interested in it. He could see he'd have to place his penis in the doll in some fashion. Not that he discovered a case of raging desire for Catherine, but the idea of being fondled by a little girl who had no idea what she was about appealed to him. Maybe he'd apply himself to that later.

"O.K., that's enough. I've got to get ready."

"That's not a happy story."

"I'll think of a better one tomorrow. I might get lonesome tonight. Leave me Andy."

"O.K." She handed him the doll and skipped out of the room.

It was as though every year corresponded to a card, Hortensia thought. All the cards played out the last fifty-two years. This has got to be the Year of the Joker. Her conversation with Carwyn preyed on her mind, as did Catherine's outburst and then Sugar's faux pas. Maybe it was the locusts, but something was in the air.

Paris strolled by her sitting room. "Good night, Mother."

"What havoc do you intend to wreak tonight?"

He wore bright white pants, the pale blue shirt without its celluloid collar. His boater raffishly pulled over one eye, he looked like a magazine drawing. "A stag party. We'll think of something."

"I bet you will."

He stepped in, prepared for a litany of his sins.

"Paris, Mary Bland Love is pregnant."

"Oh, no."

"You are named as the father. Her father spoke to Carwyn at the club."

"How do they know it's me? I'm probably not the first one."

Angry, Hortensia clipped her words. "You know a girl like that wouldn't—"

"Fuck around."

"You're absolutely heartless."

"That's your opinion. I'm not going to marry her, if that's what you're driving at."

"She says you promised you would."

"Liar." Of course, he'd promised her that. He'd have said anything to get what he wanted.

"Mr. Love will defend his daughter in any way he can. I believe he'll kill you."

"A relief for the world, I'm sure."

"I don't know why you did it, but I don't see any way out of this. The girl is insipidly genteel."

Stung by this swipe at his judgment, Paris sneered, "Selective indignation, Mother, or is it that she's not the daughter-in-law you envisioned? The Loves are one of our people. It'd be a worthy match although not a love match." He grinned at his little verbal trick.

"She's a holy bore, Paris, but you've knocked her up, in plain words, and you'll pay the consequences. Your father is on his way home and he knew there'd be no keeping you from your party unless I told you what transpired. You are to wait here for him."

"Like hell I will. I'm sick to death of his corrosive tongue."

"You'll not speak that way of your father."

"Why not? You don't like him any more than I do."

Twilight filtered into the room. Hortensia was at a loss to explain how things were coming apart at the seams. Maybe the whole fabric is rotten, she thought, the whole goddamned social fabric. "I've learned to get along with him. I can't lie about our less than perfect marriage. But we have learned to accept one another." She looked at his incredible face, like looking in a mirror. "That has nothing to do with you."

"There isn't much that has anything to do with me. This household is organized around the heir transparent."

"Don't be a silly ass."

"It's true. You love Edward and you don't love me."

"Motherhood was not my gift. I know it as well as you do and I'm sorry. I think I ignored your brother as much as yourself. In later years he's proved easier to talk to. You've . . . you've . . ."

"Been an insufferable shit."

"Yes, if you care to put it that way. This is getting us nowhere. You're in a terrible mess, my boy, and you're taking our entire family with you. You will marry Mary Bland Love, that aptly named creature."

"You didn't marry your nigger." Fire shot out of those ice-blue eyes.

Stunned, Hortensia stared at him.

"If you can get away with it, Mother dear, so can I."

She slapped him with all her might. Hortensia was tall and strong. She should have known better than to rely on his filial piety. He slapped her right back.

"Animal!"

"Whore!"

A doubled-up fist jolted his jaw. Blood trickled down the side of Paris's mouth. He was six inches taller than his mother, a solid seventy pounds heavier, and he was almost two decades younger. Quickly he grabbed her wrists. He pushed her against the wall with enormous effort. Hortensia did not give ground easily. Once he pinned her to the wall, blindly, out of control, he kissed her and pushed his body against her. She bit him, tearing his lip even more. As he pulled back she brought her knee up and caught him, mid-erection. Howling, he let go and then swiftly she kicked him with such primal force he skidded across the room, knocking down everything in his way. She picked up a fireplace poker and snarled over him like a wolf. "I brought you into this world and I can take you out."

Frightened of himself as well as her, he wiped his hand across his mouth. "For the love of God don't hit me. I don't know what got into me." Up on one elbow, he eyed her. "No, I won't say it again, but it's true. I know it's true, Mother. You love that bastard more than you ever loved me.''

Suddenly exhausted, Hortensia blinked hard. She felt she'd fall asleep. "I said, no more."

"What would you do if I told Father?"

"Do as you please." She worried much less about Carwyn than about Catherine. It flashed through her mind that Paris might try to hurt her through the child.

He got up. "I won't say anything."

No, you won't, she thought. You'll use it against me at some crucial moment. "Why did you kiss me?"

"Because I wanted to." He came up next to her. She wasn't afraid of him. His moment had passed for now. "I want you."

"For what? I can't make up for the past."

"I want *you*."

She understood. "You're insane!"

"Maybe I am, but before I die I will make love to you, I swear I will."

Revolted, she shivered. "You'll have to kill me first."

"No, I'll have you without a fight. I don't know when and I don't know how, but I will have you."

The front door slammed. Edward and Carwyn called out from downstairs.

"We're up in the sitting room," she called out, relieved they'd arrived.

It seemed to take them two years to climb the curling mahogany stairway. Hortensia replaced the poker. Paris hurriedly attempted to straighten the room. It was as though an unspoken bargain had been made.

Carwyn was first through the door. Edward was on his heels.

"What in hell's going on?" Carwyn demanded. Hortensia's hair was somewhat disheveled. Paris's bloody mouth gave him away, and if they'd noticed the foot imprint on his crotch, it would have made for even more trouble. Luckily for him, the two men noticed only his mouth. Carwyn went to Hortensia's side. "Are you all right?"

"Yes."

Edward, thunderstruck, mumbled, "Did you hit her?"

"No, she hit me." Paris smiled.

Like a cat, Edward grabbed him by the shirt and shook him. Paris hit him in the stomach. He'd longed for an excuse to sock Goody Two Shoes. Goody Two Shoes shared an equal longing, and hit him right back.

"That's enough!" Carwyn commanded, stepping between them.

With exaggerated reluctance the brothers stopped. Edward had never realized how much he loved his mother, distant though she was, until that moment. "If you hurt her I'll kill you, Paris. I'll kill you and gladly rot in jail for it."

"That's enough. My God, what's going on? Sit down! Everyone sit down." Carwyn was baffled. "I don't know what's going on in the world. Outside the club today a man shot Toddy Brittingham."

Toddy Brittingham, one of Edward's bosses, wore expensive suits that hung on him like a toga. He was one of those people who make you laugh just looking at them. That didn't keep him from being the best courtroom lawyer in Montgomery.

"Toddy?" Hortensia was surprised, if anything could still surprise her.

"Yes. Some fellow he'd sent to jail fifteen years ago."

"Is he dead?" she asked.

"No, but his kneecap is shattered. He won't lose the leg but he'll probably lose the use of it." Carwyn, usually correct in matters of dress, removed his coat and unbuttoned his vest. The news from Mr. Love and the shooting had upset him. The additional burden that his son may have struck Hortensia deeply disturbed him. "Paris, did you hit your mother?"

She answered for him. "He lost his head, Carwyn. The news about Mary was, shall we say, not well received. It's all over now."

Not sure what to do, Carwyn minutely studied his wife, then looked at the other blond. "Don't excuse him."

"I didn't exactly hit her." This was true. He'd slapped her. "I shook her a little."

Carwyn leapt to his feet and smashed Paris so hard across the face tears came to his eyes. He was gearing up to blast him with the other hand when Hortensia seized his wrist. "No, Carwyn—please, no. That's not going to solve anything."

Edward, overcome with magnetic horror, stayed riveted where he stood.

"Do you get my point, Paris?" The words slithered through Carwyn's teeth.

"Yes." A red welt raised up on Paris's cheek.

"You will marry this Love girl. If you don't, you will be disinherited and turned from this house forever."

Alive with concern, Paris almost cried. "Ruin my life! I don't want to be tied down to that simpering moon face."

"You should have thought of that before you slept with her." Carwyn bore down on him. "We had a discussion before about different kinds of women." He looked at his wife and shrugged his shoulders. The situation was so extraordinary it didn't seem strange to discuss this before her. She turned her hand palm upward. He felt better. Edward, however, was very embarrassed.

"I'd rather be disinherited." Paris's tone was emotionless now.

"That's fine with me, but you'd better get out of town fast because Mary's daddy's toting a thirty-eight."

"I'll marry her," Edward said.

Wild hope shone in Paris's eyes.

"Indeed you will not. A loveless marriage is not the way to start your life." Hortensia was adamant.

Paris wanted to say, "You ought to know," but he didn't.

Edward laughed weakly. "It's probably the only way I'll get a wife."

"You're in your last year of law school. You've got years to find a suitable wife." Hortensia brushed her hair off her forehead.

"Who's to say Mary Bland would even agree with it?" Carwyn was amazed.

Edward defended her. "I remember Mary from all the Great Witch Hunts. At least she was smart. If she'd been on our team we might have won more often."

"And so boring in bed." Paris yawned.

Carwyn, between a menace and a sigh, moved toward him.

Paris chattered, "I'm sorry, I'm sorry. Anyway, Edward wouldn't know the difference."

With a touch of his mother's acid tongue, Edward said, "As a child you were a savage wretch. In this quickly changing world, there's comfort in consistency."

"Edward, I forbid you to even consider this one second longer." Hortensia rose.

"Mother, let me make my own decisions. I'll go over there tomorrow. If she's honestly dreadful or a conniving belle I won't, but if she's intelligent and of good character, then I will try to reason with her. It's to her advantage and maybe it's even to mine."

"I can see no advantage in this to you." Self-sacrifice was not in Carwyn's nature. He admired Edward's gesture. No doubt it would help the family, but if there was another way out of this with honor, Carwyn felt bound to find it.

"I'd like someone to talk to," Edward simply and quietly said.

There was a note in his voice that reminded Hortensia of Catherine at the polo field. She suddenly felt her heart would break.

Later that night, Carwyn rapped on the door to Hortensia's bedroom. She invited him in and they sat on the bed and talked about the situation, as well as admitting to one another a sensation of foreboding coupled with a renewed drive to live. It was as though they were disengaging from life with the one hand while grasping it more firmly with the other. After ascertaining that she was all right, Carwyn kissed her on the cheek. He wanted to sleep with her but he hadn't the guts to ask. They hadn't made love to one another in ten years. As he walked out and closed her door he told himself the day had been too much for her. It would have been unseemly to ask. He was afraid she'd say no. He hoped he'd find the right moment soon. He felt so different about her now. When he was young he'd force her. He even beat her once or twice, and then was consumed by hot, licking shame. Some days he couldn't look her in the face. Tonight he wanted to make love to her for her. Swallowed up by his foolishness those years ago, he walked to his room. An uneasy idea nipped at his heels: Did Paris inherit his wildness from him? Was he to blame?

Questions about her parentage recurred like malaria. As she toyed with the heavy silver-framed photo of Hercules Jinks that sat on a little round table covered with a silk shawl, an idea struck Catherine with howitzer impact: How could she be piebald if Hercules was black and Amelie was black? The photo sat in the middle of pictures of Amelie's family. Sometimes Catherine noticed it was moved a bit and she wondered why Amelie hadn't replaced it perfectly. Amelie never left anything out of place, even crooked. She put the photo back exactly where it should be. Catherine learned in the crib that when you were under Amelie's tutelage you kept neat, clean, and above all, orderly. The only disorderly person in the house was Paris and he ventured only so far as casting dirty shirts on his bed. He never even left his shoes in the middle of the floor. She reeled in shock the first time she pushed through Piggy Latham's screen door and discovered an entrance-way that looked like the debris after a typhoon. As near as she could figure it, if you had money someone cleaned for you. If you didn't have money, cleanliness ranked you among your peers. Well, the fellow in this picture looked clean enough and rugged. She was glad Hercules was her father because she liked the way he looked. Amelie said little about him except that he was a boxer. She knew he was killed in a railroad accident. So far she only knew his first name. It seemed enough, since her embryonic classical studies dealt with people who bore one name only: Hector, Achilles, Odysseus, Hercules. But he was definitely black and so was Amelie. With dismay she realized somebody was lying to her.

Up until that moment Catherine shot straight for the bull's-eye. Ten is not too young to learn that sometimes you reach your goal more quickly if you zigzag. She went to the three-way mirror where Amelie laid on her creams with a heavy hand. Catherine previously paid scant attention to her features. She would have preferred to look like Hortensia or the man in the photograph. Amelie was of such Olympian girth Catherine didn't want to look like her. She could see her face full on, and in the side panels she could see her right and left profiles. There was no doubt she was a Negro. She could see that and it was fine with her—but that red cast to her hair, the delicate nose and those sea-green eyes. There was a white person hard by. Maybe it was a grandmother or a grandfather. She put her nose within an inch of the mirror and she discounted that since Amelie's mother, long deceased, was dark. She didn't know who Hercules' mother was, but it was a sure bet she wasn't white. An expression popped into her mind: "There's a nigger in the woodpile somewhere." She changed it. "There's a clabberface in the woodpile somewhere." She felt as though ragged glass were stuck in her throat. She swallowed and swallowed but it wouldn't go down. She knew people loved her and she loved them back, but how can people love you and lie to you?

A week limped by after the explosion. Edward, with a rare determination, visited Mary Bland Love. She refused to speak to him at first but his persistence won out. He was so remarkably different from his brother, she couldn't believe they came from the same family. But he strongly resembled his father, so she knew he was a Banastre. Mr. Love fumed like Vesuvius but reached a quiescent state as Edward's plan unfolded before him. As was customary, Edward informed the father before he said one word to the daughter. Horace Love, dazzled by this change of fortune, quite forgot his child's happiness. Edward fell like manna from heaven. He would have twisted her arm into marriage, but Edward protested that she must make up her own mind. He agreed to call upon her every evening after dinner so they might become acquainted. Sweeping women off their feet was impossible for Edward. All he could manage was to talk to her as though she were a human being with a brain in her head.

This proved intoxicating to Mary. Except for her teachers, no one paid the least attention to Mary's more than adequate mind. No, she wasn't thrilled to her toes with Edward, but the more she saw him the more she liked him and, important, respected him.

Raised to shield women from taboo topics, Edward

discovered he wanted to protect Mary but he felt he could say anything to her. He felt he could be himself. As mid-August scorched the town, the railroad tracks seemed to melt in the sun and the river steamed, Edward knew he had to take charge.

"Mary, I know this may be sensitive for you, but if you'll have me after this brief courtship we ought to get married immediately. Sunday."

Her delicate hand fluttered to her breast. "Sunday?"

"Forgive me, but if we marry now and the child comes on time, we can always say it's premature."

She caught her breath.

"I'm sorry." His voice was a low-register baritone. "If we are going to live together for the rest of our lives, I think we ought to start out on the right foot and say whatever we think. Don't you?"

Mary, giving herself up to the thrill of honesty, agreed.

"Montgomery relished its one great summer wedding. Perhaps we can do something simple. Will you be upset? I know a wedding is supposed to be a woman's pride and joy."

"I don't care about all that," Mary quickly replied. "Nor do I care if we return to Montgomery after you finish law school."

"Then you'll marry me?"

"Answer me this, since we are to speak directly: Why would you want damaged goods?"

"I don't think of you that way. Maybe I'm damaged goods myself." His thick black hair glistened.

"You? You have a flawless reputation."

"Yes, and I'm a bore."

"You most certainly are not. I think you're the kindest man I've ever met."

"You don't have to say that. I know next to Paris I appear anemic."

"Don't you say that. Don't even think that. Why, next to that—Let's not talk about him. You're a man and he isn't." Mary flushed.

"Thank you. I do so very much believe we can make a good team, Mary." He said this with such hope Mary's eyes filled.

"Edward, I don't deserve you."

"Because you're going to have my brother's baby? Listen, if I were a woman I'd probably fall for him too. He shines like a lighthouse over a dull sea of social tedium. I'm not immune to his charm, but I know him for what he is: a heartless, pleasure-seeking parasite."

She didn't reply.

"I—I really shouldn't say this, but God, I hate him. When I see you, I hate him even more."

She put her hand in his. He'd not held her hand before. It was cool and smooth.

"He looks in mirrors with no reflections."

"What?" Edward puzzled.

"It's an old country expression. It means there's nobody there; he's bloodless." She tilted her head up to the ceiling, paused a moment, then locked her china-blue eyes right into his eyes. "It's one thing to marry me. It's another thing to live for the rest of your life with another man's child."

Smiling, Edward said, "I should think we could have some of our own." Hoping he hadn't gone too far, he reassured her, "The child is half you. I would love that half, and well, the other half is Banastre blood, which isn't all bad, you know. How can I hold a baby accountable for its father?"

"Its! I'm not throwing a litter." Mary Bland was not as bland as everyone took her to be.

"Her father, then. I'd like a daughter. Having been raised in a house with only boys, I would welcome a girl."

"I'll see what I can do." She squeezed his hand. "I don't think your mother likes me."

"Mother? Oh, you'll get used to her, and she'll just have to get used to you, won't she? When I was small I was terrified of her, terrified. She seemed like a goddess to me, floating on a cloud. I never could reach her. I like her now that I'm older, but she's not one to smother you in affection. You will like her in time, Mary, I know you will. Mother's a fine, strong person. Of course she'll like you. Is this yes?"

"This is yes."

Edward kissed her on the lips, then stood and raised her up. They walked into the library off the main hall of the

Love house, where Mr. and Mrs. Love sat wishing they were flies on the wall in the next room. Mary's parents greeted the announcement with tempered goodwill. They knew full well Edward had delivered their precious Mary from a living hell. Marriage to Paris would have saved her reputation but destroyed her life.

Mrs. Love worried about such a quick and small wedding, but Mary said they were very modern. For her and her fiancé, a restrained ceremony would do.

Without its being said openly, it was perfectly understood that Paris was not attending the procedure.

The Banastre house had vibrated as though struck by lightning ever since the blowup. Carwyn told Paris he was not to show his face at the wedding, which was O.K. by Paris. He avoided his broken toys when possible. Not that he felt guilty; he simply didn't want to be bothered with leftover emotions. Paris lived without a past and with no concept of the future. Cause and effect played no part in his life.

Hortensia behaved as always toward him, cool and aloof. He veered from rage to studious nonchalance over her. When she knocked on his bedroom door before dinner one evening, it was unexpected. He let her in.

"We need a little time for things to cool down. Might we talk?"

"Yes." Paris ushered her to the green wing chair; he sat on the hassock at her feet. "Is this going to be another warning about staying away from the wedding?"

"No."

That pleased him.

"When I named you I did so because I loved the city of Paris. It's full of light, beauty and culture."

"Lucky for me you didn't love London."

She rested her chin in her hand. "England is an aquarium, not a nation. London, no."

He loved her when she lowered herself to engaging in sophisticated banter with him.

She continued. "Paris it is and I fear you'll bring our house down as did that Trojan."

"He killed Achilles first, remember."

"Your enemy is yourself."

"I leave for school in a week, so you won't have to be reminded of me, the Trojan War—or menopause, for that matter."

"Not yet, mister." She considered kicking him again. "I'm at the age where I'm called 'still beautiful' as opposed to 'well preserved.'" She relaxed in the chair although she didn't feel relaxed. "What I came up to ask you is not to say anything to Catherine. A smart, offhand comment could hurt her and there's no reason for it."

"Maybe I will and maybe I won't."

"Maybe you will, Paris. You're on thin ice."

"So you did sleep with that nigger?"

"Whatever I have done or will do is my business. And I'll thank you not to use that word in front of me. You don't know what I've done or how I've felt and further-more, my great beauty, you don't care. You don't care about anyone but yourself."

"So you admit it?"

"I don't admit anything." Her temples pounded. She wanted to smash him, but that wouldn't get her what she wanted, which was to protect the child.

Airily, he said, "Yes, well, great ladies don't even admit fucking with their husbands. Why should I expect you to tell the truth?"

"Paris, why is it the truth is told with hate and lies are told with love?"

He blinked. She could hold in him thrall. Damn, she always could. "How should I know, Mother? Am I not a reflection of you?"

"That's what I'm afraid of. I'm not the best person in this world—but I'm hardly the worst. I don't understand why you want to hurt us. Why you hate Edward, me, your father. Were we that terrible? I don't remember ever even striking you."

"Maybe you should have. At least it would have been contact."

She wondered if he was right. "I don't know. I've said it before: some women shouldn't be mothers. Obviously I'm one of them. All this prattle about instinct is just that, prattle."

"But you love Catherine. You act more like a mother to her than to me or even Mr. Wonderful." Paris slammed Edward one more time.

"I'm older now. If we had children when we were in our late thirties or early forties I think we'd all do better with them. It's easier for me to care for Catherine; I've made my peace with myself. When you're young, well, when you're young you have babies and you're still one yourself."

"Mother, I can't possibly imagine you being a baby."

"Just because someone is reserved doesn't mean they're mature."

"But you love Catherine. Admit that. You can't deny that."

"Of course I love Catherine. Can you think of one person who doesn't love her? The child's a joy."

"And I wasn't?"

"For Christ's sake, Paris, that was years ago. You can't sit here and hold resentment against a child because you were shortchanged. It's not her fault."

"Actually, I like Catherine." Her Raggedy Andy doll perched on his bed. He might try to get her to play with him using the doll, and then again he might not. It seemed like a lot of trouble and he was not attracted to children, but if he couldn't humiliate or hurt Hortensia as he wished, he was capable of trying anything.

"Promise me you will never speak of this to her."

"Why is it so important? Oh, I can see why it's important for you to cover your platinum ass, but how can it hurt her to know? All right, all right, I'm not pressing you to say you're her mother, but we both know you are. I'm not blind. She displays many of your characteristics, not so much in her looks as in her manner, and she's smart. There's never been a dumb Reedmuller or Banastre yet. I have that to my credit too."

"You're smart but not wise. Why is it so important? The child's a half-breed. Our kind will never accept her. Colored people are far more humane on that issue that we are. If she . . . gets ideas, she might try to fit in and reap nothing but pain. Can you understand that?"

"Then why the hell keep her under your roof? Amelie could have raised her anywhere away from here."

He had a point. "I want her to get a good education, to be provided for, and I hope she'll attend college."

"She could do all that on the other side of town."

Hortensia didn't say anything.

"You want her to know you." Paris's eyes narrowed to slits.

"Is that so wrong?"

"No, but I never knew you. Why should she get the chance?"

"Do you relate every event on this earth and all human exchange to yourself? She has nothing to do with you, Paris."

"She has a lot to do with you and you have a lot to do with me." He stood up and put both arms on the chair, bending over her.

"I made a vow and I intend to keep it." She did not look up at him.

"To her father?"

"To the memory of her father. He was the gentlest human being it has been my privilege to meet."

Paris sneered. It was the closest to an admission he'd ever get out of her. The idea of his mother, this paradise of flesh, in the arms of a black man practically split him wide open. He could well understand why she didn't love Carwyn. But she could have had anybody. That emotion mixed with his jealousy over Catherine—over everyone, when it came to his mother—produced a high-octane blend. "I won't tell, but I have my price."

She knew what it was and didn't know if she could bring herself to pay it. But she hoped her love for the child would overcome her repulsion for the act. "What?"

He smiled and leaned down and kissed her. She did not return the kiss.

"Paris, I don't understand this."

"Yes you do."

"I understand what you want but I don't understand why you want it. It's against all the laws of nature and man." She was trapped but resilient. Hortensia survived Hercules' death, she supposed she could survive this, but

she felt as though an iceberg were on her chest. It was
Paris who placed his hand between her breasts.

"Laws are made to be broken." He kissed her again.
Had anyone seen them, they would have looked to be
carbon copies of one another, an artistic tableau.

Carwyn and Edward awaited dinner downstairs. She
knew as long as they were both in the house she was safe.
He knew it too. He kissed her with more warmth. She
pushed him away.

"Careful, Mother." Paris was as afraid of getting his
wish as of not getting it. Tremendous desire pounded in his
body, but he was afraid of her. Hands still on the arms of
the chair, he put his knee between her legs to make it
harder for her to get up and then he kissed her hard.
Hortensia knew she couldn't be cold much longer or he
would make good his threat.

She kissed him back. He felt overcome as if by a solar
storm.

"Promise me you'll come to me when they're out of the
house." He panted, and his pupils almost overran his
irises.

"I promise if you will keep your word."

He pressed his cheek against hers and closed his eyes.
"I promise. I promise. I promise." He was shaking.

For a fleeting moment she pitied him. His need for
her—maybe it was even a love for her—was like a double-
edged sword. She didn't know which way it would cut
first. But she was utterly determined Catherine should not
feel the blade. She prayed Hercules would forgive her if
there was a heaven and if those who go there care at all for
human life. The dinner bell rang and, still shaking, he let
her go. She swept past him like a queen.

Payson and Grace returned to California in triumph.
Europe adored them. On the way home they decided at the
last minute to give the Canadians an opportunity to worship them as well. They took the Canadian Pacific from
Montreal to Vancouver, speechless like all other tourists at
the shores of the Great Lakes and the cathedral Rockies. A
few days in Vancouver convinced them they must return in
the near future, for it was a clean, beautiful city. They

sailed on a yacht from Vancouver to Seattle. At Seattle they passed through the stately train station into the *Coast Starlight* train, which ran along the Pacific coast down to Los Angeles. They were certain they looked like Mongols and would never work again, because for the entire trip their noses were pressed flat against the windowpane. Neither one could decide which was more beautiful: the coast of Washington and Oregon or the coast along Santa Barbara, California. Santa Barbara was certainly closer. As soon as this mystery picture was in the can, Payson had a week before starting in the flier picture Aaron presented them as a wedding present. Grace was doing *Oui, Oui*, set in eighteenth-century France, but she was certain she'd get off around the time Payson did. If not, she'd at least steal a weekend. They wanted to buy land and build a bungalow in Montecito or Santa Barbara. The area was eighty miles from the city and it took long enough to get there by car, but the trains were regular and Grace had already discovered an enormous tree growing next to the Santa Barbara station. She declared this a good omen. They pored over their bankbooks and were sure they could come up with the cash. A bungalow to Payson or Grace meant a mansion to anyone else.

Payson wanted to redecorate his stupendous home off Sunset Boulevard. Grace sold her house in Hancock Park. She'd had a hell of a time getting into the Park. They frowned upon movie people. Only her good Montgomery bloodlines had saved her, that and friendship with the newspaper heiress who owned one of the largest chains of papers in America. However, Payson's house had a fine view and it was much larger. She prevailed upon him not to run about willy-nilly, trying to do everything simultaneously. They'd redecorate the house when they had time. Payson's taste was elegant. Grace liked the house as it was, although she found it a bit too masculine. She could make a few changes in time.

Payson treated her like a twenty-carat diamond. He didn't want anyone to lay a fingerprint on her. If she tried to pick up any object weighing over five pounds he'd rush to snatch it from her hands. She told him over and over again she was as strong as a horse, but he regarded her more as a creature from another planet, a planet more civilized and higher than earth. She finally gave in and let him dance attendance upon her. Even former doubters of the match admitted the two got on like a house on fire. Payson was too busy to launch any new affairs with hairy-chested sportsmen, but he'd get around to it. Their understanding worked overseas. Discretion was the key word.

He arrived home late after work one night. She'd only managed to get there fifteen minutes before him.

"Gracie!"

"I'm in the bath."

"I'm starved."

"Nigel's fixing a rack of lamb. I called him from the studio. It ought to be ready in about ten minutes."

He bounded through the bathroom door. Grace was up to her neck in milk.

"Don't tell me you're pregnant?"

"This time a star will rise in the west."

"You know, I've heard of women taking these things but I've never believed it. Do you do it often?" He lit a cigarette.

"Once a month. Our whirlwind in Austria left me no time for such pamperings."

Payson stuck his finger in the warm substance and then licked it. "Mmm. Think it will keep me free of wrinkles too?"

"Why not?"

He took off his clothes and hopped in. The two of them squealed and giggled.

"Payson, you can't smoke in a milk bath. It's sacrilegious."

"I think it gives me a certain panache." He blew smoke rings.

"Well, as long as you're despoiling the ritual, give me a puff."

He placed the cigarette between her lips. She inhaled gratefully, then exhaled a cloud of blue smoke in his face.

Coughing, he said, "You're all heart."

"And a lot of liver too."

"Seriously, does this do anything for your skin?"

"It feels good. Replacing moisture is the only way to slow down aging. Slap those emollients on your face, buster."

"Ferdie dashes me with aftershave."

Grace squinched up her face. "No, that'll dry you out. You need a cream."

"Darling, I can't go around with goo on my face. Makeup is bad enough."

"I'll mix you up a batch of potion that will disappear right into your skin. Really, lovie, it helps. Looks are our bread and butter."

He splashed milk at her. The toes on her right foot reached his balls and gave him a flick. "Whee. Where's the other foot, Grace? We could start a whole new perversion."

"Hey, guess what I did today?"

"Show and tell," he sang.

"Waltzed into Darla Divine's dressing room. Done in Neolithic and the couch is about as soft. She calls it her desert look. I swear, honey, she's blasted the whole thing, walls and furniture, in some kind of sand paint—not just the color, but the texture—and the furniture is built in or rather carved out of stone. It all looks veddy caveman."

"Darla Divine neé Mildred Greenblatt. I wonder what fag designer suckered her into that?"

"When bee-stung lips go out of style, Darla will be sitting in the desert. Poor thing, Payson. She was so glad to see me. And the music she's selected to be played during her big scene with Rudy—Tchaikovsky's Sixth. She wants to be very sad. Can you see Myron's face when they tell him he's got to hire an entire orchestra, not just a quartet."

They laughed over that. The producer for Darla's picture was hysterical if the budget tipped over one penny.

"We haven't got music on our set." Payson scrubbed an arm. "I like it, though. You know Johnny used it all during The Big Parade. Said it helped him enormously. Think I'll use it for Man in the Iron Mask."

"Have you talked to anyone about that?"

"Ha. You breathe here and they steal it. I'll fully apply myself to it after our daring-men-in-the-sky number."

"We could finance it ourselves." The milk was streaming off her breasts as she sat up.

"You look like the Nike at Samothrace. If she had a face it surely would be yours."

"Winged Victory, you are a monstrous flatterer, but I love it. Seriously, Sweetcakes, if Doug, Mary, Charlie and D. W. can form United Artists, why can't we make our own picture?"

Payson took her measure. Grace was unquestionably smarter than he was about business and he was grateful. "Think so, truly?"

"Truly. If we make it, the theater chains will gobble it up like all that sweaty popcorn they sell."

"God, what an idea. I don't know how I'll live through this next six months. I can't think of anything but that story!"

"Darla told me the most extraordinary news. She said within the next three years every studio—repeat: every studio—will switch over to talkies."

"I've heard that before. I figure they'll release phonographs synchronized to the pictures. They can hide the equipment and amplifiers in all those miles of organ pipes. You know, I hate to admit this, but I detest that organ music they score for pictures. It's a pity people can't hear what we hear while we're shooting."

" 'Fuck you' would go over big in Wisconsin." She laughed.

"The orchestras." He splashed her again.

"Payson, I don't think Darla's pulling my leg. You know who she sleeps with. *Jazz Singer* wasn't a fluke. Wolfie tells her everything."

Wolfie was to Darla's studio what Aaron Stone was to Payson's studio.

The corner of Payson's mouth turned down. "I still think it's hustle and hokum. Next you'll tell me they're ready to shoot in color. By the time they are, my liver spots ought to photograph nicely."

Her laugh floated up to the ceiling. "That's at least fifty years off."

"Color?"

"Liver spots."

"Ah." He smiled.

"Our profession is as tied to science as it is to business."

"I notice you left art out of the question."

"Yes; well, no use crying over spilt milk."

"Grace!" He grimaced.

"I believe sound is around the corner. No tricks, but sound. You and I ought to make out O.K. We were both trained on the stage and we've got good voices. God knows what the rest of the gang will do. A certain pair of sisters lug around the nation's thickest New York accent."

"They could all be out on their collective ears, couldn't they?" Payson prophesied with thudding clarity.

"We ought to take a little voice training on the QT to spruce up our instruments." She sang up and down the scales.

He sang with her. Then they broke into "Row, Row, Row Your Boat." Payson slopped over to her side of the gargantuan sunken tub. He started singing "Lady Be Good" to her. She chimed in. He lay back in the milk, singing all the while, and let the tip of his erect penis rise out of the water. They both sang "Lady Be Good" between fits of giggles. Grace left off singing and sucked him off. There was no sexual act Grace found revolting, although she'd heard from a few brave females willing to even whisper about such topics that they'd gagged. Oral sex ranked low on her list, but it was all in the game. Besides, Payson returned fair exchange.

Afterward she said, "I always think of sperm as a thousand gray fish eyes."

He lolled up to his neck in milk. "Fish eyes? Is that bad or good?"

"I don't know."

"I think of your juices as flakes of crushed pearls. How's that?"

"More poetic." She sank down next to him, completely covered by the liquid except for her neck. "Of the two of us, you're the artist."

"Go on."

"You are. I envy you sometimes."

"You should envy no one. Besides, acting is no profession for a man."

"Not that again. You're an artist and that's that. You can play counterpoint with hunting or something."

"Ever since you told me the card ranking system I use it every day. I love that." Animated, he cheerily changed the subject. "You know, I think Johnny's a heart. That's why he drinks so much."

"Yes."

"What's Greta?"

"Tough one. Let me think. A spade, the ace of spades."

"Greta?"

"Lots of common sense and sturdy. The money doesn't matter. She started out without a penny, anyway."

"Most of them did, honey. I feel sorry for them. Not Greta. She'll rise like cream. Sorry, there I go this time." She splashed milk in his face. Sputtering, he continued. "They've got no perspective. It's all now, now, now. You walk into their homes and everything is decorated to the last degree. It isn't bad enough they work on a set; they have to come home to one."

"Not everybody can inherit Chippendale," Grace said.

"You'd think they could learn from those who have. Like me, for instance." His teeth looked iridescent beneath his thin black mustache.

"The Arbiter of Taste, Payson Thorpe." She tooted an imaginary trumpet.

"And I taste good." He put a wet arm around her shoulder and hugged her. "Back to the cards. They made me think of myself: Payson, the damndest things go through your mind. I wonder do they go through anyone else's?"

"Like what?"

"I divide conversations into flavors: vanilla, chocolate, strawberry."

"What's this?"

"Vanilla. It's sweet and rich and subtle. Chocolate conversations are, well, more obvious. Does that make sense?"

"Keep going, then I'll tell you."

"Champagne conversations—that's easy."

"Easy." She closed her eyes and nodded, sagelike.

"Every time I talk to Aaron Stone that's a Limburger conversation."

"How about sulfuric?"

He sparkled. "You're so quick. And I've changed my mind. This isn't a vanilla conversation at all. This is pure nectar and ambrosia." His dark eyes glowed like brandy. "I'm so happy. You make me happy. I haven't been this happy since Please."

"Please?"

"You had your little dog, Bunky, when you were a girl and when I was a boy I had a wire brush of an Airedale named Please. You should have seen people when I'd call out, 'Come here, Please!' "

Grace, warmed from her beauty ritual and Payson's personality, laughed so hard she went under the milk and came up squirting it through her teeth.

"Your hair!" he said.

"You make me happy too." She dunked her head again in the milk. Then she dunked his head. Then they both sprang out of the tub and raced for the swimming pool.

• • •

Activity in the train station was in direct ratio to the heat. Late August broiled man to beast. With the exception of the ever-singing locusts, even the bugs were too hot to move.

Blue Rhonda fanned herself in the ladies' waiting room. As was her custom, she walked to the station to watch the people and the trains. But she couldn't convince her legs to turn around and walk home. It was too damn hot.

Placide Jinks slowly pushed a cart out on the platform. A whistle sounded in the distance.

Rhonda thought railroad tracks crisscrossed meadows like a Frankenstein monster's scars. Once in a great while she'd crack a book, to Banana's disbelief. Fantastic stories appealed to her and she felt so sorry for the Frankenstein monster that she moped about for days after he was killed.

The whistle blew again, closer. Curiosity got the better of her and she went to a window to see who was leaving or arriving on this dog day.

Hortensia and Carwyn were bidding goodbye to Edward and Mary Bland Love, now Mary Bland Banastre. The train glided into the station. As the mammoth engine passed her line of vision, Rhonda could see the engineer, wearing a red bandanna around his neck. Fortunately this engine didn't need stokers. They'd have died in ten minutes on such a day. A giant screw fed coal into the engine. Anything and everything to do with trains interested Blue Rhonda. Some of her customers worked for the L & N and she'd sweet-talk them into showing her things. Her biggest thrill was when Larry Gustaffsen, an engineer, took her up to where he stood when he drove the train. Lamps, huge handles and knobs that looked like faucets covered the entire front of the engine. It was like a giant cast-iron dashboard. Rhonda's idea of real power was driving a locomotive. Bunny's idea of real power was owning your own senator.

She watched Carwyn lift up Mary from the ground while Edward reached for her from the Pullman car. Rhonda, to herself, wished the young couple well.

A familiar, reed-thin figure stepped off the train, Reverend Linton Ray. He tipped his hat to the Banastres and headed for the general waiting room. Rhonda thought he looked exactly like a praying mantis.

On a whim she entered the waiting room, hoping to catch Linton before he left the station.

"Reverend Ray." He turned around, to behold his nemesis. Schooled on manners, he raised his hat, then realizing whom he was saluting, he jammed it back on his head.

"Aren't you glad to see me?"

"Miss Latrec, I'd welcome you with far more alacrity if you'd come into the fold."

"Yeah, I know."

His small expressionless eyes observed her. "You don't look so good."

Rhonda snapped, "Don't tell me what I already know."

"If you'll excuse me, I've got to catch a cab."

"Some good shepherd you are."

"I beg your pardon." So surprised was he at that barb, he forgot to be condescending.

"Isn't there a story in the Bible about all the sheep being in the flock except one bad little sheep?"

"I recall the sheep being lost, not bad."

"It amounts to the same thing." Rhonda's eyes danced. She was cooking up a new plan.

"What about it?"

"Didn't the good shepherd search high and low for the sheep and when he found it wasn't his rejoicing great?"

"So it was."

"Then why are you running for public office instead of finding lost sheep?"

"You'll be pleased to hear I have withdrawn from the race. After journeying to discuss this matter with a brother in Christ, I am convinced my flock needs me more."

"Good." That was news!

"Now, if you'll excuse me." He hurried for the door.

Rhonda called out, "What about the lost sheep?"

Linton stopped and she drew alongside him. "I don't understand you," he said.

"Ain't I a lost sheep—or maybe you think a black sheep?"

"I suppose you are."

"I'm giving you a chance to save me." Rhonda did her level best to stay serious.

"Uh . . ."

"I'm coming to listen to some sermons. And when I don't understand something, I'm asking questions."

"Surely not during the sermon."

"No. Afterwards." She smiled. "See you around, Reverend."

Transfixed, Linton pondered this event. A cab waited outside. He walked out to hail it. The sun bounced off the windowpane and blinded him. He stumbled and fell. Rapidly shaking his head and rubbing his eyes, he struggled to his feet.

The vision of Saul of Tarsus, he thought. Yes, I've been blinded by our Lord. How could I have forgotten my true vision? Thank you, God, for letting me see thy will. I shall bring that poor creature to your bosom. This is my calling. Thank you.

"Need help, Reverend?" The cabby put his hand under Linton's armpit.

As they drove off, Linton remained overwhelmed. He was chosen. Of all men he was chosen for the task, and the reward was such that men might not see, but he, Linton, would know he had been the bugle of God.

The sunlight blazed so that a few others stumbled upon leaving the dark waiting room and coming out on Water Street. Rather than imagining themselves latter-day saints, most of them said "Goddammit" and hurried on their way.

• • •

Paris lived like an exposed nerve. Once Edward and Mary left for New Haven, Hortensia would be in the house alone. However, with her schedule of polo, clubs and civic duties, he wasn't one hundred percent sure he'd get his way, plus he had to worry over Carwyn's appointments. He had two days remaining before he boarded the train for Charlottesville, although the administration at the university would have been euphoric had he not shown up. Like a horse on a tether, he grazed closed to the house. He packed his trunk for school. He organized his bookshelves. Desperate, he even painted his bedroom. This spurt of uncharacteristic physical labor fascinated Catherine, who watched a half hour of it.

If Hortensia was avoiding being home, she didn't betray it. She knew Paris grew more unreliable with each passing day. Amelie took Catherine over to Ada Jinks Tuesday for her lesson. Carwyn would be either in his office or at the club. So Tuesday afternoon she canceled her appearance at the garden club meeting, much to Lila's displeasure. Hortensia attended the garden club to appease Lila. She liked roses and snapdragons very much but she couldn't swoon over them like her mother. Icellee fussed at Hortensia for pulling out at the last minute and Hortensia, truthfully, declared she'd rather be at that particular garden club meeting than anywhere else in the world. Icellee then saw fit to tell Hortensia in vivid detail about Grace's orange trees, lemon trees and bougainvillea. After that recital she launched into the details of the flier film now in progress with Payson and Grace. Icellee wowed her friends by telling them films are not shot in sequence from beginning to end.

Hortensia bore this with a distracted patience. After one more flurry of discontent from her mother, she climbed into her Duesenberg and drove home. No sooner was she in the house than Paris appeared at the top of the stairs.

"Home?"

"Yes, I'm home for the afternoon." She looked up at him but made no move to go up the stairs. He gripped the banister until his knuckles were white. Perhaps he feared he'd leap from the top step to the bottom.

"Are you coming upstairs?"

"Yes, Paris, I'm coming upstairs." Her footfall was so light he couldn't hear it. Once at the top of the stairway, she stopped six inches from him. Neither of them spoke. He was pinching himself to believe his time had come. She was trying to believe it was a nightmare and she'd wake up. At last he took her hand and led her down the hallway to his bedroom, which still smelled of fresh paint.

He shut the door behind them. Hortensia paused for a moment in the middle of the room and then decided to get on with it. She walked over to the edge of the bed, sat down and took off her shoes. Paris stared, immobile. When she unbuttoned her blouse he sprang to life.

"Let me do that." Carefully he removed each article of clothing. She was firm from riding, and lean. Her skin was no longer that of a young person, but otherwise time left no mark upon her or whatever mark it did leave enhanced her allure rather than detracted from it. He was afraid to breathe.

He put his shoulder to her shoulder and pushed her back on the bed. Caressing her with his right hand, he tried to unbutton his pants with his left. Fumbling and now sweating with desire, he ripped off his shirt, placed both hands at the top of his expensive trousers and ripped them off too. Naked, he leapt in the bed on top of her. He kissed her neck, her shoulders, the insides of her arms down to her palms. He sucked each finger of each hand and then moved over to circle her breasts with his tongue. He may have been rotten to the core but he was a good lover. Straining against the impulse to just shove inside her, he played with her for half an hour. Finally, he slid his left arm under her neck, his right arm tight around her waist, and he entered her. Even then he didn't hurry the job. Near delirious from pleasure, he held off. Physically the two of them were attuned to one another. He convulsed in a cataclysmic ejaculation. He thought he'd write her name in the sky with sperm.

After they both recovered their wind, Hortensia asked him, "Are you finished?"

His arm still under her neck, he whispered, "Yes."

Gently, she moved him away from her and sat up. She shook her hair.

"What are you doing?"

"Leaving."

He was alarmed; his voice got higher. "Why?"

Still sitting, she half turned toward him. "You got what you asked for."

Thinking she'd turn on him, he struck first. "Don't tell me you didn't like it."

"You're good at what you do."

Hurt by her lack of emotion, he pressed, "But you liked it."

"Physically, yes. How can I deny that?"

He moved over on the sheets behind her and nibbled at the back of her neck. She brushed him away. "You've got the morals of a tarantula."

He bit her harder. "You've got it backwards. It's the female that kills the male."

"No matter." She began putting on her clothes.

"Don't leave."

"What else is there to say? I've kept my part of the bargain."

On his feet, he wrapped his arms around her and buried his face in her hair. "Fucking you was so good. Don't go away from me. I want you more."

She extracted herself from him without answering his demand and left the room. She gathered into herself like some creature retracting into a density higher than our own and therefore impenetrable.

Dazed, Paris fell back on his bed. He'd possessed his mother but she'd never belong to him. The act by which he'd sought to bind her to him only drove her further away. He realized this and tried to keep himself together by focusing on the act itself. She was wet, she was open, she was ready for him. She had to love him. He had no way of knowing she hadn't slept with anyone for ten years.

Paris was like a bit of cloth with a thread out of line. It was as though a divine hand now pulled on that thread. Sooner or later he'd unravel into nothingness.

• • •

School days meant skirts and crinoines that melted in the heat. Each morning Amelie inspected the outfits Catherine laid out. If she put a polka dot blouse with a plaid skirt she was corrected. By this time the inspection was perfunctory, as Catherine had mastered the nuances of fabric, pattern and cut. All through early October the heat lingered, but mercifully the nights were cool. Catherine hung up on her closet doorknob a crisp blue plaid dress with a little black ribbon bow. She loved clothes but she couldn't see the point of dressing up to attend school. By first recess she generally sported some dirt on her person because she played kickball, baseball and tag. Capture the flag was her favorite game and that of every other child in the school. If you were captured and imprisoned, the only way out of prison was to lie flat on the ground and stretch as far as you could. Each prisoner touched the toes of another prisoner, forming a human chain. When the chain got long enough to cross the boundaries between teams in the middle of the field, all the prisoners ran free. The only other way to be freed was if someone from your side broke through the line and tagged the prisoners before being tagged herself. Complaints from parents about ripped clothing turned the teachers away from assigning the game but didn't stop the children from playing. If she could wear overalls her good clothes would stay good. This was unthinkable, of course. The children did remove their shoes and socks when they played, so as to save those expensive items from excessive wear. Catherine, luckily, had all her material needs tended to. She wore a different dress every day and hair ribbons to match. She religiously shined her many pairs of shoes. Most of the other children wore the same garment every day for the week. Their mothers would strip the clothes off when they arrived home, wash the dress or shirt, hang it to dry and then iron it with the heavy irons sitting on the stove lid. The children of strivers stood out in the classroom. The children who would become day laborers stood out also. With each advancing grade the two groups of children grew apart from one another although they couldn't pinpoint why until about sixth grade, when background was fully understood to be more than parents, but one's social position and future expectations.

Catherine topped the ladder on this issue and she was beginning to fathom it. While a few classmates chirped about her mixed-race heritage, all the children perceived that Catherine was rich. She could have anything she wanted and she'd go all the way to a college or a finishing school. Snottiness based on money was foreign to her. The little girls who boasted of belonging to Montgomery's black upper crust disgusted her. She liked the sons and daughters of the poor, but while she played with them she wasn't one of them. Her teachers saw this and encouraged her in her studies, which was easy to do as she enjoyed them. Whatever happiness Catherine would have in this life would probably come through solitary pursuit; some kind of work where she could excel but not be dependent upon belonging to any group. As Ada now presided over her education, this inclination became a system. Without ever being told, Catherine understood she was to be a doctor. She offered no resistance. She would have taken any path at that time, as long as it was difficult. The harder the task, the more Catherine liked it. She was already reading at an eleventh-grade level. Once Athena, home from Atlanta for a visit, took Catherine into a veterinary operating room, where instead of being repelled, the child was fascinated. A predilection for science and exactitude was a Jinks trademark.

Placide would have preferred that she become an architect, although there were fewer women in that field than even in medicine. Ada's homage to practicality won him over. Doctors eat better than architects. A child in Catherine's precarious position must become self-sufficient. Marriage would not be the solution for her that it would be for other girls. No white man would marry her. As for a black man, well, there was always that kind of fellow who was a headhunter, who looked for a light-colored wife to improve his social position. A husband like that would do her no good. She needed someone who was also a professional and who could work with her as opposed to working against her.

Ada became quite protective of the child in the short time she'd been instructing her. Once she told Placide she thought Catherine resembled them somewhat; surely Amelie's people were no relation to the Jinkses or Ada's people, the Goodwaters. Placide nodded, pretending to be uninterested, which provoked a retort from his wife that men cared only for outside things, while kin was what counted. He growled a little for her sake. Ada appreciated a tangle from time to time. This topic was soon replaced by the scandal of the Brothers of Hannibal Lodge, an elite club of Montgomery's black men roughly on a par with the Princeton or Yale Club in the white community. The treasurer absconded with all the funds. Everyone was in an uproar and feeling very guilty because Placide held that position for the last five years and was finally ousted by a caucus of younger men who said they needed a college-educated man. Ada relished the contrite faces when she walked down the street. Calling her man old was enough to get the lava flowing; insinuating that he was behind the times intellectually brought forth an eruption. Prudence, caution and long-term investing were Placide's watchwords at the lodge and in his home.

Vindication of Placide was good news enough, but even better news for Ada was the announced resignation of the elderly principal of the school. Unanimously, Ada was elected to take over.

Knowing she took her lessons with the new principal gave Catherine a shiver, even though she liked Ada. Her image of a principal was of someone who gave you the strap.

Catherine neatly packed her book bag and bounded down the three flights of stairs to the kitchen. Bacon, biscuits, grits and scrambled eggs waited on the table. Catherine sat at the table and joyously gobbled up everything on her plate. The door into the kitchen swung open on noiseless hinges and Hortensia came in.

"Amelie, that smells so good I'm eating two breakfasts today."

"Plenty here." Amelie put the frying pan back on the stove.

Hortensia sat at the table next to Catherine. "Don't you look pretty."

"Thank you. You look pretty too."

"With a tongue like that in your head you'll go far in this world, my dear." Hortensia winked at her. "Did you do your lessons?"

"Yes, ma'am."

Hortensia pointed to the book bag. "May I inspect?"

Eagerly Catherine opened her bag. She was proud of her papers. First she handed Hortensia her arithmetic book. "See, I do fractions and percents. Baby stuff."

"What neat papers. Mine were neat but they rarely had the right answers."

"I bet you were the best."

"Not at arithmetic." Hortensia replaced the book and withdrew the small Latin volume lent the child by Ada. "You're already reading."

Catherine beamed. "I can speak it too. But the reading is harder. There's so much to remember. There's endings for everything. They're like little cuff links."

"What?" Hortensia laughed.

"You know, little cuff links you pinch a sleeve with. If you didn't put those endings there, everything hangs open. The words wouldn't make any sense." Catherine drew in her breath and exhaled as she'd seen Ada do. "But, Aunt Tense, I don't understand how someone like Julius Caesar, who was so smart, couldn't figure out how to talk like we do. We don't use endings and we make sense."

"I couldn't agree with you more. I don't understand why the whole world doesn't speak English. It certainly would be more convenient." Hortensia put her arm around Catherine and hugged her closer. "Is it true you're in love?"

"Mother, you told on me!" Catherine accused Amelie.

Flipping an egg over so the yolk wouldn't break, Amelie shrugged.

"Ah ha. It's true." Hortensia tickled her. "I bet it's Piggy Latham."

Catherine gagged. "No!"

"Such a response, it must be love."

"I hate Piggy Latham. He picks his nose and sticks buggers under his desk."

"Catherine, need you be so graphic at the breakfast table?" Hortensia grimaced.

"That's right, young lady." Amelie shook a spatula at her and spritzed herself with grease. Both Hortensia and Catherine laughed.

"I take it you won't reveal the source of your heart's desire?"

"I'm not telling." Catherine pretended to button her mouth.

"It's just as well, because I bet you change your mind tomorrow." Amelie taunted her.

"How's Ruthie?" Hortensia asked.

"A pill. I don't like girls anymore. They're silly." Catherine pouted.

Amelie delivered eggs, bacon and another plate of biscuits to the table. Catherine reached up to take one before the plate was on the table and Amelie smacked her hand. "Mind your manners."

"Amelie, we'd all die without you. Starvation." Hortensia savored a mouthful of bacon.

"Did you like girls when you were in school?"

"No. I didn't like girls until I got married. Now I like them fine. It takes a long time to make true friends."

"Well, I don't think I'm ever going to like them. They act one way when we're all together and then when the boys come around they giggle or pick fights. Blah." She closed her eyes and wrinkled her nose.

"Wait and see," Hortensia advised. "Are you sure it isn't Piggy Latham?"

"No." Catherine shook her head. Deciding to devil Hortensia in return, she said with excitement, "Aunt Tense, what's that crawling up the wall over there?"

When Hortensia turned to look, Catherine stole a biscuit off her plate.

"You little sneak."

"Catherine, put that biscuit back on Mrs. Banastre's plate."

"We're only playing, Mother."

"It's fine, Amelie."

Amelie glanced up at the old railroad clock on the wall, which Bartholomew Reedmuller gave his daughter many years ago. "Sciddle daddle do, miss, you'll be late for school."

Dutifully Catherine wiped her mouth, picked up her book bag and hopped out of the chair. She kissed Hortensia on the cheek and then kissed Amelie. As she opened the back door to leave, Hortensia sang out, "Piggy Latham, Piggy Latham."

Catherine screamed in pleasure and skipped down the stairs.

"Oh, to be young again." Hortensia sighed.

Amelie, hands on hips, gazed out the screened door and wondered, too, where the years had gone.

• • •

Two stuntmen died in the flier film. Rather than squelch the story, the studio played it up. Blurbs like "the most dangerous movie ever made" began to fill film magazines. Both Payson and Grace were sickened by the entire episode. Things like this happened before, perhaps the most famous incident being the filming of the naval battle in *Ben-Hur*. Ramon Novarro still refused to talk about the poor Italian peasants who drowned during that sequence. All the while, the director had kept the cameras rolling. In the director's defense, the Italians had said they could swim before taking the job as rowers, soldiers and sailors, but work was hard to get and the Americans should have known the men were desperate. The studio hushed up the entire affair. Part of Aaron Stone's intelligence was in realizing he could push audiences and actors farther than anyone imagined. He masterminded the whole danger advertising campaign, complete with heartbreaking photos of the children of the deceased stuntmen placing wreaths on their fathers' graves. The anticipation created assured the movie's success.

People also wanted to see Grace and Payson as a team. They were good together. The studio already prepared a film for them after they completed *The Man in the Iron Mask*. It was to be their first talkie and the publicity machines popped into first gear.

Aaron also had a great gift for bringing pictures in on time and on budget. He set a record with the flier film. He was meticulous, efficient and ruthless. It was inevitable that he would become head of Pacifica Studios. The future rested with talkies. Aaron was determined to create a new caste of stars who were dependent upon him. He'd break the backs of those insufferable silent kings and queens. There'd be a few crossovers but only very few at Pacifica. Aaron feverishly searched for new, beautiful faces. He found a gorgeous young man with a flat Midwestern voice. Perfect for the hinterlands, he thought, and he tossed him into the machinery, where the young man had his hair curled, his teeth capped, his eyebrows tweezed. He emerged even more beautiful, if somewhat antiseptic. But Aaron's strongest quality was in his ability to pick women. He felt so competitive and hateful toward other men he couldn't develop them as he developed women. He devised a system for screening all prospective females. First they were divided into brunette, redhead and blonde, with a special category for exotics, i.e., Chinese. Next came their eye color and after that their vital statistics. On the upper-right-hand corner of each dossier was a small box for rating acting talent and intelligence. This was in code: TT was the highest acting rating, ZI was the lowest intelligence rating. He purposely sought women who could act but were dumb. Those creatures he could control absolutely. He also bought off their agents, which was relatively easy. Within a year's time Pacifica would burst upon the screen with an army of fresh faces, talking. Some nights Aaron couldn't sleep for planning.

Grace observed the trainees with a mixture of concern and pity. She didn't like the idea of being moved over or bumped off. Who would? But she also knew her breed was tougher than these kids. They would be squeezed dry like sponges. She was less dependent emotionally on other people's opinions of her. If audiences stopped liking her as a star, she didn't give a good goddamn. The accolades and adoration were lovely, but didn't alter her opinion of herself. The only person she envied was Payson, who she knew was a true actor. Grace was good, and with Payson, remarkably good, since he knew how to draw a performance from her. Payson would probably die if he couldn't act, although he didn't know it and griped about his profession constantly. Grace would simply go on to something else. She was a Deltaven and the security of her heritage sustained her no matter how remote or antiquated it might seem to someone else. She knew her place, she knew her people and she knew what was expected of her. Southerners always had the wisdom to realize that form is as important as content. In moments of crisis or confusion, form can literally keep you alive until you figure things out. For that she was grateful, although she still hated the pecking order. If you listened to every jumped-up Southerner in Alabama, they'd tell you their family came over with Smith at Jamestown, Virginia. No state could possibly have spawned as many refugees as Virginia, but the name reverberated, a great golden bell. Try getting someone to admit their family really started with an English horse thief dumped in Georgia by Oglethorpe. While she thought all that ridiculous, Grace did believe her people first settled in Virginia.

She leaned on a reclining board so as not to disturb her sumptuous, fatiguing costume. How anyone walked around in the France of Louis XIV was beyond her. The crew adjusted lights one more time. Payson became obsessive with detail. The picture had to be authentic. They'd been shooting for two weeks, but it was already apparent that the performance of everyone in this project was remarkable. Even the extra playing an old beggar woman seemed real. Sometimes Grace would blink to remember she lived in the United States and it was the twentieth century.

Each picture becomes a small nation. The citizens live together, eat together, suffer together, and more often than not, sleep together. The tone of the group is set by the director and the stars. Payson created an environment where everyone wanted to give his best. Despite all the screen magazine photos of stars cavorting in a round of endless pleasure, filming was grueling labor. Payson took pains to provide for the physical comforts of his people. No one was too lowly for him not to inquire about him, settle a dispute or play a practical joke which restored people's good humor.

Since he wore a mask, he had to rely on gesture and body posture to convey emotion. He also played the twin brother, the king. One slight twitch at the corner of the mouth suggested duplicity. Rather than create the king as an outright villain, he played him as a sophisticated, bloodless man. Put the mask on Payson's head and everything changed. He exuded despair, courage, warmth, decency, without overplaying his hand. The other people, actors and technicians, usually stayed on to watch him even if they had no part in the scene.

Grace bought him an Airedale puppy at the beginning of the film. They named her Thank You and the dog had the run of the set. Before she was four months old she was fat. People fed her constantly and the creature enjoyed endless attention. Life was wonderful.

Linton Ray, high in his pulpit, pinch-hit for God. His sermon this week was his interpretation of the Sermon on the Mount. Blue Rhonda had been attending these performances for a few weeks now. Morbid fascination brought her back again and again. Browbeaten into reading the Bible as a child and attending Sunday school or face a beating from her father, she was surprised at how much she remembered. For the last six weeks she'd been reading books about Buddhism, finding it attractive.

Banana Mae almost took smelling salts when she discovered Blue Rhonda reading and then inspected what she was reading. Banana Mae pooh-poohed this latest phase of Blue Rhonda's, but she didn't know Blue Rhonda was dying. Rhonda would never grovel before a Hebrew or Christian God, but matters of the soul, previously scorned, became of great importance.

Linton intoned that the meek shall inherit the earth. Blue Rhonda thought, No doubt after the rich have squeezed it dry.

The faces of Linton's parishioners resembled glazed fruit. They certainly didn't listen to what he was saying, but rather thought that the act of sitting in the pew for an hour on Sunday insured against descent into hell. Rhonda wondered if the origin of all religion was in the stark fear of death. It was much on her mind these days and gave her an aura of intuition she previously lacked or perhaps blocked. She could tell who was happy, who was lying to himself, and strangely, who was dying. Bartholomew Reedmuller was dying. Whether he knew it or not Rhonda couldn't say, but the last time she saw him disembark from the Birmingham train she thought he resembled a dark lighthouse. Bartholomew never had the guts to break away and design the buildings he should have designed. Status and reward kept him in line. It all seemed very foolish now and Rhonda felt pity for him. He was an old man and lived an exemplary life, but what's an exemplary life when you've betrayed your deepest impulses? Rhonda had not betrayed hers. She'd wanted a good time. She was sorry she hadn't wanted anything more profound. Linton thought his life lived on a par with the archangels. He conceived of himself as a noble creature sacrificing his life to lift up mankind. Rhonda figured it was a sop to his ego. For her that wiped out all the grandeur of his imagined martyrdom. At least she was honest. The worst liars are the people who lie to themselves.

After each sermon Blue Rhonda would wait discreetly in the chancery to ask Linton questions or simply to torment him. She couldn't figure out what drew her back to these sparring matches, but she did enjoy getting one up on him. He lacked a sense of humor and that made him an easy target. Rhonda wondered why God didn't laugh. The laughter of the Greek and Roman gods boomed through the heavens. You can't trust a person who has no sense of humor and she applied that to this Hebraic-Christian deity with its icy benedictions. Once in a tussle with Linton he asked her why she turned everything into a joke, why she tried to make everyone laugh. She said, ''Because we're afraid." That went right by him. Linton lived in a world of tight rules, neat systems. He had an answer for everything. And what he couldn't answer he explained away by saying God's will was impossible for a human mind to comprehend. This was supposed to give you comfort. Your child dies. God wants the little sweetheart in heaven. You waken in the middle of the night, your heart racing, and feel a nameless dread. It's God telling you to mend your ways. Millions of people die in World War I. We deserved it. We're evil vermin that need to be periodically cleansed. All this because Eve picked that apple off the tree. Suffering is woman's fault. Men are bad but women are worse. And smarter. Adam was a dumbbell. You've got to beware of women constantly. The female principle is powerful, gifted and evil.

Sometimes evil came out of good and sometimes good came out of evil. Blue Rhonda recognized that hers was not a great mind, but she was reasonably intelligent and she knew there were no easy answers.

Having shaken the hands of his flock as they filed out the front door, Reverend Ray turned his attentions to Rhonda, waiting in the little room off the entrance.

"How did you like today's sermon?"

"I would have liked it a lot better if the man sitting in front of me hadn't farted his way through it."

Linton's face curdled. Bad enough humans sin. Worse that they had body functions. "The Sermon on the Mount is the most beautiful passage in the Bible."

"In the New Testament maybe," Rhonda replied, "but my favorite passage is the twenty-third Psalm or that one about speaking with the tongues of angels but if you lack charity you sound like a cymbal."

"First Corinthians, thirteen." Linton exuded authority.

She had little to say to him this Sunday. "I suppose no one's even faulted you on your memory, Reverend. I'll see you next Sunday if I'm up to it."

"Have you changed your ways, Miss Latrec?"

"No."

Frowning, he reminded her, "Don't continue to defile yourself. Remember your body is a temple."

"That's right, and mine's open twenty-four hours a day for worship." She left him fuming.

Riding home on the streetcar, she thought over her successive arguments with Linton. If she was a whore, why wasn't it God's will? But Linton's version of life was that when you do wrong it's your fault and when you do right God takes credit. God bears no responsibility for evil. Well, Rhonda couldn't much be bothered with theological refinements today. She figured it didn't matter if what she believed was true or false. It gave her the will to live.

She alighted from the trolley and walked the rest of the way home. The sun sparkled on every windowpane. On the side of one wooden building the letters ICE were painted in blue, with white ice painted over the top of each letter. She must have passed that building a thousand times in her life in Montgomery, but today she noticed how perfectly beautiful it was. Everything seemed so crystal clear and alive.

She could see far up the street that Lotowana, Bunny and Banana Mae sat on the front porch. Her mums, zinnias and other fall flowers spilled unrestrained onto the grass from their flower beds. As she came closer the three waved. She decided to have a little fun with Lottie by asking her the first question Buddhists practice on the Way. The Way to what was never quite clear to Rhonda, since Nirvana sounded like a skin disease, but who was she to quibble with people's versions of heaven, afterlife or oblivion? She'd trade them all in for life eternal on earth. Bad as it may be, Blue Rhonda loved earth.

"Rhonda, Minnie Rue and Leafy Strayhorne had a huge fight this morning," Bunny dryly reported.

"Broke every window in the living room," Lottie said.

Rhonda took her seat. "Why would those two get into a fight? One's as bad as the other."

"Yeah, they're like the difference between the Democratic and Republican parties, syphilis and gonorrhea." Banana smiled.

"Nobody's talking," Bunny supplied, "but it will come out sooner or later. Everything does."

"Yeah." Lottie agreed with her boss.

"Still reading all those books?" Bunny asked Rhonda. What Rhonda didn't know was that the three had been discussing her in her absence. They weren't stupid. Her appearance had changed. Rhonda, thin to begin with, was now dangerously skinny. Her spirits stayed high but she looked ill. Banana called Rhonda's doctor on the sly but the doctor wouldn't say anything other than that Rhonda was severely anemic. When Banana pressed the doctor, he said what transpires between a patient and his client can't be revealed to anyone else. Banana was actively worried. She and Rhonda lived together for so many years that she took Blue Rhonda for granted like sunshine. Bunny and Lottie, too, felt a gnawing concern. Bunny kept a quiet eye on Rhonda while Lottie continually deviled her, told stories, did anything to get Rhonda to laugh.

"Lottie, I've got one for you. This is the first question a Buddhist is asked. Kind of like the First Commandment but different. Are you ready?"

"Yes." Lottie's shoulders stiffened; she was eager to apply herself.

"What's the sound of one hand clapping?"

Lottie slapped her in the face. "There, you silly twit."

Rhonda blinked and then burst out laughing. Lottie was right.

. . .

Ada rearranged her family photos in her semiannual bash of cleaning. Spring housecleaning and fall housecleaning loomed as large on her calendar as Christmas did on other people's calendars. Usually she kept the pictures of her children upstairs, but on a whim she brought them down and scattered them throughout the parlor. After an afternoon of polishing the ornate frames, she set them up in a semicircle.

A few months before, she started taking her purse to bed with her. Placide raised holy hell over that so she put the purse under the bed but carefully placed the money in her pillowcase. She didn't tell him about that. He couldn't understand why she'd want to sleep with her purse, but Ada said it made good sense; if they were robbed in the night, who would look for a purse in the bed? Placide assured her they would not be robbed in the middle of the night.

Catherine finished up her lesson but didn't move. She couldn't get up until Ada dismissed her, and Ada was taking a long time to go over her papers. Catherine heard children calling to one another outside in the crisp fall air. She longed to get home to her pony.

"Here, you misplaced the accent. See." Ada pointed to a little scratch on the page.

"I won't do it next time."

"So that makes your score ninety-nine instead of one hundred."

Catherine should have been disappointed, but she was too anxious to play. "I'll do better next time. Is that all for today, Mrs. Jinks?"

Ada looked at her wristwatch, an anniversary gift from her husband. "You've been here an hour. Do you understand today's lesson?"

"Yes."

"All right." Ada got up and retrieved Catherine's coat.

"Did you change your furniture around?" the child asked.

"Yes. Haven't you got ready for winter yet? Time to put away all the summer drapes."

A familiar face beckoned from across the living room. Catherine walked over to look at Hercules. The pose was different from the one in Amelie's photograph, but the man was unmistakably Hercules. Catherine was careful not to touch anything.

"Mrs. Jinks . . . is his name Hercules?"

Ada, stacking her books, didn't look up. "Yes. He died in nineteen eighteen."

"He was a boxer, wasn't he?"

"Catherine, who's been talking to you about my son?" She sighed. "Well, I suppose he's still a hero around these parts. He was the best athlete anyone's ever seen and probably ever will see."

"He's my father," Catherine stated simply.

"What?" Ada almost knocked a book on the floor.

"Mother keeps his picture on a table. How come you don't know?"

Ada sat down hard. Of course, Catherine looked like a Jinks. But Amelie? Something was very wrong. "Who told you that Hercules was your father?" Her voice was kindly. She didn't want to frighten the girl. Discovering her grandmother like this was enough.

"Mother. She doesn't say much. But he was a good man . . . wasn't he?"

"He was a very good man." It was hard for Ada to think of him as a man. For her he would always be her boy.

"You're my grandmother then, aren't you?"

"It certainly looks that way." Ada motioned for her to come near her.

"I never had a grandmother who was a principal."

Ada hugged the child. She'd found a bit of life she thought she'd lost so very long ago. Hercules returned to her in a flood. She could see him in this child and wondered that she was so blind as not to make the connection before. She knew immediately that Amelie was not Catherine's mother and she perceived Placide knew a great deal more than he was telling. She'd settle that with him when he came home.

"Catherine, who else knows about Hercules?"

"Oh, we never talk about it. Mother says people pry, so it's best to shut up no matter what the subject."

"Amelie has good sense." Ada lightly inquired, "Does Mrs. Banastre know?"

"I don't know."

"She's kind to you, isn't she?"

Catherine's eyes brightened. "Oh, yes, Mrs. Jinks. She's the very best person I know. She looks at my papers and she always asks how I do in my Latin. She rides with me too, and someday I'll ride as good as she does."

"I'm sure you will."

"Mrs. Jinks?"

"Honey, call me Grandma. I would love to hear that name."

Shyly Catherine said, "Grandma, I like you. You're very smart. Can I tell you a secret? Something I've never, ever told anybody. Not even my mother."

"Of course you can tell me, and I promise not to repeat it."

"Someone's lying to me."

"Lying?" Ada wasn't sure what to expect.

"People say I'm half and half. I can see that. I've got light eyes. How can I be half and half when Hercules was dark and so is Mother? Did I do something wrong?"

Ada hugged the child tighter. "No, precious, you didn't do one single thing wrong. The wrong has been done by others. Now don't you worry over it."

"But you think I've been lied to, don't you?"

Ada didn't want to further upset the child, but she was not one to duck an issue. "Yes, Catherine, I think there's a great deal that must be answered. Whether that means you've been lied to, I don't know. Often in this world older people believe they must protect children by not telling them the truth or by waiting until they're older. I don't think anyone is trying to hurt you."

"I'm old enough. If I can do Latin, I'm old enough."

"I suspect you are. But sometimes you learn more in silence than you do by asking a question."

Catherine looked at Ada. "Maybe."

"Just for now, Catherine, let's not upset the apple cart. I think if we both are quiet we can solve this mystery without, well, without hurting a great many people."

Catherine wasn't sure why her finding out about her bloodlines would hurt others, but she had faith in Ada and agreed with her for the time being.

Before allowing her to go home, Ada made sure the child was all right. Catherine's resilience amazed her, but then she remembered her own childhood. Not knowing was always worse than knowing. Catherine was solid. The adults around her were another matter.

When Placide sailed through the door, whistling, Ada, arms folded across her chest, waited on the davenport.

"Placide, I want to talk with you."

"I can see that." He hung up his coat. "Everything's ready for winter."

"Yes. Catherine Etheridge came for her lesson today."

"Good."

Arms still folded, Ada asked him, "Why didn't you tell me?"

He noticed the pictures in the room and said nothing.

"I'm the girl's grandmother. I have a right to know. All these years. How it would have eased the pain to know Hercules left something behind."

"It's not that easy." He wearily sat in the chair opposite her.

"Blood calls to blood. What else is there?"

"There's her mother's blood too." He would not be drawn into a fight with her.

"Amelie? Ha!"

"I didn't say Amelie."

"Well, who then? Who is more important than you or I? We could have raised her and we should have raised her."

"No. You and I had our children."

"What's that got to do with Catherine?"

"A child belongs with her mother."

"Well, then goddammit, who is her mother!"

"Hortensia Banastre."

Ada collapsed back in her chair. If she'd thought about it she would have registered suspicions long ago, but she never thought about it. Such couplings usually occur in reverse and women like Ada were accustomed to raising the offspring, or miscellany. "I can't believe it," she said, even though she knew it had to be true.

"If you could have seen her at the funeral home you would find it painfully easy to believe." Placide swallowed.

"My boy, my sweet boy, what in God's name was he doing? What was he thinking of?"

"Neither of them were thinking," Placide said.

A flurry of indignation aroused her. "She has two sons of her own. The child belonged with us."

"No, the child belongs with her mother." Placide was firm.

"What kind of mother? Catherine thinks Amelie is her mother."

"I know," he sighed. "These things work their way out in time or they stay hidden forever. That's not your affair."

"It most certainly is."

"Ada, the woman had nothing. Everything and nothing. I pity her. I pitied her then and I pity her now. Catherine is her life."

"What about her sons?"

"You know as well as I do that Paris is riding to hell in a handcart. As for Edward, he's turned out all right—but Catherine is her life."

Ada did know of the Banastre estrangements. In Montgomery even the trees whispered, and the blacks knew a great deal more about the white families than the white families could ever hope to know about one another or the black families. Struggling for survival makes the senses keen.

"You should have told me."

"I did what I thought was right." Placide stared at the photo of Hercules.

"You and I share everything. I—I'm stunned that you betrayed me." Ada's eyes filled with tears.

"I deceived you; I didn't betray you. I'm sorry, Ada. I believe I did the right thing. I didn't know myself that Hortensia was pregnant until she remained in Chicago for so long. It didn't take much to put two and two together. I was afraid you'd try to take the baby from her. And I made the judgment that she needed that baby more than you did."

Ada quietly sat for a long time. Then she whispered, "They must have been mad, the two of them. Utterly mad."

"They were in love."

Ada quoted from her favorite ancient Greek playwright: " 'Those whom the gods wish to destroy they first make mad.' "

"Honey, we both know that more people cross that thin line between madness and sanity, between black and white, than anyone will ever admit. Who's to say if they were wrong? If Hercules were alive today we'd tell him he was wrong, but was he? Was he really wrong?''

Absentmindedly, Ada hugged herself. ''Oh, God, I don't know.''

He tiptoed over and sat next to her. ''What's there to know? Men make one set of rules and the human heart makes another set. People are pulled in two directions at once. I don't even try to understand anymore.''

Ada, fiercely intellectual, would never be content with such a viewpoint, but for now she had nothing to offer in its place.

He asked her, ''Do you think Catherine will be O.K.?''

''Yes. Catherine will be just fine.''

In the asylum of his personality, Paris suffocated. A golden-red Albemarle County fall provided him with no pleasure. His weekly, then nightly, visits to Marguerita's made his cravings worse. No prostitute could give him what he wanted.

He began to lose weight and he rarely attended classes. That was nothing new, but his haunted look was. His fraternity brothers assumed he was taking drugs. They were very easy to obtain, especially if one had money and put the touch on an upper-class physician. Laws restrained only the middle class and the poor. The rich could always get what they wanted.

He wrote hundreds of letters to his mother and then tore them up or threw them in the tiny fireplace of his room behind the serpentine walls. He once thought of going up to New Haven to kill his detestable prig of a brother, but that wouldn't do him a bit of good and the last thing he wanted to do was get caught or wind up supporting his child. Why people couldn't fuck and not conceive was a mystery to him. Conception loomed large in his mind as an evil that befalls mankind. There ought to be a button you could push when you were ready to have children. They should have absolutely nothing to do with sex. He'd never thought about it until Mary Bland Love came down with child, like distemper. Why he ever got within ten feet of that bookworm now tormented him. And worse, his brother was actually happy with that ever-fattening creature. Edward was happy while he writhed. Edward was too dull to be happy; he was probably only content. This thought didn't please him all that much. He couldn't bear for Edward to have anything.

He thought of Hortensia two decades earlier, conceiving him, Paris. She probably closed her eyes and wished Carwyn would roll off. She was too beautiful to have married Carwyn. She should have been chaste, like Artemis or Athena. The thought that another man slept with his mother drove him out walking in the night. He used to pace before Edgar Allan Poe's old room and wonder if the poor devil ever felt as wretched as he did. Could Poe have even dreamed of sleeping with his mother? What was Ulalume compared to that?

Paris inhabited blue-neon nights, red-shaded dreams. He wouldn't last long.

• • •

Hanging out of her bedroom window this Halloween twilight, Catherine watched the white children wend their way down to Court Square. They looked like ants on the trail of honey. The Great Witch Hunt was only for whites. No one said so, but it just was, that's all. The odor of turning leaves excited her. A night like this was too good to waste. She wasn't all black. In fact, she was pretty sure she was half white. Therefore she ought to be allowed in on half the hunt.

A quick look in Amelie's closet convinced her there was nothing to use for a costume. Anyway, Amelie was big as a house. Catherine ran to the mirror and decided she'd better cover her face. Keeping that in mind, she skipped over to the linen closet, retrieved a worn sheet, as she knew her mother would kill her if she took a good one. She cut holes for eyes, made a crooked smile with her watercolor set, took all of three seconds to admire her work, and then folded the sheet under her arm. She tiptoed down the back stairwell. Nearing the kitchen, she heard Amelie singing to herself. She'd have to slip out the back door, which meant crossing the kitchen. Amelie puttered about, choosing the right frying pan. Catherine waited and waited, but the woman betrayed no signs of vacating the kitchen. Finally, she headed toward the pantry. That fast, Catherine zipped out the door, noiselessly closing it behind her.

Free of the house, she donned her makeshift costume and ran all the way down to the big fountain in the middle of Court Square. The children were being divided into teams. Catherine heard names called out. Another ten-year-old, Gretchen Sommerfield's name was called. Catherine answered and was assigned to the Orange team. Gretchen lived a few houses away from Catherine and she knew Gretchen had the mumps. When one of the children said how glad he was she was feeling better, a knot came up in her throat and she whispered, "Thank you."

The two teams received their first clues. Randolph Baker, captain of the Oranges, read it aloud. That one was easy. As they raced from one little shop to another, Catherine felt so happy. This was fun. The children were giggling, screaming and romping. The next clue read was: "Stars fell on Alabama in 1833. But where I stand, there's only one star for me."

The older children kept silent. Those were the rules, as clues were progressive. Catherine wanted to speak, but was afraid someone might recognize her voice. Even though she attended the black school and the children around her were all white, sometimes they did play together. The little ones were puzzled. Finally, daring to risk it, Catherine spoke firmly. "It's Jeff Davis's six-pointed star." A murmur rippled through the crowd. Randolph asked for discussion. It seemed obvious once Catherine pointed it out. "Good work, Gretchen," he said. "Let's go to the west portico and check." A herd of Oranges rumbled to the capitol, where the star gleamed up at them. It was on this spot that Jefferson Davis took the oath of office to become President of the Confederacy.

A white envelope was attached to the star. Randolph plucked it up and read the next clue. From blocks away they heard the shouts of the Blacks. This always spurred teams to further action. Harold Richards headed up the Blacks and Randolph dearly wanted to best him in this

Great Witch Hunt. Harold had just stolen away the young lady of Randy's heart.

Catherine felt a shiver when she heard the yells. She jumped up and down in one place in her excitement. Another ten-year-old reached out and took her hand. She quickly looked down, but the other child said nothing. He didn't notice my hand is darker than his, she thought to herself. The fear was soon interrupted by a solution to that clue, and off they went.

The clues stiffened with each finding. The eighth clue reduced the Orange team to sitting in a circle pulling their hair. Randolph read it one more time in desperation: "I'm old as Egypt yet brand new. My men wear skirts for mysteries true."

David Hutter, a sixteen-year-old, called out, "What mysteries? There isn't even a fun house around here."

"I don't know any man who wears a skirt," moaned another voice.

Catherine pondered this. Egypt held her attention. She felt that was a bigger clue than the skirts. The Oranges had to win, they just had to. She vaguely remembered being in Bartholomew Reedmuller's office maybe two years ago. That's a very long time when you're ten, but she remembered a drawing. On a huge slanted table were drawings of Egyptian motifs and Bartholomew kindly explained to her what all those symbols meant and why he was using them. Using them on what? A building. Now she had it on the tip of her tongue. She could see the drawing all at once. Where was it and what was it called?

A roar from faraway Blacks deepened their gloom.

Catherine shot up and bellowed, "It's a building. It's a temple—the Scottish Rite Temple!"

Randolph stared at her. The kids her own age stared at her. She didn't sound like Gretchen Sommerfield, and Gretchen was already known among her peers as dumb. How'd that dodo bird come up with this? There was little time to worry about the source of the answer.

"It's our only chance. Let's hope you're right, Gretch."

In confusion, anxiety and hope, the team tore over to the new limestone structure. Pinned to the great doors was the next clue. Fired by their conquest of that tough one, the Oranges whipped through the ninth clue and received the tenth about five minutes before the Blacks received the identical tenth clue. Their spies reported back to them that they had a slight edge. After hasty deliberation, they decided the Episcopal graveyard was the target.

Nearing the end of the search, Randolph, running in the lead, looked ahead into the graveyard and beheld a man swinging from a tree, hanging by a rope. Jolted, he herded his team in front of the rectory and took two other large boys with him. One sentry was posted to alert Harold Richards if the Blacks came up too quickly. They did just that and Harold fussed and fumed until the sentry whispered in his ear. He then took two of his best friends and left his team to eye the Oranges suspiciously. By now nerves were at a fever pitch. Who would win and what was happening?

Harold walked over to Randolph and saw what his opponent had seen: a man hanged by the neck, dressed in a witch's costume. There was no clue or message. This wasn't the end of the search and it wasn't a joke. That man was good and dead, his tongue dropping further each second.

"We'd better call the police," Randolph said.

Harold quickly agreed. He felt green around the gills. "I'll go back and keep the teams in check."

Randolph and his friends rang the bell at the rectory. When the Reverend Fitzhugh heard the news he, too, had to run out and see. He then ran right back in and called the police. Once he was off the phone, Randolph asked him if this was the end of the hunt. Was the Great Witch here? Owners of the finish line, whether a house, a graveyard or a railroad shed, were always consulted by the Great Witch Hunt Committee. The reverend said the Great Witch was not in his graveyard.

Back outside, Randolph consulted with Harold again. A few curious teammates were severely reprimanded for trying to sneak into the graveyard. Hardly anyone knew what was going on.

Harold spoke loudly to both teams. "It seems we've both taken a wrong turn. We'll have to study the clue again and see who wins. This is not the place."

"Oranges, over here," Randolph called.

As they conferred once more, Cedrenus Shackleford drove up with the police ambulance. The children were more than curious. Just to get them out of there, Randolph shouted, "I've got it. Follow me."

Harold, taken in, charged after him with the Blacks.

Whether by luck or angelic assistance, Randolph led his team into the Lutheran graveyard, where they found a very alive Great Witch, Icellee Deltaven, in her glory. The Blacks were but a hair's breadth behind.

Randolph and Harold informed Icellee of events. She then did an extraordinary thing. "Boys and girls, quiet, please. Tonight has been a very unusual night. You all arrived within a split second of one another. As the Great Witch and with the power invested in me, I declare both teams the winners for nineteen twenty-eight."

Caps and masks were tossed in the air. Children danced. Costumes were ripped. In the thrill of the moment, Catherine forgot and tore off her sheet. No one noticed until the badges started being pinned on the children by Icellee and the marshals. A little boy said, without intending to be cruel, "Hey, there's a pickaninny here." No one paid much mind, as they were still celebrating. Another voice piped up, "Great Witch, Great Witch, there's a nigger here." That word froze out the group in no time.

Randolph walked over to the object of intense scrutiny. "Were you the little ghost who said you were Gretchen Sommerfield?"

Terrified, Catherine answered, "Yes."

Randolph turned to the celebrants and said, "We Oranges owe some of our success tonight to—what's your name?"

"Catherine Etheridge," came the wavering reply.

"She deserves a medal and that's that."

Silence followed and then one of the older girls cheered, "An Orange is an Orange. Thank you, Catherine." Half-hearted cheering followed, but the children were upset. Something had been violated and they were entangled in a web not of their own making. Most of them wanted to like Catherine, especially the Oranges, but a few people were outraged. But even the ones who wanted to like her wondered to themselves: Why did she do it? or: Why not leave well enough alone? or: They have their ways and we have ours.

The party broke up shortly after that and Catherine stood at the edge of the group, fighting back a huge need to cry and hit people at the same time. Icellee, God bless her, walked over and said, "Come on, honey, I'll walk you home. It's too dark now for a young lady to walk alone." Catherine put her sheet back on.

Catherine slid her hand in Icey's bejeweled mitt and the Great Witch and a little ghost flickered down the streets of Montgomery. On the way home Catherine quietly cried. Icey knew it. And she also knew there wasn't a damn thing she could do or say about it.

The hanged witch turned out to be one of Alabama's prosperous rum runners.

•••

By now Rhonda ventured from Water Street less frequently. She kept up appearances and took her daily stroll down to the train station. Once she put a nickel into a new pay phone and called home. When the receiver was lifted, Blue Rhonda gaily called out, "I love you."

"What?" answered an unfamiliar voice.

"Is this Banana Mae Parker?"

"No, this is Annie McNeary."

"Wrong number?"

"I should say," was the indignant reply.

"Wasn't it nice to hear 'I love you' anyway?" Blue Rhonda hung up the receiver.

Her excursions to Linton's church slowed down too. In a fit of pastoral responsibility, he'd stop by the house once a week. Banana Mae usually left the room since she couldn't abide the man. Once on the way up the stairs Linton bumped into a priest of his acquaintance and jealously questioned Blue Rhonda about him. Rival prophets of Christianity did not interest Rhonda and she flatly told him so. It wasn't until days later that Linton realized the good father was there to relieve himself of bodily need. Linton was sure whatever guilt the man felt would be exorcised by confession. In Linton's book, when you sinned you sinned and the stain marked you forever. Even if humans could have remained in the womb untainted by the world, the copulation that resulted in their life was sin just the same. Rhonda's resistance to sin, guilt and other forms of misery provoked in him a surprising intensity of emotion.

Her crack about the priest sent him into twelve hours of nonstop prayer. It was a dark moment for Linton; would he never get through to this soul? Rhonda said the priest was a man of the cloth while she was a woman of the sheet. It wasn't that her comment was so bad; it was just further proof to Reverend Ray that he was up against a formidable challenge.

• • •

The Man in the Iron Mask was released around Thanksgiving. Payson had little time to enjoy the avalanche of praise because of his contract at Pacifica Studios. Aaron propelled him into his first talkie, which he wanted released almost simultaneously with *Mask*. No one was allowed to see the rushes other than Aaron and the director. Unbeknownst to Payson, Mr. Stone handsomely paid off the sound man and the director. Sound equipment was crude, but not so crude that it couldn't be tampered with. Payson's voice, a rich baritone, squawked like that of a deballed tenor.

Neither Payson nor Grace was prepared for the thunderclap of derision which greeted *Talk of the Town*. Grace's voice rang out beautifully. Audiences howled every time Payson opened his mouth. Within the space of two weeks Payson's career turned around 180 degrees.

At first, the two of them tried to finance another silent film, just as they'd done for *The Man in the Iron Mask*. Silents were over. A few studios were stuck with some in production, but already silents were referred to in the past tense, the way family does when a patient is dying but hasn't yet crossed over the line.

Grace accepted the end of the era better than Payson. When he finally gave in to it, he assumed he'd have other chances at talkies if he worked feverishly at lowering his already low voice. Neither could possibly know that the fault was with Aaron Stone. They figured, as did everyone, that for some strange reason Payson's voice didn't "take." Since he was under contract to Pacifica Studios, he couldn't jump over to another studio. He tried to buy out his contract, but for pure spite, Aaron refused.

To further insult Payson, Aaron offered him menial parts in new projects.

On the surface of it, Aaron lost money on *Talk of the Town,* but the victory was his. He finally ruined Payson, he made an example of a star and cowed the rest of the people in his employ. Enough people went to see the movie because they heard it was awful so Aaron didn't lose as much as he put about. Some silent actors and actresses retired immediately even though they were young. The business had changed and they didn't or couldn't change with it.

Grace survived the transition. If anything, sound fleshed out her appeal. To further humiliate Payson, Aaron gave her a huge vehicle all her own, *Worldly Woman.* She told Payson the hell with it. She'd quit. But he'd have none of it and encouraged her to work. The real misery was when they'd go to parties and people would shun him because they were afraid he'd ask for a part in a picture. No one could understand how his deep voice came across the way it did on the screen, but hardly anyone had an inkling of what had been done to Payson.

"Honey, let's go home to Montgomery for a week or two."

Payson looked up from a script. "What about your shooting schedule?"

"Aaron Stone can stuff it up his ass."

"Grace, you don't have to do this for me."

"We'll tell him I'm pregnant and I want a week home with my mother to consider the future."

Eyes alight, he barely asked, "Are you?"

"No, but it's as good an excuse as any."

Sinking back in his chair, he sighed, "I wish you were."

"Keep working on it." Grace smiled. She picked up the

phone and dialed the big boss. His secretary performed the usual irritating screening routine. Nobody, but nobody, answered his own phone in Hollywood. Why, to even touch the thing would give you leprosy and your hand would fall off. After a wait, the toneless voice announced Mr. Stone would return her call, he was in conference.

"In conference, shit! Mabel, you tell that son of a bitch I'm taking a week or two off, starting today."

Mabel mumbled, switched off the line. Right fast, Mr. Stone was on the other end of the telephone. "What do you mean, walking out in the middle of shooting? You can't do this to me. You can't do this to Rod. You can't do this to—"

"I'll do as I damn well please."

Payson sat upright in his chair, enjoying the tussle.

"This will cost us a fortune, Grace," Aaron griped.

"Mr. Stone, if you'd have the goodness to shut up, I'll tell you why I'm going home. I'm pregnant."

"Oh, no," was the mournful reply.

"I want to visit my mother and think this over. This may not be the appropriate time to have a child."

Never spoken of openly, abortion was quite common among the upper classes. Aaron brightened considerably. "Perhaps you're right, Grace. I can understand your desire to see your family. It's an important decision. Naturally, a child at this time would destroy your career. We'll shoot all the scenes without you."

"That's what I want to think over." Grace ignored his attention to shooting sequence.

"Try to make it less than two weeks. Bye," Aaron crooned into his loudspeaker on his desk. She'll never have the kid, he thought. Not now, not when they're down and out and she's the breadwinner.

"Pack up, buster." Grace slapped her husband on the back.

Icellee was overjoyed to see her two sweetcakes, as she called them. It didn't take her long to notice that Payson was not as buoyant as he had been. On a calculated stroll through her gardens, which she paid a fortune to maintain but never tended herself, Icellee put her arm through her daughter's arm. "He's drinking a bit, isn't he?"

"Nothing serious, Mother."

"Hmm."

"You should have known him before I married him." Then Grace thought, God, no; you'd have died of shock.

"What do you mean?"

"He drank a great deal then. All the fellows did. It was the manly movie star thing to do. He gave up all that when we got married. I can't hold it against him if he's taking a nip or two during this hard time."

"It's the strangest thing—his voice, I mean. Such a deep voice and that awful squeak on the screen." Icellee put her foot in it.

Grace tightened her shoulder muscles, then relaxed. After all, it was true. "We're praying they perfect sound. He's a great actor, Mother."

"Yes." Icellee fondled a boxwood. Although it was high afternoon, it was rather cool. Winter was giving notice. "I remember when I took my marriage vows with your father: 'For richer or for poorer, in sickness and in health, for better or for worse until death us do part.' It's so easy to say them and so hard to live up to them." She turned to her daughter, whose black hair caught the soft winter's light. "You do love him, don't you?"

"As a friend first, then as my husband. The husband part came later."

Icey's eyes flickered. "I wish I could say the same. Your father died before you could really remember him. You were so little. I married a fine-looking man in a cloud of angelic love feathers. One day I woke up and discovered a real, live, faulty human being sitting opposite me at the table. I was terrified."

"You?"

"Me. Where was the romance? Where was Prince Charming? I'd married a very ordinary man. That's when I really learned to love him—after the honeymoon, so to speak. I think you were wise to be friends first." Her voice cracked. "It's so very hard to be friends with men."

"Yes." Grace paused, then turned back, with her mother on her arm. "But you know, I think it's even harder for them to be friends with one another."

Icellee patted Grace's arm and they walked toward the house, truly mother and daughter.

There were few moments in Hortensia's life when she looked inward. It seemed narcissistic to her. When Hercules died she felt a violent undertow, as though the ocean were rolling backward. When Paris fully revealed his twisted self, and then recently when Catherine was unmasked at the Great Witch Hunt, she was pushed into herself. How much of this was her own doing? Oh, not Hercules' death, but Paris. Had she consciously denied the child love? She didn't think she did, but she'd never felt close to him, not once. Perhaps he looked too much like her. That's supposed to make for attraction, but in Hortensia's case, she was attracted to those unlike her. Paris displayed her wit, her ability to straddle all social strata no matter what the occasion, and also her tremendous magnetism. He was her son. But this need for her? This disregard for anybody but himself? Once the shock wore off, she felt a faltering bond with him, some slight touch with his encompassing loneliness. The act wasn't all that bad. In fact, making love was making love. Perhaps she was a monster herself for not being more repelled and destroyed by the fact that she'd slept with her own son. What devoured her nerves was her fear for Catherine. Yes, Paris was right. She loved that child in a way she had never loved him or his brother. Edward she'd learned to admire and cherish, but she could never love Paris. He was the wrong person to be her son or she was his mother at the wrong time or it was some cosmic cruelty, but he didn't belong to her as a son belongs. For Catherine she tied the blood knot. How many times she wanted that child to know that she was her mother! She loved her.

As she wandered into the stables, vicuña coat tossed over her shoulders, she looked up at the loft. For the first time she put herself in Catherine's shoes. How would I like to be lied to? How would I feel if I were told who my real parents were? All those years of deception, for my own good, of course. Could I ever trust anyone after that? Could I look at my mother and respect her?

Hortensia realized she could lose the person she loved most in this world, and lose her by the means she employed to protect her: kind dishonesty. What do you tell a child, and when? How can you explain the races and their bramble bush of involvement? The races, hell—how can you explain the sexes?

As she looked up at the loft, she remembered her lover: his mouth, his smooth hard back and his tightly curled hair—she remembered it all. What did we do? Did we know what we were doing? What legacy have we left our child—or any child, for that matter?

She stood there still and then thought, I'd do it all again, everything, for I wouldn't know what I now know. The knowledge was worth the pain that purchased it.

As for Catherine, she didn't know how or when, but somehow she must tell her the truth. For herself, Hortensia feared no one, not even Paris, whom she felt creeping closer like a malignant fog. For Catherine she feared, but then what parent doesn't? We all want to leave our children the Garden of Eden and we wind up giving them hardscrabble.

Touching the flanks of her brilliant bay, the successor to a long-dead Bellerophon, Hortensia finally understood she was no longer young, but she did know who she was.

• • •

After much deliberation, while still home in Montgomery Payson decided to try out for a play. Icellee encouraged him and Grace prayed once audiences heard his voice they'd want him back on the screen. If only some critic would be good enough to notice, as well. An old New York friend came through and Payson got the lead in a new play bound for Broadway, with any luck at all.

Edward and Mary Bland Banastre came to see the tryouts in New Haven. Payson was terrific but the play was a stinker. It folded before seeing the far side of Manhattan.

Payson felt like a fraction reduced to its lowest terms. They'd worked hard on this play, weeks of rehearsal, little sleep, the pressures and episodes that go into making the theater the exciting, heartbreaking life it is. What deepened his dread was that all this came on the heels of his greatest triumph, *The Man in the Iron Mask*. He bestrode the world, a glorious Colossus, just a year before. Perhaps it was all too much, with him worrying about middle age. He and Grace had been apart for almost one month now. He'd never realized how much he needed her. Chorus boys were fun, but Grace, Grace was the North Star. He couldn't beg her to come East. Aaron gave in once. Twice would be like parting the Red Sea. Besides, what woman wants a man who's flat on his back, defeated? He was weak. That's exactly how he felt and his self-loathing grew in proportion with each passing day. He didn't deserve Grace. She should have a real man, not a has-been actor. His drinking became worse. He had pride enough to hide it, but how long can you hide gin fumes? If Payson had less pride he might have borne this trial better.

Sitting in his hotel room, half lit, he called home. The butler answered the phone and informed him Grace was still at the studio. Disheartened, Payson hung up.

Since he'd been clear of alcohol for so long, his system had lost some of its famous tolerance. The bottle of gin catapulted him into a severe depression as well as producing the typical unpleasant effects of too much liquor.

He yanked out all the drawers of the desk in the suite until he found writing paper, which was right where he should have expected it, the long middle drawer. He also took out the Bible placed in the deep right-hand drawer. He tried to read it but couldn't focus. Then he started a letter to Aaron in which he assaulted him in a variety of ways, beginning by addressing him as the ''Sperm of Judah.'' When he exhausted his supply of invective he turned to the Old Testament. But the anger passed quickly and despair, unfamiliar and terribly frightening, took its place. He crumpled the letter.

Then he rang room service for another bottle. He thought to himself that he'd mortify his body to purify his soul. After that he didn't think much at all.

Hours later, in the middle of the night, the telephone

awakened him from his stupor. He knocked it over trying to pick it up. Eventually he got the receiver to his ear.

"Payson."

"Gracie," he mumbled.

She knew what he'd done and there was no point in making him feel worse. Grace decided that no matter what the cost, she'd keep him talking. "How was the last show?"

"All right. I really wish we'd made it."

"There will be other shows."

"I don't know."

"Are you all right?"

"I'm fine. I don't feel so hot. Picked up a little bug."

"I'm coming out to get you."

"Huh?"

"The picture can wait two weeks."

"No, no, Grace, don't do that. One of us in the doghouse is enough."

"Honey, you're not in the doghouse. We both have to be patient and wait for sound to be perfected. You've got the most beautiful voice."

He didn't reply. He felt he would black out. "I'll call you in the morning. I feel terrible."

Desperate, Grace shouted, "Payson, are you all right?"

"Yes, yes, I said I was. I picked up a bug. I'll be good enough to go down to New York tomorrow."

"Call me before you leave. Promise."

"I promise." He hung up the phone and conked out. When he woke up the next morning he looked and felt wretched. He called Grace and managed to get her in her bungalow on the set. She relaxed upon hearing him hung over as opposed to still drunk. He took a hot shower, packed his bags and caught the train down to Grand Central. The ride through the Connecticut countryside was soothing although it was cold as a witch's tit out there. He did not have a drink on the way down.

He'd loved Grand Central Station since the first time he'd seen it. The physical structure drew the sound up into the ceiling, and voices sounded vaguely religious to his ear. Pale winter light shone through the arching glass over the walkways. He motioned the porter to follow him and went to the counter to find out about departures for Savannah, Georgia. Then he remembered he'd have to leave out of Pennsylvania Station for that, so the porter loaded his bags into a taxi. As they drove across Forty-second Street, Payson felt lost. He used to own this city, any city. He'd disembark from trains amid popping flash-bulbs, female screams and champagne. Today he snuck off the train like a thief. True, studio publicity departments helped considerably in these displays of mob affection and he could probably have orchestrated something had he really wanted it. But now the city seemed a place of sinister solitude. He didn't want to see his old friends and he didn't want to make new ones. He wanted to see Savannah. He didn't wish to see his mother so much as to walk around the parks, hear the cadence of his country and smell the water. Winter in Savannah was a most agreeable affair. In fact, anything in Savannah was agreeable. He wondered why he'd ever left.

Luckily, he got a stateroom that had been canceled not one minute before he stepped up to the counter. He settled in to enjoy the ride. By the time they hit Philadelphia he was depressed all over again. He rang for the porter, lavishly tipped him and awaited the return of ice and two bottles of potent gin. He told himself this was to calm his nerves. One shot.

One shot led to two and after a time he lost count but he still felt depressed. He hadn't eaten anything that day, so the gin hit him like a medicine ball. He sat and stared out the window. At Washington, D.C., he took out some of the paper he filched from the hotel in New Haven and wrote a note to Grace. All he wrote was:

Dear Grace,
    In chess it isn't the moves that kill the king; it's the rules by which the game is played.

Love,
Payson

Then he settled down to hard drinking. He believed it was his duty to protect Grace. Had he only shared the ragged edge of his sorrow with her, they would both have been better off. Playful, high-spirited and imaginative,

Payson was conventional when it came to Grace. How could she respect him if he blubbered, wailed and descended into self-pity? He didn't know the line between self-pity and true sorrow, so it was better to just stiff-arm the whole emotion. It was bad enough he was prevented from doing the one thing he most loved—and he was so down now he couldn't see it might be temporary. He could act on the stage. But the laughter of those movie audiences seared into him like a poker brand on a roped, trapped bull. As for switching to another career—real estate, the stock market—he wasn't cut out for that and he knew it. Business was unnatural for him. He was an actor and that was all he'd ever be or want to be, much as he hated taking orders from directors and all the rest of it. What was he to do? Sit around the house and wait for plays to fall into his lap? If he moved to New York, where the theater was, then he and Grace would be separated, and that he couldn't stand. How could he in clear conscience ask her to give up her career, and a career that was bringing in millions? She said she'd chuck it and she would, but Payson was afraid she'd someday resent having given it all up for him. He didn't think he was worth it. But Grace wasn't like him. She didn't love acting all that much. He could never understand that she didn't really love it, that she loved him, in her way.

By the time the train roared through the southern end of Virginia, Payson was drunk, sick and at the end of his resources. He wrote two letters and tacked one on the outside of his door. In that he instructed the porter to wake him as the train pulled into Savannah. The other was addressed to his mother. Then he swallowed a fistful of pills and polished off the second bottle of gin.

An arsonist's dawn awakened the beautiful Southern city. The porter rapped at the door. There was no answer. After deliberation with his superior, they opened the door, which was not locked, and found Payson, dead, sitting straight up in his seat, looking out the window.

The letter to his mother read:

Dear Mother,

   I couldn't take it anymore. Forgive me and care for my Gracie. Please bury me next to Please.

Love,
Payson

The fragrance of pine curled through every room of the Banastre house. Garlands wrapped up the stairway to the second floor, draped across every mantelpiece and even hung about portraits of founders of the family—all from Virginia, of course. An immense and perfectly shaped tree sat square in the middle of the parlor. Hortensia, Amelie, Lila and Catherine were decorating it. Bartholomew, feeling unwell, watched from the couch but was in good humor. Carwyn was working late.

Lila inspected the balls for breakage. "Icellee left for Savannah this morning."

"How is she?" Hortensia asked.

"Good, all things considered. She'll bring Grace back here after the arrangements."

Catherine listened to all this. "What arrangements?"

"Oh, a friend's suffered a loss. There's no need to let it spoil your Christmas," Hortensia answered.

"Wouldn't it be awful to die on Christmas Eve?" Catherine considered this the saddest possible exit.

"I think it would be pretty awful to die anytime," Bartholomew called from the couch.

"Let's change the subject," Hortensia commanded.

"I really think Edward should come home. She won't deliver for another three months. Mary Bland is not all that delicate." Lila snapped open the little stepladder and climbed up.

"They're doing what they think best," Hortensia said.

"We all know why they aren't coming home," Lila placed a red ball at the end of a bough.

"I don't know," Catherine innocently remarked.

Lila observed Catherine. She was at the age where she not only asked questions but began to find answers. "Well, dear, there's no sense in hiding it. Edward and his brother do not get along."

"Oh." She sat cross-legged on the floor and divided the balls into colors.

"When is Paris coming home?" Bartholomew picked up the evening's paper.

"Tomorrow," Hortensia answered.

Lila continued hanging balls. Since no one knew what to do about Paris, they'd given up talking about him.

Catherine opened a little carton and plucked out a large golden star. "The Star of Bethlehem?"

"If it isn't, it certainly should be." Hortensia took it from her hand. "Mother, can you put this on the top or do you want me to do it?"

"You're taller. I think I'll let you perform the honors." Lila climbed down and Hortensia got on the ladder. "Now don't get on the top. It's unsafe."

"Mother, I've been doing this for years and haven't fallen yet."

"There's always a first time." Lila smiled but with that authoritative edge.

Catherine, hands on hips, watched the procedure. She asked the gathering, "Do you think there was a Star of Bethlehem?"

"Yes," Lila said.

Amelie caught Catherine out of the corner of her eye. What was she going to come up with next?

"The Bible says so." Hortensia leaned over and delicately twirled the twine around the base of the star and the topmost part of the tree.

"I suppose," Catherine said. "But it says, too, that Lot's wife turned into a pillar of salt and I don't believe that. Salt would just fall all over the ground. It couldn't stand straight up."

Bartholomew laughed. "Ah ha, the seed of doubt and rationality."

Lila ignored him. "Things do seem strange sometimes, but the Star of Bethlehem isn't one of them."

"Oh," Catherine resumed her spot on the floor and sorted more Christmas balls.

Hours later, they carefully placed candles at the ends

of the branches. Those wouldn't be lit until Christmas Eve.

"Beautiful," Lila exclaimed.

"I think this is our best tree yet." Hortensia stepped back to admire their labor.

"I can't wait until Christmas. It takes so long to get here." Catherine licked her lips.

"A few more days, miss." Amelie put her hand in the middle of Catherine's back and pushed her in the direction of the stairway. "Now say good night."

"Do I have to go to bed?"

"Yes." Amelie pushed harder.

"Good night, Mrs. Reedmuller. Good night, Mr. Reedmuller." She kissed them both. "Good night, Aunt Tense." She hugged and kissed her. Halfway up the stairs, she called down to the group. "Do you really think Jesus got here without, uh, without a real father?"

"Catherine!" Amelie, in front, pulled her up the stairs.

The little assemblage downstairs watched this with amusement. Once Catherine was in her room, Amelie chewed her out. "Why do you go saying such things? Proper young ladies do not discuss religion."

"Well, I wasn't discussing religion, exactly."

"What do you call it, then?"

"I was wondering about Jesus. He got here without a father, a human one. I was thinking maybe I got here in some strange way too."

"That's silly talk. You know who your father is."

"I've seen his picture." Catherine pressed her lips together. She did believe Hercules was her father, but she was struggling over how she could look the way she did.

"I don't want to hear any more of this, Catherine. I'm tired and so are you."

"I'm not dumb, Mother."

"Now what!" Amelie, exasperated, threw her hands in the air.

"If my father was dark and you're dark, there's no way I can look the way I look. I'm not dumb."

Amelie, restraining her desire to just give the child a smack, said, "Now you're being silly. People can come out in as many combinations as a litter of kittens."

Unconvinced but tired, Catherine said, "Sure." She went into the bathroom to wash her face.

Amelie wearily removed her shoes and thought to herself that Catherine was too clever by half.

Paris was home long enough to admire the tree and long enough for everyone who saw him to wonder what was the matter with him. He appeared as though his heart were continually racing. Hortensia treated him as she always did.

The first night he couldn't sleep and Carwyn heard him prowling around the halls. He got up and put on his robe.

"Who's there?"

"It's me."

Recognizing his son's voice, Carwyn said, "What's the matter?"

"I can't sleep."

"Go down to the kitchen and drink a glass of milk."

"I already did that." Paris didn't get too close to his father.

"You'd better go to bed. You'll wake up everybody in the house."

Paris padded back to his room and closed the door.

Christmas Eve kept everyone busy. Carwyn, at the office, was the only person exempt from chores. By late afternoon, most of the work completed, Catherine and Amelie went up to the third floor for a nap and Hortensia repaired to her small sitting room. She picked up a book but put it down. She couldn't concentrate. Instead, she wrapped her legs in an afghan and closed her eyes for a few moments.

Paris quietly opened her door and kissed her gently.

Startled, then angry, she glared at him. "What right have you to come in here like this?"

"I was lonesome."

"Be lonesome somewhere else. I'm tired."

"Too tired to kiss your loving son?"

"Don't disgust me, Paris."

"And don't get high and mighty, Mother. I can still ruin your life—or worse, your precious daughter's life."

"Apparently you've already ruined yours."

His hands were shaking. "Blood's thicker than water."

"Yes, you can choke on it."

He paid no attention. He sat opposite her and put his feet under the afghan.

"I asked you to leave me alone. I want to take a nap."

"I can't leave you alone."

She tucked her feet underneath her to get farther away from him. He got out of the chair and knelt beside her. He put his arms around her neck and she took them away. "For God's sake, stop it."

"All those months at school I haven't been able to think of anyone else." he reached up for her again and she knocked his hands away.

"You're a raving lunatic."

"I'll have you and I'll have you any time I want you." He straddled her.

With a swift upward motion she knocked him off. "Enough!"

Not to be cast aside so easily, he came for her again. As they fought and swore at one another, Amelie and Catherine heard the commotion. Alert, Amelie ran down the back stairway to the kitchen, where she phoned Carwyn. As the noise increased, she called up Cedrenus Shackleford. She knew she might be overstepping her bounds, but there was something in Paris's manner that made her skin crawl and she'd rather be embarrassed than sorry. It was only after she'd made the calls that she realized Catherine was not by her side.

"Catherine!" Amelie called out. There was no reply.

Catherine had run down the front stairway. Seeing the fight between Hortensia and Paris, she leapt on Paris like a little terrier. Outraged, he tried to shake her off. Hortensia beat him around the face. Finally, he wrenched the child around and now held her in front of him.

"Careful, Mother. You wouldn't want to hurt your darling."

Catherine kicked backward and caught him on the shin.

"Goddammit!" he yelled, and smacked her on the face.

"Leave that child alone!" Hortensia bellowed.

"Your precious bastard. Why don't I just kill her and take the thing you love most?"

In the state he was in, Hortensia wasn't sure he wouldn't do it. She started for him again, but he grabbed Catherine around the throat. Catherine was too mad to be scared and she bit him so hard her teeth went through to the bone on his thumb. He dragged her out of the room and began beating her. Hortensia chased him but she couldn't get close enough to stop him. She remembered Carwyn's .38, kept in the top drawer of his bureau, and raced down the hall. Catherine, afraid that she was leaving her, screamed, "Come back."

Paris spat in her ear, "That's your mother for you. She'll ditch you the same way she ditched me."

Amelie, in the front hall, didn't quite know what was going on, but when she got a good look at Paris hurting the child, she grabbed a vase, ran up the stairs and threw it at him. He was so crazed it had no effect. Wild, Amelie started throwing anything she could get her hands on. Family portraits, little paperweights, anything.

Hortensia flew out of her husband's bedroom. Paris was dragging the child down the stairs, with Amelie beating on him from behind.

Very calmly, Hortensia walked to the top of the stairs. "Amelie, get out of the way."

Amelie looked up, and fat though she was, she jumped on the other side of the stairs.

Paris saw the gun too, but didn't believe she'd use it.

"Paris, free that child."

"You stinking whore. You nigger-lover. You—"

"Let the child go."

"Never. I'll kill the bitch. I'll kill her because you love her!" He choked her harder.

Hortensia raised the gun, squeezed the trigger and hit him in the shoulder. He was knocked backward. Catherine scrambled free. Amelie leapt up the stairs, two at a time, picked the child up in her arms and ran down again. Paris got up and looked for Catherine. Hortensia fired again and blew off the back of his head. He dropped where he stood. Catherine screamed and stuck her head in Amelie's bosom. Hortensia motioned for her to get the child out of the hallway. She walked down the stairs to inspect Paris. He was dead. Blood gushed over the stair runner. She sat down next to his body and put her head between her knees, breathing deeply. As she cleared her mind, the front door opened as if a hurricane were behind it and Carwyn burst through. He rushed to Hortensia. Gently he took the gun from her hand and sat next to her. Within five minutes Cedrenus Shackleford was also through the door.

Carwyn stood up. "He went quite insane. I shot him."

Hortensia, without raising her voice, contradicted him. "Cedrenus, don't listen to him. I did it."

Cedrenus looked from one to the other and then leaned over the body. Catherine could be heard sobbing in the kitchen. "Just tell me what happened."

"He tried to kill Catherine," Hortensia said.

Cedrenus nodded. "Excuse me." He walked into the kitchen, asked a few questions of Amelie, then reemerged. "Let's forget it. He shot himself cleaning the pistol."

Hortensia opened her mouth. Cedrenus, still looking at the body, said quite simply, "I owe Catherine's father one."

• • •

After they took the body away, Hortensia and Carwyn sat in the library.

"I have a great deal to tell you," she said to him.

"No, don't." His eyes were ringed with sorrow. "Whatever has happened, I am as much to blame as you."

"Do you forgive me?"

"Forgive you! I wish I'd shot him myself." A burst of anger passed through him like a sudden gust of wind.

Hortensia knew he chose not to understand. If he ever wished to know she would tell him, but until that time she would respect this compact of silence.

"If you'll excuse me, I'll go look in on Catherine. She had a terrible fright."

"Yes, yes, of course, the poor little thing." He stood up as she rose to leave the room.

Amelie stroked Catherine. She was under the covers,

which were pulled up to her chin. When Hortensia came in, Amelie discreetly left.

"How are you feeling?"

"Better," Catherine said.

"You were very brave and I'm proud of you." Hortensia brushed her forehead.

Catherine stared at her. "Thank you for saving me."

Hortensia kissed her and said, "I don't think he meant to kill you, Catherine. He hadn't been right for some time. These things happen. I don't know why."

"Is it true what he said? You're my mother?"

"It's true."

Catherine lay quietly for a long time, then she said, "I'm glad you're my mother, but I don't know if I'll think of you that way."

"I'm sorry, Catherine. I broke a rule and you seem to be paying for it. I wouldn't blame you if you never thought of me as your mother."

"It would get you in a lot of trouble if I called you Mother, wouldn't it?" Her jaw was set firm.

"I suppose it would, but I don't much care."

Catherine sat up in the bed and placed two pillows behind her. "Aunt Tense." She stopped as if to call her by another name, and then continued, "I don't feel like I belong to anybody but myself."

Tears filled Hortensia's eyes. "You can belong to me if you want to."

"I don't know," Catherine said thoughtfully.

"As long as you like yourself, then if you do belong only to yourself perhaps you're ahead of the game."

"I like myself." Catherine smiled, kissed Hortensia and then lay down and went right to sleep.

Epilogue

Blue Rhonda lasted until March 1929. Banana Mae hired a nurse to look after her and the woman had a job of it. Rhonda was still very modest about herself. Even though she was confined to bed she would take the washcloth and try to sponge herself.

Linton paid his visits. She looked forward to it. The sheer hostility of their conversations sparked her.

Bunny and Lotowana spent as much time with her as they could. Lottie was on the verge of tears the whole time, but Rhonda wouldn't let her break down.

"Where's my hairy honey?" Rhonda demanded.

"I'll fetch him." Lottie went out to look for Attila.

The nurse, a woman of Junoesque proportions, disapproved. "Miss Latrec, you shouldn't have that dirty cat in the bedroom. How do you ever expect to get well?"

"I don't expect to get well."

"Tsk, tsk. Such talk," came the professional response.

Bunny and Banana Mae sat on opposite sides of Blue Rhonda. Lotowana came back with Attila, who happily jumped all over Rhonda, pushing his head against her chin, purring loudly.

"Sweet Tillie." She stroked him.

"Did Linton bestow his presence upon you today?" Bunny asked.

"Yes. I exposed myself to his friendship." She whispered, "I also made him madder than a wet hen when I told him there is only one God and that's Time."

Lotowana mouthed the sentence to herself to try and understand it.

Blue Rhonda said, "In my day I could suck the paint off a Chevy. Isn't that the truth?"

"You bet," Banana agreed.

She dozed off. When she awakened again they were still sitting around her. If they stayed that long, Rhonda knew the end was near. She smiled at them and held out her hand for Banana.

"Would you have done something different?" Banana asked.

"I don't know," Rhonda breathed. "If I knew when I was a kid what I know now, maybe. I don't think I hurt anybody. Did I?"

"No," Banana soothed her.

"You're the funniest thing ever lived," Lottie said. "You couldn't have hurt anybody."

The nurse bustled over. "You rest, honey. All this talk will tire you out."

Rhonda looked up at the figure leaning over her and said, "Christ, what tits," and died.

True to what she always said, Rhonda had the last laugh. When they prepared the body for burial they discovered she was a man. Her genitals were uncommonly small, but they were those of a man nonetheless.

Banana, shocked initially, saw the humor in it. At Rhonda's request she read a letter she'd written before she was too weak to write. Rhonda had asked that the contents be read the day after she died, to Lotowana, Bunny and Banana.

The three sat in the living room, empty without Rhonda, yet full of her memory. Banana Mae carefully opened the sealed envelope with a letter opener, unfolded the letter and began:

"Dear Friends,
    "I'm not the man I used to be. (You're supposed to laugh.)"

Lottie sobbed loudly. Bunny patted her hand to quiet her. "Come on, Lottie, she wanted you to laugh."

"Oh," Lottie gulped.

Banana Mae began anew.

"I was born James Porter with very little, as you know. I never felt like a boy and never wanted to be one. God played a joke on me and put me in a man's body, and not much of a man's body at that. I ran away from home when I was fourteen and passed myself off as a girl. I fooled you all, so I guess I did a good job. I didn't really want to fool anyone. I just wanted to be a woman and I think I was.

"Banana Mae, stop drinking. I know that will sound funny coming from me who abused myself shamelessly. I regret that. Life is too beautiful to put anything between yourself and it. No more booze. And take care of Attila.

"Bunny, I hope when you die you die as rich as Midas, and Lottie, I hope you find someone to love.

"Give Reverend Ray thirty pieces of silver.

"As I write this I know I'm dying. I ought to be filled with awe or remorse or great questions but I'm not. I wish I could live forever. If not forever, then a little longer. All my recent readings and tangles with Linton haven't given me any answers. I guess you can't look for the answer; you must be the answer.

"I love you."

Blue Rhonda Latree

ABOUT THE AUTHOR

RITA MAE BROWN lives and writes in Charlottesville, Virginia. Her neighbors are surviving.

The brilliant new novel by the author of
RUBYFRUIT JUNGLE

SUDDEN DEATH
by Rita Mae Brown

A Bantam Hardcover

Filled with incisive wit, deep warmth and penetrating insights, Rita Mae Brown's new novel is a moving love story set against the glittering, cutthroat world of international women's professional tennis. Carmen is a charming twenty-four-year-old tennis champion at her peak, determined to win the Grand Slam. Harriet is an irreverent, gutsy, strikingly attractive professor of Greek religion. Carmen and Harriet are in love. But when Susan Reilly, Carmen's first lover and chief competitor for the Grand Slam, leaks word of her relationship with Carmen to the press, the true depths of the feelings of all involved are tested on and off the court.

Buy SUDDEN DEATH, available wherever Bantam hardcovers are sold or use this handy coupon for ordering: